Edgar Hilsenrath is a survivor of Leipzig in 1926, he was later take escape Nazi persecution. When G deported to the Ukraine and sent to a liberation he went to Palestine on one of the first refugee trains. He subsequently lived in France and the United States and is now resident in Berlin. His books were initially underground classics, since the 1980s they have been standard literature for German courses in universities, especially in the United States. *The Story of the Last Thought* won the Alfred Döblin award in 1989, given by the Günter Grass Foundation.

Hugh Young has translated numerous works over the last twenty years, principally from German and also from Italian, French and Danish. A prisoner-of-war in Italy and Germany, his post-war career in the Colonial Office and later the Diplomatic Service took him to the West Indies, East Africa and Pakistan. He lives in Suffolk. His translation of *The Story of the Last Thought* won the Schlegel-Tieck Prize.

THE STORY OF THE LAST THOUGHT

by

EDGAR HILSENRATH

Translated by HUGH YOUNG

An Abacus Book

First published in Germany as *Das Märchen vom letzten Gedanken*
by R. Piper GmbH & Co. KG, München 1989

First published in Great Britain by Scribners, a Division of
Macdonald & Co (Publishers) Ltd, London & Sydney 1990
Published in Abacus by Sphere Books Ltd 1991

ISBN 0 349 10253 8

Typeset by ⚠ Tek Art Ltd, Addiscombe, Croydon, Surrey

Printed and bound in Great Britain by
Cox & Wyman Ltd, Reading

Sphere Books Ltd
A Division of
Macdonald & Co (Publishers) Ltd
165 Great Dover Street
London SE1 4YA

A member of Maxwell Macmillan Publishing Corporation

PROLOGUE

'I am the story-teller in your head. Call me Meddah.'

'And now be quiet, Thovma Khatisian. Quite quiet. For it will not last much longer. It will soon be over. And then . . . as your lights gradually go out . . . I will tell you a story.'

'What sort of story, Meddah?'

'The story of the last thought. I shall say to you: Once upon a time there was a last thought. It was there in your last cry of fear, hidden there.'

'Why, Meddah?'

'Well, why do you think, Thovma Khatisian? What sort of question is that? Are you really that stupid? It's quite simple. It had hidden there to sail out into the open with your last cry of fear . . . through your gaping mouth.'

'Where to, Meddah?'

'To Hayastan.'

'To Hayastan, hmm?'

'Yes, Thovma Khatisian.'

'To the country of my ancestors? To the country at the foot of Mount Ararat?'

'That's where.'

'There, of all places?'

'Where else, Thovma?'

'To the holy land of the Armenians, desecrated by the Turks?'

'Desecrated, Thovma. They desecrated it.'

'The place where Christ was crucified the second time?'

'As you say, Thovma.'

'For the last time, perhaps? Finally!'

1

'That can't be certain.'

'Tell me, Meddah – what really happened?'

'What, Thovma?'

'Where are the Armenians from Hayastan?'

'They've disappeared, Thovma.'

'But that can't be right, Meddah.'

'Why can't it be right, then?'

'Because I know they're still there. Their wounded bodies lie rotting deep under the sacred earth.'

'You're quite right, Thovma. You're actually not half as stupid as you look. You seem to know quite a lot.'

'There's so much I know, Meddah.'

'Then why do you ask me?'

'I was just asking, Meddah.'

'Are you trying to make me look silly?'

'No, Meddah.'

'Tell me, Meddah.'

'What is it now?'

'When my last thought flies out into the open . . . will it find Hayastan?'

'But Thovma Khatisian, what a stupid question. Of course it will find it.'

'Are you really sure?'

'I am quite sure.'

'You must tell it: it's where the sunflowers grow as high as the sky.'

'As high as the sky?'

'Or up to the gates of heaven.'

'But Thovma Khatisian, that's a great exaggeration.'

'Do you think so?'

'I do indeed.'

'Hayastan . . . where the watermelons are bigger and rounder and juicier than the fattest old dear's arse?'

'That's where Hayastan is.'

'Where they put honey in the bulgur? And dry the juice of ripe mulberries on the roof garden?'

'Yes, Thovma Khatisian.'

'Where they shake the milk in goatskins to turn it into butter?'

'Of course. That's where it is.'

'Or in earthen churns, like at my grandmother's? She rocked it on her lap, the way she used to rock my father. And she used to sing the butter song: *Garak geshinem* . . . I'm making butter . . . I'm making butter for Hagob . . . for Hagob?'

'That's right.'

'Where the women have full breasts, pearly, damp . . . like fresh pomegranates, early in the morning?'

'Only when they're young, and when they're sweating.'

'Well, it's all the same.'

'All the same, Thovma.'

'Where old men and young men hang around the village wells when the women are scooping up water? For the women bend down so low over the side of the well, deeper than anywhere in the world.'

'Yes.'

'Hayastan. Where the mountains touch the sky. Where strong men brace themselves before the *kuthan*, the big Armenian plough – there in the barren fields – to set the oxen racing. Where my great-grandfather threw the chaff in the air at the threshing and the Armenian wind just took it away to the mountains or down to the sea. Where there were fat-tailed sheep and mutton and yoghurt. Do you know that still? The yoghurt that grandmother called *madsun*?'

'*Madsun*. Yes.'

'Tell me what I look like, Meddah.'

'You look ugly, Thovma Khatisian. No woman would fall in love with you, except your mother. Your eyes keep rolling and looking down at the floor. There is stinking spittle running out of your half-open mouth. Soon you'll be opening it wide, to let go that last thought which – like I told you – sails out into the air with your last cry of fear.'

'And my hands? Tell me, Meddah. What are my hands like?'

'They don't sweat any more. They're as good as dead.'

'And my feet?'

'The same.'

'Yet you're not old, Thovma Khatisian. Born in 1915. You're

seventy-three. A young brat still strong enough to piss against the wind. What's wrong with you?'

'I don't know, Meddah.'

'Your ancestors weren't like that, Thovma Khatisian. One of them especially, your grandfather's great-grandfather. He was quite a different sort of man. He lived to over a hundred.'

'Yes, Meddah.'

'He did really, Thovma Khatisian. These Armenians from Hayastan grow very old indeed from lots of fucking and lots of yoghurt – *madsun*, they call it, and they drink it by the bucket.'

'Yes, Meddah.'

'They only die young if the Turks or the Kurds cut their heads off.'

'Yes, Meddah.'

'Or else they die some other way – by the crooked butcher's knife, for instance.'

'Yes, Meddah.'

'Listen, Thovma Khatisian. This one ancestor of yours especially, your grandfather's great-grandfather, he was such a different kind of man. When he was ninety-seven he could still have two women, one before he went to sleep and one first thing in the morning.'

'How was that, Meddah?'

'Like this: before going to sleep he had your grandfather's great-grandmother, for he was clever, like all Armenians, who are even cleverer than the Jews and Greeks, as everybody knows. Your grandfather's great-grandfather said to himself: if I don't do it with her, then tomorrow she'll put dried cowshit in the bulgur instead of honey. And I'd rather not risk that, although my stomach is still good and healthy, and I can fart like a kid of seventy-three.'

'Was that so?'

'It was.'

'And first thing in the morning?'

'While your grandfather's great-grandmother was still asleep, he sneaked out to the cowshed. And there he had the little Kurdish girl. She was nine and had a cunt the size of a pigeon's egg. Oh yes, Thovma Khatisian. That's the sort of chap your ancestor was. But one day the little Kurd didn't want it and went and stuck herself against the back wall of the shed.'

'And what happened then?'

'Your ancestor charged up to her furiously, with a stiff prick. But the little minx quickly dodged out of the way. And so your ancestor rammed a great hole in the shed wall, as big as his cock. That's the sort of chap he was.'

'Was the cowshed wall made of wood?'

'No. It was made of earth and dried cow's dung, what people in that part of the world call *tezek*.'

'No more of that, Meddah. Tell me again what I look like.'

'I've told you once. You look like somebody that only his mother can love. In a mother's eyes even an old bugger like you is the sweetest little angel. Your mother doesn't see those jellyfish eyes, she doesn't smell that stinking spittle. Can you feel it, Thovma Khatisian? Your mother is still with you. She's stroking those hands of yours that can't sweat any more. And she's stroking your cold feet. She's stroking that ugly bald head of yours and kissing your half-dead eyes.'

'Where is my mother?'

'She's already gone, Thovma Khatisian.'

'Tell me, Meddah, how did I come into this world? For I never knew my mother.'

'Hayastan bore you, Thovma Khatisian. And the wind from the mountains of Kurdistan. The dust bore you. And the hot sun that shone over the country road.'

'So I didn't have a mother.'

'You never had one.'

'Is that the truth.'

'That is the truth.'

'And yet it can't be, Thovma Khatisian. For even our Saviour, Jesus Christ, was born of woman. Or do you believe that the spirit of God had shaded the sun? Or the wind from the Kurdistan mountains? Or the dust on a poor country road, in Hayastan?'

'No, Meddah.'

'Now you see, Thovma Khatisian, a woman bore you, and yet

you never had a mother, none at least that ever sang you a lullaby, none that ever suckled you or rocked you to sleep.'

'But someone must have suckled me?'

'Of course someone suckled you. But it wasn't your natural mother.'

'Who was it then?'

'A Turkish woman. She found you. On the country road. And she took you with her. And she suckled you. And she sang many lullabies to you.'

'Armenian lullabies?'

'No. Turkish.'

'Are they as tender as Armenian lullabies?'

'They are just as tender.'

'I have an idea, Thovma Khatisian. I've an idea that you, Thovma Khatisian, came into the world by Caesarean section.'

'What nonsense you're talking, Meddah. Who would there be on a poor country road who could do a Caesarean section?'

'A Turk, Thovma Khatisian. They were specialists in it. This is how I see it: it is August 1915. A hot day. Thousands of half-starved Armenians are stumbling under the whiplashes of the Turkish police along a country road on the way to Mesopotamia, still in the Armenian highlands, on the border of the Kurdistan mountains. Your mother is among them. She is pregnant. In her ninth month. The pains are just coming on. It's about midday.'

'Go on, Meddah. Go on.'

'I don't know exactly how many Armenians there were on that road that day; but there must have been several thousand. They had been on the road for weeks, for the saptiehs – that's what the Turkish gendarmes were called – were deliberately driving them in a circle. They came from all directions, those Armenians, from Erzurum and Mush, from Mersifon and Kharput, from little towns and big towns, villages and market-places. Hundreds of thousands of them had been driven out, millions even, but there were not many of them here. Several thousand, as I said before, for I'm only telling you about this one road.'

'Tell me, story-teller. Tell me, my Meddah. Can your eyes see my father at this moment?'

'No, Thovma Khatisian. Your father wasn't in the column, for the saptiehs had shot all Armenian men, all those who were still half-able to stand on their legs, who were not yet grey-haired or still had teeth in their mouths.'

'Did they shoot my father, then?'

'No, Thovma Khatisian. Your father was an exception.'

'In what way was he an exception?'

'I'll tell you that later.'

'Later?'

'Yes, later.'

'Your mother was there. She was bigger than most of the women in the column.'

'Did she have a pretty face?'

'She didn't have a face at all. She just had eyes.'

'What sort of eyes?'

'The mirror-eyes of a pregnant woman. Big eyes, that reflected what she carried in her womb, for in the middle of that eye-mirror the little, unborn Thovma Khatisian sat and waved.'

'Had her time come?'

'Her time had come.'

'It was about midday, Thovma Khatisian. You peeped through your mother's eyes at the long lines of women, children and old men, and then you asked yourself, where are all these funny people going? Why does the sun shine, when nobody's laughing? And why do all the people go barefoot? Why isn't there any water anywhere, and why do the saptiehs keep beating the people, who after all aren't trying to defend themselves? Aren't they going fast enough for them? And why should they go any faster, since anyway they're only being driven round in a circle? And why does my mother stop now? And why does she suddenly sink to her knees? Look out, mother! Be careful, or you might lose me out of your eyes.'

'When your mother collapsed and stumbled here and there screaming, when she suddenly realized that she would have to give birth, in the middle of that country road, with her last strength she cut the baggy trousers off her body, lay down on her back, lying in

7

the dust of the road, opened her legs and raised her feet towards the sun and the sky.'

'Yes. And that is how it was,' said the story-teller. 'The guards were furious, because your mother was holding up the whole column, and one of the saptiehs pulled his horse round and thundered over to the place on the road where she was lying in the dust screaming, her feet raised up to the sky and the sun. He drew his sabre out of its sheath and jumped down off his horse.'

'Did the saptieh cut my mother's head off?'

'No, Thovma Khatisian. The saptiehs often did cut Armenians' heads off, but they also liked to slit their bellies open, especially the bellies of pregnant women. Apparently that amused them. Now, Thovma Khatisian. Your mother was lucky. The saptieh actually put the point of his sabre on her naked stomach, but playfully rather than angrily, and he only scratched her a little bit. And behold . . .'

'Behold?'

'There you were already, Thovma Khatisian, just slipped out of your mother's body. When the saptieh cut the umbilical cord, with his sabre, just by way of a joke, you began to crow like the first cock God ever made, to greet the first day on the first ever manure heap. And the saptieh looked and laughed and sheathed his sabre again, since he was basically no worse than most people who serve the state and carry out their duty obediently.'

'It may have been different, of course.' said the story-teller. 'It might even be that your mother had survived that hot day without finally letting you go. Not until it was evening and gradually growing dark did the column halt, for even the saptiehs were tired, and the horses were restive. The saptiehs ordered the prisoners to sit down; they wanted to feed and water the horses.

'In that region,' the story-teller said, 'it gets dark quickly, for the Kurds up in the mountains are smart, and they bring the sun home every evening with their black goat's-hair ropes, because they are afraid that the devil-worshippers, of whom there are a lot in that region, might steal the sun. During the night the Kurds hide the sun in a big tent, also made of black goat's-hair, and they only let

8

it go when the golden eagle wakes up and gives its first cry, which re-echoes far over the mountains and is heard down in the gorges, valleys and meadows of the land of Hayastan.

'So it quickly grew dark,' said the story-teller. 'Your mother had fallen asleep, together with the others. They were all lying in the dust of the road. Many of them were really asleep, others just lay there listlessly. Many were silent, others called out for water. When it was quite dark, your mother's pains began.'

'So I was born in the middle of the night, when the Kurds still had the sun hidden in that big, black tent?'

'That's right, Thovma Khatisian. When your mother saw how you were slowly disappearing from the mirror of her eyes, just going back deep in her womb in order to push out into the open as an independent being, she staggered over and squatted in the ditch.'

'Then did she bear me squatting?'

'Many people in that region give birth squatting.'

'How is that, Meddah?'

'They simply shit their children out.'

'And how was it with me?'

'It was just the same, Thovma Khatisian. Your mother simply shat you out. What else was she to do? Suddenly there you were lying there in the ditch, a little bit of shit crowing in the dark. The saptiehs didn't notice anything, a lot of the women in the column had small children with them who crowed the same as you. In the morning, after the Kurds had let the sun out and the dawn had crept down from the mountain to the country road, the wretched crowd moved on. They simply left you behind.'

'Why didn't my mother take me with her?'

'I don't know. Perhaps she thought the deserted country road was your only hope. And so it was, Thovma Khatisian. For later in the day the holy Virgin Mary came by. She came in the form of a Muslim Turkish woman, and she was accompanied by her husband, who was called Yussuf. And Mary noticed you at once, and Yussuf noticed you too, and said to his wife:

"Look, this one here is the most helpless witness in the world, and the silliest, too, for he doesn't know what he's seen."

"It doesn't matter whether he knows or not," said Mary. "What matters is that one day he will bear witness that men are not all wicked." And Mary smiled and got down off her donkey and took you in her arms. And later, in their camp, she made Yussuf caress you, and she rocked you to sleep.'

Now it became absolutely quiet in my head, and I thought my time had come. I thought about my last thought, which would soon take flight to the land of my ancestors, to seek out all those I had never known. But I was mistaken. For something happened to me. It was just a thought, and I had to laugh out loud, and I let out a fart.

'That was your last,' said the Meddah.

'Is it all over?'

'Not quite,' said the Meddah.

'Maybe I'll fart again,' I said.

'Maybe,' said the Meddah. And the Meddah asked: 'What made you laugh like that, Thovma Khatisian?'

'Because, just a second ago, I was talking to the Turkish prime minister.'

'Did he tell you anything?'

'Yes.'

'I caught him out in the end, the Turkish prime minister. His voice sounded quite dangerous on the telephone. And he asked: "Who dares to telephone me here?" I was at the other end of the line, the safe end, and I said: "I do."

"And who are you?"

"I'm your Armenian psychiatrist."

"And what do you want from me?"

"Nothing at all."

"Does that mean I want something from you?"

"That's right."

"Then I'll come to your consulting room tomorrow."

"Please do."'

'I'd given him my address. And he came. Punctually.

"I have nightmares," he said.

"All Turks have nightmares," I said.

"Why?"

10

"Because of the Armenians."

"So it's because of the Armenians?"

"Yes."

"What's the matter with the Armenians?"

"They were wiped out by the Turks."

"That's nothing to do with me. It's nothing to do with anybody, none of the present-day Turks."

"I never said it was."'

'"It was really a very long time ago," I said. "In 1915. During the First World War. A whole people was destroyed."

"Simply destroyed?"

"Simply destroyed."

"I've heard something about that some time or other," said the Turkish prime minister, "but I've always thought it was a lot of lying stories put out by our enemies."

"It's no story," I said.

"Genocide?"

"That's it."

"A spontaneous outburst of anger by the Turkish people?"

"No."

"Then it wasn't a popular movement?"

"It came from the top," I said. "It all came on the orders of the Turkish government of the time. Everything was highly organized. We're talking about the first organized and planned genocide in the twentieth century."

"I thought it was the Germans who invented that."

"They didn't invent it."

"Then were the Turks their teachers?"

"That's it."'

'"There's nothing about it in our history books," said the Turkish prime minister.

"I know," I said.

"Is that on account of the gap?"

"On account of the gap in history," I said.'

'"And that's why I'm so frightened," said the Turkish prime

11

minister. "I dream about nothing but gaps and holes."'

'"Sit down," I said.
  "Where?"
  "Anywhere in my consulting room."
  "But this isn't a consulting room. It's a Turkish history book."
  "That doesn't matter."
  "Must I really sit down?"
  "Yes."
  "Or lie down?"
  "If you like."'

'"It would be best if you sat on that stool."
  "But I can't see any stool."
  "Then sit down on my couch. You can lie on it."
  "But I can't see a couch."
  "Then for all I care you can sit on the floor."
  The Turkish prime minister nodded. He was just saying: "But I can't see any floor." And then he began to scream.'

'No one can hear you, Thovma Khatisian,' said the story-teller, 'for your speech is silent. But I can hear you.'
  'Did you hear his scream, too – the Turkish prime minister's scream – as he fell into the abyss?'
  'I heard that too.'

'I've met the Turkish prime minister again,' I told the story-teller.
  'When?'
  'A few seconds ago.'
  'And where?'
  'In the great conference hall of the United Nations. It was during their General Assembly.'

'He was sitting next to the representative of his government, unobtrusively, to one side. I discovered that he wasn't prime minister any more but archivist in the United Nations, chosen officially by all the member nations. When he saw me he got up and went down to the archives. I followed him.

"I'm looking for that Armenian file," I said. "It's a question of a report on the forgotten genocide."

"The forgotten genocide?"

"Yes."

"And when is that supposed to have happened?"

"In 1915."

"That really is a long time ago. This is 1988."

"Yes," I said.

"Look here," he said.'

'And then he took me over to the filing cabinet. He said: "Our filing cabinet doesn't have a lock. These are open shelves, available to anybody; we have no secrets here."

"Then show me where I can find the Armenian file."

"I'm afraid that's impossible," he said. "A file as old as the Armenian file will have been covered in dust for ages, so dusty we can't find it any more."

"Then send for your cleaning lady and get her to dust the file."

"I did that a long time ago," said the archivist, "but it's not so simple."

"Why?"

"Because all the United Nations cleaning ladies have asthma and won't dust the old files, especially if they're as old as the one on the forgotten genocide. That would raise clouds of dust and make them cough."

I said: "I can understand that."

"What's forgotten mustn't be dusted," said the archivist. "It's too dangerous." And with those words he disappeared.'

'Later I went up to the conference hall. I got up out of the audience several times to interrupt the Turkish speaker, but the marshals put me out of the hall.'

'Once I managed to slip in again. I stood beside the secretary-general and made a stirring speech. I spoke about my people whom the Turks had wiped out, and the representatives of all the nations listened to me for a long time. But then they began to get bored, and one after another they left the hall. In the end I was all alone.'

13

★   ★   ★

'And then the cleaning lady came in. She really did have asthma, and said to me with a cough: "What are you doing, still here?"

"I've been waiting for you."

"For me?"

"Yes, for you."

"Are you one of those diplomats who try to get off with the cleaning ladies?"

"No."

"Then what do you want me for?"

I said: "I want you to dust something that has been forgotten."

She just laughed.'

'While the cleaning lady scrubbed the floor I told her my story, because I thought to myself that cleaning ladies are talkative people and she would pass my story on in the lobbies and corridors of the United Nations, so that it would come to the ears of the representatives of all the nations. But the cleaning lady didn't listen to me. She turned her backside on me while she scrubbed and then left the great hall.'

'Now I was alone again. Rather at a loss, I strolled past the tables of the different nations, reading the name plates, and finished up in front of the secretary-general's desk. I went up behind the desk and spoke to the empty chamber.'

'I told the silence the story of the genocide. I made the silence aware of how important it is that it should be spoken of in public. I said: "Everyone ought to know!" For how will genocide be prevented in future if everyone declares they knew nothing about it, and they did nothing to prevent it because they couldn't even imagine such a thing. I spoke at length and minutely. I claimed nothing for my people, and I demanded no punishment for the persecutors. I said: "I only want to break the silence."'

'Not until much later did I start to talk about myself. I told the empty chamber my story and the story of my family. I spoke about my father and mother, my grandparents and great-grandparents, my aunts and uncles. I spoke about all those people I had never known until I was exhausted, stopped and closed my eyes and rested my head in my hands.'

'When I looked up the secretary-general was standing beside me. He said: "You didn't see me, but I was standing beside you all the time."

"Then you heard it all?"

"I heard it all."'

'"Will you pass it on?"

"No," said the secretary-general, "I won't pass it on."'

'Then we smoked a cigarette together. The secretary-general said: "I found the story of your family particularly confused and incredible; how they lived, I mean, before the great massacre and then were wiped out. Just like that."

I nodded and said nothing.

"It's simply extraordinary, Mr Khatisian," said the secretary-general, "that you should remember everything so clearly. If I'm not mistaken, you never knew any of your family, not even your own mother. For when you came into the world, Mr Khatisian, in 1915, they were all either dead or had disappeared."

"My mother was with me."

"How do you know that?"

"I don't know it, Secretary-General, and yet I know it exactly."'

'"You told the empty chamber just now that two Turks found you on the road."

"Yes, Secretary-General. A man and a woman."

"And later – so you said – the two of them put you in an orphanage, some orphanage or other. There were a lot of them in those days."

"Yes."

"Shortly after the Great War two women from the Red Cross came and took you to Switzerland? That's what you said just now?"

"That's right, Secretary-General."

"And you stayed there, and today you're a Swiss citizen?"

"Yes."

"A Swiss, then?"

"No, Secretary-General. I'm Armenian. An Armenian with a Swiss passport.'"

'"But your family, Mr Khatisian! You didn't even know them! You didn't know any of them. Not even your family's name."

"That's right."

"At some time you adopted the name Khatisian, because you believed that that was what your family might have been called."

"Yes, Secretary-General. The name Khatisian is a very common Armenian name."

The secretary-general smiled. He said: "You don't even know where your family came from, not even the name of the town or the village. You know nothing about them. Nothing.'"

'"Look, Secretary-General," I said. "When I was thirteen I began trying to find out. And for the past sixty years I've done nothing but investigate."

"Have you found any clues?"

"I've found a great many clues, but they all lead nowhere."

"Then it's true that you don't know who you are."

"It's not true," I said. "I know who I am.'"

'"For sixty years I've been getting survivors of the massacre to tell me their stories, stories about Hayastan, which is also called Turkish Armenia or Anatolia – whichever you like – and from all those stories I've put my own story together. And so one day I had a genuine family history. I knew my roots. I had a father and a mother again, and I had many relatives. I also had a name with a tradition, one that I could pass on to my children and grandchildren. You see, Secretary-General, this story is still a bit confused in my head. But soon it will take shape, and then it will be just as real as all real stories are."

"When will that be?"

"It will be soon."

"Ultimate clarity always comes too late," said the secretary-general. And he added, almost as a joke: "It only comes with

16

the last thought."

"But that's not too late," I said. "With the last thought everything will become clear. And I see it already: the last thought will clarify all the confusion in my head. And that state of order in my head will gently rock me out of this life. People will say of me: look, this man died like a tree. A tree can shed its leaves, but never its roots. And why should it be different for men?"'

And now I am back lying on my deathbed. And the Meddah in my head says: 'You are full of expectations, Thovma Khatisian. You are waiting for the last thought like a bride waiting for the bridegroom, who then comes to her to show her his own roots. But I warn you, Thovma Khatisian: the last thought is short, less than a fraction of a single second.'

'Can it be prolonged?'

'No, Thovma Khatisian.'

And the Meddah said: 'But I could tell you now about the last thought, which sits there in the last cry of fear and will fly back to your father and your mother and all those whom you never knew. And I can also tell you now that your last cry of fear will be changed.'

'How do you mean?'

'Into a cry of joyful expectation.'

'Then I will die without fear?'

'You will not die in uncertainty.'

'Is that the same thing?'

'It is the same.'

And I said to the story-teller in my head: 'Tell me about the last thought, to fill in the time of waiting and prolong that which is going to flash through my head in less than a fraction of a second at the last moment. After all, you promised me that.'

'I only promised you a story.'

'The story of the last thought?'

'The story of the last thought.'

And the Meddah said: 'Once I held your great-grandfather on my lap. It was in the market-place of Bakir, a big Turkish town. I told him a Turkish story and said to him: *bir varmish, bir yokmush, bir varmish* . . . Once upon a time there was someone, once upon a time there was no one, once upon a time . . . That's how all stories begin in that part of the world. And why should the story I'm going to tell you now begin differently?

'And now listen, Thovma Khatisian. I'm saying: *bir varmish, bir yokmush, bir varmish* . . . Once upon a time there was someone, once upon a time there was no one, once upon a time . . .'

BOOK ONE

CHAPTER ONE

Once upon a time there was a last thought. It could fly every way in time, into the future and into the past, for it was immortal.

As this last thought flew through the gaping mouth of the dying man, with his last cry of expectation, it said to itself: before you fly into the future, you should first pay a visit to Bakir, that great Turkish city, where your parents are expecting you. And so it happened.

The last thought flew back in time and came down in the wartime year 1915, on a spring day, on the dome of the city gate, the eastern gate called Bab-i-Se'adet, the Gate of Happiness. It was a big wrought iron gate in the thousand-year-old stone of Bakir's city wall. No one saw the last thought come down on the dome of the gate, because it could neither be seen nor be heard. And so it spoke quite freely to the story-teller.

'Where are you, Meddah?'

'I am with you,' said the story-teller.

'But I have no body.'

'That makes no difference.'

'Where are you?'

'I am within you. And you are a part of Thovma Khatisian, who is just breathing his last.'

'Breathing his last – how long does that take?'

'Less than a fraction of a second.'

'But that isn't long.'

'It is not long. That's true. Or maybe it isn't true. For it is possible that eternity is shorter than a fraction of a second. It's measured in a different way.'

'Tell me where I am, Meddah.'

'You're on top of the Bab-i-Se'adet Gate, the Gate of Happiness. If you look to the south-east, you're looking straight towards Mecca, the place to which all faithful Muslims must make a pilgrimage at least once in their lives, for that is where the Prophet lived and worked. And the sacred Ka'aba is there.'

'The Ka'aba? And Mecca? The Gate of Happiness? But then I don't understand . . . why there are three Armenians hanging right under this gate? Their mouths are wide open, as if their last cry of fear was still between their teeth. They are dangling on long ropes, swaying slightly in the evening wind and staring straight in front of them.'

'They are traitors.'

'Is that true?'

'The Turks say so.'

'Is my father one of those three Armenians?'

'No. He's not down there.'

'Are you taking me to my father and mother now?'

'Not yet,' said the Meddah. 'Wait just a little while.'

'Your dreams have always told you that Bakir is the most beautiful city in the world,' said the Meddah. 'The Turks call it the city of a thousand and one mosques. A thousand and one storks perch on the golden domes in summer. At daybreak, when the sun breaks loose from the Kurds' goat's-hair rope and prepares to lick up the last traces of night with its fiery beams, when the first bird tries out its song, then the storks on the domes of the mosques bathe their white wings in the morning light, clatter with their long bills and call up the muezzins to shout their *Allahu akbar* to the heavens from the minarets.'

'But I don't see any storks.'

'They're still in Mecca; they'll only come when it gets warmer.'

'And I can't see so many mosques. Did you say a thousand and one?'

'A thousand and one.'

'But I can only see eleven. I've counted them exactly. There are eleven mosques in Bakir.'

'That, my son, is because the Turks love to exaggerate, just like

22

the Jews and the Greeks and the devil-worshippers and the Gypsies, all the people in this part of the world. There are in fact only eleven mosques here. You're quite right. I've counted them too. There are eight in the Turkish quarter, two in the Kurdish quarter and one in the Armenian *mahalle*, though it doesn't really belong there.'

'Why, Meddah?'

'Because the Armenians are Christians. You know that, Thovma Khatisian. And you've just seen the Armenians' churches.'

'I haven't see them yet.'

'Then look round, Thovma Khatisian. Look round. You will see churches everywhere, most of all in the Armenian *mahalle*. They just aren't so conspicuous.'

'Why do you call me Thovma Khatisian?'

'Because you represent him here.'

'And why do you call me "my son"?'

'That doesn't mean anything. I could just as well call you "my little lamb" or "my little pasha". I could call you by lots of names, though you've only got one real name.'

'What name is that?'

'Thovma Khatisian.'

'Soon the sun will disappear, for the Kurds are already hauling in the evening, fumbling with their goat's-hair rope. Shall I tell you what always happens in Bakir on an evening like this?'

'Yes, Meddah. But make it short, I want to go to my father and I want to go to my mother.'

And the Meddah said: 'At this moment four gentlemen are sitting in the office of the Mudir of Bakir, on the top floor of the *hukumet*, the government *konak*, a weatherproof building in the Rue Hodja Pascha, as the upper-class French-speaking Turks call the street, though otherwise it's simply called Hodsha Pasha Sokaghi. One of the gentlemen wears a khaki uniform and has a fur cap on his head; he's the one-eyed Mudir of Bakir, governor and commander-in-chief of the local gendarmerie. The other gentlemen are in civilian dress and just have the red fez on their heads. Two of them – the Kaimakam and the Mutessarif – are senior officials in the complicated Turkish administrative hierarchy, responsible for the different areas and districts into which the Vilayet of Bakir is divided. But the fourth gentlemen is the Vali himself, the provincial governor of the whole Vilayet of Bakir, a *vilayet* as big as the Vilayet of Erzurum or the Vilayet of Van. The gentlemen are sitting on an expensive carpet, each with a gaily coloured cushion stuffed with feathers under his backside; they sit cross-legged, drinking sweet coffee from tiny copper cups and smoking their *chibouks*.

"I'll have this Vartan Khatisian beheaded first thing in the morning," the Mudir is saying. "And then I'll run a spear through his head with my own hands and stick it up on the city wall."

"Whereabouts?" asks the Mutessarif.

"At the Gate of Happiness," says the Mudir, "off to the left above the heads of the three Armenians I had hanged yesterday." The Mudir laughs and looks expressionlessly at the two gentlemen with his glass eye.

"I shouldn't do that if I were you," says the corpulent Vali, and makes a weary gesture with his hand. "That Vartan Khatisian has actually got a lot to tell us."

"The Vali is right," says the Mutessarif. "Vartan Khatisian can tell us a lot so long as he's alive, but once he's dead there's no more he can do."

The Vali makes another tired movement with his hand. He says: "Efendiler. I've just been trying to dig out a confession from a dead man, but he was dumber than a fish from Lake Van. Even I, the Vali of Bakir – even I couldn't squeeze anything at all out of him.'"

The gentlemen fall silent, slurp their sweet coffee and smoke their *chibouks*. They couldn't know that the last thought of Thovma Khatisian had come out in goose-pimples all over his back, even though being a creature with no body he had no real back; but he had been horrified by their words, and so he asks the Meddah now: 'Who are they talking about?'

'About your father, my little lamb. About your father.'

'Where is my father?'

'He's in prison.'

'In prison?'

'In prison.'

'When will you take me to him?'

'Soon, my little lamb.'
'Will they chop his head off?'
'That we shall soon see.'

'And now listen, my little lamb,' said the story-teller. 'While the four gentlemen in the government building go on talking about the fate of your father, in many houses in Bakir they are lighting the first oil lamps. The traders in the bazaars are closing down their stalls and loading their goods on to mule or donkey-carts or, many of them, just into big flour sacks, which they either carry home themselves or have dragged by a *hamal*, giving him a couple of lousy paras. These Bakir *hamals* are the laziest porters in all Turkey, even worse than the ones in the harbour at Constantinople, and do you know why? I'll tell you, my little lamb: because most of them are Kurds. A Kurd is either proud and free and lives high in the mountains, depending on his sheep or on robbery, and owning a horse and a gun; or else he gives up his pride and his freedom, and with them his dignity, and becomes a *hamal* in Bakir. That's how it goes. These Kurdish porters in Bakir rank lower than a donkey.'

'Why are you telling me all this, Meddah?'

'To sharpen my tongue before I tell you more about your father, who is waiting for you without being aware of it, and whom you will soon see.'

'When?'

'Soon.'

'You don't mind, do you, if I call you Thovma,' said the story-teller to the last thought, 'or "my little lamb" or "my son" or that sort of thing?'

'No,' said the last thought. 'Call me whatever you like. The great thing is, you're taking me to my father.'

'Don't you want to see your mother too?'

'Of course,' said the last thought. 'Her especially. But I think it's more important just now that I should see my father, or they may chop his head off before I've seen him.'

'You're absolutely right,' said the Meddah. 'But first, just look round.'

'I've done that already,' said the last thought.

'And what do you see?'

'I see all those Turks in the Grand Bazaar, just closing down their stalls.'

'They aren't Turks,' said the Meddah, 'they're Armenian traders, most of them anyway. They've been living with the Turks in the same country for centuries, and often you can hardly distinguish them from the Turks. Just look: most of the men are wearing a red fez, and their baggy trousers or *chalvars* are tied with string at the knee. The sleeveless jackets they wear under their coats are the same as the Turks wear. Many of them strut around in western clothing, just like the new generation of Young Turks, and wear a fur cap or a fez with it. Their shaggy moustaches strike fear into the women; they're no less impressive than those of the Turks or the mountain Kurds. The cigarettes or pipes they smoke, the *chibouk* for instance, are the same as even the Vali of Bakir and the Mutessarif and the Mudir smoke; or else they smoke the *nargile*, the water-pipe with the coiled tube, but you need time and leisure for that. And if you ask an Armenian what tobacco he fills his *chibouk* with, he will naturally tell you it's the Persian Abu Ri'ha tobacco, the father of fragrance, and that is the same answer you will get from any Turk who thinks anything of himself.'

The Meddah said: 'My little lamb. All those are external things. If you want to know whether anyone is Armenian, look in their eyes.'

'Soon the bazaar will look as if it had died,' said the Meddah, 'and only the watersellers with their goatskins half full of water will be running here and there up to the departing traders, still shouting *lyi su, soghuk su, bus gibi, on para* – good water, cold water, like ice, ten paras. The watersellers are always the last at the bazaar, they take the Prophet at his word, the Prophet who said: all haste is from the devil.'

'Yes, my little lamb: all haste is from the devil, and in this country only the deaf-mutes seem to be in a hurry, when they rush off to the mosque in the evening to make the wordless *namaz* prayer because they didn't hear the call of the muezzins shouting themselves hoarse from the balconies of the minarets.'

'Where do the deaf-mutes pray, Meddah?'

'Wherever the other Muslims pray,' said Meddah. 'Many of them probably go to the Hirka Sherif Djamissi, the Mosque of the Holy Mantle, in the Turkish quarter, or to the Kurusebil Sokaghi, the Avenue of the Dry Well, or the the Deli-Avret-Djami, the Mosque of the Foolish Woman, down in the Kurdish quarter. I don't know, my little lamb, but I suppose most deaf-mutes go to the Mosque of Muhammed Pasha the Miracle Doctor, Djerah Muhammed Pasha Djami.'

'It's a pity you weren't here this morning,' said the Meddah. 'A lot of new recruits came through the Armenian quarter. They came out of the barracks, marched to the Bit Bazari with a military band – that's the flea market or junk market – turned into the Divan Yoli, the street of the council, then marched through the Armenian quarter where the craftsmen work, along the streets of the potters and the silversmiths; they even came past the *urbadjis*, the Armenian tailors of Bakir, where your great-grandfather made himself a suit of real wool which your grandfather later inherited, and your father after him. And now guess where the recruits were going?'

'How should I know that, Meddah?'

'They went to the Top Kapi, to the fortified gate in the west of the city. And if you go through that, you get straight to Erzurum.'

'What is there in Erzurum?'

'That's where the Turkish Third Army is stationed.'

'What for, Meddah?'

'To stop the Russian steamroller, my little lamb. The one that's rolling straight across the Caucasus, on its way to Constantinople.'

'Regiments were marching through Bakir all the morning,' said the Meddah, 'mostly Rediffs, reservists of the first class, but also Mustahfis regiments, the lowest class of reservists, and in those I saw old men and others who looked like children, and I saw lame men and other cripples. And, believe it or not, the screaming women followed the Mustahfis, and then came the dervishes of the Rufai sects, who were suddenly there yelling *Ya ghasi, Ya shahid, Ya Allah, Ya hu* – O warriors, O martyrs, O Allah, O he. And the Vali

27

and the Mutessarif, the Kaimakam and the one-eyed Mudir, were there standing on the *hukumet* balcony, and they really would have crossed themselves if they'd been Christians.'

'But now the Mudir is not standing on the balcony. Nor are the Vali and the Mutessarif and the Kaimakam. They are back again sitting in the Mudir's office discussing your father.'

'Have they come to any conclusion?'

'Not yet, my little lamb, not yet. For the gentlemen have had a visitor, a bit late, a German officer of the rank of major, one of the instructors of the Turkish army. And now they are all sitting on that expensive carpet with cushions under their backsides, drinking coffee and smoking *chibouks*.'

'"This morning," says the German officer, "when I rode into the town with my men, I saw three Armenians under the Gate of Happiness. They were swinging on long ropes."

"They're traitors," says the Vali.

"All Armenians are traitors," says the Mudir, "and actually they all ought to be hanged."'

'"How many Armenians are there in this area?" asks the major.

"Five million," says the Vali.

"There can't be," says the German major. "According to the statistics there are only 1.2 million of these remarkable people living in the whole of Turkey."

"Those were Sultan Abdul Hamid's statistics," says the Vali. "The Young Turks scrapped those long ago."

"Does that mean that Abdul Hamid wanted to play down the minorities' question?"

"That's it, Binbashi Bey," says the Vali.'

'"These Armenians are dangerous people," says the Vali. "And they live on both sides of the frontier. 4 million on our side and 1 million on the Russian."

"That's a wild exaggeration," says the major.

"No, Binbashi Bey," says the Vali. "There could be even more, for these people breed like rats." The Vali smiles and slurps sweet coffee. "And they're all related to each other."

"What do you mean by that?"

"What should I mean, Binbashi Bey?" says the Vali. "Well, it's like this. The Turkish Armenians have aunts and uncles on the other side of the frontier. Many have sons and daughters over there. Parents and grandparents and all sorts of relations. They're all related to each other."

"And if they weren't related to each other – officially, I mean," says the Mudir now, "all the same they are still related to each other, because, you see, they are a special race who have practised inbreeding for thousands of years. They all have the same blood."

"It's bad blood," says the Vali, "it comes from the devil."

"And they're all in league with one another," says the Mudir, "all Armenians, both sides of the frontier. And they're all in with the Russians."

"Does that mean," asks the major, "that the Armenians here on the Turkish side are waiting for the Russian invasion . . . or that they will actually support it?"

"You've guessed it, Binbashi Bey," says the Vali. "The Turkish Armenians are waiting for the Russian invasion and the invasion of their relatives over there, fighting for the Czar. And this invasion has their full support."

"Do you have substantial evidence of that?"

"We don't need it," says the Vali. "It's enough that we know it."

"A dangerous situation," says the major.

"And near the front, too," says the Mudir. "Millions of Armenians with Turkish passports in our rear. Millions whom we know to be on the enemy's side."

"A highly dangerous situation," says the major.'

'"You understand, Binbashi Bey," says the Mutessarif now, "why we had to make an example of those three Armenians you saw hanging."

"I can understand that," says the major.

"And the Gate of Happiness is just the right place."

"Yes," says the major.

"We hanged the three of them in such a way that they weren't looking at Mecca."

"Which way were they looking?" asks the major.

"The wrong way," says the Mudir.'

'"On one of those hanged Armenians we found a bottle of Russian schnapps," says the Mudir. "That's a serious crime, as Russia is enemy territory."

"He said he got the schnapps from his brother-in-law," says the Mutessarif, "his wife's brother, who has a distillery over there on the wrong side."

"He said he'd got the schnapps before war broke out," says the Mudir, "but he had no evidence to prove it."

"And what crime had the other two Armenians committed?" asks the major.

"On the second one we found a letter," says the Mudir.

"A letter from Russia, from his grandmother."

"Contact with the enemy?"

"Just so, Binbashi Bey."

"And how did the letter get into Turkey?"

"Well, of course, Binbashi Bey, the letter came by post."

"Before the war, then?"

"Of course, before the war."

"Was the date with the Russian postmark still on the envelope?"

"No, neither the date nor the postmark was on the envelope."''

'"There wasn't any envelope, in fact," says the Mudir, "because the postman had opened the letter and chucked the envelope away."

"And what did he do that for?"

"Because the Armenian wouldn't give him a tip, and he wanted to keep the letter until he got his tip."

"*Baksheesh?*"

"Of course. *Baksheesh*. The usual tip. What else. These postmen are little, underpaid officials, easily corrupted, dependent on tips. What good does it do that, since the change of government, we Young Turks have been doing everything possible to change things, to root out corruption, when a postman like that one still lives in the spirit of the deposed Abdul Hamid and can't get hold of the new ethics?"

"Right," says the Vali.

"You see, Binbashi Bey," the Kaimakam says now, "the postman had kept the letter for two years and only delivered it last week. And when we found the letter, a letter with no envelope, we naturally believed it was a letter that had been smuggled in. What else should we think? For no legal post comes over the frontier in wartime. And we had no way of knowing that the letter had actually come in peacetime."

"Didn't the postman say anything?"

"Oh yes, Binbashi Bey. But he only said it when the Armenian was swinging up there in front of the gate. In front of the Gate of Happiness. And looking the wrong way. Not towards Mecca."

"So that's it," says the major.

"That's it, Binbashi Bey," says the Kaimakam. "And may Allah be my witness."'

'"And what about the third traitor?"

"He's an Armenian priest," the Mudir says now. "We picked him up in the middle of a sermon."

"So you must have sent informers into the Christian church?"

"There's a war on, Binbashi Bey. There's a war on. What are we to do?"

"And what had the priest done?"

"He had prayed with his congregation for victory. Only we didn't know for which side."

"But I don't understand that, Mudir Bey."

"At the end of the service he called for cheers for the sovereign, and what he actually said was: Long live the Padisha! But we didn't know which Padisha he meant. You'll understand, Binbashi Bey. There's a Russian Padisha and a Turkish one. In Russia there's the Czar and in Turkey we have the new Sultan that Enver Pasha has put on the throne. How were we to know which Padisha the priest meant?"

"It really is hard to decide," says the major.

"But we decided it," says the Mudir triumphantly, "for as he spoke of the Padisha the priest touched the cross."

"What cross?"

"The long cross that dangles on his chest. And so we knew that he could only have meant the Russian Czar. Only that one."

"I'm not so sure about that," says the major.

"Well, we're quite sure," says the Mudir.'

'"It has astonished me" says the major, "that the Armenians haven't gone on strike. Only today I went shopping in the Armenian quarter. All the shops were open."

"And why should they be closed?"

"Because three of them had been hanged."

"But, Binbashi Bey," says the Mudir, "those rats are much too cowardly to make a public protest."'

'"A few weeks ago I was in Galicia," says the major, "on the Austrian front. And do you know, Mudir Bey, what happpened there?"

"No," says the Mudir.

"There are too many Jews there. And you know what it's like haggling over things with Jews?"

"No," says the Mudir.

"Just like Armenians," says the major. "Those two peoples are so alike you can almost mix them up. It's incredible."

"No doubt," says the Mudir.

"Do you have any problems with Jews here?"

"No," says the Mudir. "Here we have problems with the Armenians."'

'"Those Armenians are worse than rats," says the Mudir. "Wherever they live they infiltrate the local people, undermine them and finally destroy them."

"Quite right," says the Vali.

"They exploit us Turks and act as if they were our lords and masters."

"Quite right," says the Vali.

"And those Armenians are rolling in money, believe you me. Their women are all dressed in silks and satins and wear the most expensive jewellery. You know what they say: every Armenian woman is a walking jeweller's shop." The Mudir laughs. "And everything is in their hands. The banks and money exchanges, the crafts and trade. They are the doctors and the lawyers, and they send their sons and daughters to good schools."

"And they're in league with the enemy," says the Mutessarif.

"Yes," says the Mudir. "Every Armenian is a Russian in disguise."

"They're just waiting to stick a dagger in our back," says the Vali. And he adds quietly: "Something has got to be done!" And he sips his coffee contentedly, draws on his *chibouk* and says: "Something has really got to be done."'

'"And what about that spy you've had in prison so long?" asks the major. "Is he an Armenian?"

"Of course he's an Armenian. What else?"

"What's his name?"

"He's called Vartan Khatisian."

The major laughs. He says: "But that's a very common Armenian name."'

'"The Armenians are a very ancient people," says the German major. "If I'm not mistaken, they were already living in this region when Mohammed was enlightened."

"You're right there," says the Vali.

"Even before that," says the major. "I believe . . . when Christ preached the sermon on the mount, as early as that."

"That is true," says the Vali.

"Even before that," says the major, "before your calendar, even before ours."

"Yes," says the Vali.

The Vali draws thoughtfully on his *chibouk* and smiles. "Are you trying to say that the Armenians were already here, in this region, before the Turks came?"

"I'm not trying to say anything," says the major.

"Well, that may be right," says the Vali, "but what does it mean now?"

"It doesn't mean anything," says the Mudir. "They're nothing more than rats, and even the rats were here before the Turks came."'

'"So we're back with the rats again," says the Mudir. He smiles

33

and says: "Do you know, efendiler, a little time ago I was chasing a rat in the cellar. I had a club with me of course, because I wanted to kill the rat." The Mudir closes his one eye for a second, opens it again and looks innocently at the major. "When I was down in the cellar I saw another rat. There were two of them. And then there were four. There were more and more of them. Hundreds and thousands. Wherever I went there were rats. Suddenly there were millions. They ate all the clothes off my body, they gnawed away my club, they went for my arteries and completely devoured me."'

'"And then you woke up?" asks the major.
    "No."
    "But that can only have been a dream?"'

'For a time no one said a word. Only when the Mudir nervously clapped his hands and told the saptieh who rushed in to fetch fresh coffee, did the Vali clear his throat in an embarrassed way and ask the major the question that had been hovering in the air so long:
    "How is the war going, Binbashi Bey? Will the Germans occupy Paris now or not?"
    "It can't last much longer."
    "And St Petersburg?"
    "We'll soon be in St Petersburg."'

'"And how is it going in the Caucasus?"
    "Enver Pasha's army has had to withdraw temporarily."
    "The Turkish soldier there is the best in the world."
    "It's on account of the cholera," says the major. "And the cold winter."
    "But the winter must be over?"
    "Yes," says the major.'

'"As long as Enver Pasha was commander-in-chief of the army in the Caucasus, everything went well," says the Vali. "Enver Pasha ought to have marched on and on until he met the Kaiser in St Petersburg. I simply don't understand why the front collapsed and Enver came back to Constantinpole."
    "Nobody understands it," says the Mudir.

34

"Because of the cholera, perhaps," says the Vali. "Or because of the shortage of winter clothing. Or because of the Armenians. The Armenian soldiers have bewitched our troops. It's all their fault."

"Yes," says the Mudir.'

It has grown silent all round me, and although I, Thovma Khatisian, am still only a thought, and timeless, I can hear a ticking sound.

'That's only the time,' says the Meddah, 'and whether you like it or not, time always passes. And soon the decision will be made.'

'What decision?'

'The decision of the provincial governor, the Vali of Bakir, who will order the Mudir either to behead your father or not to.'

'Are you taking me to see my father now?'

'Soon, my little lamb. Soon.'

And the Meddah said: 'Do you see that old blind beggar by the Gate of Happiness?'

'Yes, I can see him.'

'He's called Mechmed Efendi. He's a clever chap, this Mechmed Efendi, so clever that people say of him . . . he may be a Turk, but he has the intellect of an Armenian.'

'And the child at his feet?'

'That is his grandchild, Ali.'

'Two hungry mouths that Allah has forgotten?'

'You're mistaken, my little lamb. Do you see that beggar's cloth on the kerb, held down with four stones so that the wind won't blow it away? There are only a few lousy paras in it. But that beggar is rolling in money. I suppose you won't believe that?'

'No, I don't believe it.'

'Well, believe what you want,' said the Meddah. 'But it's true. And this Mechmed Efendi wanted to ransom your father, because your father had once saved his life. But I'll tell you about that later.'

'Did the beggar ransom my father?'

'No,' said the Meddah.

'Why not?'

'Because no one can ransom your father. He's too important to the Vali.'

35

'So it's no use.'
'It's no use.'

'Of course other people tried to buy your father out. Your mother, for instance. And the whole family. They all tried. But it was no use. And yet people say that Turkish officials are corrupt.'

'Are they corrupt?'

'Of course they're corrupt, my little lamb. In this country you can get almost anything done with *baksheesh*. Only nobody can ransom your father.'

'Because he's important? To the Vali?'

'Not only to the Vali. Also to the others, especially the Mudir. The officials have a lot of plans for him.'

'If he's so important, then he must surely still be needed, and if he's needed they won't be so stupid as to behead him too soon?'

'Just so, my little lamb. You've got it right. I thought of that too.'

'At this moment, my little lamb . . . at this moment . . . the old blind beggar gives a jump. Did you see it?'

'Yes. I saw that.'

'He goes like that, as if something had startled him, but it's only a game. He likes to play jokes on his grandson. And can you hear what he's saying to his grandson?' And I hear the blind beggar say to the child:

'Ali, my darling. I believe death is near.'

'Nonsense, Dede,' says the child. 'Death can't come until you've told me where you've hidden your money.'

'You're right, my darling,' says the blind man. 'And you understand things too. You inherited that from me.'

'Yes, Dede,' says the child.

And the beggar says: 'What happened just now was because I got a cold feeling in my throat.'

'What sort of cold, Dede?'

'A cold wind.'

'But there's no wind blowing, Dede.'

'Yes there is, my darling. There's a cold wind blowing. And it comes from the Gate of Happiness.'

'From the Gate of Happiness?'

'Yes, Ali, my darling. That's where it comes from. And I'll wager with you there is death on the arch of the gate.'

'There's death underneath the arch, Dede.'

'And what does it look like?'

'It looks like three Armenians swinging up there.'

'So that's what it looks like?'

'Yes. That's what it's like.'

'Tell me, my darling, what are the dead men wearing on their heads?'

'Only one of them has anything on his head, Dede.'

'And what is that?'

'A *kühla* of Persian lamb.'

'Do you think it's worth anything?'

'Yes, Dede. But not much.'

'Do you think the *kühla* could fall down here?'

'Yes, Dede. But only if the dead man wagged his head.'

'Even my blind eyes can see that much.'

'Yes, Dede.'

'Perhaps the dead man would wag his head if the wind blew again?'

'Yes, Dede.'

'Tell me, my darling. Can you catch the *kühla* if the dead man wags his head and the *kühla* falls down off him?'

'No, Dede.'

'Why not, my darling?'

'Because there's a guard standing under the dead man's legs, with a gun.'

'A gendarme, one of those stupid saptiehs?'

'Yes, Dede.'

'Are there any other people standing under the dead man's legs?'

'Yes, Dede. A lot of *hamals* and other Kurdish riff-raff. Also a couple of Turks and even an Armenian.'

'And what are they doing there?'

'They're looking up at the dead man, waiting for him to wag his head and throw his *kühla* down to them.'

'Looking up at him, are they?'

37

'Yes, Dede.'

'And what about the dead men's clothes?'
  'It's not easy to get at them.'
  'And what about their shoes?'
  'Just the same.'

'Something will have to be done, my darling, to get at the old clothes
or the shoes. And your old Dede always thinks of something. Or do
you think I'm too old and won't get any more ideas?'
  'No, Dede. I don't think that.'

'Now, be careful, my darling. We can give up any idea of getting
the clothes. It surely isn't easy to undress the dead man with one
of those stupid saptiehs watching you . . . And there are all those
people under the hanged men waiting for loot. Not at all easy, my
darling.'
  'True, Dede.'

'But it's different with shoes.'
  'How different, Dede?'
  'Just different, my darling.'

'Tell me, my darling. What sort of shoes are there on the dead men's
feet?'
  'One of them is barefoot, Dede. He's an Armenian priest and
looks like a Persian king, in one of those long robes with a cross on
his breast, but not wearing a crown.'
  'But Persian kings don't wear a cross, my darling. They really
don't wear a cross.'
  'Maybe, Dede. I didn't know that.'
  'And what sort of shoes is the second one wearing?'
  'He's got a pair of red velvet slippers on.'
  'They must have taken him when he was in bed.'
  'Yes, Dede.'
  'Those Armenians sleep in their slippers if the fire goes out in
their *tonir*.'
  'Yes, Dede.'

'You don't get much for slippers, my darling. So let's forget about that.'
'Yes, Dede.'

'And what has the third one got on his feet?'
'A pair of yellow leather boots.'
'Yellow leather, did you say?'
'Yes, Dede.'

'Now be careful, my darling. You will now climb the thousand and one steps, I mean the steps that lead to the arch of the gate, the arch of the Gate of Happiness.'
'Up there where the dead men are tied?'
'Yes, my darling.'
'To the end of those long ropes?'
'Yes, my darling.'
'But I can't see a thousand and one steps.'
'That doesn't matter, my darling.'
'There aren't as many as that, Dede.'
'So much the better, my darling.'

'And now be careful, my darling. You'll climb up there and untie the dead man, the one with the yellow boots.'
'Yes, Dede.'
'And then he'll tumble down. Right at the saptieh's feet. And he'll wonder where the dead man came from. And the stupid saptieh will get a tremendous fright and believe that the Prophet himself has sent the dead man from paradise, although in fact he had to hang right here on earth, on the Gate of Happiness.'
'What will the saptieh do?'
'He won't do anything, my darling. He'll just scratch his head and look at the dead man.'
'And what shall I do?'
'You'll run down the thousand and one steps, as fast as your legs can carry you. And you will run over to the saptieh and talk to him.'
'What shall I say to him?'
'You will promote him to the rank of captain. For these saptiehs are stupid, and that makes them specially conceited. You will say

to him: "Yusbashi Bey. We can't just leave the dead man lying here in the street. But you know that better than I do, Yusbashi Bey."

'And the saptieh will feel flattered and will stroke your hair, and he'll say to you: "Of course I know that better than you."

'"I know you'll hang the dead man up again," you will say to him, "for it can't be right that the Mudir had three people hanged and now there are only two hanging under the arch."

'"That can never be, my dear," the saptieh will say. "If the Mudir has had three people hanged, then there simply have to be three."

'"Then I'll help you tie the dead man up again."

'"That's not a bad idea," the saptieh will say. "But have you seen those thousand and one steps?"

'"I've seen them," you will say.

'"It's a lot of steps."

'"Yes, Yusbashi Bey."

'"And you'll really help me go up all those steps to the top of the arch with this dead swine, this uncircumcised infidel, whose soul will burn for ever in hell, if indeed he ever had one?"

'"Yes," you'll say.

'And that's how it will be. Since you're still small and weaker than the saptieh, you'll take the lighter end of the dead body, which of course will be the feet.'

'You mean the feet with the yellow kidskin boots on the end of them?'

'That's it, my darling. The saptieh will be taking the heavy end, holding the body under the arms, and the two of you will plod panting up the steps dragging your package. But then you'll suddenly stop.'

'Why, Dede?'

'Because you want to say something to the saptieh.'

'What shall I want to say?'

'You'll say to him: "Yusbashi Bey. You're going up the steps backwards. You can't do that."

'"Why can't I do that?" the saptieh will say.

'"Because only an ass goes up steps backwards, when you try to drag it forwards, the right way, on the rope, which of course the ass generally has round its neck."

'"You wouldn't be meaning that I'm an ass, by any chance?" the saptieh will say.

'"No, Yusbashi Bey," you'll say. "A clever man like you is certainly not an ass, and he certainly doesn't go up steps backwards."'

'And what happens then, Dede?'

'Well, this is what should happen. The saptieh will turn round and pick up the body the other way round, and then he'll go up the steps the way any normal man goes up steps, looking in front of him, I reckon . . . towards the arch, where he wants to hang the dead man again.'

'I see, Dede.'

'The saptieh will turn his back on you and so won't be able to see you. He'll plod on up the steps, swearing and spitting. He'll curse all dead men that have been hanged by the Turks in the course of history. And he'll curse the unbelievers, especially the Armenians. And he'll grumble about the war and about the authorities and about the Vali of Bakir and the Mutessarif and the Mudir and the Kaimakam, about all the high-ups who get lots of *baksheesh* while he, the saptieh, mostly goes hungry or picks up the bones the bigwigs leave for him. And he'll curse the day he was born. And he'll curse all mothers who have borne people like the Vali or people like the Mutessarif, the Kaimakam or the Mudir, people who lead a good life while he, the saptieh, lives no better than a dog, with little *baksheesh* and a monthly wage of a few paras, which the authorities in Constantinople mostly forget to pay. As I've said: he will curse, and he will sweat. And while he curses and sweats and puffs his way up the steps, I reckon he will quite forget the other end of the body; the dangling end of the body, the legs that a little boy is holding.'

'But I hang on to the boots, the yellow kidskin boots?'

'That's right, my darling. You hang on to the boots. And you take them off the dead man, no hurry about it, the saptieh can't see you. You drop the boots on the steps. And, believe me, the saptieh won't notice anything, not a thing. But I shall follow up behind you, although I'm blind. That won't bother me at all, I've known the thousand and one steps for years and years. How often I've been up and down them! So I shall go up behind you. And I'll

41

stick those lovely boots in my sack.'

'In the sack?'

'Well, where else, my darling?'

'And that is how it happened,' said the Meddah to the last thought. 'The boy Ali untied the dead man. And the dead man plumped down at the feet of the stupid saptieh. He behaved just as the blind beggar Mechmed Efendi had said he would. He just scratched his head and looked down at the dead man without a word. His lips muttered something or other that only the last of the prophets understood.'

'I see the boy Ali,' said the Meddah. 'I see how the boy runs down the thousand and one steps and rushes over to the saptieh and speaks to him. And I see how the two of them carry the dead man up the thousand and one steps, the saptieh at the heavier end and the boy at the lighter. Everything happened like that, just like that. The saptieh turned round, because only an ass goes backwards. He picked the dead man up the other way round and carried the body properly. While the saptieh cursed and sweated, the boy slipped the boots off the stiff feet. And the blind beggar was already behind him to make the yellow boots disappear in his sack.'

'When the two of them reached the last of the thousand and one steps with the dead man, the saptieh turned round.

"We ought to have a better rope," said the saptieh.

"Yes," said the boy.

"This rope will break again."

"Yes," said the boy.

"We ought to have a rope like the goat's-hair rope the Kurds catch the sun with."

"Yes," said the boy.

It was only then that the saptieh noticed the dead man's bare feet.

"Where are his boots?" asked the saptieh.

"I don't know," said the boy.

"Do you think a dead Armenian can still work magic?" asked the saptieh.

"Yes," said the boy.

"It really is like magic," said the saptieh.'

'They laid the body down on the top step, but in such a way that the dead man was looking at the sky.

"I must just have a breather," said the saptieh, as he wiped the sweat off his brow, "then you can help me tie the dead man up again."

"Yes," said the boy.

"First we'd better turn him over so that he's not looking at the sky," said the saptieh, "otherwise his clothes will disappear too."

"Yes," said the boy, and he helped the saptieh turn the dead man over.

"So an Armenian can actually work magic," said the saptieh. "As long as they're alive they magic the money out of our pockets, and when they're dead their boots disappear."

"Yes," said the boy.

"They're all devil-worshippers," said the saptieh, "like the Yezidis in the village of Birik, the next-door village to Terbizek, the village where my blessed mother gave me life. May Allah be my witness."

"But the Armenians aren't like the Yezidis," said the boy.

"Where did you learn that?"

"From Mechmed Efendi. He knows the Armenians. Mechmed Efendi told me that the Armenians pray to Jesus."

"And who is Jesus?"

"The god of the unbelievers."

"Who told you that?"

"Mechmed Efendi told me."

"Did he tell you anything else?"

"Yes. He said that this Jesus hangs nailed to a cross and can work miracles."

"May Allah have mercy on me," said the saptieh.

Then the saptieh lit a cigarette, one of the Amroian brand, the cheapest cigarette, made here in Bakir by the Armenian Levon Amroian. "Do you think this Jesus has taken the boots off this hanged man?"

"It's possible," said the boy, "for Mechmed Efendi told me that Jesus certainly needed a pair of yellow boots of real kidskin, because

43

he hangs on the cross bare-footed."

"Bare-footed, did you say?"

"Yes," said the boy.

"May Allah have mercy on me," said the saptieh.'

'And so it came to pass,' said the Meddah. 'While the two were tying the dead man up again – and that took quite a time, because the saptieh was not a very dexterous man and didn't know the Turkish hangman's knot, and also because the boy Ali didn't know how a knot can be wound round a rusty hook so as to be foolproof, a hook said to be as old as the Gate of Happiness, and that was very old, older than the first scream of the first man hanged under the arch – so while the two of them laboured, especially the saptieh, who was only doing his duty, so that there should not be two of them but three of them hanging under the Gate of Happiness, in accordance with what the Mudir had ordered – while all that trouble was being taken not to annoy the authorities and everything was being sorted out as it ought to be, while all this and that was going on, darkness had fallen on the town from the Kurdish mountains. Darkness never came secretly there, like a thief in the night as they say – no, my little lamb, darkness always came quickly to Bakir, because the *djinn* in the mountain gorges are impatient spirits which could hardly wait until the Kurds had secured the sun. As soon as the *djinn* saw that the sun had been overpowered, they came up laughing from their mountain gorges, picked up the long shadow that the sun had left in front of the great tent, simply picked it up and threw it over the town.'

'It was all one to the three hanged men whether the sun was still shining in Bakir,' said the Meddah. 'And they were not concerned about the long shadows that the *djinn* with a single heave had thrown over the city of a thousand and one mosques, nor about the countless little oil lamps and the street lights that were being lighted one after another in the darkness of the town. They saw nothing, for they had no more sight. And yet their dead eyes looked in a certain direction.'

'How can anyone look in a certain direction if they have no sight?'

'Direction makes no difference if you can't see, my little lamb.'

'Which way were they looking, then, with no sight?'

'In various directions, my little lamb. Each of them was looking a different way.'

'The one in red is called Mushegh Inglisian. He was the richest grain merchant in Bakir. Now guess which way his eyes were looking?'

'How should I know that, Meddah?'

'Those dead eyes were looking at the *askeri ambari*, my little lamb, the military supply depot, for Mushegh Inglisian had for years supplied the Turkish army with the region's best grain. The soldiers used to say, and not without reason, this *ekmek* is the best bread in the world, for the flour comes from the stores of the rich Armenian Inglisian. It's true enough that all Armenians are cheats, but this Inglisian is an exception, he's an honest man.'

'But I can't see any military supply depot, Meddah.'

'You must look the right way,' said the Meddah to the last thought. 'Then you'll see it. It's not far away.'

'How far?'

'You could smoke four cigarettes as you go there, my little lamb. If you go through the Armenian quarter, straight through the *mahalle*, first through the streets of the coppersmiths, potters and tinkers, then through the alleys of the goldsmiths and silversmiths, the money-changers and jewellers, then past the hatmakers, then through the alley under the arches – the Kemer alti Sokaghi – if you go quickly across the flea market – the Bit Bazari – then back along the alleys of the tobacconists, outfitters and saddlers – the *tutunshis*, *urbajis* and *sarajis* – if you keep going all that way in no more than the time it takes to smoke four cigarettes, then you come out at the Turkish quarter. Then it's only another two cigarettes past shabby clay huts, a few shops, most of them already shut, past some fruit and vegetable stalls with nothing left on them, and over a little, rickety wooden bridge, and finally you reach the barracks.'

'The barracks?'

'Yes, my little lamb. The Turks call them *kishla*. You can't overlook them, can't miss them, because coming out of the barracks just now is a sound of janissary music.'

'Janissary music?'

'Yes, my little lamb,' said the Meddah. 'The janissaries were once the élite of the Ottoman army. But that was a long time ago. There are no janissaries now. All that remains of them is their marching music.'

'Now I can hear it, Meddah.'

'Good, good, my little lamb. Now you're going to the barracks. And then a bit further. And then you'll see it.'

'What shall I see?'

'The military supply depot. There, where the grain merchant's lifeless eyes are looking. It's empty, of course.'

'Why is it empty, then?'

'Because there's a war, my little lamb. And the Turks have no more supplies. All that was left was sent to Syria last week, to Fourth Army Headquarters . . . and on to the south, to the British-Turkish front.'

'And what about the Russian front?'

'You mean the front on the Caucasus?'

'That's what I mean.'

'There's nothing there but hunger and cholera. And the Turkish soldiers plunder the Armenian villages and take anything they can still find.'

'And the second hanged man, the priest, he's also looking in a certain direction. And do you know where?

'No, Meddah.'

'He is looking up to Heaven, my little lamb, just as Jesus looked up to Heaven when He was hanging on the cross.'

'And what do His dead eyes say?'

'They say, Father, forgive them, for they know not what they do.'

'And now, take a look at the third hanged man, my little lamb. What do you see?'

'It's too dark, Meddah. I can't see anything.'

'Then, just imagine: this third hanged man looks like your father.'

'Is it my father?'

'Of course not, my little lamb. Your father is in prison. This man here is his brother Dikran . . . Dikran Khatisian . . . your own

46

uncle. The two of them always looked very much alike.'

'Really my uncle?'

'Yes, indeed.'

'The one whose yellow boots were stolen by the blind beggar?'

'The very one.'

And the Meddah said: 'Your uncle was not rich. He was a poor shoemaker, who had to feed twelve children.'

'And the yellow boots?'

'They were his pride and joy. They were the finest kidskin boots in all Bakir.'

'"Listen, my darling," the blind beggar Mechmed Efendi is saying to the boy Ali. "You did that really well, that trick with the boots. These boots are worth a fortune."

"Because they're real kidskin?"

"No, my darling. Because there's gold in the boots."

"How do you know that?"

"Every Armenian sews a gold coin in his boots," says the blind beggar. "Often two or more."

"How do you know that?"

"Everybody knows that," says the blind beggar.

"And what do the Armenians do it for?"

"Because they are a persecuted race," says the blind beggar, "like the Jews and the Gypsies in other countries. An Armenian never knows when a Turk is going to burn his house down over his head. So he's always ready to jump."

"Ready to jump – how do you mean?"

"Well, my darling, haven't you ever seen an Armenian jump?"

"No, Dede."

"An Armenian jumps like a billy-goat if his house suddenly catches fire. I once saw one jump out of the window."

"Can an Armenian run too?"

"Naturally he can run. And that's just it. The Armenian runs with the gold coin in his boot. And so of course the gold runs with him."

"Would that always happen?"

"It has to happen, my darling. When the great *tebk* comes – that's what the Armenians call a special event . . . even a bad accident or a massacre – then he's got no time left to pack up all his belongings. He doesn't have time to bury his children when they're killed. Or his wife. Or his parents and grandparents. All he can do is run. And somewhere or other he will stop and take the gold out of his boots."

"What for, Dede?"

"To start a new life, take a new wife and beget children again."'

'And only now does Mechmed Efendi stick his old hands into the old sack, which is even older than his hands. He feels the boots for a very long time, and then he says: "I know the man who owns these boots. There was only one pair of boots like this in all Bakir."

"How do you know him?"

"Because the man who owns them often used to talk to me. Whenever he needed good advice, he always came to me. He wasn't rich, so he only threw half a piastre into my begging cloth each time."

"Have you seen his boots, then?"

"No, my darling. But I've felt them with my hands. I'm telling you, I know every fold of these unique boots."

"What's the man called?"

"Dikran Khatisian. An Armenian shoemaker."

"And why did they hang him?"

"Because of a bottle of Russian schnapps. It must have been talked about."'

'"We've stolen the boots from a friend, Dede."

"That's true, my darling. But the boots are better stuck away in my sack than in a saptieh's saddlebag."

"Why would they be in his saddlebag?"

"Well, my darling. It's like this: tomorrow they'll cut the dead men down. Or perhaps the day after tomorrow. Or next week. I don't know what the officials have decided, and how long the dead men have got to hang. But sooner or later they'll be cut down. And then the saptiehs will fight over their clothes. The strongest of them would have got the boots, and would surely have taken them round to the stable and slipped them in his saddlebag. But what's the use of a pair of expensive boots in a saptieh's saddlebag? It would be a waste of good boots."'

'And the blind beggar says: "I'll sell the boots tomorrow. But first I'll take the gold out of them."

"But this Armenian shoemaker wasn't rich?"

"No, my darling."

"Then perhaps there won't be any gold in his boots?"

"Yes, there will, my darling. Even the poorest Armenians find a gold coin from somewhere to hide in their boots."

"Can you feel the gold piece?"

"I've been trying all this time, but I can't feel anything."

"He must have sewn it in very cleverly."

"Yes, my darling. Maybe it's in the heel. And that's made of wood."

"Take it off."

"Not yet, my darling. Not yet."'

'"Tomorrow I'll sell the boots," says Mechmed Efendi. "Or I won't sell them, but give them back."

"To the Armenian shoemaker?"

"I mean, to his wife, who has a right to the boots."

"You'll never do that, Dede. You've never yet given anything back once you've got it in your sack."

"You're right there, my darling. The devil has always tempted me. But Allah is great. Perhaps this time it is his will that I should give the boots back, to win a little place in paradise. That wouldn't be bad, eh?" And Mechmed Efendi says:

"*Inshallah*. Only Allah knows what I shall do."'

'And then Mechmed Efendi gathers up the few paras in his begging cloth, pockets them, pushes the cloth under his turban, picks up his blind man's stick out of the gutter and hangs his old sack over his shoulders.

"Guess where we're going now," he says to the boy Ali.'

'As they went through the dark town the beggar told the boy a story.

"Long ago," he said, "I lay dying under the Gate of Happiness.

No one did anything for me. All day long Armenian and Greek merchants drove by on their *arabas* to the bazaars of Bakir. Most of them came from the district of Diyarbakir – the town of the big watermelons. But camel caravans passed by too, and Kurdish horsemen from the hill country and mendicant Kurds from the villages of the semi-nomads, all coming into town to make their fortune. But others came too, a motley mixture of peoples, even Gypsies. Of course there were Turks too, especially saptiehs, who wore coloured trousers in those days, and *bashibazouks*, guerilla bands, most of them Circassians. It was a hot day, and no one gave me water. But late in the afternoon one single man stopped where I was lying. He gave me water to drink, a whole bucket of it. Then he lifted me on to his donkey-cart and took me with him."

"Where to, Dede?"

"He drove to Yedi Su, an Armenian village, two days' journey from here."

"An Armenian, then?"

"Yes, my darling, an Armenian. He was called Vartan Khatisian, and is the brother of the hanged man."

"He saved your life?"

"Yes, my darling. He took me to his village. Then he handed me over to his *kertastan*, that is the Armenians' extended family. There were many women and children. They looked after me until I was well."

"And where is this Vartan Khatisian?"

"He's in prison, my darling."

"Are we going there now?"

"That's where we're going."

"What is he doing in prison?"

"He's waiting to have his head chopped off tomorrow."

"How do you know that?"

"From the people in the street."

"So he'll die tomorrow?"

"If it is Allah's will, my darling."

"And if it is not Allah's will?"

"Well, then he won't die."'

At this moment the last thought asked the Meddah: 'Can the blind beggar do anything for my father?'

'That we shall see,' said the Meddah. 'He'll probably only snoop around among the saptiehs in the prison, to find out what's to be done. And then he will pray to Allah for good advice. We must wait and see.'

'Where is my father?'

'I've told you that already. He's in prison.'

'In a cell?'

'Of course. In a cell.'

'What is he doing there?'

'He's swinging on a long rope.'

'Then he's dead already?'

'No, my little lamb. He's not dead.'

CHAPTER TWO

When the last thought saw his father for the first time, he thought: the Meddah is right. He really isn't dead, although the Turks have hanged him. But they haven't hanged him by the neck, only by the legs. And the fact that he's hanging upside down ought to make you happy, for legs have no neck, and if they're broken it's not fatal.

And the last thought cheered up and said to the Meddah: 'My father is alive!'

And the Meddah said: 'Yes, your father is alive.'

'My father's eyes are open!'

'Yes, my little lamb. But his eyes don't see anything.'

'Are his eyes blind?'

'No, my little lamb. Your father is only unconscious. But that doesn't matter. He'll come round soon. And then he'll see the floor of his cell. And nothing else.'

'But I hate this floor.'

'So do I, my little lamb. It's a filthy floor. A floor of trodden clay and full of shit and piss.'

'If it were light,' said the Meddah, 'and not pitch dark, and if your father could see the little barred window in the corner on the left and actually look through it, he would see a high wall. It dates back to the Seljuk period and is made of the same stone as the ramparts of Bakir. Of course he'd see the prison yard too, and the top storey of the government building.'

'The *hukumet*, you mean?'

'That's it, my little lamb.'

'Does the *hukumet* stand on the prison yard?'

'Of course not, my little lamb. It's the other side of the wall, but

52

so near that when the Mudir is in his office, he only needs to open the window to hear the screams of the Armenians quite clearly, from the prison torture chambers.'

'Does he like that?'

'I don't know, my little lamb. But it's good for his digestion. Not so long ago he said to the Vali: "Do you know, Vali Bey, since the government finally decided to interrogate the Armenians, I don't need any more castor oil, for the screams of those infidels being tortured act as a most effective aperient."

"By Allah," the Vali said. "They do the same to me."

"Don't you take castor oil any more?"

"No, Mudir Bey. I've swallowed enough oil in my long life."

"Do you think, Vali Bey, that Allah in his far-sightedness gave a screaming mouth to the Armenians to improve our digestions?"

"Allah's reasons are unfathomable," said the Vali. "But your suggestion, Mudir Bey, is not outside the bounds of possibility."'

'Only a few months before, a German officer inspecting the prison had asked the Vali: "How is it there are so few Armenians among your prisoners? Didn't you recently declare that all Armenians are swindlers?"

"Armenians are smart," the Vali had said, "and hard to catch."

"And what about murderers?"

"Just the same."

"Is it possible that it isn't all true?"

"What do you mean?"

"That in fact there are fewer murderers and thieves and swindlers among those people than among the others?"

"Everything is possible," the Vali had said.

"It may be that the Armenians are all honest and peaceful, and people simply don't want to believe it?"

"We must ask Allah," the Vali had said. "Allah knows the answer."'

'And it is a fact,' said the Meddah, 'that when the Germans inspected the prison, there were only three Armenians in custody.'

'Who were the other prisoners?'

'No Armenians,' said the Meddah. 'Most of them were Kurds,

but there were also Turks, Arabs, Gypsies and others, especially many of the *mohajirs*, the Muslim emigrants from Macedonia, Bulgaria, Greece and the Caucasus. Only there were hardly any Armenians in the Bakir prison.'

And the Meddah said: 'It's true, my little lamb. Your people were never a people of robbers and thieves. What is it they say: if you're looking for a robber, look among the Kurds, especially among the wild highlanders. Any one of them would cut your throat without a second thought to get your boots or your hat, provided your hat didn't have a brim, for it is improper for a Muslim to wear a hat with a brim. And among the others, too, you don't have to look long before you find a thief or a swindler, not that that means that there aren't also honest people among the others. Very many of them are honest, but not as many as among the Armenians. How could it not be so, when only a few months ago there were no more than three Armenians in this prison?'

And the Meddah said: 'When the great wave of arrests began and hundreds of Armenians were picked up as they lay in bed to be interrogated about espionage and other such nonsense, the Mudir, after talks with the Vali and the Muntessarif, had all the prisoners moved out of the main prison by the *hukumet*.'

'Where to, Meddah?'

'Into the empty prison down by the river.'

'Why, Meddah?'

'Well, why indeed, my little lamb? To make room, of course. The Mudir had to have somewhere to put all those Armenians. And he wanted to have them near the *hukumet*, because they all have their offices there, the Vali and the Muntessarif and the Kaimakam and the Mudir. And because it's only a few steps from the *hukumet* to the main prison the other side of the wall, which is as old as the ramparts of Bakir.'

And the Meddah said: 'The prison is full now. If they arrest any more Armenians they'll have to put them all in chains and keep them in the yard.'

'Isn't there a third prison?'

'There's only a women's prison.'

And the Meddah said: 'Not all the Armenians have cells to themselves like your father. And not all the Armenians are hanging upside down, on a long rope fastened not round the neck but simply round the feet.'

And the Meddah said: 'But now that's enough chatter. I'll leave you alone with your father.'

I am alone with my father. I would like to talk with him. I would like to say to him: *Father*! But I say nothing. It is pitch dark in the cell, and it's only by his groans that I know he's still alive.

I do not need a watch, for I am timeless.

Some time in the night the cell door is opened. An ugly, grinning saptieh, with a face like a horse, comes into my father's cell with a torch. And two more men come after him: the fat Vali and the one-eyed Mudir.

The Mudir points at the prisoner. 'Why is he hanging upside down?'

'Because you ordered it, Mudir Bey,' says the saptieh.

'And when am I supposed to have ordered that?'

'This morning,' says the saptieh.

'And what sort of reason could I have had, if I really did order it?'

'I don't know, Mudir Bey,' says the saptieh.

The Vali says: 'Perhaps because he refused to make the confession that we demanded from him. This Armenian is one of the obstinate ones.'

'That's possible,' says the Mudir.

'Perhaps you had him hung upside down so that the blood would run to his head?'

'That must be it,' says the Mudir.

'So that his brain would have plenty of blood, his memory would be stimulated and his tongue loosened?'

'That's possible,' says the Mudir.

*   *   *

The horse-faced saptieh says: 'If the deaf-mute Issek Efendi chops his head off tomorrow, the prisoner won't need his memory any more.'

'Just so,' says the Mudir.

And the Mudir says to the horse-faced saptieh: 'Can you imagine what the prisoner will look like tomorrow after Issek Efendi has cut his head off?'

'Yes, Mudir Bey,' says the saptieh.

The Mudir says: 'But we shan't chop his head off.'

'And why not, Mudir Bey?'

'Because the Vali wants to interrogate the prisoner again tomorrow.'

'That's correct,' says the Vali. 'And also not correct.'

'What's not correct, then?' asks the Mudir.

'I'm not going to interrogate him, Mudir Bey. You're going to interrogate him again.'

The Mudir walked thoughtfully up and down the cell. In front of the latrine bucket he stopped. The saptieh came with the torch.

'Why is the bucket empty?'

'Because it's typical of an Armenian to shit on the floor.'

'Is it possible that he just wasn't able to use the bucket?'

'That's possible, Mudir Bey.'

'Because he was hanging at the end of a long rope, tied by the legs?'

'That's possible, Mudir Bey.'

Only now did the Mudir see the food bowl next to the latrine bucket. He bent down and sniffed at the remains of the bulgur.

'This bulgur stinks like the shit on the floor.'

'That's possible, Mudir Bey.'

'Is it perhaps not a bulgur, but shit?'

'That's possible too, Mudir Bey,' said the saptieh.

'When did he eat any of it?' asked the Vali.

'Before I hung him up,' said the saptieh.

'Then he could have poisoned himself.'

'That's possible,' said the saptieh.

'It would be as well,' said the Mudir, 'if the prisoner spewed that muck up, so that I can examine him tomorrow. If he's dead tomorrow he won't be telling me anything.'

'That's true,' said the saptieh.

'Maybe he's spewed it up already?'

'I must just have a look.'

The saptieh shone his torch on the dirty floor under the prisoner's head. Then he turned to the Mudir and shook his head.

'He hasn't spewed anything up, Mudir Bey.'

'How is that?'

'I don't know, Mudir Bey.'

'But it's just not possible.'

'Why, Mudir Bey?'

'Because he's hanging here upside down, head down, and he would simply have had to bring his food up.'

'Perhaps he couldn't bring it up, Mudir Bey?'

The Mudir turned to the Vali. 'What do you think?'

'Nothing at all,' said the Vali.

'The best thing,' said the Vali, 'would be if the prisoner vomited. Otherwise you won't be able to interrogate him tomorrow.'

'Yes,' said the Mudir.

'Do something, Mudir Bey!'

'Get a move on!' said the Mudir to the saptieh. 'Come on, look sharp! Do something!'

'What shall I do, Mudir Bey?'

'Anything, you bloody fool!' said the Mudir.

'I could push a spoon into the prisoner's mouth,' said the saptieh, 'but I can't see a spoon.'

'How did the prisoner eat his food?'

'With his fingers.'

'And where is his spoon?'

'He hasn't got a spoon.'

57

* * *

'Can you get hold of a spoon somewhere?'

'No, Mudir Bey. Not in the middle of the night.'

'Can you stick your finger in his mouth?'

'I can, Mudir Bey. But I've got short fingers. And you'd have to stick something longer in his mouth, long enough to make him choke.'

'What about your bayonet?'

'It would have to be something soft, Mudir Bey.'

'Or the muzzle of your rifle?'

'That isn't soft, Mudir Bey.'

'The saptieh is right,' said the Vali. 'You'll hardly be able to interrogate him tomorrow if we shove the muzzle of a rifle or the hilt or the point of a bayonet down his throat. These Armenians have delicate throats. I know from experience.'

'You mean, the prisoner wouldn't be able to talk tomorrow?'

'That's just what I do mean, Mudir Bey,' said the Vali.

'Have you got anything soft?' said the Mudir to the horse-faced saptieh. 'Something soft but still long enough to make the prisoner vomit, something you can poke right down in his throat without seriously hurting him? We want to interrogate him tomorrow.'

'I could fuck him in his mouth,' said the saptieh.

'Can you manage to fuck?' asked the Mudir.

'Yes,' said the saptieh.

The saptieh gave the prisoner a little push, with one hand, since he was holding the torch in the other. The prisoner swung to and fro, and it looked ghostly; at least the Mudir thought so, and the Vali also found it ghostly, not least because both of them, the Vali and the Mudir, were no longer looking at the prisoner or the saptieh, who was holding the torch in one hand, but at the opposite wall.

'A shadow play,' said the Vali. 'Look, Mudir Bey. A silhouette on the bare wall, swinging to and fro.'

'A Turkish shadow play,' said the Mudir.

'*Karagös*,' said the Vali.

'Yes, *Karagös*, the classic Turkish shadow play that Europeans have always admired.'

'An ancient art,' said the Vali.

'Yes,' said the Mudir.

'Shall I put the torch in the hole?' asked the saptieh.

'What hole?'

'The hole in the floor, where the dog's head is.'

'What dog's head?'

'The one the prisoner wouldn't eat.'

'Who gave him a dog's head, then?'

'You gave him the dog's head, Mudir Bey,' said the saptieh.

'Put the torch in the hole with the dog's head,' said the Mudir, still staring fascinated at the opposite wall, and the Vali too was looking spellbound at the wall where the silhouette danced to and fro.

And suddenly there were two silhouettes, for now the saptieh was standing in front of the torch, which he had stuck in the hole, the hole in the floor where the dog's head was.

'Look, Vali Bey,' said the Mudir. 'It's almost incredible, what's being played on the wall. And yet it's only a wall.'

'That is art,' said the Vali. 'Real art. There's no people in the world that can surpass us in the shadow play.'

'*Karagös*,' said the Mudir.

'*Karagös*,' said the Vali.

'You have to imagine it all,' said the Vali. 'You just have to imagine that that second man is taking his trousers down.'

'And is opening the mouth of the first silhouette as he hangs upside down from the ceiling.'

'That's right,' said the Vali.

'You have to imagine that snake that the second silhouette is bringing out between his silhouetted legs.'

'You don't have to imagine that,' said the Vali. 'You can see that.'

'True,' said the Mudir. 'I can see a snake too. And now the snake is turning into a stick.'

'And the stick's getting longer and longer.'

'And thicker.'
'It's almost incredible.'
'*Karagös*!'
'*Karagös*!'

'Do you know, Vali Bey,' said the Mudir, 'this saptieh with the silly horse-face is the son of a famous man.'
'Really. Who?'
'He's the son of Hassan the One-legged, who was partly responsible for the great massacre in those days in Bulgaria.'
'When was that, then?'
'In 1876.'
'The Bulgarian rising?'
'That's it.'
'His father still had both legs then. But during the massacre and all the rape and murder, one of those Bulgarian women drew a revolver and shot Hassan's leg off.'
'You don't say!'
'Yes, Vali Bey. Simply shot it off.'

'The British press attacked the Turks furiously at the time. They said our troops had burnt down whole villages. They said that headless bodies had been found, women and children had been burnt.'
'Is that true?'
'Of course it's true. But it wasn't the Turks.'
'Who was it?'
'It was *bashibazouks*, the mercenaries of the Sultan of that time – mostly Circassians.'
'But the *bashibazouks* were under the Turkish high command?'
'Naturally they were under the Turkish high command.'

'Those Circassians couldn't stand the Russians,' said the Mudir, 'because Russian Cossacks had burnt their villages down.'
'Understandably,' said the Vali.
'They fled from the Caucasus and took refuge in Turkey. And many of them became *bashibazouks*. The Sultan sent them to Bulgaria when the rising broke out. And the Circassians couldn't

stand the Russians, and because they thought all Bulgarians were Russians, they massacred the women and children.'

'Understandably,' said the Vali.

'We had a lot of trouble with them at the time, particularly on account of the British press.'

'Yes,' said the Vali.

'And the British are no better now. They want to conquer the whole world. Their *bashibazouks* are just called by different names.'

'And there was Hassan the One-legged, who still had two legs then. Actually he was only an ordinary *choush*. But the British papers exaggerated the Turkish word in their unbelievers' language, and so they called Hassan the One-legged a sergeant, and that's something special in England. And so they pilloried him in the press.'

'To hell with the British press,' said the Vali.

'And this saptieh with a face like a horse, who's just now having it off with that Armenian in his mouth, he's his son.'

'His real son?'

'Yes, really.'

'He's a bit queer, this son of Hassan the One-legged,' said the Mudir. 'But then he comes from the village of Sazan-Köy, where they say there are the most beautiful boys.'

'True enough,' said the Vali.

'Once he buggered a three-year-old boy, and the kid almost died.'

'Did he die?'

'No.'

'It's remarkable,' said the Vali. 'I see this horse-face every day, and yet I never knew that the man that face belonged to was actually the son of Hassan the One-legged, and on top of that a queer who almost killed a three-year-old boy having it off with him.'

They stared at the shadow play. The Mudir's voice was soft, almost amused, the Vali's loud and throaty. In the background they could clearly hear how the prisoner was vomiting, and as each gurgling burst of vomit issued from the man's mouth as he hung head down, the Mudir gave a start, and his glass eye snapped forward as if it wanted to jump out against the bare wall and the shadow play.

It had given the last thought a shock when the Mudir's glass eye threatened to jump out of his socket, and so the story-teller soothed him with his fairy-tale voice. He told the last thought: 'His glass eye won't really jump out against the bare wall. It just looks like that.'

'My father's got glass eyes too,' said the last thought. 'And each time the saptieh pokes his prick down into my father's throat, his eyes start out of their sockets, and I'm afraid they'll fall on the floor and get broken.'

'It just looks like that,' said the story-teller. 'Eyes don't just fall out of those holes under the forehead where the good God planted them.'

'But they're glass eyes. Did the good God plant glass eyes under my father's forehead?'

'They're not glass eyes, my little lamb. They're just the eyes of a man who has lost his mind.'

'What has happened to his mind, then?'

'The Turks have blown it away. But don't worry. Tomorrow morning the good God will restore his mind to him.'

Next morning my father was no longer swinging on the long rope. Before daybreak several men in uniform came into his cell, cut him down and carried him over to the paillasse under the barred window. There they laid him down. They stood in front of the bed for a while, looked at him and said nothing. Soon afterwards a man in civilian clothes, with a red fez on his head, came in. It was the Kaimakam himself. The uniformed men stood to attention and saluted.

'This Armenian stinks like ten dead lambs in the midday sun,' said the Kaimakam. 'He can't possibly go to the Mudir's office in that state.'

'That's true, Kaimakam Bey,' said one of the uniformed men.

'But he's got to be interrogated. This man is a dangerous spy, and his confession is extremely important.'

62

'But he'll have to be washed first.'

'All Armenians are filthy,' said the Kaimakam, 'because they don't wash five times a day as the Prophet laid down. They are as unclean as the pig's meat they eat.'

'Yes, Kaimakam Bey.'

'All the same, he'll have to be washed. First of all he'll have to be woken up.'

'Yes, Kaimakam Bey.'

'Do you think he will still be able to wake up?'

'We can't be sure, Kaimakam Bey.'

'If he doesn't peg out,' said the Kaimakam, 'if he really does wake up, feed him up a bit. Give him a decent breakfast and a decent lunch. He's got to be ready to be questioned this afternoon.'

'Yes, Kaimakam Bey.'

'He's got to be in a good mood.'

'How do you mean?'

'Make him good-tempered.'

'How are we to do that?'

'Bring him a loaf of Armenian *lavash* for breakfast. That ought to make him happy.'

'Do you think so?'

'I'm sure of it.'

'And what shall we give him for lunch?'

'That stuff Armenians eat on their holidays, the Armenian national dish. It's called *harissa*. Every Armenian becomes good-tempered automatically if you stick that mess of overcooked meat and pearl barley under his nose.'

'But, Kaimakam Bey, how are we to cook the Armenian national dish here in this prison? I've heard about this food, and I know it has to be boiled and stirred all day.'

'That's true,' said the Kaimakam.

'We could get it in the Armenian *mahalle*, of course. But that's very awkward.'

'Do what you can,' said the Kaimakam.

'Everything I see,' said the last thought to the story-teller, 'I see with your eyes. And everything I hear I hear with your ears. But are a

63

story-teller's eyes and ears just as fanciful as his tongue? Why do you tell me tall stories, although I know quite well you want to tell me the truth?'

'Because I am the story-teller,' said the story-teller. 'And because I always tell the truth differently.'

And the story-teller said: 'Call me Meddah.'

'Tell me, Meddah. Did my father really swallow the saptieh's prick?'

'His mouth fought against it, my little lamb. You saw it. And his throat fought against it. And his gullet. Yes, and his stomach too. But he had to swallow the prick. However, my little lamb, your father wasn't aware of any of it, he was unconscious the whole time.'

'Then he doesn't know anything about it?'

'Yes he does, my little lamb. He will dream about the prick. And then he'll wake up, and he'll shout out loud.'

'And what about the shadow play? First I saw the silhouettes of two men, but then I saw a bat.'

'Did you really see a bat?'

'Yes, Meddah.'

'That was just the two silhouettes, which joined together to form one shadow. They turned into a bat. And the bat fluttered and fluttered when the saptieh's prick began to twitch and the genes of Hassan the One-legged spurted into your father's throat, so deep down that your father vomited again.'

'When they cut him down,' said the story-teller, 'and laid him down on the paillasse, your father fell into a deep, refreshing sleep. It wasn't until nearly midday, when his sleep grew lighter, that he began to dream, and he shouted out loud while he was still half asleep, and that woke him up.'

CHAPTER THREE

'Early in the afternoon the guards carted him out of the cell. He was washed and scrubbed. He got new clothes. Then they took him into a different cell, one that had already been cleaned.'

'Did they give him breakfast?'

'Yes.'

'And did he get *lavash*, the delicious Armenian bread, and later on *harissa*, the Armenian national dish?'

'Of course not, my little lamb. They gave him ordinary *ekmek*, the usual flat loaf, though there was some grape jam spread on it; and a lot of spiced tea, and later on mutton and beans.'

'Your father has a tough nature,' said the story-teller. 'Late in the afternoon he was fit to be questioned, in his right mind once more. Then they put chains on his ankles again, though with so many saptiehs to watch him he couldn't possibly have run away, and they took him across the great prison yard through the gate in the old wall.'

'To the *hukumet*?'

'Just so. Where the Mudir has his office.'

'My little lamb . . . I've already told you about the Mudir's office, and I've described the talk the gentlemen had yesterday afternoon, do you remember? The gentlemen – all important people – smoked their *chibouks* and talked about one thing and another, and about your father's head, whether or not to chop it off. I didn't describe the office, because I didn't want to bore you. It's not what is in a room that matters, but who is in it. And just now it is the Mudir and your father. But one thing I must tell you: this one-eyed Mudir is a western-oriented man, a fanatical supporter of the Young Turks

65

and their new party *Ittihad ve Terraki*, the Committee for Unity and Progress. Therefore there are two proper chairs in his office and also a wide desk, although that is unusual in a Turkish office. Of course there is also a divan in the office and lambswool rugs lying on the floor, and even a short hand-knotted carpet. Hanging on the wall are an old sabre, a picture of the Sultan, a couple of texts from the Koran and, of course, a poster of the war minister, Enver Pasha. As you see: Enver Pasha, mounted on his horse, in smart khaki uniform and fur hat. Enver's face is as soft as a girl's, his narrow moustache could have been stuck on. His hands, holding the reins of his horse, look gentle, and the long thin fingers might be a pianist's. An attractive man, a man with sensitive hands and a sensitive face. He is the hangman of the Armenians.'

'The saptiehs have handed over your father, as they were ordered. Now they stand face to face: the Mudir and your father. The Mudir is polite. His glass eye looks your father straight in the face. He makes a welcoming gesture with his hand and says: "Take a seat, efendi."'

'After a little while a third man comes into the office. He is the Bash-Kiatib, the chief clerk.

You will be wondering, my little lamb, why the Bash-Kiatib isn't wearing western clothes, like most of the Young Turks' supporters; he hasn't even got the usual red fez on his head, as is appropriate for a man of his rank. Well, he's an old man, as you can see, and a little old-fashioned, and he can't give up the baggy trousers and the robe like a kaftan, a clean one hiding the dirty clothes underneath. And he couldn't give up the white turban with the green ribbon of a strict Muslim. The Bash-Kiatib carries a little basket with everything in it he needs, the big inkpot with the usual purple ink, a Stamboul pen, a sponge and powder for blotting, and of course: your father's file. In addition he has a square writing board under his arm. The Bash-Kiatib doesn't bother to look for a third chair, first because there isn't one, and secondly because he is accustomed to sit cross-legged on the floor. So he sits down, sticks a cushion under his backside and another behind his back, leans against the divan, puts the square writing board on his lap and puts the inkpot with the purple ink on it, lays the Stamboul pen beside it, together with the sponge and the blotting powder and, of course, your father's file.'

'Your father is a man whose age is hard to estimate. But I can see, my little lamb, that the Bash-Kiatib has entered the figure 1878 in the file, neatly in purple ink, so I take it that your father is thirty-seven years old. That's what it says in the file: Vartan Khatisian, born 1878 in the village of Yedi Su, in the Vilayet of Bakir, accused of espionage and high treason.

Yes, my little lamb. That is what is written there. If you think about it, he really doesn't look at all like a spy, but then who can say for sure what a genuine spy looks like? As far as your father is concerned, my little lamb, he looks like a typical Armenian from the hills.

His face is long and thin. His hair and skin are dark, although just now his face is almost yellow, but that comes from his many weeks in the prison cell; his chin and his aquiline nose look as if they wanted to escape from his face, to anywhere where the moutains are higher and the air cleaner, where your head almost touches the clouds and where the whisper of the wind is different from that down in the valley of the Turkish landowners, the Deres Beys. Your father has beautiful, almost delicate hands, which don't go with his face at all. Enver Pasha also has beautiful, delicate hands. But ought I to compare your father's hands with a hangman's? No, my little lamb, I won't do that. So I tell you now: your father has sensitive hands, but they are quite different from Enver Pasha's hands. They are sad and tortured hands, for hands have an expression, just like eyes. And we can see the same thing in his eyes, my little lamb. At the moment they look like the glass eye of the Mudir. They have absolutely no expression. But don't be disappointed, my little lamb. You ought to have seen his eyes before he came here to prison.'

'"An Armenian's eyes are lecherous, spiteful, greedy, cunning, sly, just like the eyes of the Jews and the Greeks. These three people personify the evil of the world."

Well, my little lamb, I didn't say that. It was said by the Vali of

Bakir. And he went on to add: "It's the Armenians' eyes that annoy me most. Even if there was no other reason to root them out, their eyes would be a reason."

I should like to have asked the Vali of Bakir: "Tell me, Vali Bey, have you ever seen an Armenian's eyes when he is caressing his child?" And the Vali would be sure to say: "No, I've never seen that."

"When do you look these people in the eyes?"

"Actually, only when I'm changing money or when my prick itches."

And then I say to the Vali: "Vali Bey, if you look an Armenian in the eyes, then you're looking in your own eyes!" And I see how the Vali turns pale. He says: "In my own eyes?"

And I say: "In your own eyes!"'

'I see a cross, my little lamb. And hanging on the cross is, not Jesus Christ, but the eye of an Armenian. A Turk nails it up.'

'It is late afternoon, my little lamb. The sun peeps into the Mudir's office. It winks at the Mudir, and its winking irritates his glass eye. He rubs at it, and then polishes his nose. The Sultan, too, in his picture-frame, and Enver Pasha on the poster, wink at him . . . mocking, encouraging . . . even the texts from the Koran above their heads smile and wink. The Mudir's one eye looks at your father, the other squints at the Koran texts, as if the Mudir had never noticed the Arabic writing before. Do you hear, my little lamb, how the Mudir is trying to persuade your father? It is a long monologue, and your father is listening and nodding his head. It's astonishing how polite the Mudir's speech is. He asks your father whether he slept well, whether the paillasse was still full of shit and piss from all the people who had slept there before your father and had pissed and shat themselves there. He explains to your father that this is regrettably due to the current shortage of straw, and so of paillasses, for there's a war on and straw is very short because of the Turkish cavalry, which is the best in the world, for the Turk is a brave solider, but his horses do consume the straw.'

'The Mudir enquires about his teeth – your father's teeth, I mean.

They haven't been pulled out, we're humane here. And how is his throat, and his gullet, and his stomach? Whether he'd noticed how his stomach had been pumped out in the middle of the night? Whether he'd noticed anything peculiar? No. Your father hadn't noticed anything. For he was lying, or hanging, deeply unconscious at the end of a long rope. And whether he had a dream, the Mudir asked, of a long tube, for example, that was limp and mushy but got bigger and bigger and stiffer, and whether he knew, the Mudir asked, who Hassan the One-legged was, and his son, the one with a face like a horse, who sometimes squirts the genes of Hassan the One-legged, the famous *bashibazouk* and butcher of 1876, into the stomachs of unbelievers? And your father didn't understand any of this and only nodded his head and looked tired, with glassy eyes. Finally the Mudir said: "We have already questioned you a number of times, efendi . . . the Vali and I . . . each in his own manner and style, and this time we are trying yet again. But it is your last chance."

The Mudir waved at the chief clerk with his left hand. Actually the Mudir only raised his hand imperceptibly, but the chief clerk, who had known every movement of the Mudir's for years, had observed it, and so shook himself, put his board with the writing materials on the floor, fetched the Mudir's *nargile*, a new style of water-pipe from Erzurum, and took it to the desk, passed the Mudir the tube with the mouthpiece, lit it for him, went back and sat down again on the cushion in front of the divan, picked up the board with your father's file, the inkpot and the Stamboul pen, the sponge and the powder for blotting, put everything straight again, even the cushions, the one under his backside and the one behind his back – both cushions, that is.

The Mudir puffed for a little while in silence. Then he said: "It really is your last chance, efendi. It will be best to start again at the beginning . . . as in all the previous hearings, not the Vali's but the ones I've conducted . . . although it is boring, I admit, always to have to start again from the beginning."'

"'So your name is Vartan Khatisian?" said the Mudir. "Is that right?"

"That's right," said your father.

"And you come from an Armenian village where only one single Turk has lived?"

"A Turkish family."

"And all the others were Armenians?"

"Yes, Mudir Bey."

"I suppose there was a church there?"

"Yes, Mudir Bey. The church of the holy Sarkis."

"Is this church still standing?"

"It is still standing."

"And the Armenians?"

"They're still there too, at any rate most of them."

"And the Turkish family?"

"Still there too. Hardly anything has changed in my village."'

'"So you come from an Armenian village, a village with an Armenian majority, where the few Turks are compelled to go to church?"

"No, Mudir Bey. No one compels a Turk to go to church."

"But you convinced this Turk that Allah has a son, although it says in the Koran: Allah begets not, nor is begotten."

"The Armenians don't try to convince anyone of anything, Mudir Bey. They live by themselves and are glad to be left in peace."

"Then what's all this lying rubbish? Don't the Armenians in Yedi Su tell every stranger that goes by that this village is typical of the whole of Turkey, and that there are really no Turks left in Turkey, only Armenians?"

"No, Mudir Bey. How could the Armenians in Yedi Su say anything like that? Nobody would believe it."

"But they do say that this country once belonged to them?"

"I don't know about that, Mudir Bey. Anyway it isn't true. The whole country never belonged to them, only a part of it."

"A part of it?"

"Yes. But that is history, Mudir Bey. It's too long ago."'

'"The Armenians are a race of traders and swindlers. The trustful Turk is defenceless against them."

"My father is a farmer, Mudir Bey. Most Armenians are simple farmers and artisans."

"And what about all those Armenian traders in the big cities?"

"I don't know about that, Mudir Bey."'

'"This Turkish family in your village. I'm sure you've tried to chivvy them out of the village?"

"No, Mudir Bey. They are neighbours of my family, and friends of ours."

"Friends?"

"Yes, Mudir Bey. There has never been any trouble between us and the Turkish family as far as I remember. We have helped each other. Once – it was after a bad harvest – my father lent the Turks some corn. We gave them a couple of sacks of wheat flour and some bottled vegetables."

"Have you ever given them anything else?"

"Yes, Mudir Bey. We've taken them whole pots of *tan*, *patat* and *harissa*."

"What is that, efendi?"

"*Tan* is made from *madsun*, the Armenian yoghurt. It's the same as Turkish *ayran*. But it tastes a bit different because my mother sprinkled a few spices in it, but I don't know the secret of it. It tasted a bit sweetish, and I suppose she put a little bit of honey in it."

"An Armenian magic potion, is it?"

"I don't know, Mudir Bey."

"And what is *patat*?"

"The same as the Turkish *sarma*. These are ordinary cabbage leaves stuffed with meat and rice and bulgur. There are vegetables in it too. We call it *patat*, but believe me, Mudir Bey, it's exactly the same as Turkish *sarma*."

"And what is *harissa*?"

"That's the Armenian national dish."

"Does it have pork in it?"

"No, Mudir Bay. It's made from mutton or chicken."

"And your Turkish neighbours ate this muck?"

"It wasn't muck, Mudir Bey. It was real *harissa*."

"And there was really no pork in it?"

"No, Mudir Bey. There wasn't."'

★　　★　　★

'The Mudir made another gesture to the chief clerk. This time he just turned his head slightly to the left, towards the chief clerk, twitched his glass eye, and the chief clerk knew at once what his lord and master wanted. He cleared his throat, flicked through the pages of the file and read: "Vartan Khatisian, by profession farmer, also active as *tezek*-merchant and poet."

"Is that true?" asked the Mudir.

"That is true," said your father.

"Can you make it a bit clearer to me?"

"I can," said your father. And your father smiled for the first time, and his glassy look lightened up a little. "We all had to help in the fields when we were children," said your father, "so every one of us was a farmer whether he liked it or not. And we were roped in for all sorts of other work that had to be done. We even had to milk the sheep, cows and goats."

"Did you also have a donkey?"

"Yes, Mudir Bey."

"And was that milked too?"

"Yes, Mudir Bey."

"But no one can milk a donkey."

"That's so, Mudir Bey."

"Are you trying to make a fool of me?"

"No, Mudir Bey."

"Then was it a jennet?"

"Yes, Mudir Bey."'

'"And what about the *tezek*?"

"It's a matter of dried cow dung. We Armenians actually call it *atar* or *chortrik*, but in our district we use the Turkish word *tezek*. It makes wonderful fuel for heating."

"*Tezek*," said the Mudir. "I suppose you think I don't know what it is. It's ordinary cowshit."

"Well, Mudir Bey, so it is. Rich people use wood for heating and poor people use *chortrik* or *atar* or *tezek*."

"Aren't there also some rich people who use cowshit for heating?"

"Very many, Mudir Bey. The richer a man is, the more economical he is. And wood is scarce in this district and costs a lot of money."

"More than this *tezek*?"

"That actually doesn't cost anything, unless you buy it from a merchant."

"An Armenian, for example?"

"Possibly, Mudir Bey."

"They understand how to turn cowshit into money?"

"Yes, Mudir Bey."'

'"I started dealing in *tezek* when I was still a boy. I brought it to Bakir in sacks, because they paid better prices in Bakir than in our neighbouring villages, where the farmers' children pick up the cowpats themselves and the farmers generally have all they want. I dealt in it for several years. Then I emigrated."

"To America?"

"To America."'

'"That's correct," said the chief clerk. "I've got all that in his file. You can see for yourself, Mudir Bey. All neatly set out."

"Yes," said the Mudir.

"Vartan Khatisian," said the chief clerk. "Born in 1878, farmer, cowshit-seller and poet. Emigrated to America in 1898."

"You read it differently before," said the Mudir.

"I've written this sentence several times," said the chief clerk.

"Polishing your style?" asked the Mudir.

"Yes," said the chief clerk.'

'"How does a farmer with a sideline in cowshit become a poet?" asked the Mudir.

"I don't know, Mudir Bey."

"Is that just one of those Armenian lies?"

"No, Mudir Bey."'

'"So you emigrated to America in 1898?"

"Yes, Mudir Bey."

"To get rich quick, I suppose? To sell shit to the Americans the way you sold shit to the Turks here in Turkey?"

"No, Mudir Bey."

"Why did you emigrate, then?"

"Because I had an uncle over there who sent me the journey money. It was my father's brother Nahapeth. To be precise, Nahapeth Khatisian."

"A trader, I suppose, this Nahapeth Khatisian?"

"Yes, Mudir Bey. He was a trader."

"And did he deal in cowshit?"

"No, Mudir Bey."

"Why not?"

"The Americans don't use *tezek* for heating."

"Aren't there any cows in America?"

"Oh yes, there are plenty of cows."

"I suppose the cows shit gold coins over there?"

"No, Mudir Bey."

"So your uncle wasn't a dealer in cowshit?"

"That's correct."

"What did he deal in?"

"In rags."

"So, a rag-and-bone man?"

"Yes."'

'"Are all the Armenians in America rag-and-bone men?"

"No, Mudir Bey."

"What do the Armenians over in America do?"

"I don't know exactly, Mudir Bey, but I think they do the same things as other people do. Some are businessmen, others are artisans. Many of them work in factories or do something like that. I still have some relatives over there, one uncle is a tailor, another is a driver. And a cousin of my mother's is a hatter."'

'"You were born in 1878. In 1898 you were twenty?"

"I was twenty."

"You were still single then?"

"I was single."

"I know your file by heart," said the Mudir. "Now I've caught you out in a lie. Actually you were married."

The chief clerk cleared his throat, and the Mudir looked round at him.

"Isn't that right, Bash-Kiatib Agah?"

"He was a widower," said the chief clerk.

"That doesn't sound at all right," said the Mudir.

"He married when he was fifteen," said the chief clerk, "something that is quite common in those backward villages. His wife died in childbirth, in the first year of their marriage, so he was already a widower when he was sixteen. Four years later, when he was twenty, he emigrated."

"To America?"

"To America," said the chief clerk.'

'"And what does a twenty-year-old Armenian cowshit-merchant do in America . . ." asked the Mudir, "a man who was also a farmer and claims to be a poet?"

"I went to school at night to learn the foreign language and to complete my education."

"Do all Americans go to school at night, instead of in broad daylight like normal people?"

"Not all, Mudir Bey. Only those who have something to catch up with, or who work somewhere during the day."

"Weren't you a bit too old to be going to school still?"

"There were many of them older than me, Mudir Bey. Many of them were married and had wives and children."

"Married, did you say?"

"Yes, Mudir Bey."

"And not divorced or widowed?"

"Many of them were properly married."

"That can't be true, can it? When is a married American like that going to have his wife, if he goes to school at nights?"

"I don't know, Mudir Bey."'

'"And what did you do during the day?"

"During the day I worked."

The Mudir looked at the chief clerk again. "Is that true?"

"It's true, Mudir Bey. By day he was a street-sweeper, in a street that hasn't got a name."

"Then it isn't true," said the Mudir. "Every street has a name."

"Over there the streets have numbers," said Vartan Khatisian.

"Numbers?" asked the Mudir.

"Numbers," said Vartan Khatisian.'

'"The streets had numbers," said your father, "and we street-sweepers had numbers, though we didn't wear the numbers on our chest or sewn to our clothes or anything like that. We just had them in our head. And the people in the street all looked alike, although a lot of them were black and others white. And they had numbers too, somehow or other."

"So there were only numbers in this American town?"

"That's how it seemed to me," said your father, "at least for my first few months in America. Later it didn't look like that any more, for you can get used to anything."

"What's that meant to mean?" asked the Mudir.

"The longer I lived over there, the more I got used to the numbers. After a time the numbers had faces and I could distinguish them clearly from one another."

"Are you trying to make me look silly?"

"No, Mudir Bey."

"Had the people got faces again?"

"Yes, Mudir Bey."

"And the numbered streets?"

"Those too, Mudir Bey."'

'"An Armenian street-sweeper in an American town," said the Mudir, "someone who's as tricky as all Armenians but who couldn't sell any cowshit to the Americans, because the Americans aren't Turks."

"I don't know about that, Mudir Bey."

"And you're trying to tell me that you'd been a street-sweeper for sixteen years until you came back to Turkey?"'

'"No, Mudir Bey. Later on I did all sorts of things. I worked in factories and restaurants, and I also carried loads."

"You were a porter too?"

"Yes, Mudir Bey."

"A common *hamal*?"

"Yes, Mudir Bey."

"And what were you after that?"

"I was a night-watchman."

"A night-watchman?"

"Yes."

"Where, efendi?"

"In a skyscraper."'

'"What is a skyscraper?" asked the Mudir.

"It's a house that looks as if it would collapse any minute," said your father. "It's not low-built like they are with us here . . . or square . . . but like a monument whose plinth is on the ground and whose head rises into the clouds. There are lifts going up and down inside, the entrance doors go round in circles and suck people in and spit them out again, and when you go into one of those houses you think you're in a bazaar."

"I don't understand that," said the Mudir.

"Behind those damned revolving doors," said your father, "there are a lot of shops, like a bazaar, only it's a different sort of bazaar from the ones we have here."

"And what is there above the bazaar?"

"There are offices."

"A lot of offices? Five or six?"

"About five hundred."

"There's no such thing," said the Mudir.

"But there is," said your father. "There is such a thing."'

'"And what does a night-watchman do all night in a hell of a house like that?"

"Not much, Mudir Bey. He can count the hours until it gets light. He can read, to pass the time. And he can also write poems."

"Poems?"

"Yes, Mudir Bey."

"Did you write poems?"

"Yes, Mudir Bey."'

'"Every Armenian poet is a conspirator," said the Mudir. "He's got nothing in his mind except stirring people up against us. And so I suppose you published your poems in those lying Armenian papers that there are everywhere . . . especially in America . . . Armenian exile papers that stir people up against us and give us a bad name.

Am I right?"

"No, Mudir Bey."

"Where did you publish your poems?"

"Nowhere, Mudir Bey."

"I suppose they weren't good enough?"

"I don't know, Mudir Bey."

"Presumably no one wanted to print them."

"But they did, Mudir Bey."'

'And now your father's face lit up. It seemed as if he was looking at the Mudir for the first time, and his gaze penetrated deep into the glass eye. Then your father sank back again, and his voice became very soft. "Poems should not be published," he said to the Mudir.

"Why is that, efendi?"

"Would you cut a hole in your breast, so that the curious could look in your heart?"

"No, efendi."

"And would you cast holy things to the wolves?"

"Surely not, efendi."

"Or thoughts – that are no one's business . . . among the gossipmongers?"

"No, no, efendi." The Mudir smiled. For one second his one eye looked at your father full of understanding. Then his expression changed and it looked as if the Mudir had two glass eyes. He said: "Let's get to the point, efendi."'

'But the Mudir still took his time, for he suddenly stood up, like someone who can't sit still and has to move. He went over to the window and opened it. Whether by chance or not, at the moment he opened the window a machine-gun opened fire somewhere, and that made the Mudir jump.

"You'd almost think the Russians were in the town already," he said to the chief clerk. "Only yesterday it said in the paper that the Russians had been beaten."

"They're not in the town yet," said the chief clerk. "It must have been a Turkish solider, probably one of those young recruits letting off a few rounds into the air to show the bystanders what

78

he was capable of."

"Have you ever seen a machine-gun?"

"No."

"They're German."

The Mudir smiled. He stood by the window and looked into the yard. And now the scream of a tortured prisoner reached him over the prison wall.'

'The Mudir shut the window. He came slowly back to his desk, walked round the water-pipe, pushed it to the side a little, and sat down at his desk opposite the prisoner, folding his hands over his lap.

"Let's get to the point," he said.

The glass eye opened wide. "Let's get to the point, efendi."''

'"So you spent sixteen years in America, and in spite of the outbreak of the World War you came back to Turkey. Isn't that rather strange?"

"I wanted to see my family again," said your father, "and I wanted to get married again."

"And you couldn't find any other time to choose for your return than the outbreak of the Great War?"

"A pure coincidence, Mudir Bey."

"What did you really want in Turkey? And who sent you here?"

"No one, Mudir Bey."

"Who are you working for?"

"Nobody, Mudir Bey."

"Why do you tell lies, efendi?"

"I'm telling the truth."''

'"I particularly wanted to get married," said your father. "And I wanted a woman from my home village. That was the real reason I came back. I wanted to marry again and take my wife back with me to America."

"Aren't there any women in America?"

"Oh, yes, Mudir Bey. There are plenty of women there. But somehow they're different."

"Different in what way?"

"Well, Mudir Bey. They don't obey their husbands. They think they're independent. And they show everybody their legs."

"Like the Franks?"

"Yes, Mudir Bey."

"All Franks are the same," said the Mudir, "never mind if they're German or French or Italian. All Franks are unbelievers, eat pork, and their wives don't do what they're told and show everybody their legs."

"It's true, Mudir Bey."

"And it's the same in America?"

"It's a lot worse over there, Mudir Bey."

"Then it must be really bad," said the Mudir.

"Yes," said your father. "It is bad."'

'"But we believe that this question of your family and your marriage is only a pretext," said the Mudir, "and that there's a quite different reason why you were sent back to your homeland on the eve of the Great War."

"What sort of reason, Mudir Bey?"

"You know, efendi. And you know more than I do."'

'"Let's begin with the murder of the heir to the Austrian throne," said the Mudir. "He and his wife were shot in Sarajevo, on 28 June 1914, an event that gave rise to the Great War." The Mudir smiled blandly. "How does it happen, efendi, that on that day . . . that very day . . . you were in Sarajevo? Was it just chance?"

"Pure chance, Mudir Bey."

"You do admit, then, that you were in Sarajevo on that day? We've seen your passport with the Austrian visa, permit for a two weeks' stay, then an extension to that, as well as confirmation of your registration with the Sarajevo police, and your hotel bill, dated 28 June."

"I admit it, Mudir Bey. But it's pure chance. I was in Sarajevo to visit my uncle."

"Which uncle?"

"My father's brother. His name is Simeon . . . Simeon Khatisian . . . and he runs a coffee-house."

"Runs a coffee-house, does he?"

"Yes, Mudir Bey."

"Do Armenians have an uncle everywhere?"

"We are a big family, Mudir Bey."

"And what did you want with this uncle?"

"Nothing at all, Mudir Bey. My other uncle, the one in America, wanted to send his brother some money, this brother in Sarajevo . . . and he asked me to hand the money over personally . . . You understand . . . on account of the currency restriction."

"And why did you stay in a hotel?"

"Only the first days, Mudir Bey. I didn't want to be a burden, but then my uncle fetched me out of this hotel, simply came in a carriage, sent the driver up to my room, had my trunk carried out, didn't even ask me. You know how it is, one just can't refuse."

"Hospitality, eh? Or family feeling? All right and proper, isn't it?"

"It is indeed, Mudir Bey. We Armenians are hospitable, and we also have family feeling. In this way we are like the Turks. And one can't refuse an invitation from a relative."

"I understand that," said the Mudir.'

'"And you had nothing to do with the murder of the heir to the Austrian throne?"

"Nothing at all, Mudir Bey."

"It was just chance?"

"Just chance, Mudir Bey."

"You didn't see how the Archduke and the Princess were shot?"

"No, Mudir Bey, I didn't see it."

"And you didn't hear the shots?"

"Oh yes, Mudir Bey. I did hear the shots."'

'"We were in the street by the bridges on the quay, Mudir Bey. My uncle and I. There were thousands of people in the streets to see the royal couple. I do believe that everyone who had eyes was there. You don't see that sort of thing every day."

"True enough," said the Mudir. "You do not see that sort of thing every day."

"It was a terrific, world-shattering event."

"Yes," said the Mudir. "It certainly was."'

* * *

'"And you say that it was all just chance," said the Mudir. "And was it also just chance that on 25 July exactly, just one month later, you arrived in Constantinople, at the very time that the Austrian ultimatum to Serbia expired?"

"Chance, Mudir Bey."

"Three days before the outbreak of the Great War! Chance, efendi?"

"All chance, Mudir Bey."'

'"It's true," said your father, "that I stayed rather a long time in Sarajevo and didn't arrive in Constantinople until 25 July. But that was due to my illness."

"What sort of illness?"

"I don't know exactly. It looked like some venereal disease. I was convinced I'd picked it up from one of the girls who sat about in my uncle's coffee-house."

"From a prostitute, you mean?"

"Yes. And, you see, I really only wanted to stay in Sarajevo a day or two. But then I didn't dare go back home."

"You mean you didn't dare to go to Turkey, to your relatives and your bride?"

"That was it, Mudir Bey. I wanted to get my illness cured first."

"And had you actually got venereal disease?"

"No, Mudir Bey. It was all in the imagination."

"And when did you find that out?"

"A few weeks later, when I finally decided to go to a doctor . . . The end of July, it was. I went to my uncle's doctor, and he had a thorough look at me and said it was all my imagination."'

'"So, just chance again? No more than a mere coincidence that a month later, by which time the whole world knew that there would be a war, you arrived in Constantinople."

"Chance."

"And I suppose it was just a chance that you didn't go straight on to your family up country?"

"An accident. Naturally I wanted to go straight on, but my clothes were dirty after my long journey. And I didn't want to go home in dirty, creased clothes. So I had them cleaned."

"And of course that took several days?"

"That's right."

"And on those days, when you were waiting, you had nothing better to do than go for a trip on the Bosphorus. By steamer, of course?"

"I was a tourist, why shouldn't I take a steamer trip?"

"And you happened to have your camera with you?"

"Yes, I had it with me."

"And you actually went to the Dardanelles on your trip, and as far as the Gallipoli peninsula?"

"It was the usual steamer route."

"And you took photographs there? On the day before war broke out? Out of boredom, I suppose?"

"From sheer boredom."

"Although you knew there was going to be a war?"

"Everybody knew that."

"And of course you didn't know anything about the strategic importance of the Dardanelles and the Gallipoli peninsula?"

"I didn't know anything about it."

"Not even that the enemy wanted to land there because they thought we should be vulnerable there?"

"How should I know that?"'

'"We've found your pictures, efendi, though we don't know if these are the whole lot."

"They're quite harmless pictures."

"You took photos of the Bosphorus, the Golden Horn, the coast of the Dardanelles with the fortifications. Also of the Gallipoli peninsula."

"All harmless pictures, Mudir Bey. I didn't even think about it. Those are just a few of all the pictures I took during the journey."

"To impress your bride?"

"I suppose so, yes."

"And your family?"

"Yes, Mudir Bey."

"All quite harmless, aren't they?"

"Yes, Mudir Bey."'

* * *

'"And a few days later, efendi. What happened then?"

"Then I packed my trunk to move on. By then the Great War had broken out. It was the beginning of August."

"We weren't at war by then," said the Mudir. "Not yet, in August, although we had mobilized on 3 August. The war didn't begin for us until later."

"In November," said your father.

"In November," said the Mudir.'

'"That's right," said the Mudir. "Turkey was not yet at war. And you, efendi, found no difficulty in travelling to Bakir, in the interior of the country, and on to the village of Yedi Su. Your American passport was in order. You had also very wisely had a home pass issued, a *teskeré*, as is usual here. And your *teskeré* was in order too, and later, as you went on . . . every single stamp for every *vilayet*. You paid the prescribed fees. And you went home, to your relatives. And you married Anahit Yeremian, the girl from your village."

"That's right, Mudir Bey."

"And then you had a honeymoon trip to Syria and took photos of the cliffs on the Mediterranean coast?"

"That is correct, Mudir. All harmless pictures."

"And later you met Pesak Muradian?"

"I'd met him before. He came to my wedding. He's my sister Aghavni's husband."

"So he's your brother-in-law?"

"My brother-in-law, yes."

"He's a conspirator. Did you know that?"

"I knew nothing about that."

"But we know it," said the Mudir. "Your brother-in-law is accused of high treason."'

'There was a question mark in your father's eyes, and it was reflected in the eyes of the Mudir, in his one real eye, which now flashed dangerously, but also in his glass eye.

"Your brother-in-law hasn't told us anything," said the Mudir, "because he's actually disappeared. If you were to let us know where he's hiding, it would make things a good deal easier for you."

"I have no idea," said your father.

"Naturally," said the Mudir. "You were arrested before him."

"I was," said your father.

"And you have no idea where he might be hiding?"

"How should I know?"'

'"You don't know anything at all."

"I am innocent, Mudir Bey."

"Tell us what you do know."

"I don't know anything, Mudir Bey."'

'"But I'm sure you've heard about the Ochrana?"

"I've never heard of it before."

"That's the name of the Russian secret service."

"Oh? I didn't know that."

"There are men from the Ochrana working behind our front line. They're mostly Russian Armenians sent over the border by the Russians, who can mix easily with the Turkish Armenians. Many of them have lived in Turkish territory at some time, before they went to Russia. They speak Turkish and Armenian, and you can hardly tell them from the Turkish Armenians. They possess valid papers. Still, we pick up some of them every day. We find them everywhere, among the Armenian traders, among the artisans, even among the farmers."

"I don't know anything about that, Mudir Bey."

"We thought at first, efendi, that you had been sent by the Ochrana. But then we said to ourselves, the Ochrana just send their own men over the Turkish-Russian border. They are easily smuggled in. Why should they take the trouble to bring a man over from America?"

"Yes, Mudir Bey."

"And actually send him to the Bosphorus, to the Dardanelles and the Gallipoli peninsula?"

"Yes, Mudir Bey."

"Or even to Bosnia, a former Turkish province that the Austrians have annexed, and whose capital is Sarajevo?"

"Yes, Mudir Bey."'

*　　*　　*

'"Do you see, efendi? We therefore concluded that you were working for the Americans, although America is neutral and we don't understand why the American president wants to instigate a revolt of the Armenians here."

"I don't know anything about a revolt, Mudir."

"So we said to ourselves, perhaps you're working for the British and the French."

"What British and French?"

"Well, just the British and French."

"I don't understand a thing, Mudir Bey."'

'"It all looks very complicated," said the Mudir. "But complicated things are sometimes the simplest."

"Yes, Mudir Bey."

"That's a cliché, of course. I expect you've often heard people say something like it?"

"Yes, Mudir Bey."

"And yet clichés are sometimes true."

"It's possible, Mudir Bey."

"Now look here, efendi."'

'"I'm a genius," said the Mudir. "Only they don't know that in Constantinople."

"I understand, Mudir Bey."

"I've always been a genius, but nobody wanted to know, and no one has even noticed it."

"Yes, Mudir Bey."

"I have ideas."

"Yes, Mudir Bey."

"Do you believe that, that I have ideas?"

"Yes, Mudir Bey."'

'"A little time ago I said to the Vali of Bakir, this man Vartan Khatisian is not working for the Ochrana or any other sort of Russian secret service. And he wasn't sent by the Americans, or by the French and British. This man Vartan Khatisian is simply an agent of the world conspiracy by the Armenians."

"An Armenian world conspiracy?"

"Yes, efendi."

"I've never heard of that before."

"You don't seem to have heard of anything before, do you, efendi?"'

'"When I was still studying abroad," said the Mudir, "I met certain people who told me something about the protocols of the Elders of Zion. And they told me about the Jewish world conspiracy. And do you know what, efendi? I laughed at those people. I told them, the Jews are harmless businessmen. I know some of them, from Smyrna, Stamboul and Bakir. But you ought to see our Armenians and Greeks. And later, since coming back to Turkey, I've often thought about those gentlemen again, and the things they said about the Jews. And the more I thought it over, the more I crossed them off the list of offenders. And then, surprisingly, the Greeks too. That left only one people responsible for every misfortune."

"What people?"

"The Armenians."'

'"The Armenians are everywhere," said the Mudir, "wherever evil turns up on the wheel of world history. They've got all the levers in their hands."

"I never knew about that, Mudir Bey."

"And the worst thing is, they want to wipe us Turks out."

"I don't know anything about that, Mudir Bey."'

'"There is a worldwide conspiracy by the Armenians," said the Mudir. "They are the real manipulators of this war. Their aim is the destruction of humanity. But most of all they want to harm us Turks. That's what they planned this war for. And you, efendi, are their agent."

"I'm not an agent, Mudir Bey. I've no idea what you're talking about."

"What are you then, efendi?"

"I was a farmer, Mudir Bey. And later I read books, and even wrote poems, and I've done all sorts of things. I've never had any proper profession."

"Tell us who sent you, efendi."

"No one sent me, Mudir Bey."

"And tell us what you know about the Armenian world conspiracy."'

'The Armenian world conspiracy! At those words the chief clerk's Stamboul pen jumped a couple of times, so he crossed the sentence out and wrote it again. The Mudir didn't like it when the chief clerk crossed things out simply to write the same sentence again, but what was he to do? A shaky sentence like that, with squiggles, loops, curves and hops and leaps could simply not be allowed to remain in the text, especially when this text was written in the holy purple ink. The chief clerk looked anxiously across at the Mudir. He suddenly heard that buzzing in his ears again, as he had before when a similar sentence about the Armenian world conspiracy had occurred; there was a fluttering in his stomach, a pricking like a thousand and one needles, as if all the Armenians in the world were engraving the history of the Armenian world conspiracy in his stomach with a thousand and one needles. It made him feel sick, but he swallowed it down bravely, so as not to annoy the Mudir. He was still writing down the sentence in which the prisoner said "I don't know anything, Mudir Bey . . ." when he heard the buzzing in his ears again and felt the pricking and scratching of the thousand and one imaginary needles. But fortunately the interview was over, for Allah took care that nothing more occurred to the Mudir, so that the chief clerk didn't have to hear anything else that absolutely should be, or must be, written down. And Allah, praised be his name, took care that at the right moment the Mudir clapped his hand . . . three times . . . and three saptiehs rushed in with fixed bayonets, as if the Armenian rebellion had already broken out, actually in the Mudir's office, right here, and after all why not . . . but no, just to make sure that the world of the Ottoman office was still in order.'

'The saptiehs led the prisoner out, that is to say, they dragged him off that handsome western Frank chair, had a look at the fetters, made sure the prisoner couldn't run away, shoved him over to the door and disappeared with him into the corridor. The Mudir remained sitting at his desk and examined his bitten fingernails.

Then he took a little silver-plated nail file out of his uniform pocket and began to file his nails. The chief clerk packed his gear away, cleared his throat and swallowed.

"Is there something wrong with you?" asked the Mudir without looking up.

"I've got a pain in my stomach," said the chief clerk.

"You eat too much *baklava*," said the Mudir.

"Yes, Mudir Bey," said the chief clerk.

"And who sells that *baklava* to you?"

"The Armenian bakers," said the chief clerk.

"Those Armenian bakers put needle points in their *baklava* to make us Turks believe it's the fault of our own stomach, which won't digest anything unusual."

"Yes, Mudir Bey."

"That's another bit of the Armenian world conspiracy," said the Mudir.'

'After the Mudir had dismissed the chief clerk with a gracious wave of his hand, the chief clerk went to his office on the second floor of the *hukumet*, handed over Vartan Khatisian's file to Osman, the office boy, saying: "This contains important state secrets, lock it up carefully; I hold you personally responsible." He handed over the inkpot and the Stamboul pen as well, the blotting kit and the writing board and said: "If anyone asks for me . . . I'll be in the lavatory." Then he turned round and staggered along the empty corridor, tortured by stomach cramps. He met some saptiehs, who were lounging about and chatting. At the end of the long corridor he saw three gentlemen, whom he greeted obsequiously. One of them was only a chemist, a common *ejaji*, but he was brother-in-law to the chairman of the court, Halil Bey, and it was remarkable enough that this *ejaji* should be here in the *hukumet*, let alone in the company of two gentlemen who were on close terms with the Vali of Bakir; the *defterdar* Aly Bey, the chief accountant, whom all the officials sucked up to, and the *avukat* Hassan Agah, reputedly the best lawyer in the *vilayet*, a man of Armenian extraction who enjoyed the confidence of the Vali despite his Armenian great-grandmother's bad blood. What did that chemist want here? Then it occurred to the chief clerk that the *ejaji's* pharmacy was in a house that belonged to an Armenian, a house, that is, that was to be confiscated and auctioned. What was going on here? Did Halil Bey's brother-in-law want to take over the Armenian's house? Why were the three gentlemen standing here in the corridor? And just by the door of the Vali's office? The chief clerk staggered past the group. The lavatory was at the end of the corridor. He tried to pull the door open. It was locked!

The chief clerk listened at the door angrily for a bit, to make sure that the lavatory was really occupied or whether the door had just got stuck somehow, but he could find nothing suspicious. There was no keyhole in the door, but it could, as he knew from experience, be bolted on the inside. The chief clerk stood there by the lavatory, undecided and unhappy. Finally he discovered a crack in this panel without a keyhole. He took off his glasses, bent over and pressed his shortsighted eyes against the slit in the wood. A pair of legs, he thought. You can't see any more. Anyway, the lavatory's occupied. So, wait till the chap comes out.

The chief clerk walked up and down outside the lavatory. His stomach was still hurting him, but somehow the pain had grown less sharp and seemed to be slowly wearing off. However, the chief clerk felt no relief. He tried to have another look through the crack in the door. Now he could also see the red fez the man had on as he crouched over the hole with bent knees, his head between his knees. Like a spider, he thought. Suddenly the other man raised his head and stared straight at the crack in the door. Alarmed, the chief clerk took a pace back. For the man in the lavatory was none other than the governor of the province himself, the Vali of Bakir.

A foolish man would have knocked on the door, to let the Vali know that someone else needed the lavatory and that he ought obligingly to hurry up, but the chief clerk was much too nervous to take that sort of risk and annoy that great, powerful man. And he was not one of those foolish men who believed what the Young Turks preached: equal rights for all Osmanli. No, he knew exactly where his place was, a chief clerk's place, and he knew that a single wave of the Vali's hand would be enough to destroy him. And so he just turned round to look for another lavatory.'

'There was in fact a second lavatory in the Bakir *hukumet*, a brand new one that had only been completed a fortnight before, a great achievement in the middle of the war, as even the Turks' enemies would not deny. Responsible for this extravagance in hard times when everything had to be saved and scraped for was the architect Haidar Efendi, who with the aid of the crafty lawyer Hassan Agah, third scion of an Armenian great-grandmother of bad blood, the most notorious *avukat* in the whole Vilayet of Bakir, had arranged to make money available in Constantinople in order that the high and mighty in Bakir Vilayet should have a second lavatory in the government building. In November 1914, when war broke out, such an undertaking had been regarded as impossible, but now even the doubtful could convince themselves that there really are things of which you can say, when you see them, you can hardly believe your eyes. The lawyer Hassan Agah had naturally had convincing reasons for this construction, reasons that the Stamboul Young Turks could not possibly turn down without the support of the ruling triumvirate – Enver Pasha, Talaat Bey and Jemal Bey. And they did not have that backing. The reasons indeed were plausible, for – so the lawyer wrote – you could not possibly expect the saptiehs of Bakir, the upholders of law and order, to stand in a queue for hours in front of the one-man lavatory, just because their seniors had precedence there, which – so the lawyer wrote – was opposed to the ideas of the Committee for Unity and Progress, and equally, one could not expect the representatives of law and order to go, as they generally or indeed nearly always did, for better or worse, on account of the endless queue, to the prison yard, the other side of the *hukumet* wall or the prison wall – which was basically the same wall, it depended on which way you were looking at it – in order to perform their natural functions in the prison yard, on a latrine that was not even roofed in. And – so the lawyer wrote – it was not justifiable to expect such a thing, for the saptiehs and representatives of law and order had to squat there on the unenclosed latrine in front of the prisoners, nearly all Armenians and, as is now known, traitors. That was bad for the morale of the troops, wrote the lawyer, for those Armenian were cunning, mixed with the Turks, had no fingernails because, quite rightly, they had long since been torn out, stank of filth, were unwashed, had infectious diseases, burns, ulcers and lice, often they no longer had tongues and sometimes no eyes and yet they talked and seemed to see, since Armenians can work magic, as everybody knows. And moreover, so wrote the lawyer, the unenclosed latrine had no shelter from wind and weather. The saptiehs caught cold, their uniforms got wet and wore out more quickly, and that cost the state money.

A lot of words to say very little; the Vali of Bakir, who was secretly behind the complaints made against him, received the money from Constantinople, put the greater part in his pocket and with the rest built a second lavatory for his saptiehs and junior officials, not a one-man lavatory but a roomy, democratic, big lavatory with ten holes to accomodate ten bottoms, putting an end to the queuing, just the right kind at the time of the Young Turks' revolution, a revolution that had declared war on reaction in the true spirit of the Committee for Unity and Progress.

And that's where he went now: the Bash-Kiatib, called in civil life Abdul Efendi, son of Mirza Selim, he, the one-time *yassiji*, public letter-writer in the Bakir bazaars, now chief clerk in the *hukumet*.'

'Most of the offices in the *hukumet* had already finished work, so it was not surprising that even the new lavatory was chock-full, for it was just before time for the evening prayer, and the junior staff and saptiehs were in the habit of relieving their bladders and their bowels before hastening to the mosque. For many of them the evening visit to the toilet was a sacred duty, for it was part of the cleansing like the prescribed washing. Since the lavatory had been built in the spirit of the Committee for Unity and Progress – as was generally known – it had no door to form a queue in front of. As people said: a democratic lavatory intended for everybody, who can go in and out whenever they like.

As the chief clerk arrived before the new lavatory he collided with a German officer, who came straight out of the lavatory, pushed past him and disappeared into the long corridor of the *hukumet*. By Allah, thought the chief clerk, you've seen that handsome fair-haired lieutenant before some time; but he couldn't remember when or where it was. Or was it? Of course. Yesterday, in the steam bath. No doubt. What was that German looking for here? A German officer?

He went hesitantly into the stinking, smoke-filled room. There were ten bottoms hanging over the ten holes. All occupied, thought the chief clerk. He noticed some people leaning against the walls of the lavatory and waiting. So there is a queue, he thought, it just doesn't look like a queue. He found a place among the waiting men. They all knew him. One of them said: "Cigarette, Bash-Kiatib Agah?"

"I'm a non-smoker," said the chief clerk.

"But you could smoke one, Bash-Kiatib Agah. Or do you want to hurt my feelings?"

"No," said the chief clerk. "By Allah, I don't want to do that." The chief clerk took the cigarette and had it lighted. Scared of everybody, he thought, even of a common saptieh. Why was he so anxious not to hurt the man's feelings?

"Well, how do you find the cigarette?" asked the saptieh.

"Good," said the chief clerk.

"It's Bulgarian," said the saptieh. "Those infidel swine the Bulgarians are traitors and pro-Russians, but they do have good tobacco."

"Yes," said the chief clerk. He choked a little as he smoked. He didn't like it, and the pain in his stomach started up again, and the story of the Armenian world conspiracy pricked him worse than ever with those thousand and one needles.'

'He squatted between a saptieh and the interpreter Faruk Agah. The interpreter Faruk Agah also offered him a cigarette, and once more he didn't dare to refuse.

"Did you see that German?" asked the interpreter Faruk Agah. "He left the lavatory just as you came."

"Yes," said the chief clerk.

"That chap often comes here to show off his bottom."

"Really," said the chief clerk.

"He's as queer as a Greek *arabachi*, one of those products of the union between a queer Greek priest and a bearded nun. Have you ever known a Greek *arabachi*?"

"No," said the chief clerk. "Most of the *arabachis* in this part are Armenians. I hardly ever take an *araba*, those hackney-carriages are too expensive."

"You walk, then?"

"I always walk," said the chief clerk.'

'"Don't you ever travel?"

"Not often."

"And how do you travel, if you don't take an *araba*?"

"On the Baghdad line that the Germans built for us."

"And how do you get to the Baghdad line? From what I'm told, there are no trains going across the Taurus Mountains, and it's more than a day's journey to the next station."

"I go there in an *araba*."

"You don't really?"

"Yes, I do."

"You're an odd sort of chap."

"I only meant that I never take an *araba* in the town."

"And if you go to the next station? Don't you go there with a Greek, a Greek *arabachi*?"

"No," said the chief clerk. "I always go with the same *arabachi*. And he's an Armenian."'

'"To go back to that German," said the interpreter Faruk Agha. "Don't you think he's beautiful, beautiful as a blond angel?"

"I didn't look at him all that closely."

"The saptiehs are absolutely crazy about his bottom."

"That may be," said the chief clerk.'

'"Those Germans are extraordinary people," said the interpreter. "Have you ever noticed how the pockets of their uniforms bulge, especially their trouser pockets?"

"Yes," said the chief clerk.

"And hasn't anything occurred to you?"

"No," said the chief clerk.

"How's that, nothing struck you?"

"I don't know," said the chief clerk.'

'"German uniforms look as if the men wearing them have stuffed them with walnuts. But it isn't walnuts, of course."

"What is it, then?"

"Newspaper."

"Newspaper?"

"Yes."

"By Allah! Who wants to stuff his pockets with newspaper?"

"The Germans do."

"But why?"

"Because they say there's no lavatory paper in Turkey."

"Lavatory paper? What's lavatory paper?"

"The paper that Europeans wipe their arses on."

"But you don't wipe your arse with paper!'

"Of course not. That's what I said to the German.""

'"Those Germans are so scared of lavatories without paper that they never leave their barracks without newspaper. They always take a whole stockpile with them."

"Yes," said the chief clerk. "That sounds just like the Germans."

"They fuss about everything," said the interpreter Faruk Agha. "Everything is planned with them, considered in advance."

"Yes," said the chief clerk.

"A German said to me once, 'You Turks wipe your arses with your bare hands, the left hand of course. Then you pour well-water on your left hand. And you get the water out of the water-can there is in every lavatory.' 'That's right,' I said. 'Why don't you have paper in your lavatories, even if it's only newspaper?' 'Because there's nothing in the Koran about newspaper,' I said. 'And what does it say in the Koran?' he asked. 'I don't know exactly,' I told him, 'but there's something in it about water and sand. That's what men must cleanse themselves with before Allah.' And do you know what the German said?"

"No," said the chief clerk.

"'You don't have proper lavatories here at all,' he said."

"What did he mean by that?" said the chief clerk. "Are we sitting in the Sultan's divan then? Isn't this a lavatory?"

"'With the Franks,' the German said, 'in the whole of Frankistan, people sit on a wooden or porcelain donkey with no head or tail, and the donkey has a huge hole in its back.'"

"Do you mean to say that the Franks sit over a hole when they give back what they haven't digested to Allah?"

"Just that," said the interpreter.

"Those unbelievers have vile habits," said the saptieh. "They shit sitting down, don't wash their bottoms afterwards, eat pork, don't believe in the Prophet and stuff newspapers in their pockets."

"They invented printer's ink, too," said the interpreter.

"What's printer's ink?"

"For printing their newspapers."

"So that they can stuff their pockets with them?"

"Exactly."

"So they can wipe their arses on them?"

"That's it.'"

'The interpreter now told the chief clerk self-pityingly about all the work he had, how overloaded he was, all his hours of overtime and his overdue salary.

"Have you not had any salary for the last three months either, Bash-Kiatib Agah?"

"The last five months, Faruk Agah."

"What do you live on then?"

"Allah only knows," said the chief clerk.

"Our pay disappears into the bosses' pockets," said the interpreter.

"There's no evidence of that," said the chief clerk cautiously, looking anxiously round him.

"Well, maybe there isn't," said the interpreter.

"Have you really got so much work?"

"Yes," said the interpreter.'

'"Mostly with all those Kurds," said the interpreter. "That lot don't speak a word of Turkish. And who has to translate Kurdish into Turkish? I do, of course."

"I only know Kurds who speak Turkish."

"There aren't so many of them."

"And how do you get on with the other minorities?"

"Not so badly," said the interpreter. "There's hardly ever any difficulty with Jews and Greeks, and even the Gypsies from Lake Urmia who come over the old Persian border speak a few words of Turkish. The least trouble is with the Armenians."

"How do you get on with the Armenians?"

"They can all speak Turkish. Some of them speak our language better than we do ourselves."

"You don't say!"

"But you know that, Bash-Kiatib Agah."

"Of course I know it, but I still get a great surprise every time anyone reminds me of the fact."

"A lot of those Armenians speak better Turkish than we do," said the interpreter, "and if I didn't know that they're all traitors and unbelievers, I'd believe they were the true Turks."

And now the interpreter crawled, still squatting, over to the place on the white-tiled wall where the water-can stood, took the can, splashed some water on to his left hand with his right, washed his backside, did that three times, dried the wet place with his coat sleeve, pulled his trousers up, put the water-can back, nodded to the chief clerk, shuffled past the waiting men leaning against the lavatory wall and disappeared through the open doorway. He had hardly gone when another man had taken his place, let his trousers down and squatted groaning over the hole in the floor.'

'Maybe the interpreter Faruk Agha is right, thought the chief clerk, when he says it sometimes looks as if the Armenians were the true Turks. Pity the interpreter hadn't squatted by him a little longer really, for now he would like to have said to him: "Do you know, Faruk Agha, there are people who even say that the Armenians are our best citizens, true Ottomans, people we can be proud of." But then he thought that such an idea was dangerous, even though it didn't originally come from him. And then he thought that it was just as well that the interpreter Faruk Agha had washed his behind and left the lavatory so soon. And then it came back to him: yesterday, in the steam bath. He went there quite often, because he had been a widower for years, had no wife, loathed the brothels, and because the eunuch Haji Efendi would lick his prick for a few paras.

"Now, Bash-Kiatib Agha," the eunuch had said, "a high-up gentleman like you really ought to go to the Armenian *hamam* –the one in the Armenian *mahalle*. Those rich Armenians have got a real marble swimming pool there."

"Yes, Haji Efendi," he had said. "That's true. But the time is past when a circumcised man can mix with the uncircumcised."

"But we have uncircumcised people in our *hamam*," the eunuch had said, and the eunuch had pointed out a German officer, some way away, reclining on one of the high levels between some Turks. "That man is a lieutenant. He is young and fair, and what's more he's queer. They say he also hangs around the *hukumet*, even in the new gentlemen's lavatory."

"Really," the chief clerk had said. "I didn't know that."

"And he doesn't bother about being uncircumcised and sitting among circumcised people."

"Well, yes," the chief clerk had said.

"He asked me once if I'd lick his prick for three piastres. But do you know what I told him, efendi?"

"No."

"I said: 'I wouldn't even lick your uncircumcised prick for five lira. No way. Let the devil lick it. Don't you know that all sorts of dirt collect under the foreskin of an uncircumcised prick, pus for example, and piss, and that all the flies in Turkey amuse themselves there, settle there to feed the way they do on the festering eyes of a blind beggar?' – 'But, efendi,' the German said, 'isn't this a *hamam*? A steam bath? And what is a steam bath really for? Surely to clean off all that piss and that pus and those fly droppings. Now look, I'm absolutely clean, I wash my prick five times a day, the way you Turks do your sweaty feet before prayer. And I'll give you ten piastres.' 'No,' I told him. 'At no price.'"

"Was he upset?"

"He calmed down long ago."'

'Later, after the eunuch had massaged him, whipped him with willow switches, kneaded him powerfully and then licked him, he joined the group sitting round the German.

The German was just saying to one of the Turks: "Those three hanged Armenians on the Gate of Happiness have changed the look of the city."

"That's true," said the Turk.

"If the war situation gets any worse and the front withdraws a bit nearer, there will be more people hanged. Not only in Bakir. Armenians will be hanging everywhere, in every public square in the country."

"That could be," said the Turk.

One of the other Turks said: "They all ought to be hanged, the whole pack of Armenians."

"That wouldn't be practical, efendi," said the German. "The government couldn't afford so many gallows."

"Then they can hang them on trees."

"That's a problem too, efendi. Don't forget that most of Turkey is very poor in trees; in some parts there are no trees at all. It's as if Allah had been economical with trees in those areas so that man would not forget his creation."

"What do you mean by that?"

"That Allah created trees for mankind," said the German, "like everything in nature, but obviously not with the intention that man should string his neighbours up on them."

"Only Allah knows the purpose for which he created the tree," said the Turk.

"He surely knows that," said the German.'

'The chief clerk had sat down quitely among the people in the *hamam*, breathing in the steam and keeping his ears pinned back. He had come two or three times in the toothless mouth of the eunuch and felt fully restored.

"Do you know," said one of the Turks, who up till then had taken no part in the conversation. "Do you know, efendiler, I don't understand the whole thing."

"What don't you understand?"

"Why the Armenians are being harassed at all."

"A lot of people don't understand that, efendi. But you don't have to understand everything. Do you understand for instance why the Armenians are pro-Russian and secretly pray for the Czar?"

"No, I don't understand that."''

'A one-armed Turkish major sitting next to the German said: "Efendiler. You see this arm, the arm that I've lost. Allah has taken it from me. In November it was, during the first Russian offensive in the Caucasus. We were surrounded, in a hopeless position. And do you know, efendiler, whom Allah sent to save my life and rescue me?"

"No, efendi."

"An Armenian."''

'"My Armenians were my best soliders," said the major. "And I've heard the same thing from other officers."

"But, Binbashi Bey, if that's so, if the Armenians are loyal soldiers, why have they been chucked out of the army?"

"I don't know, efendi."

"There must be some reason."

"There isn't any reason."

"Is there some baseless reason?"

"It looks like it."

"But that's absurd."

"It isn't absurd. Allah knows all reasons, even reasons that aren't reasons."

"It's also possible that some baseless reason is in fact a reason, and we just don't know what the reason is."

"That could be a possibility, efendi."

"Could it not be that even the government doesn't know the reason, and has no idea why it's harassing the Armenians?"

"That will be it, efendi."'

'The chief clerk remembered that he had dozed off out of sheer exhaustion. He had had a little dream about the eunuch's mouth, and then had woken up again. The gentlemen had stopped talking, and were dozing. The one-armed major had moved away a bit with the young German, on to the highest, hottest level. They were sitting there snuggled up close to each other. When he could see more clearly through the steam, he saw that the Turk had got the German's prick in his fist, so that he could no longer get his prick free. By Allah, thought the chief clerk, shaking his head, and it struck him that the German's prick was like an extension of the great German Kaiser's prick. And we Turks are hanging on to it, he thought. That's how things are. Because the Kaiser gives us cannon, and without those cannon we couldn't wage war.

Some time before the chief clerk had asked a dervish to tell him about the devil and about temptation. And the dervish had said: "If you take the devil by the prick, the prick will never let you go."'

'After the steam bath he had strolled down to the Gate of Happiness. There were three Armenians there hanging on long ropes. A blind beggar was squatting at the side of the road. He also knew the little boy who was crouching at the old man's feet.

"So, how are you, Mechmed Efendi?"

"Oh, it's you, Bash-Kiatib Agah. Thank you for asking. I'm very well. Allah has taken the sunlight from me, but in its place he has given me good health."

He threw a half-piastre piece in the begging cloth and then went and mingled with the onlookers. Among the crowd he noticed two Turkish dignitaries whom he had often seen in the *hukumet*. One of them was mayor of a nearby village, the other a notary. They were accompanied by a German in civilian clothes, wearing a monocle.

"Did you know, efendiler," said the German, "that the Armenians were the first actual Christians?"

"No, efendi."

"From the political point of view, anyway. The Armenians were the first to adopt Christianity as their state religion."

"Really?"

"Yes. A fact. Even before Rome."

"That's very remarkable."

"Later they quarrelled with all the other Christian churches. They don't believe in the dual nature of Christ."

"What does that mean?"

"They are convinced that Christ had only one nature, the divine."

"Really?"

"A so-called monophysite religion."

The German scribbled something on a sort of writing pad with a pencil, but the chief clerk couldn't see clearly what it was.

"Four thousand years ago there was a dolichocephalic race living here," said the German. "But later the dolichocephalic race was driven out by a brachycephalic people."

"Driven out?"

"Yes."

"And what are the Armenians?"

"Brachycephalic. Armenoid, anyway. Thought to be mixed with Dinaric."

"I don't understand a word."

"You can see it in those hanged men. Receding chin. Strong, rather hooked nose, light brown skin, curly, rather frizzy dark hair . . . Big, expressive, velvety eyes."

"But, efendi. Those men's eyes are dead!"'

★   ★   ★

'At that moment a man in the lavatory shouted: "Look out! The Mudir!" That shook the chief clerk out of his reminiscences. The Mudir was actually standing in the doorway of the lavatory, smiling, one casual hand on his hip.

The chief clerk seemed paralysed. He wanted to reach for the water-can, but he did nothing, simply remained squatting, in the same position. He saw the shocked men pulling up their trousers and leaving the lavatory. Soon he and the Mudir were alone.

"Those pigs are in such a hurry they've forgotten to wash their bottoms," said the Mudir.

"Yes," said the chief clerk. He reached for the water-can, but the Mudir asked him to stay where he was.

"Just wait a minute," said the Mudir. "I'd like a word with you."'

'The lavatory looked deserted. The Mudir squatted down by the chief clerk. He was smoking a Russian cigarette with a paper mouthpiece.

"That's something that could cost another man his head," said the Mudir, tapping the Russian cigarette. "But mine come from pre-war times, and anyway I'm beyond suspicion."

"Obviously," said the chief clerk.

The Mudir smiled. "What were you dreaming about just now, Bash-Kiatib Agah? I was standing at the entrance quite a long time watching you."

"I wasn't dreaming, Mudir Bey."

"Don't you ever have daydreams?"

"Never, Mudir Bey. As chief clerk I can't allow myself that sort of thing."

"But I was watching you, Bash-Kiatib Agah. And I'm telling you, it looked as if you were dreaming."'

'"Even animals dream," said the Mudir. "My cat, for instance. It mews in its sleep."

"Yes, Mudir Bey."

"But those weren't daydreams. Only men can dream when they're awake."

"Do you think so, Mudir Bey?"

"Yes, Bash-Kiatib Agah."'

*   *   *

"'I had a daydream a little time ago," said the Mudir. "I saw a big tree. A very big tree. And it was growing in the heart of Turkey. A giant tree. And hanging on the tree were all our troubles."

"What did our troubles look like, Mudir Bey?"

"They looked like Armenians. Like Armenians."'

"'Let's get to the point," said the Mudir, and turned his head towards the chief clerk, blowing smoke in his face, regardless of the discomfort it caused him. The chief clerk didn't dare to cough. He didn't even dare to think that it was bad manners and he ought to protest. He only thought: "That's just what the Mudir said to that prisoner, the Armenian Vartan Khatisian, who had no profession and professed to be a poet. 'Let's get to the point,' the Mudir had said to him."

"Let's get to the point, Bash-Kiatib Agah," said the Mudir.

"Yes, Mudir Bey," said the chief clerk.

"What do you think of that Vartan Khatisian?"

"I think he's an obstinate fellow."

"He is, Bash-Kiatib Agah."

"You'll never get anything out of him, Mudir Bey. Not a thing. The man says he's innocent and doesn't know anything."

"Innocent or not," said the Mudir, "he'll make a confession. That I guarantee you."

"Do you think so, Mudir Bey?"

"I swear it by the head of my mother," said the Mudir, "my mother who bore me. And I swear it by Allah, who in his wisdom has given me a tongue to swear with. That Vartan Khatisian will make a confession, and more than that. I will take care that he is sent to Constantinople. And he will confess there too."

"Confess what, Mudir Bey?"

"That there is an Armenian world conspiracy."

"And how will you get him to confess, not only here in Bakir but also in Constantinople?"

"I have ways and means," said the Mudir.

"By Allah," said the chief clerk. "Allah knows ways and means of loosening the tongues of the most stubborn."

"And I have spoken with Allah," said the Mudir. "And Allah

has inspired me."'

"'I'll dictate Vartan Khatisian's confession to you first thing in the morning," said the Mudir. "The prisoner doesn't know about it yet, and his confession . . . written, in purple ink . . . will come as a complete surprise to him. Then he'll just have to sign it."

"Will he sign?"

"Obviously."

"Will it be signed by witnesses?"

"But of course. I will sign that I was a witness and have read the confession, and that his signature was made in my presence. And you will also sign that you were a witness. And others will sign."

"Will there be a verbal confession?"

"That too. But afterwards. First we want the written one."

"And what about witnesses for the verbal confession?"

"No different."

"Who will the witnesses be?"

"Myself, for one. And you. But also the Vali and the Mutessarif and the Kaimakam. Possibly also some Turkish and German officers."'

"'The Christian holidays are coming soon," said the Mudir. "The next one, just round the corner, is Ascension Day. I happened to learn that from one of the prisoners. And do you know, Bash-Kiatib Agah, each time one of these holidays comes round, the Christians get more stubborn. That's why the Armenian Vartan Khatisian will be making his confession this week."

"Yes, Mudir Bey." And the chief clerk asked: "And what is Ascension Day?"

"It's the day when that odd saint of theirs sailed up to heaven, like our Prophet on his white horse El Buragu."

Both men fell silent. The Mudir smoked thoughtfully, and the chief clerk looked out of the lavatory window, which had no curtains and was only the size of a ventilator, no more than a hole in the wall through which the pale evening light oozed. Now and then voices and cries reached them in the half-dark room from the nearby prison, mingling with the other voices from the offices and corridors in the *hukumet*. Just as the Mudir threw his cigarette between his feet into the shit-hole under his bottom, at that very moment the muezzins began to sing on the minarets. One of the muezzins could be heard clearly, for his cawing song came from the minaret of the closest mosque, the Hirka Sherif Djamissi, the Mosque of the Holy Mantle, the Avenue of the Dry Well. *Allahu akbar*, sang the muezzin, God is great. And the muezzin was calling all the faithful, even the Mudir and the chief clerk. Four times the muezzin called. The chief clerk shut his eyes and listened. The cawing voice of the muezzin filled the room with a thousand and one crows. They flew round the Mudir and the chief clerk like huge grey butterflies, hovering over their heads and fluttering over the shit-holes. *Allahu akbar*, called the muezzin for the last time. God is great. I declare that there is no god but Allah. I declare that Mohammed is his prophet. Up to prayer! Up to salvation! *Allahu akbar. La ilah illa 'lla.* God is great. There is no god but Allah.'

CHAPTER FIVE

The Mudir had gone home. The chief clerk had gone home too. And all the petty officials in the *hukumet*, and the others, the petitioners and visitors and cleaning women and saptiehs, everyone who had nothing more to look for here late in the evening, they had all gone home. Everybody had gone home. Only the night watchman was there, and the sentry outside the main gate. It was very quiet in the *hukumet*. The song of the muezzin had long since died away, the cawing birds had disappeared from the lavatory and the big grey butterflies too. Through the silence there sounded only the voice of the story-teller. He said: 'My little lamb. As you see, they have all gone to bed. Night has crept up on Bakir.'

'Your father too had heard the call of the muezzin, in his cell. When the muezzin called "God is great" for the third time, your father had peacefully gone to sleep. But in his dreams he saw the glass eye of the Mudir, and it said to him: "Do you see this glass eye, Vartan Khatisian? It sees no more and no less than the eye of God. For I bet that God, who is great, has seen nothing of the dead Armenians on the city gate and in the market-places. Nor will he see the others that will be hanged, no matter whether they are guilty or not. The government will hang many more. And many will also be shot and beheaded. Many will simply be beaten to death. And I am telling you, God has glass eyes. And I'm saying: the government will light a great fire. And millions of bodies will be cast into that fire. And it will all take place before the eyes of God, which are glass eyes. And I see a big lamb, with its throat cut. And I see how the lamb cries out to the glass eye. And in the glass eye there is no response." And when your father heard that, he woke up, and knew that he was lost.'

*   *   *

'Not much happened for a day or two. Your father was decently treated. He was neither beaten nor tortured. And his food was not poisoned. The saptiehs grinned when they looked into his cell. And your father was frightened. On the third day he was taken before the Mudir.'

'"This is your confession," said the Mudir, and pointed to the document lying on the desk in front of him. "As you see, I've already signed it. The chief clerk too has not hesitated to append his signature to the confession. The Vali has signed too, and the Kaimakam and the Mutessarif. All these gentlemen have signed to the effect that they have seen you, Vartan Khatisian, read the confession and then sign it with your own hand. All we need now is one more signature. And that is yours."

"But I haven't confessed anything," said your father.

"That doesn't matter," said the Mudir.

"May I at least read the confession I haven't made?"

"Naturally," said the Mudir.'

'After your father had read the confession, he said: "I shan't sign that."

"But you're mistaken," said the Mudir. "The witnesses have declared that you have signed. The witnesses saw it."

"But the witnesses haven't seen anything at all," said your father. "When am I supposed to have signed this confession?"

"This morning," said the Mudir. "It's even got the time on it."

"That's true," said my father. "It has got the time on it."

"Well, there you are," said the Mudir.

"But on the document it says 9.22 in the morning. And it's afternoon now."

"We can turn the clock back," said the Mudir. "Believe me, efendi, it is all one to Allah what time it is in reality. For what is reality? Do you really know? Allah's sun is always the same."

"I'm not going to sign."

"But you must sign," said the Mudir. "Otherwise the witnesses' signatures are wrong. And after all we're talking about the Vali and the Mutessarif and the Kaimakam, the chief clerk and myself. Do you want to say that we've all lied and haven't seen anything? We've all seen you sign with your own hand!"

"I'm not saying a thing," said your father.

"Are you signing now?"

"No," said your father.'

'The Mudir clapped his hands angrily. The chief clerk stood up, opened the door and called the saptiehs who were hanging around outside. Actually they must have heard the Mudir clap his hands themselves. The Mudir said something to the saptiehs that your father couldn't hear, so your father thought they were going to take him away now. Perhaps they would tear his fingernails out or give him the usual bastinado. He had already heard a lot about that. They whipped the soles of your feet and then rubbed oil and salt in them. But nothing like that happened. The saptiehs disappeared for quite a while, to fetch the *kahveji* – the coffee-seller who generally stood outside in front of the *hukumet*. They couldn't find him, so they fetched the *kahveji* from the nearest coffee-house, the *kahvehane* El Rashid, the Coffee of the Just. The *kahveji* came straight back with the saptiehs. He was wearing a dirty turban, a sleeveless jacket and baggy trousers. His unwashed feet were stuck into leather sandals. The mourning bands under his toenails were blacker than the strongest coffee, and that was black and strong in these parts. The *kahveji* brought three cups of coffee and *baklava* and a sweet, light brown pudding of highly dubious origin. He served the Mudir and the chief clerk, and the prisoner too. The Mudir threw the *kahveji* a silver *mejidye*. Then the saptiehs grabbed the *kahveji* and shoved him out again. Guzzling and swilling, the Mudir said: "I'd advise you to sign."'

'"How can I sign that there is an Armenian world conspiracy?" said your father. "How can I sign that I am their tool and that I came to Turkey just before the outbreak of war on the instructions of this world conspiracy? And what have I got to do with the murder of the Austrian Crown Prince? I can't sign anything like that."'

'"If you don't sign," said the Mudir, "we'll have you executed. But not in public, as we are going to do before. We'll simply

109

let you disappear."

"I'm an American citizen."

"That doesn't mean much, efendi."

"They will protest!'

"Nobody's going to protest, efendi, if somebody accidentally and regrettably dies of a heart attack. Don't forget, America's a neutral country. But we are at war. The Americans won't get involved here, especially not in a matter of espionage in an area just behind the front."

"And the American press?"

"Who cares about the press? The press is a whore and always makes a great fuss about everything."

"The consulate will protest."

"You are mistaken, efendi. The consulate will very wisely keep quiet. There's a war on, efendi. And you are a spy."

"I am not a spy."

"Well, never mind that."'

'"And supposing I do sign?"

"Then you're guilty."

"Then shall I be executed?"

"No. On the contrary. If you admit your guilt, then we send you to Constantinople. And there you will say what you've said in your confession. There will be a trial. A great trial. A public trial. The whole world will be listening. Even America and its respresentatives. Even the American ambassador in Constantinople . . . Morgenthau, a Jew, a man who, naturally to our annoyance, stupidly supports the Armenians, in an astonishing way. He'll be there too. And they'll all recognize that the Armenians are guilty."

"But they aren't guilty!"

"That's a matter of opinion, efendi."'

'"Look, efendi. If you're guilty, then you're very useful to us. And so long as you're useful, you can live. It will be a very long trial. So you may live a long time."

"And after the trial?"

"Then it's all over," said the Mudir. "But if I were you I shouldn't worry about that just now. A long trial is a long trial. And if one

110

day it comes to an end, by then the war may be over. And then, from our point of view, it's all one whether you're allowed to live or not. It could well be that you'd be exchanged, perhaps for one of our men taken by the Russians, or the British or the French. So you see, there's hope for you. That's how things are, efendi. The guilty may hope."

"But I don't really understand, Mudir Bey."

"You don't have to understand anything, efendi. There are times when the innocent have to die and the guilty are allowed to live. At such times it's better to be guilty. Do you understand that?"

"No, Mudir Bey, I don't understand it."'

'"That Armenian doesn't understand a thing," said the Mudir later to the chief clerk, after Vartan Khatisian had been taken back to his cell. "Do you understand why I don't understand that that Armenian doesn't understand anything, although in fact he must understand what any idiot understands?"

"No," said the chief clerk.

"It would be easy enough of course to persuade him to sign," said the Mudir, "a matter of a few seconds. I'll give you an example: I could threaten him with a pistol. I could press my pistol against his forehead. And do you know what would happen then?"

"No," said the chief clerk.

"He would sign at once."

"Do you think so?"

"I'm sure of it."'

'"But that wouldn't make sense," said the Mudir.

"Why not?"

"Because we want to take him to Constantinople," said the Mudir. "And because when he's there he's got to say before the whole world what he's said in his confession. Do you understand that?"

"No," said the chief clerk.

"Oh, well," said the Mudir. "That's how it is. That stubborn Armenian has got to say before the whole world that there is an Armenian world conspiracy that is plotting against mankind, against every nation, against justice and order, against morality.

But above all against us."

"Against Turkey and the Turks?"

"That's it. And that's why we must first convince him. That means he must believe in his confession."

"Why?"

"Because otherwise his confession would be pointless, and his evidence in Constantinople unconvincing. Don't you see? He can't give convincing evidence if he himself isn't convinced."

"I do understand that," said the chief clerk.'

'"And what's the best way of convincing a man?"

"I don't know that," said the chief clerk.

"Frightening him," said the Mudir.

"Frightening him?"

"Of course. Frightening him."

"But that man is completely frightened."

"He's not frightened enough."

"And if you pressed your pistol against his forehead . . ."

"No, no, Bash-Kiatib Agah. A few seconds' fear like that won't last until Constantinople."

"You mean, by the time he's in Constantinople he'll have forgotten that fear again?"

"Let's say, got over it."

"He could be threatened with execution?"

"We've done that already. It's not enough."

"He's really extraordinarily obstinate."

"Yes, he really is."'

'"Of course we could tear his fingernails out. Or give him the bastinado. But, believe me, that will be no good with a chap like that. And anyway it wouldn't work."

"Why wouldn't it work?"

"Because he can't arrive in Constantinople with no fingernails or with the soles of his feet kaput. World opinion might think we were barbarians. Or that we'd blackmailed him. Or something like that. No, Bash-Kiatib Agah. This man must arrive in Constantinople in good condition. And what he says there has got to convince everybody, even the observers from neutral countries, the American

112

representative for instance, in Constantinople."

"Who exactly do you mean there?"

"We know who it will be: the Jew Morgenthau."

"Oh, that man?"

"Yes, that man. He's an Armenian at heart. At any rate he supports them."

"A difficult problem."

"Yes, it is a bit difficult."'

"'Have you seen the Armenian priest we hanged on the Gate of Happiness?"

"Yes, I've seen him."

"We've picked up another one now."

"An Armenian priest?"

"Yes."

"Will you hang him too?"

"No. I've got something else for him."'

"'The priest is sitting in his cell barefoot. And so I say to myself, an Armenian ought not to go around barefoot, not even in a cell. The Armenians are a sensitive race."

"Right, Mudir Bey."

"So I say to myself, we'll shoe the Armenian priest."

"How do you mean?"

"Well, the way you shoe a horse. We'll nail horseshoes to his bare feet."

"What sort of horseshoes?"

"Either the Anatolian sort, you know what I mean; the thin ones made of ordinary metal, with three holes . . . or, if I were to ask one of the German officers, a shoe from the German cavalry. The German horses have different shoes. They're two fingers thick, and don't bend."

"But we haven't got any bellows in the prison, nor here in the *hukumet*."

"We can get bellows from anywhere. If necessary we'll cold-shoe the priest."

"You won't need bellows for that."

"No," said the Mudir.'

*　　*　　*

'"When we're shoeing the priest, I'll make Vartan Khatisian look on. Perhaps that will convince him."

"Perhaps," said the chief clerk.

"If not, we'll have to think of something else."

"What?" asked the chief clerk.

"I don't know yet," said the Mudir.'

'"Couldn't that Vartan Khatisian be convinced by clever words?" asked the chief clerk.

"No," said the Mudir.

"Will nothing work but fear?"

"That's it," said the Mudir.'

'And the Mudir said: "A frightened man only listens to his own voice, and that is the voice of fear. So I speak to the frightened man in his own language."

"And if the frightened man should suddenly lose his fear?"

"That doesn't happen," said the Mudir. "For then he wouldn't be really frightened. Or else he'd be a saint, whose heart had been cleansed of fear by Allah."

"That Vartan Khatisian is no saint."

"He isn't," said the Mudir. "He certainly isn't."'

And all at once it became completely silent in the Mudir's office. There was only the scratching of the Stamboul pen, for the chief clerk had begun to make a copy of the confession. The Mudir lighted his *chibouk*, leaned his head back against the headrest of his Frankish chair, closed his good eye and only stared at the ceiling with his glass eye. The only voice in the room was the voice of the story-teller. And he said: 'Do you see the Mudir's glass eye, my little lamb? And do you see the chief clerk's Stamboul pen? And his sponge, and the powder? When the copy is finished, it will be powdered and dried and blotted, and then it will find its way to Constantinople, and it will get there before your father gets there. And I bet you it will land on the desk of Enver Pasha, the war-god and redeemer of all Turks. And do you see, my little lamb, how the chief clerk suddenly puts his Stamboul pen down in the inkpot, as if he had writer's cramp, or as if he needed to think something over? And shall I tell you what he is thinking now? Although these are thoughts that the Mudir mustn't hear. But don't worry. No one can hear my voice.'

And the Meddah said: 'The chief clerk is thinking about one thing and another. He is thinking: "By Allah! We're all frightened. I'm frightened of the Mudir, and indeed of all my superiors. And the Mudir is frightened too, though I don't know who and what he's frightened of. But he is frightened. And that's why he wants to frighten other people, so that they can be more frightened than he is."'

And the Meddah said: 'I am the Meddah and the story-teller. It is one and the same. And that is why I am telling you now: there were once two children. They went into the forest. And there was a gingerbread house there, and a witch lived in it. And the witch had a big cooking-pot. A very big one. And when she saw the children in the forest, not far from her hut, she thought, I'll tempt the children into the hut. And then I'll put them in the big cooking-pot. And I'll boil them and eat them.

Well, my little lamb. The witch lived in Frankistan and not in Anatolia. Everything here is different.'

'It really is different here, and small children are not boiled in big cooking-pots. And yet for many people here it is worse, more frightening, than for small children who are to be boiled in big cooking-pots. Here, fear does not rise from the steam of a cooking-pot, it hangs in the air everywhere. The people breathe it in, whether they will or not.'

'And I am telling you, my little lamb. There was once a man who set out to learn about fear. But he did not come as far as Anatolia.'

'It was in the spring of 1915,' said the story-teller. 'It was the period of preparation: preparation for the wiping out of a people, or for the sacrifice of the lamb whose name was to be blotted out in the book of names. It had not gone so far yet. Men would still talk with other men; with your father, for instance, who was a common

farmer, or an uncommon one, for he was also a seller of cowshit, a
night watchman and lots of other things. He was also a poet. It had
not gone so far yet. They took an interest in him. They took him
round the prison and showed him how a priest was shod. They
showed him other methods of torture, which I will not tell you about
now, for what after all are fingernails torn out or teeth pulled out
or stomachs that burst because too much swill has been poured into
the mouths. What after all are festering feet that have been whipped
for days by the Turkish warders and finally have to be sawn off
because the warders could not bear the stink. Your father saw it
all, and he also saw the hearses that left the prison every day. And
he heard the dogs in the street howling, because the prison walls
couldn't hold back the stench of putrefaction and decay.'

And the story-teller, who was called Meddah, said: 'Your father is
sitting in his cell alone. And yet he is not alone, for he is
accompanied by his fears. Shall I tell you about his fears?'
    'Yes,' said the last thought.
    'And about his daydreams too, which whisper his fears in his
ear?'
    'Yes,' said the last thought.
    'Or shall I let his fears tell their own story?'
    'As you like,' said the last thought.

And the fears of Vartan Khatisian told the story-teller the story of
the daydream that Vartan Khatisian dreamed in his cell. And the
story-teller told it to the last thought.

'One morning,' said the story-teller, 'the cell door burst open and
the Mudir came in, accompanied by two saptiehs. But there was a
third saptieh outside, and a little bow-legged man whom the third
saptieh took by the scruff of the neck and pushed into the cell. So
now there were five of them: the Mudir, three saptiehs and the little
bow-legged man. Your father was desperately frightened when he
saw the bow-legged man, for he looked like the angel of death as
he had dreamt of him as a child. But he heard the Mudir say: "By
Allah! We've been waiting for that chap." Then he fainted.'

*   *   *

'When your father came to, he saw that the angel of death was himself frightened. He was a little man with a bald head. And he had big, black, frightened eyes. And he had a hooked nose and extraordinary bow legs. The Mudir said: "This is the cement expert."'

'The Mudir kicked one of the saptiehs on the bottom with the toe of his boot. "Do you know what cement is?" he asked.

"No, Mudir Bey," said the saptieh. "By Allah, I don't know."

And he asked the other saptiehs: "Do you know what cement is?" And the other saptiehs said: "No, Mudir Bey. By Allah, we don't know."'

'The Mudir asked the angel of death, who was actually only a frightened little Armenian, a man with bow legs and a hooked nose and a big bald head and big, black eyes: "Do you know what cement is?"

And the little man said: "Yes. I am the cement expert."'

'"There's no cement in this area," said the Mudir to your father. "But there's cement in Constantinople, and also in some other big cities. This man" – and he pointed at the nervous little Armenian – "was in Smyrna, where he worked for a big foreign builder, and he's brought a bag of the bloody stuff with him."

"I've brought a bag with me," said the little man.

"Tell this man what cement is, then," said the Mudir, pointing at your father, "and what you can do with it."'

'"Cement is a powder," said the little man, "which was invented in the west, where every damned thing was invented . . . If the powder is mixed with sand and a little water, after a time it goes solid. Then it's called concrete."

"Concrete?"

"Yes, concrete."

"How hard is concrete?"

"It's very hard, Mudir Bey."'

'"What happens if while you're mixing the cement you accidentally stick your finger in the paste?"

"What paste?"

"The cement paste?"

"Nothing at all, Mudir Bey. Nothing happens, so long as you pull your finger out again."

"And if you don't pull your finger out, but leave it in?"

"Then your finger would get stuck in the paste. After a time the paste turns into concrete. As I just told you."

"Not pasty any more?"

"That's right."

"A firm, hard mass?"

"That's right."

"Does that mean you'd never be able to pull your finger out again?"

"Yes, Mudir Bey. Never again."'

'"And what would happen if you stuck your prick into the cement paste?"

"Nothing at all, Mudir Bey. Nothing at all would happen, if you pulled your prick straight out."

"And if you didn't pull it out?"

"Then your prick would get stuck in it."

"And you wouldn't be able to pull it out again?"

"That's right."'

'"So your prick would be stuck fast for ever and ever?"

"Yes, Mudir Bey. For all eternity."'

The story-teller said to the last thought: 'Do you see what will happen to your father?' And he said: 'What did I tell you? The man who set out to learn about fear never came to Anatolia.'

'"Only unbelievers could invent something like that," said the Mudir, "and people who are possessed of the devil."

"Yes," said the little man, "that is true." And he said, "I am the cement expert."'

'"This cement expert is an Armenian," said the Mudir to the

118

saptiehs. "He belongs to a race that is cunning, and that has conspired against mankind. The Armenians are arrogant and rebellious, but when you beat them they crawl at your feet. Fundamentally they are a frightened race, and the fact that they are frightened has to do with their fertility. That man there" – and he pointed at the little concrete worker again – "has thirteen children. And he knows quite well what I shall do with his thirteen children if he doesn't do whatever I tell him."

"I'll do everything you tell me," said the cement expert.'

'The Mudir said: "Armenians believe that they are all brothers and sisters. Tell your brother what I've told you to do, and what you will be doing to him."

"You've told me to seal up his orifices."

"What orifices? Explain to your brother."

"The one orifice," said the cement expert, "where undigested food comes out. And the other orifice where his water comes out."

The Mudir turned to your father laughing. "Now will you sign that confession?"

"No," said your father, "I won't sign anything."'

'Everything that would happen in a daydream,' said the story-teller, 'can be foreseen, and we two – you and I, my little lamb – really only need the imagination of an unimaginative saptieh, of a simpleton, to picture the next scene of this daydream. The Mudir has your father fettered. The saptiehs stuff wool up his anus, because cotton-wool is scarce and can only be found in the German hospitals. The saptiehs also stick wool into his penis – they have no tweezers and have to use matches sharpened with a knife – they stuff the orifices full, pressing it in well, regardless of your father's screams, regardless too of the cement expert, who meanwhile has fetched his bag and a wooden bowl, and now begins to pour the fine powder into the bowl, then goes out to fetch water and a little sand, and a long wooden stick, and mixes it all into a grey paste.'

'We two,' said the story-teller to the last thought, 'are only observers, and I, the story-teller, can do everything that you, my little lamb, can't do. I can even read thoughts. But I won't read the thoughts of the cement expert. Let me just say that he isn't really thinking at all, because his thoughts frighten him. Or else, he does think, for instance that the wool ought to be enough to stuff up the orifices. Why does the Mudir want him to smear concrete over them as well? "I shan't need much. The pisshole is narrow and the arsehole is a bit bigger, but not big enough to need my entire supply. I've got a whole bag full."'

'Later your father, dressed only in a prison overall, hung before the barred window. The saptiehs had hung him up by his arms, and he hung there like washing hung out to dry.

"How long does this stuff take to dry?" asked the Mudir.

"Several hours," said the cement expert. "Then it's concrete."

"Will he never be able to shit or piss again?" asked one of the saptiehs.

"No, never," said the Mudir.'

'"You've got a few hours to think about this business of your signature," said the Mudir to your father. "If you sign quickly, we can remove the cement. But you must get a move on. Once the stuff is dry, it's too late. You'll never be able to shit again. Or pee again. I know you're an Armenian, but there are some things that all humans need. And before Allah snuffs out your lights, you will be screaming. You'll scream so loud that the birds will fall out of the sky."

"When the sun shines through the barred window," said the cement expert, "the paste will dry quicker."

"The sun isn't over the prison yard yet," said the Mudir.

And one of those silly saptiehs said: "I think it's because it's early in the morning. The sun doesn't shine here until just before the midday prayer."'

'Your father hung in his cell alone. Somewhere there was his mother's voice. He heard it clearly: "My son. Why did I ever bear you?"'

'He was five, and he was sitting on his mother's lap.

"How did I come into the world, mother?"

"I don't know, my little pasha."

"Who does know?"

"Your grandmother."'

'"Grandmother, how did I come into the world?"

"All Armenian children are born somehow."

"But how, grandmother?"

"Well, now. Armenian girls are born under fig-trees."

"And Armenian boys?"

"Under grapevines."

"But there aren't any grapevines here."

"True," said his grandmother. "This is hill country, and there are only poor fields here."

"Where is my grapevine?"

"Beyond the Kurdish mountains. Over the other side. Where the sea is."

"Is it a long way away?"

"No, my little pasha. Two days in the donkey-cart."

"Beyond the mountains, where the sea is?"

"Yes, my little pasha."

"Is that the land of the grapevine?"

"Yes, that's the land of the grapevine."'

'"When Armenian children are born, the Mother of God smiles and blesses every fig-tree and grapevine, and all the birds in the land of Hayastan chirrup with angels' voices."

"Tell me what it was like when I came into the world?"

"I don't really know, my little angel."

"And who does know?"

"Well, who should know it? Your grapevine, of course. Your grapevine knows it, my little angel."'

'And his parents got into the donkey-cart to go and fetch him. His mother was in the family way, in her ninth month. The pains had already begun, and she was groaning and crying. She said to his father: "Drive the donkey hard. It must go fast. For my little Vartan is lying under the grapevine, waiting for us to fetch him." And his father said: "I'll make the donkey go as fast as possible.

But a donkey is a donkey, and there's no stick, not even the best of sticks, that can make it hurry."

The donkey went through the country of the Kurds at its own pace. The mountains got higher and higher, their peaks touching the sky.

"A donkey is a donkey," said his father.

"I can't stand it any longer."

"Then pray to our Redeemer."'

'And his mother prayed to him who died for all of us. "Jesus," she whispered, "help me." And she heard Jesus say: "I will help you. You will feel no pain." And in fact the pains ceased. The donkey drew the cart slowly through the clouds. The Kurdish mountains were so high, it made them dizzy to look down into the villages of the Kurd semi-nomads, or still further, to where the Armenians lived, right down in the valley.

"I have no pains any more," said his mother to his father. "The Lord heard me."

"That's very good," said his father.

"Will it really take two days to get to the grapevines?"

"Yes, so long as the donkey doesn't decide to stop."

"Do you think our Vartan will wait so long?"

"Certainly he will wait."'

'But during the journey much milk had flowed into his mother's breasts. And her breasts swelled and grew bigger and bigger, until at last they hung like two heavy sacks over the floorboards of the donkey-cart.

"The milk can't wait any longer," said his mother to his father.

"The milk is looking for the little mouth of our dear little Vartan," said his father.

"But our Vartan is still lying under the grapevine."

"That's where he's lying," said his father.

"We ought to have brought a puppy with us," said his mother. "That's what the Gypsy women do. If they have too much milk, they get the puppy to suck at their breasts."

"We'll soon be there," said his father. "The milk can wait that long."

"How long?"

"Until you take our little Vartan in your arms and give him your breast."

"He'll have a hungry little mouth?"

"Yes," said his father.'

'But the milk would not wait. And the donkey grew stubborn and went slower and slower. Often it just stopped and wouldn't go any further. But the milk could not wait.'

'And suddenly his mother's great sacks of milk burst. And whole streams of milk flowed down the mountain and poured into the Anatolian valleys. And more and more milk flowed down. And the streams became rivers. And the rivers, seas. The whole world drowned in his mother's milk. Only the grapevine, where little Vartan lay, remained dry. And little Vartan cried and cried. He cried for his mother's milk, which was everywhere except where he was.'

'Vartan Khatisian hung in his cell, drying. He wanted to relieve himself, and couldn't. He cried for his mother. But only a saptieh came. And he asked: "What's the matter?"

"I can't stand it any more, Saptieh Agah."

"Shall I fetch the Mudir?"

"Yes."

The Mudir came into the cell.

"Shall we open your holes?"

"Yes, Mudir Bey."

"And what about the confession? Will you sign?"

"No."

"But, efendi, don't you understand? We shan't open your holes until you're ready to sign."

Vartan Khatisian began to howl, and the Mudir let him howl for a little while.

"Actually I'm doing you a favour if I let you sign," said the Mudir. "It's a big favour, and you must beg for it."

"I can't stand it any longer, Mudir Bey."

"Will you sign, efendi?"

"Yes, Mudir Bey."
"Do you beg for it?"
"I beg you, Mudir Bey."'

'Vartan Khatisian was untied. The cement, which was not dry yet and so not hard, was washed off, the wool was pulled out of his penis and his backside. The saptieh brought him a pair of trousers and helped him put them on, but before he could do the buttons up, the inevitable happened.

"He's done it in his trousers," said the saptieh.

"It doesn't matter," said the Mudir. "That was only to be expected."'

The last thought had tried to get the feeling of his father's fear; but since he was already beyond fear, he could feel nothing. The story-teller had sat down at the Mudir's writing-desk, and since there was no one in the office now, and the door was closed, and because the story-teller had cast a dark magic cloth over the whole *hukumet* and the wall and even the prison where his father's cell was, he could see nothing and couldn't even imagine anything.

'So is that a true story or not?'

'Everything that happens in a man's head is true,' said the story-teller, 'though there is another truth that often seems impossible to us.'

'I don't understand that.'

'It's not important,' said the story-teller. 'I have told you before: it's only the fears of your father that have told me this story that I've told you. It is his nightmares that have told a nightmare. It is, if you like, a nightmare's nightmare.'

'Why can't my father frighten his fears away?'

'Because he's worn out, my little lamb. Because his soul has no more strength. Because he has seen too much in this prison and because he knows that the Mudir can make nightmares come true if he wants to.'

The story-teller waited for the last thought to ask the important question: 'Did my father sign? Will he confess?' But the last thought didn't ask. So now the story-teller said: 'Your father had seen how the priest was shod, and he had seen other things even worse, and

124

he had heard the screams of men being tortured, at first only at intervals, then all day, and later all night too. The whole prison was filled with nothing but screams. And, as I've told you, your father was worn out. The worst thing was, he didn't know what the Mudir intended to do with him, and that almost drove him to madness, for he began to imagine unimaginable things. And one morning . . .'

'What happened, one morning?'

'One morning the Mudir sent for your father in his office. He asked him in a friendly way: "Do you know how your wife is?"

"I don't know," said your father. "I get no news about her."

"We know she's pregnant," said the Mudir . . . "in the fifth month, isn't she?"

"In the sixth month," said your father.

"Is it going to be a son?"

"We hope so," said your father.

"You want an heir, don't you?"

"Yes," said your father.

"What will your son be called?"

"We want to call him Thovma," said your father.

"Thovma Khatisian," said the Mudir. "A real Armenian name."

"Yes," said your father.

"We've arrested your wife," said the Mudir. "She's in the Bakir women's prison now."

"It's not possible," said your father. "That's really impossible."

"And why is it impossible?"

"Because she hasn't committed any offence."

"Plenty of people say they've committed no offence," said the Mudir . . . "and they've been arrested just the same."

"Yes," said your father.

"We're just holding your wife as a hostage," said the Mudir . . . "until you have confessed."

"As a hostage?"

"Yes," said the Mudir.'

'"Don't worry," said the Mudir. "Your wife is under my personal protection. Nothing will happen to her. We will only kill the unborn child if you don't confess."'

125

"My son Thovma?"

"Your son Thovma."

The Mudir smiled, opened a drawer in his desk and took out some things of your mother's. There was her inland pass, what they called *teskeré*, and there were a few bits of jewellery that your father had bought her; even her wedding veil was there, all familiar things. "You see," said the Mudir, "we really have arrested your wife. Do you believe it?"

"Yes," said your father.

"And with your wife we have arrested your son, even though he's not born yet."

"My son Thovma?"

"Your son Thovma."

"My son?" said your father. "My son."

"He's always there, wherever your wife goes."

"Thovma," said your father. "My little Thovma."

"We won't do anything to your son if you sign. Will you sign?"

"Yes," said your father, "I'll sign."'

'Your father signed, and he put his signature next to those other signatures that already declared that the signatories had seen him sign with his own hand. The Mudir was very friendly. He said: "Of course this isn't enough. You will also . . . in Constantinople . . . give evidence before the general public."

"Yes," said your father.

"And you know what will happen to your son if you withdraw anything in Constantinople?"

"I won't withdraw anything," said your father.'

'"And there's one other thing," said the Mudir. "The day after tomorrow there are some gentlemen coming to my office. Those gentlemen would very much like to hear from your own mouth what's in the written confession. So you will learn by heart the written confession, which you have signed with your own hand, and then repeat it verbally before those gentlemen. It's a sort of dress rehearsal so that we know what you'll be saying in Constantinople. So that you won't make any mistakes, do you understand?"

"I understand."

"Take the copy of the written confession to your cell, efendi. And learn it by heart. And tell those gentlemen everything that's in it."

"Yes, Mudir Bey."

"There are a few gaps in the written confession. Think about filling them in, and answer all the questions that the gentlemen or I put to you clearly. It has to sound credible and natural, in no way as if it had been learnt by heart. Do you understand?"

"Yes, Mudir Bey."

"And remember your little Thovma."'

'What was to be staged in the Mudir's office two days later was not the great trial,' said the story-teller, 'because of course that had to take place in Constantinople, and because the gentlemen in the Mudir's office were not judges, but witnesses. The Mudir said it was just the dress rehearsal of a verbal statement, but in effect it wasn't even that. It was merely the first confession, made before witnesses, of a whole string of other confessions which your father still had to make before the real dress rehearsal of the verbal confession took place before the ears of the examining magistrates in Constantinople, which would then be repeated later in court, and thus before the general public. Do you understand that?'

'No,' said the last thought.

'All right,' said the story-teller, 'I'll explain it. Your father was to make a confession about which we two – you and I – know virtually nothing. We know only that the Mudir had dictated the confession and that it had something to do with a mysterious Armenian world conspiracy, in which your father was said to be involved. This confession, as I've said, is purely invented, by the Mudir in collaboration with the Vali, the Mutessarif, the Kaimakam and the chief clerk. It is purely invented, but it is based on suspicions that are plausible. The Mudir had his invention taken down in writing and signed by your father. The other gentlemen, the Vali, the Mutessarif, the Kaimakam and also of course the Mudir himself and the chief clerk, have declared by their signatures that the confession is in order, though their signatures were appended before the actual signature by your father.'

'I understand that,' said the last thought.

'This is something I've already said once, but I'll say it again.

And what I say again is that your father now had to repeat verbally what was in the written confession, so that he could say the same thing later in Constantinople. He will repeat it over and over again until his confession sounds so convincing that even the gentlemen in Constantinople will run no risk with him when they make him say it before the general public. The performance in the Mudir's office is thus not a dress rehearsal, although the Mudir calls it one, but only the first rehearsal of many rehearsals leading up to an eventual dress rehearsal and then to the final confession before the general public.'

'I'm beginning to get it,' said the last thought. 'But what will my father actually confess?'

'You'll hear that soon,' said the story-teller.

'So you must picture them,' said the story-teller, 'all assembled in the Mudir's office, all those whom the Mudir had invited as former witnesses, the Vali of Bakir, the Kaimakam, the chief clerk, the Mutessarif, some Turkish officers and three Germans, including the little gay lieutenant and also the major and friend of the Vali's as well as an Austrian journalist who had found a billet here, not far from the front. The Kadi is there too, a Muslim judge, but only there as a witness and observer, for there will be no trial, only a hearing. You must also picture the room as smoky as a Turkish coffee-house; the little gay lieutenant – a non-smoker – keeps on coughing, and so does the chief clerk, who as you know is also a non-smoker. You must picture coffee being served in dainty little cups . . . with sweets and *raki*. Three Turkish officers sit on the divan with the Kadi, while all the others sit on the floor, on soft cushions, even the three Germans and the Austrian journalist. They don't want to attract attention and are glad to be allowed to sit on the floor and not on the divan, for instance, or even on the two Frankish chairs by the desk. The three Germans and the Austrian have noticed long ago that no one dares sit on the Frankish chairs. That would be improper. Two empty, useless chairs. There is no more than a sound of whispering, of the gulping of coffee and *raki* and even a bit of lip-smacking. Many of the gentlemen are enjoying the *baklava*, others just smoke their *chibouks*. The Germans and the Austrian take a good look at the prisoner as he sits by the desk, not fettered, but restless and frightened.

"What's all this show about?" whispers the lieutenant to the major. He speaks German and knows that none of the Turks understand him.

"The Mudir wants to make a name for himself in Constantinople," says the major. "They've been trying for months in Constantinople to find some special offender, and they can't trace him."

"What has the prisoner done?"

"We shall hear soon."'

"'Efendiler," said the Mudir, "I have unfortunately no maps, although I have been asking for them for years. But, as you see, I haven't got any. And why? Why indeed: because the official in Constantinople responsible for Turkish maps is an Armenian, and has deliberately not sent me any."

The Mudir pointed to his desk. "Look at this desk. It's covered in dust. The responsible saptieh only dusts it in one corner, where I usually sit. And I myself . . . I haven't noticed it for years. And look at all the dirt on the desk! There are still dead flies on it from 1912 and 1913 – the years of the Balkan War – hidden by the dust, embalmed so to speak, as you see. And what do I do when I want a map? Well, guess. Simple: I draw the map with my finger in the dust on top of the desk, quite easy. Look here. Do you see this map of Turkey? There it is."

The gentlemen stood up now and examined the map. The Germans were especially astonished; what they really saw was a map, drawn with a finger in the dust and the tomb of dead flies from the time of the Balkan War.

"As a Turkish patriot," said the Mudir, "I know the map from memory, and at any period. So this map is correct."

Now the Mudir walked up and down in front of the desk, while the gentlemen sat down again. "And who is to blame for these conditions?" said the Mudir. "Who makes us Turks so comfortable and lulls us to sleep? Just guess."

"The Armenians," said the Vali.

"Correct," said the Mudir. "The Armenians are to blame for it all. They have hypnotized us."

"So they have," said the Vali.'

*   *   *

'The Mudir called the gentlemen back to the map. He drew a circle with his finger in the heart of Turkey.

"This area in the heart of Turkey we call Anatolia, but the Armenians call it Armenia, or Hayastan."

"The name Armenia is still on lots of maps," said the German major.

"There's Greater Armenia and Lesser Armenia," said the Austrian journalist. "Greater Armenia is reckoned to extend over the Persian and Russian borders, but I can't describe it exactly. I don't carry the map in my head like the Mudir."

"Just so," said the Mudir, "but at the moment we're only interested in the Turkish part of this alleged Armenian empire."

"There was an Armenian empire once," said the Austrian journalist, "and actually in this region."

"But that was a long time ago," said the Mudir. "So long that it can't be true any more."

"A legend, you mean?"

"A legend," said the Mudir.'

'"But now the Armenians want to restore the legend of the Armenian empire to the present day," said the Mudir. "They hope that with Russian help they will be able to set up an Armenian state here, right here in the heart of Turkey."

"Is there proof of that?"

"There are indications," said the Mudir. "Indications of the Armenian treason which point towards the proof."

"But is there proof or is there not?"

"That is irrelevant," said the Mudir. "All that is relevant is faith, faith in a proof which is based on credible indications. Do you understand that?"

"Not altogether," said the Austrian journalist.'

'Your father's tongue was weighed down by fear,' said the story-teller. 'But the fact that something could hurt his son if he didn't say everything the Mudir wanted to hear, combined with a few gulps of *raki* which the Mudir had given him to drink, lifted the fear from his tongue and launched it into the room disguised as lies.

"I shot the Austrian Crown Prince and his bride in Sarajevo," said your father. "And I did it out of my convictions and in the name of the Armenian people."'

'Your father fell silent and gulped down a couple of tots of *raki*. The gentlemen were silent too, until one of them began to laugh. It was the Austrian. "But, gentlemen," he said, "that is ridiculous. It's completely incredible. I'm only the foreign correspondent of a Viennese newspaper, but I do know the facts that led to the outbreak of war. The Austrian Crown Prince and his wife were shot by a Bosnian nationalist, Gavrilo Princip, a high school pupil, a young hothead, a crazy fanatic. And behind the attack was a clique of Serbian officers and the secret society *Crna Ruka*, the Black Hand, whose commander-in-chief is a Serbian colonel, Dragutin Dimitrijevich."

"The press is ill-informed," said the Mudir. "The Bosnian fanatic Gavrilo Princip did indeed shoot at the heir and heiress, but it was the bullets fired by this Armenian that struck the Crown Prince and his wife."

"And how are you going to prove that?"

"This man will prove it."'

'"I emigrated to America in 1898," said your father. "I emigrated in the hope of getting work over there, to save money and come back to my country as a rich man. That was my only reason for emigrating. I didn't emigrate because the Armenians were oppressed here, because there never has been any oppression of the Armenians in Turkey. That is a lie put out by the Armenian world conspiracy. It just invented this lie to harm the reputation of the Turks in the world."

"But that isn't true," said the Austrian journalist. "Even the Young Turks and the present government admit that the Armenians were oppressed under the last government, which has just fallen."

"Under Abdul Hamid's government," said the German major.

"Are you talking about the so-called massacre in 1895, in which 300 Armenians are supposed to have died?" asked the Mudir, and he asked it very cautiously.

"The statistics put it at 300,000," said the German major.

"Those are just figures," said the Mudir. "Figures don't mean anything."

"Let's not discuss the last government," said the Vali. "The last government, Abdul Hamid's government, is dead. Now we have a modern, progressive and just government."

"Yes, Vali Bey," said the Mudir. "You're saying just what we all feel."

"The Armenians have always got on pretty well," said the Vali. "Who does the most business in Turkey? Whose hands is all the trade in? Who live like lords at the cost of the Turkish people?"

"The Armenians," said the Mutessarif. And the Kaimakam nodded, and said: "The Armenians."

"And what right have the Armenians to complain, when they're doing well and always have done well? And even if the last government did kill off some of them, beat them or shot them or whatever, the Armenians have caught up long ago, for they are a fertile race and have lots of children. And where did all those millions of them come from? And why do they go on living here, if they're so badly treated, or if they were badly treated some time ago?"

"Just so," said the Mudir.'

'"It's been all right for all of us," said your father. "The persecution of the Armenians under Abdul Hamid is greatly exaggerated. And if those lies are being brought up again now, it can only be something dreamed up in the perverted brains of the Armenian world conspiracy."

"What do you know about the Armenian world conspiracy?" asked the Mudir.

"Not much," said your father. "In America I found that Armenian welfare organizations were always collecting funds. They used to call at my home and ask for a donation."

"What for?" asked the Mudir.

"They said it was for orphans."

"And of course you knew that wasn't true?"

"Yes," said your father. "There can't have been so many orphans. It was clear to me right away that all this money was definitely for buying weapons, and got into the hands of Armenian nationalists."

"What sort of nationalists?"

"The Dashnaks – members of the Armenian nationalist Dashnak Party. Dashnakzagan, they're called."

"How do you know that?"

"I heard it from my brother-in-law Pesak Muradian, with whom I was briefly in contact and whom I later spoke with personally."

"When did you speak with him?"

"After my return. In 1914."'

'"This Pesak Muradian is one of the Dashnaks," said the Mudir, "a dangerous nationalist and a traitor. He's one of those who want to set up an independent Armenian state, here in the heart of Turkey. We've been looking for him for some months. But this man has disappeared without trace."'

'"The Dashnaks!" The Austrian journalist burst out laughing. "The Armenian nationalist party! That's really too funny, Mudir Bey."

"Why is it so funny?"

"Because the party really exists," said the journalist. "But to the best of my knowledge it's a legal party, or was at least up to the outbreak of war, a party that has been officially recognized since 1908, since the seizure of power by the Young Turks."

"True," said the Mudir.

"The Dashnaks gave up their efforts to gain independence long ago," said the Austrian journalist. "They gave them up when the Young Turks took over the government, in order to make common cause with the oppressed minorities."

"That's true," said the Mudir.

"Because the Young Turks offered them equal rights, equal rights for all Ottoman citizens, even the Armenians."

"That's true," said the Mudir.

"So what would the Dashnaks want weapons for?"

"Because they are secretly in league with the Russians," said the Mudir. "And because they may act as if they're working with the Young Turks, but in reality they are preparing an uprising."

"Do you have proof of that?"

"We have indications," said the Mudir.'

'"I didn't bother with politics over there in America," said your father. "But it did seem suspicious when those men kept collecting money. I had no idea so much money was needed for orphans, which don't exist anyway."

"They've collected milliards," said the Mudir, "for Armenian bankers and businessmen in America and all over the world give them tremendous financial support."

"Yes," said your father. "That's true."

"And how does he know that?" asked the Austrian journalist.

"I've told you already," said your father. "I heard it from my brother-in-law, Pesak Muradian, though really all Armenians know it, even those who say they don't know anything."'

'"At that time of course I didn't know anything definite about an Armenian world conspiracy," said your father, "although I knew well enough that there was one. But, as I've said, I didn't bother about politics over there."

"He's a poet," said the Mudir. "Poets believe they're above things, that they don't have to concern themselves with real things, practical things. But it's those very poets that are so dangerous when they do involve themselves in things that ought to be left to practical people."

"That's how it is," said your father.

"When did you get involved with the practical side of the Armenian objectives?"

"Later," said your father. "In June 1914, when I decided to shoot the Austrian Crown Prince."

"And his wife?"

"And his wife."

"That undertaking must have fascinated you as a poet?"

"Yes," said your father. "As a poet I had a rather hazy picture of the world, and even of those relationshps that people were so excited about. I was excited by the thought that I was going to take part myself."

"How did it actually happen?"

"Just by chance," said your father.

"But, efendi," said the Mudir, "there is no chance. Everything is fate and predestination."'

'"In the spring of 1914 I decided to turn my back on America for a time," said your father. "I wanted to see my family in Turkey again. And most of all I wanted to get married, and to marry a woman from my own village."

"You'd been married before, hadn't you?"

"Yes. But my first wife died in childbirth."

"So you had no heir?"

"That's it. I had no heir."

"You wanted a son, didn't you?"

"Yes, Mudir Bey. I wanted more than anything to beget a son, with a woman from my own village, a decent woman who doesn't show her legs to every stranger."

"And her face?"

"Yes, her face too."'

'"The crossing lasted several weeks," said your father. "It was a German liner called the *Graf Schwerin*. It was a very big ship – like a floating city, it was – and it sailed so smoothly that it felt as if we were sailing on a lake, a calm lake."

"Yes, the Germans know how to build ships," said the Mudir, "and it's all the same whether they're passenger ships or warships. Think of the *Goeben* and the *Breslau*, those two German warships that now sail under the Turkish flag. Not even the British, those bastards, can build them like that. Isn't that true, gentlemen?"

"Quite true," said the Vali. "We bombarded Odessa with the *Goeben* and the *Breslau*."

"Everything the Germans make has quality," said the Mudir. "You can't deny it. And I can well imagine that that great German liner, the *Graf Schwerin*, sailed as if she was on a lake."

"You can always rely on German efficiency," said the Vali. "I'll bet you, efendiler, that nobody was seasick on that great German ship, and that even the unbelievers didn't bring up the roast pork they were served with, a sign that Allah himself, who is great – praised be his name – shuts his eyes on the Germans, so that no one ever thinks of doubting their efficiency."

"Nobody was seasick," said your father. "You're quite right, Vali Bey."

"What did I tell you, gentlemen?" said the Vali.'

"'I met several Armenians on board," said your father, "but they were all harmless people who had nothing to do with any Armenian world conspiracy, for all I could see. They were businessmen. I talked to them, because they spoke Armenian. We met on deck, in the dining salon at meals or on social evenings. It was a really pleasant journey on that big German ship.'"

"'Like most tourists, I'd brought my camera with me," said your father, "to impress friends and acquaintances at home, especially my family, with my travel pictures . . . a childish trick, nothing behind it, nothing political, and of course no idea of harming the Turks by photographing anything forbidden, or of passing valuable photographs to the English or the French or the Russians. Really not, efendiler. I was a completely harmless tourist; and anyway, who knew then, at the beginning of 1914, that there was a great war coming, a war that could spell disaster for many nations. No, efendiler, I knew nothing at all about that when I took my camera with me on the journey, believe me."

"We don't want to talk about your camera," said the Mudir. "Tell us about Sarajevo.'"

"'I took the train to Paris," said your father, "and wondered whether I shouldn't take the Orient Express to get to Constantinople via Vienna, but then it struck me that I'd got to go by Sarajevo."

"Because you had an uncle there that you had to give some money to, wasn't that it?"

"Yes, Mudir Bey. From his brother in America, another of my uncles. I'd promised to do that."

"A sort of currency swindle?"

"I'd never thought of that."

"A trivial affair?"

"Yes, Mudir Bey."

"Tell us more."

"At first I didn't really want to make this trip to Sarajevo, but then I thought it could be quite enjoyable, since my uncle ran a coffee-house."

"What's so enjoyable about a coffee-house?"

"It was a coffee-house with private rooms, what they call *séparées*. There were girls sitting around in the coffee-house who were prostitutes, and you just had to take them into one of the private rooms."

"And you knew about this?"

"The whole family knew about it. This uncle was the black sheep of the family. His American brother was the only one he was on good terms with. He had lent him money and even paid for his journey to America."

"I see."

Some of the other gentlemen were laughing now. The Turkish officers were whispering to each other.

"So you didn't only want to hand over the money to your uncle in Sarajevo, you were also out to enjoy yourself?" The Mudir gave him a friendly smile. "I suppose a bit of fun . . . before you get married again . . . is good for the soul, so to speak; a last taste of freedom."

"As you say, Mudir Bey. I thought to myself: first go to Sarajevo, hand over the money, then have a bit of fun . . . in that coffee-house. After all, I'd spent all those years in America, years of hard work, of loneliness . . . I said to myself, just have a few carefree days before you go back home, get married and finally tie yourself down."

"We understand, efendi."

"We understand," said the fat Vali, who was now beginning to give little excited giggles. His gross face lit up. "There are pretty girls in Bosnia," he said, "though you can't get them so young as you can here, in the brothels in Bakir, which all belong to Armenians."

"Not all," said one of the Turkish officers.

"Tell us about Sarajevo," said the Mudir to your father.'

"'When I arrived in Sarajevo," said your father, "the papers were full of headlines about the state visit of the Austrian Crown Prince

137

and his wife. Even the date of the visit was fixed for the 28 June 1914. In Sarajevo no one seemed to have any idea that something was going to happen that would change the world. Certainly it was true that the streets were cleaned and the dirt and rubbish cleared away, especially in the Muslim quarters and the narrow alleys of the bazaar. It was true too that there were more policemen on the streets than usual, and units of the regional Austrian garrison, but a few days before the state visit it wasn't so very striking."

"What struck you yourself particularly?"

"What struck me personally was that so many Armenians appeared in Sarajevo. Armenians who didn't live there."

"How did you know those Armenians didn't live there?"

"From the waiters in the coffee-house, and from my uncle and from the other customers, especially the girls. They kept talking about all the strangers."

"You see, efendiler," said the Mudir, and looked triumphantly into the circle of gentlemen. "On the day of the assassination Sarajevo was swarming with Armenians. Armenians who didn't normally belong there. Where did they all come from? And why did they come?"

"But, Mudir Bey," said the Austrian journalist. "It was actually a special occasion, a state visit. Visitors came from all over the world, especially the newspaper reporters. I myself wanted to go to Sarajevo."

"Were you in Sarajavo?"

"No," said the Austrian journalist. "My paper sent one of my colleagues. I regret it to this day."

"It certainly was a great event," said the Vali.

"Yes, it was," said the Mudir.'

'"The Austrian heir had been warned," said the Mudir. "We Turks had warned him too; those Bosnians are dangerous people. They are as unpredictable as the Serbs. It was known at the time that the possibility of an attempt on his life couldn't be ruled out. I would go so far as to say that everybody knew that an attempt would be made."

"Quite true," said the Vali. "Everybody knew. The Archduke knew it himself. But he was too proud to cancel his visit."

"He was a proud man," said the German major, "the archetype of a German officer."

"An Austrian officer," said the Austrian journalist.

"He knew that he was unpopular, too," said the Vali. "But he still went to Sarajevo."

"It was an open Austrian challenge," said the Mudir. "For there was nowhere where the Austrians were disliked more than in Bosnia and Herzegovina."

"A challenge," said the Vali. "But also the gesture of a great country that had to show a small one who was master."

"Right, Vali Bey," said the Mudir. "Where should we get to if the great let the small see they were afraid?"

"Nowhere," said the Vali.

"Look, efendiler," said the Mudir. "Let's be quite frank. To whom did Serbia belong? To whom did Bosnia belong, and Herzegovina? To whom, efendiler? Those provinces belonged to us Turks."

"Correct," said the Vali.

"And who staged a rebellion in the seventies? Was it the Turks? No, efendiler. It was a Serbian uprising. Against whom? Against us Turks. And why, if I may ask? Well, I'll tell you, efendiler. It was sheer bravado. There was no good reason. We always treated those subjects well, even though they bred pigs and let their pigs run around in the open, in a country ruled by true believers."

"Correct," said the Vali.

"Then the Serbs became independent," said the Mudir, "although those breeders of pigs weren't able to govern themselves, and those bastards of Russians helped them. That was at the end of the seventies."

"Yes," said the Vali.

"But the Austrians spiked their guns when they marched into Bosnia and Herzegovina in 1878."

"Spiked their guns," said the Vali.

"Because the Serbs wanted to include Bosnia and Herzegovina in their new state, and then they weren't able to."

"Because the Austrians had caught them out by occupying those two provinces?"

"Naturally," said the Mudir.

And the Austrian journalist also said: "Naturally. We didn't hesitate to occupy those two provinces claimed by the Serbs."'

'"Those two provinces strictly belong to us," said the Mudir. "Even the capital of Bosnia, the old city of Sarajevo, is a Turkish city. All the same, I often laugh up my sleeve when I think what it was like in 1878, when Austria occupied those two provinces. I laugh because I'm so pleased that it wasn't the Serbs who got those two provinces."

"It was a kick up the arse for the Serbs," said the Vali.

"A kick in the balls," said the Mudir.

"Nothing has embittered the Serbs so much," said the Vali, "as the loss of Bosnia and Herzegovina. It's really as if the Austrians had cut the Serbs' balls off by occupying the region."

"And consequently there's no country in the world where they hate the Austrians as much as they do in Serbia."

"That's true," said the Vali.'

'"There's been a state of unrest in Herzegovina and Bosnia for thirty-six years," said the Mudir. "Thirty-six years. A powder-keg, efendiler. Sooner or later it had to explode."

"Sooner or later," said the Vali. "Only the precise time wasn't certain."

"It became certain when the Archduke went to Sarajevo."

"Just so, Mudir Bey."

"So let's talk about Sarajevo."

"Yes. About Sarajevo."'

'"We have established," said the Mudir, "that there was likely to be an attack on the Archduke. For, to my mind, the Bosnian nationalists could never put up with such a provocation: an official Austrian state visit in their capital city!"

"A monstrous provocation," said the Vali.

"If I were not an Austrian," said the Austrian journalist, "and loyal to my Emperor, I could almost have some sympathy with those Bosnian nationalists. But, efendiler, what has all this got to do with the Armenians?"

"Explain to the gentlemen," said the Mudir to your father, "what the Armenians' position was, and why the Armenian world conspiracy had a special interest in the attack on the Crown Prince and his wife . . . even though that was an internal affair of the Bosnian nationalists."

"I'll explain it to you, efendiler," said your father.

"Then explain it!"

"Yes, Mudir Bey."

"It's very important, efendi."

"Very important," said the Vali.'

'Your father looked round nervously. He was sweating, and wiped the sweat off his forehead with the sleeve of his coat. For a second his eyes met the eyes of the chief clerk, and in the chief clerk's eyes he read the following sentences: This man is lying like mad. There are lies in all his pores, and when the sweat comes out on his forehead those lies are printed so big that everybody can read them. All lies! Although he tries to wipe them away with the sleeve of his coat. And he could read other sentences: This man is frightened. If he doesn't say what the Mudir wants, his unborn son will be killed before ever seeing Allah's light. This man is to be pitied. But he has no choice.

"Efendiler," said your father, "the Armenians who came to Sarajevo from all those foreign countries and cities just before the state visit were the long arm of the Armenian world conspiracy!"

"We know that, efendi," said the Mudir. "But tell us rather, what interest did the Armenian world conspiracy have in the murder of the Austrian Crown Prince and his wife? And why did they pick you out to shoot the Archduke and his wife?"

"All right," said your father. "I'll tell the gentlemen."'

'"The Armenian world conspiracy sent its agents to Sarajevo at the right moment to make sure that the matter of the murder attempt was carried out according to plan."

"So the Armenian world conspiracy knew that an attempt was going to be made?"

"The whole world knew that."

"And in Sarajevo?"

"Also in Sarajevo, of course. Everybody knew it. When the

papers announced the visit, everything was ready. There was whispering in the streets and people discussed it and talked about it in the coffee-houses. There had been no such provocation of the Bosnian people for a long time."

"And what about the Armenians?"

"There were suddenly swarms of Armenians in Sarajevo," said your father. "They met in restaurants and coffee-houses, especially in the ones that belonged to Armenians. Some of those visiting Armenians met every day in my uncle's coffee-house."

"Officially?"

"Yes," said your father. "They met every afternoon, drank coffee and played cards, joked with the girls, but then went into one of the *séparées* for a time."

"With the girls?"

"No. Without girls."

"And what did they do there?"

"They discussed their plans."'

'"Before the assassination I was still living in the hotel," said your father, "but I spent all day sitting around in my uncle's coffee-house. A couple of days before the state visit my uncle took me aside and spoke to me."

"What did he say to you?"

"I had once told him I was a dead shot," said your father. "The Armenian farmers in my home village weren't allowed to own a weapon, because in those days, when Abdul Hamid was in power, before the revolution, it was strictly forbidden, but we had a few rifles and even revolvers hidden in our village. We needed them to defend ourselves against Kurdish robbers. I once shot a Kurd when I was a boy."

"And since then you've never shot anyone else?"

"No. Only the one Kurd. Otherwise I just shot wild duck, wild geese, and often, for fun, a sparrow on the wing. The farmers in the village used to say that Khatisian's son could shoot the flies out of a sparrow's beak."

"So you were a dead shot?"

"Yes."

"And what did your uncle want you to do?"

"He said the visiting Armenians in the *séparée* were looking for a sharpshooter."

"Didn't that surprise you?"

"I was absolutely astonished," said your father.'

'"Later the Armenians talked with me. They said that Bosnian fanatics were planning an attempt on the Archduke's life, and that there was a group of Serbian officers behind the Bosnians. They said they were in touch with this group of Serbian officers."

"And what did they want from you?"

"They said that neither the Serbian officers' group nor the Bosnian nationalists, who were all in it together, that neither of them would be able to carry out a proper attempt because they were all crazy hotheads. Therefore, so the Armenians said, an outsider would have to do the job, someone like me whom no one would suspect, a dead shot, someone who could be relied on to bring it off. The Armenians said I should not be nervous, because the whole thing would be blamed on the Bosnians and the Serbs. I was just to carry it out properly, coolly, skilfully, from an ambush . . . and then disappear in the crowd."'

'"The Armenian conspirators explained it to me like this: the murder of the Austrian Crown Prince and his wife on the orders of a group of Serbian officers – that would be the official version – must lead to an Austrian invasion of Serbia, for the Austrians had been looking for a long time for some pretext to settle things with the Serbs. But since the Russians had a military defence pact with Serbia, that would automatically bring Russia into the picture. But a Russian mobilization would be sure to disturb the Germans, and then they would mobilize. And England and France wouldn't just keep quiet. So the Armenians knew that the murder of the Crown Prince and Princess in Bosnia, in Sarajevo in fact, would lead to the World War." Your father broke off shortly. Then he said: "Of course Turkey could not keep out of such a war. And since the Turkish army had been trained by German officers for the last century, it was easy to foresee that sooner or later Turkey would come into the war on the German side."

"Extraordinary foresight on the part of this Armenian conspirator," said the Vali.

"Yes," said your father.

"And what was the Armenians' interest in this World War?"

"The Armenians wanted to involve Turkey in a war with Russia," said your father. "It was clear that if Turkey went to war on the side of the Germans and Austrians, that would mean war between Turkey and Russia."

"That's clear," said the Vali.

"And, to the Armenians, a war between Russia and Turkey means their liberation from the Turkish yoke."

"What do you mean by the 'Turkish yoke', efendi?"

"I don't mean anything, Vali Bey," said your father. "I'm only trying to explain the way the Armenian conspirators saw it."

"And how did they see it?"

"They saw it like this: they looked mainly at the front on the Caucasus. They thought that no one could hold up the Russian steamroller. So the Russians would cross the Caucasus, advance into Turkey and liberate the millions of Armenians on Turkish soil."

"The occupation of Anatolia by Russian troops?"

"Exactly. The occupation of Anatolia. The liberation of millions of Armenians in the border area."

"And what did the Armenians expect from the Russians and their so-called liberation?"

"The setting up of an Armenian state on Turkish soil, for this area had once belonged to the Armenians."

"That's true," said the German major. "Armenia did once belong to them."

"East Anatolia or Armenia or Hayastan. It's all the same."

"And this Armenian state would be independent?"

"Not completely," said your father. "An Armenian state under Russian protection. That was only to be expected."

"And the Armenian conspirators were all agreed on this?"

"Only as a temporary solution," said your father. "What they were aiming at was an independent Armenian state, but they didn't think the young state could manage without Russian protection.'"

"'And were there any Russian citizens among the Armenian

conspirators in Sarajevo?" asked the Vali.

"Some of the Armenians had Russian passports."

"How do you know that?"

"They spoke an Armenian dialect that's only spoken the other side of the Russian border. I found out from my uncle that they were actually Russian Armenians and that they even had Russian passports."

"Could it be that these Armenians with Russian passports were in the Russian secret service?"

"Possibly."

"In the Ochrana," said the Mudir.

"I don't know," said your father.

"And the Dashnaks," asked the Vali, "the Armenian nationalists?"

"They were to support the Russian invasion," said your father.

"An Armenian rising behind the Turkish lines?"

"Yes," said your father. "They were counting on the millions of Armenians in the border area, and also in the base area behind the lines, to attack the Turks in the rear as soon as the Czar's army in the Caucasus was on the move."

"And how did you know that?"

"I got some of it from the Armenian conspirators, and a lot from my brother-in-law Pesak Muradian . . . later, when all the connections became clear to me."'

'"So the Armenian conspirators came to Sarajevo when the business of the state visit by the Austrian Crown Prince and his wife became known? When even the date became known?"

"Yes," said your father.

"And they were in touch with a clique of Serbian officers, if I understand you correctly?"

"Yes," said your father.

"But you believed that those officers and their agents would not have been able to carry out an attack of that kind successfully. And so you had to do it, didn't you, efendi? You had to shoot the Archduke and his wife?"

"That was it."

"Because you wouldn't be suspected? Because you were an

outsider? And because people would blame the Bosnians and the Serbs?"

"Yes, Mudir Bey."

"And you still declare that you shot the Austrian Crown Prince?"

"Yes, Mudir Bey."

"And his wife?"

"That's correct, Mudir Bey."'

'"As I was saying: several days before the state visit – it must have been four days before – the conspirators took me into their confidence. I suppose it was because my uncle had told them I was all right, I was a patriot and what's more a poet."'

'"The conspirators talked to me for a long time. They explained to me that the liberation of the Turkish Armenians depended on the Russian invasion, and that was what must be set up. They said if I would do it I could be the saviour of the nation. In the end I gave in. I was excited by it. I actually saw myself as the saviour of the Armenian people. And I saw my name in the history books of the future."

"Yes," said the Mudir.'

'"The Armenian conspirators gave me a revolver," said your father. "They'd bought it from Serbian officers they'd been in contact with, and the revolver, a Browning, came from the armoury of the Serbian army."

"When did they give you the revolver?"

"On the day the Crown Prince arrived in Sarajevo."

"Just before the attempt, then?"

"Yes."

"All Sarajevo must have been in the streets that day?"

"There was a tremendous crowd of people in the city streets," said your father, "especially on the bridges on the quay. There were police everywhere. There were road-blocks everywhere. When the open car with the Crown Prince and his wife came from the direction of the City Hall and turned into Franz Joseph Avenue, I was standing quite close. I had my camera with me, and also the revolver, which I'd hidden under my jacket behind the camera. The crowd was restless. You could see hate on their faces. When the line of cars approached, the crowd where I was standing broke through the police file and stormed up to the Crown Prince's car. Of course the people were pushed back by the police, but the car stopped."

"And that was when you shot?"

"No, efendiler. I was still hesitating. The open car that Franz Ferdinand was sitting in, on the back seat next to his wife, drove on again, but it was going very slowly. I tried to run up to the side of the car, but I was forced back at once. I ran and ran. I ran up to the side of the car. And then, at the corner of Franz Joseph Avenue and Rudolf Avenue, it stopped."'

"'Suddenly I saw a young man with a revolver in his hand. He looked like a student. He was standing right next to me. I saw him run up to the car, break through the ranks of police, and I saw him shoot the Prince and Princess."

"Those were the historic shots in Sarajevo," said the German major, "the fatal shots by Gavrilo Princip, who shot the Archduke and his wife."

"On the instructions of the Serbian officers' clique," said the gay lieutenant.

"It must have been him," said your father, "but he didn't hit the Archduke. Nor his wife. Only a few seconds after the Bosnian fired the shots, I fired too. But I was a dead shot, and I hit the Archduke, and I also hit his wife, sitting next to him."'

"'But that can't be true," said the German major. "Everybody knows who shot the Crown Prince and Princess. The bullets have been identified. They come from the revolver of the Bosnian nationalist Gavrilo Princip. There's no mistake about it."

"Our prisoner had a revolver exactly the same as the Bosnian's," said the Mudir, "supplied by the Serbian officers' group from the armoury of the Serbian army. They are identical weapons."

"Are you prepared to say that the bullets that were later removed from the bodies of the two victims came from this man's revolver?"

"That's what we're saying," said the Mudir.

"And how will you prove all this?" said the German major.

"This man's confession is the proof."

"But that's not enough, Mudir Bey. Where is his revolver?"

"He threw it away."

"That's true," said your father.

"And the witnesses?"

"There are no witnesses," said the Mudir. "The Armenian conspirators are well away by now, and we don't even know their real names. And as for the prisoner's uncle, he's died since then."

"He has died, unfortunately," said your father. "And I don't know the conspirators' real names. They weren't stupid enough to let me know them."

"What about your uncle's family?"

"They had nothing to do with it. None of them were in any way involved."

"And the waiters?"

"Nor were they."

"And the girls?"

"The girls weren't involved either."

"All the same, they ought to be questioned."

"It would be a waste of time," said your father. "Neither the girls nor the waiters could know what they were talking about in the *séparées*. It could have been business matters, any sort of business. And at the shooting, I was alone. All alone. No one spotted me in that great crowd. No one saw me."'

"'It's monstrous,' said the major. "This is a prosecution with no witnesses and no evidence."

"This man is the witness," said the Mudir.

"It's monstrous," said the major. "No one will believe this confession."

"We'll take care that it's believed," said the Mudir.'

"'After the assassination I stayed on in Sarajevo," said your father. "Nobody had seen my revolver, which I'd stuck under the case of my camera. They'd heard the shots, of course, but in all that crowd and that noise they confused them with the Bosnian's shots. And then I disappeared in the crowd."'

"'Yes, I stayed a few more weeks in Sarajevo," said your father.

148

"Because you had venereal disease," said the Mudir.

"We thought it was venereal disease," said your father.

"Didn't you have any other reason for putting off your return to Turkey?"

"No," said your father.'

"Of course I was waiting for the Austrian ultimatum," said your father. "But I could just as well have waited for that in Turkey. There was no political reason for putting off my journey."

"What was that about the ultimatum?"

"It should have been presented," said your father, "but it was put off. I was beginning to think that the Austrians had got scared of the consequences at the last minute and the war we all wanted wasn't going to break out."

"But war had to break out?"

"That was it.""

"At the end of July I finally decided to go on, and so on 25 July I found myself in Constantinople."

"On 25 July. Three days before war broke out."

"Yes."

"By chance?"

"Pure chance."

"You didn't perhaps think that this chance would attract the attention of the Turkish authorities?"

"I never thought of that.""

"Then you took photographs in the area of Constantinople . . . on a steamer trip: the Bosphorus, the coastal strip of the Sea of Marmara as far as the entrance to the Dardanelles, if I'm not mistaken?"

"Yes, Mudir Bey. But no one had told me to. I did it off my own bat."

"To what end, efendi?"

"It wasn't really clear to me at the time. But I thought to myself, if war breaks out you can give them to your brother-in-law Pesak, who is in contact with the Russians."

"So that the Russians can land in the Dardanelles?"

"I suppose so."

"Or the British or the French, who have better fleets?"

"I hadn't thought it out as much as that."'

'"The Austrians and the Serbs mobilized," said your father, "and a few days later the two countries were at war. But on 25 and 26 July, only a few days before war broke out, people in Constantinople hardly knew anything about it. Tourists could still tour the Bosphorus, take steamer trips, take photographs. It was as if the Turks still hadn't really woken up. I stayed there a few days taking photos. I'd taken my clothes to be cleaned as an excuse in case anyone asked me why I had to stay in Constantinople for a few days."

"Because you were waiting for your clothes?"

"That's it."

"Because it would never do to arrive home in dirty clothes?"

"Yes, Mudir Bey."'

'"Then I went home to my family."

"To Anatolia? To Bakir and on to Yedi Su?"

"Yes, Mudir Bey."

"Did you get married there?"

"Yes, I got married."

"And you took a honeymoon trip to the Syrian coast?"

"Yes, I did."

"And there you took some more photographs?"

"Yes."

"Mostly the coasts, wasn't it? They're mostly steep cliffs, but there are a few bays where the enemy could land?"

"I photographed those landing-places."

"That is high treason, efendi," said the Mudir.

"High treason," said the Vali.'

'The Mudir turned to the group of men. "We found a whole lot of photos in his house, efendiler, but they were harmless pictures. We haven't found the most important ones." The Mudir smiled slightly, and to the men in the group it looked as if even his glass eye was smiling.

"Tell the gentlemen why we haven't found the most important photos," he said to your father.

"Because I gave them to my brother-in-law," said your father.

"There you are," said the Mudir, satisfied. "He gave them to his brother-in-law Pesak Muradian, one of the most wanted leaders of the Dashnaks, as you know, one of the people who are planning a rising here behind the front, and who are collaborating with the Russians. That lot are just waiting for the Russians to give them the signal: the signal to launch their attack."

"It's just as the Mudir says," said your father.'

'Then one of the Turkish officers said: "The Russians always go overland. Their fleet isn't strong enough to try to make a successful landing."

"It's the British who like to go by sea," said a second Turkish officer. "So we can take it that the Russians will pass the pictures on to the British."

"Right," said the Vali.

"A British landing on the Syrian coast, but also in the Dardanelles and on the Gallipoli peninsula as well, would make the Russian push easier. So it will be in the Russians' interest for the British to get the photos."

"That's right," said the Vali.'

And then there was the story-teller's voice in the room, and it was louder than the other voices. The story-teller said: 'Let them talk, my little lamb. Soon they'll get hungry, and break up. Meanwhile they'll drink *raki* and coffee and eat their sweet *baklava*, and they'll smoke *chibouks* and cigarettes and *nargiles*. The Mudir keeps on clapping his hands and the saptiehs run up and down bringing fresh *raki*.'

And the story-teller said: 'They broke up towards evening. The saptiehs took the prisoner back to his cell. They all went off. The Germans and the Austrian strolled down to the Gate of Happiness. There were some other Armenians hanging there now. There weren't three any more, but five.

"What do you think of the accused's confession?" asked the major.

"Nothing at all," said the Austrian. "The accused was under pressure. His confession is just one lie from A to Z. It seems to have been dictated to him."

"By the Mudir?"

"I suppose so."

"In Constantinople they're looking for someone to incriminate."

"Do you think Enver Pasha can do anything with the accused's confession?"

"No. I don't believe so. It isn't credible."

"And the Mudir?"

"He's a pompous little fool, one of those intellectuals who have studied in the west and want to make a name for themselves in Constantinople."

"He seems to have the Vali's support, and the Kaimakam's, and the Mutessarif's."

"Naturally. If the Mudir brings it off and convinces Enver, they'll take the credit."

"And if not?"

"Then the Mudir will get the blame."

"This Mudir's an ambitious man."

"He surely is."'

'During their talk the men had stopped underneath the hanged men. The little gay lieutenant led the major and the Austrian a little to one side; they were bigger than he was, a head taller, and he seemed to be afraid they might bump into the feet of the dead men with their field-grey caps.

"Look," said the Austrian. "This idea of an Armenian world conspiracy is lurking in a lot of people's minds. But what we have here is something mystical, something incomprehensible. The war minister, Enver Pasha, is a fanatic, and in a way he's an idealist, but he's not stupid, certainly not stupid enough to shift the blame for the assassination in Sarajevo on to the Armenians when the whole world knows who the actual murderer was. No, gentlemen, Enver Pasha can never believe such rubbish, even staged in a public trial."

"You're quite right," said the major. "Nor could anyone else in his government."

"And Talaat Bey especially, the interior minister, he'd never get involved in such lunacy. Talaat is a firm realist with a cool head. Such a man wouldn't even begin to believe in ideas like this world conspiracy. He simply sees the Armenians as the home enemy."

"The home enemy. That may be. But an enemy that has the support of the Armenians in exile. And in a way that is a world conspiracy, though not one with all this mystery."

"Either way," said the Austrian, "the government won't get mixed up in a trial that's a farce and will disgrace it."

"What will the government do, then?"

"They'll find a convincing pretext, one based on evidence, to justify certain government measures in the eyes of the world, especially of the Allies."

"But there's no pretext convincing enough to justify measures against a whole people."

"They'll work something out in Constantinople."

"They haven't got long, though, have they?"

"How do you mean?" asked the Austrian.

"Well, I mean . . . actually the government's measures have already begun, and still nobody knows yet what crime the Armenians have committed."'

'"I was talking to the German consul yesterday," said the German major.

"About the Armenians?"

"About the executions, and all these arrests."

"What did the consul say?"

"He's already informed Berlin and emphasized it at the highest level. But they've known about it there for a long time."'

'"Couldn't the Kaiser do something to stop all these arrests and executions?"

"The Kaiser doesn't interfere in things here. And anyway, there's a war on. Arrests are the order of the day everywhere."

"And executions."

"Those too."

"But not on this scale."

"You're right there, not on this scale."'

'"Did the consul say anything else?"

"Yes. He said the Turks were preparing a massacre."

"Of the Armenians?"

"Yes."

"There have always been massacres here. It won't be anything new."

"True."

"Did the consul say anything else?"

"Yes. He said the Turks were preparing a massacre such as world history had never seen. It would put every other massacre in history in the shade."

"And how does he reckon to know that?"

"He has his sources."'

'"So, a huge massacre?"

"Yes."

"When?"

"That isn't known."

"What are the Turks waiting for?"

"For a credible accusation."

"Something the whole Armenian people can be accused of?"

"Yes."'

'"Then the Kaiser will have to intervene?"

"He'll have to."

"After all, the Turks shoot with German guns."

"You're right there."

"The consul ought to inform the Kaiser. He ought to telegraph to say there's a massacre on the way such as world history has never seen. The victims are Christians."

"It wouldn't do any good."

"Why not?"

"Because the Kaiser isn't interested in things that might happen."

"You mean, it's got to happen first."

"Yes."

"They need facts? Concrete reports?"

"That's it."

"Before they can ask him to intervene here?"

"Yes."

"But won't it be too late by then?"'

'The Germans and the Austrian went on talking for a while about the forthcoming massacre, then the young lieutenant left them to pick up a *hamal* in the Kurdish quarter, one of those tough Kurdish porters whose spearheads under their dirty baggy trousers did more than just tickle. The German major and the Austrian journalist also thought about a little relaxation and strolled off towards the town brothel.

"Do you think a German contraceptive will give protection against the French disease?" asked the German major.

"You just have to try," said the Austrian.

"The Turks call syphilis the French disease."

"Yes, I know," said the major.

"Someone ought to send a telegram to Kaiser Franz Joseph," said the Austrian.

"About syphilis and the danger to German troops?"

"No, that's something for Kaiser Wilhelm II to deal with."

"Then what would the telegram to Franz Joseph be about?"

"About the Armenians. Maybe he could intervene before it's too late."'

'. . . before it's too late!' The story-teller burst out laughing. 'Do you know, my little lamb, if the powers on this earth are too idle to shift their arses . . . or if shifting that part of their body runs counter to their special interests, then their arse will stay put, its movement will be put off, and their conscience, somewhere above their arse, will be soothed with the word "Later"! And I assure you, my little lamb, later always turns out to be too late, and it will be no different this time.'

And the story-teller said: 'Those German officers and the Austrian had got the point.'

'What point?'

'That the extermination of the Armenians in Turkey – the execution of a whole people – depends ultimately not only on their

155

exterminators but also on the silence of their allies.'

'The great massacre!' said the story-teller. 'Everyone in this country knew it was coming, but only a few could really foresee anything definite. What were the Turks planning to do to the Armenians? Would they just slaughter them like sheep? Before the eyes of the whole civilized world? Who would help the Armenians? Kaiser Wilhelm II, perhaps, who took care not to do the least thing that could upset his Turkish allies? Or Kaiser Franz Joseph, who was old, and having trouble pissing? Could the Russians help, or the British or the French? Weren't they too far away . . . on the other side of the front? Or would there just be an outcry in the world's press, just to be chucked out with all the other rubbish of old newspapers? But believe me, my little lamb, it's all one what happens to us; the historians will laugh up their sleeves, especially those responsible for contemporary history, for they need new material to work on to relieve their boredom. Given their lack of imagination, they'll just look for figures to delimit the masses of the dead – as they will say, to record them – and then they'll look for words to describe the great massacre and classify it pedantically. They don't know that every human being is unique, that even the village idiot in your father's village has the right to a name. They will call the great massacre "mass-murder", and the scholars among them will say it's called "genocide". Not one smart alec among them will say it's called "armenocide", and in the end some crank will look up his dictionary and finally announce that it's called "holocaust!"'

BOOK TWO

CHAPTER ONE

'But meanwhile your father is back in his cell, lying on his paillasse. He knows the Mudir wants to take him to Constantinople so that he can declare before the general public that the Armenians are guilty. Sooner or later, then, he will be taken to Constantinople. But many days will pass before that, and maybe they won't need his confession any more until then, for it's possible that the gentlemen in Constantinople will have found other people in the meantime, other witnesses to a quite different and more credible charge.

Your father can't sleep. He thinks of his unborn son Thovma, who will be seeing the light of the world at some time, under the grapevine. And it occurs to him that he too was born under the grapevine, but not as it was in that nightmare that his fear had told him, that lying story of his mother's bursting breasts. No . . . no! His mother's breasts had never burst.'

The story-teller said: 'His mother's breasts never burst. That was a lie.'

'Are you talking about my grandmother's breasts?'

'Yes, Thovma,' said the story-teller. 'I'm talking of those good breasts.'

'There was once a boy,' said the story-teller, ' . . . who lay still unborn under the grapevine. He was to be called Vartan, and he was your father.'

'There was once a woman. She was in her ninth month. As the impatience of the good God made itself felt in pain – what are commonly called "the pains" – and as it seemed as if her body would burst, she said to her husband: "Let us quickly get into the donkey-cart so that we can go and fetch our Vartan. For he's lying under the grapevine and won't wait any longer."'

'Where is the grapevine?'

'In the land of grapevines.'

'There was once a donkey. He ran as fast as an Arab horse. He went like the wind to take the pregnant woman and her husband to the land of the grapevines. The breasts of the pregnant woman swelled on the way, but they did not burst. For it was the will of the good God that the milk should wait.'

'There was once a pregnant woman. She came to the land of grapevines with her husband. And she saw the one grapevine that had grown into a cradle for the one who was to be born. The woman saw the grapevine first, for the mother's eyes are sharper than the father's. She ran up to the grapevine, and her husband ran behind her. When the husband saw his wife take their son in her arms, he sobbed and said: "That can only be our Vartan."'

'It was little Vartan. There was no doubt, for his wife was no longer pregnant.

"Your fat belly has disappeared," said her husband.

"And the pains have disappeared too," said the woman.'

'They washed little Vartan in the spring by the grapevine. The woman laughed happily. And the man laughed too. And when later the woman held little Vartan to her breast, her nipples opened.'

'And little Vartan drank his mother's sweet milk. And the parents gave thanks to the good God that the milk had waited.'

'On the way back to their home village the donkey went quietly. The landscape soon became more barren, the slopes poorer and less cultivated, the bare rocks shone in many colours. Soon the land of grapevines was far behind them. The donkey track that they were following lost itself in the high mountains, whose peaks lay just under the clouds. They didn't drive the donkey hard, for now they had time. And they didn't have to guide the donkey, for the donkey knew where it was going. After a few hours they had a rest. The man fetched the waterskin from under the woollen cushion, and also a woven bread-basket. They drank from the waterskin and ate some of the *lavash* bread that the woman had made in the *tonir* at home. After they had eaten and drunk, the man took the child away from the woman, laughed and held him up high.

"Do you think our Vartan knows where he is?"

"No," said the woman. "Give him back to me."

"He ought to know that he's in the land of our ancestors," said the man.

"That makes no difference to him," said the woman, and now she took the child away from her husband and pressed him to her bosom.

"All the child needs to know is that he is with his mother," said the woman. "Nothing else matters."

"And what about his father?"

"Of course," said the woman. "He must also know he is with his father."'

'"If our Vartan could already understand," said the man, "and if his eyes knew what they saw, then I should like to show him the landscape now."

"But his eyes are still half-closed," said the woman, "for the good God does not want him to see too much at once, in case he's frightened."

"But you've washed his eyes."

"I didn't wash them properly."

"When will they really open, so that he can see the world?"

"In a few days, perhaps," said the woman.'

'"If our Vartan could understand me, and if he had eyes like an eagle, I should say to him now: 'Look, Vartan. This is the land of our ancestors.' And I would point to the east and tell him: 'Do you see that great snow-covered mountain? That is Mount Ararat!'"

"But he hasn't got eagle's eyes. And he doesn't begin to understand what you're saying. So what sense would there be in showing him the land of our ancestors?"

"There doesn't have to be sense in everything."

161

"So you would show him Mount Ararat?"

"Yes."

"And what else?"

"The town of Bakir," said the man, and pointed to the north-east with his finger, "and also the town of Erzurum, which is only a few days' journey in the donkey-cart from Bakir. And I would also show the Armenian royal city of Ani, the city of a thousand and one churches. And I'd say to him: 'Ani is a ruined city. Ani is dead, as the Armenian kingdom is dead, the kingdom of the goddess Anahit and the kingdom of the first Christian church.'"

"It is not dead," said the woman. "Our priest, Kapriel Hamadian, has just said: 'The kingdom of Armenia is not dead.'"

"So where is it, if it's not dead?"

"It's in a trance," said the woman.

"Who told you that?"

"The priest, Kapriel Hamadian."'

"'And I'd show our son Vartan all the Armenian villages and towns, all there are in this area. Do you see, the Turks have taken all that away from us. There, for example, there is Urfa, and there is Diyarbakir, and further off is the town of Konya, and the town of Sivas belongs to the Armenians too, and that isn't far from here. And if our Vartan asked me: 'What are those mountains called?', I should say: 'I don't know, my son. Many people call them the Kurdish mountains, others say the mountains of Hayastan. But a scholar from Frankistan who was in our village once and showed such a funny map to our mayor, the Mukhtar Ephrem Abovian, he said: 'Those are the Armenian highlands. They're in Turkey, but they stretch right over the Russian and Persian border all the way to Kurdistan.'

"'And I'd tell him: 'You see that river down there, that is the Karasu, and there is the Murat. And a little further away there flow the Euphrates and the Tigris. And if we went down the other side of the mountains in the donkey-cart, we should get to Malatya. And somewhere the mountains end and the land becomes flat. It becomes as flat as the palm of my hand, and so hot that you need seven waterskins if you go for a ride there. I think it's called Mesopotamia.'"'

162

★   ★   ★

'"And I'd say to him: 'There are Armenians living everywhere, but mostly in our area. But there are also Turks living here and Gypsies and Kurds and Persians and Arabs and Jews and Greeks and devil-worshippers called *yezidis*, and many others. Most of them you needn't be afraid of. Only be careful of the Turks and the Kurds.'"'

'"You're right," said the woman. "As soon as he can see the world properly and perhaps begin to understand what we say to him, and when he's got his first teeth and can walk and not just kick his feet about, then we'll tell him: 'Be careful of the Turks and the Kurds.'"'

'"And what about the devil-worshippers?" said the woman. "Is it true that they can bewitch our Vartan?"

"No," said the man. "That's not true, any more than the Gypsies can bewitch our Vartan."

"Who can bewitch him then? The Turks perhaps, or the Kurds?"

"No," said the man. "At most they can cut his throat. Or just beat him to death."

"So who can bewitch him?"

"Only people with the evil eye," said the man. "And you find them among all peoples."

"Even among the Armenians?"

"Even among the Armenians."

"I've known that for a long time," said the woman.

"Then you shouldn't have asked me," said the man.'

'When they had eaten the man felt he would like a fish, and so he said to his wife: "I'm still hungry after the *lavash* bread. I could swallow a whole fish, and I bet you our little Vartan could too."

"I bet you he couldn't," said the woman.

"Every time I think of a good fat fish," said the man, "I think of that great Armenian lake, not far from the Russian border."

"You mean Lake Van, just a stone's throw from where my brother lives?"

"I don't mean that one," said the man. "I'm thinking of a lake I first saw only a little time ago. And how could it have been Lake Van? Surely I should have visited your brother, living so close to the

163

lake? But I haven't seen your brother for years."

"Then it must have been some other lake?"

"It was a different lake," said the man. "I've simply forgotten the name. But since all the lakes in this area are Armenian, it doesn't matter. It was just an Armenian lake."

"And what happened there?" asked the woman.

"Nothing special," said the man.'

'And the man said: "It's not very far from here. You were in your first month with our son Vartan. I took the donkey and rode through the mountains for three days. I went through many fertile valleys, I went past rivers and streams and came to some lakes too, some quite small, some bigger."

"But that isn't possible," said his wife. "You haven't been out of the village for two years."

"But it was so, " said the man.

"Maybe you dreamt it."

"Well, that's possible," said the man.'

'And the man said: "So I came to this great lake. And I met a fisherman there, casting out his nets. His name was Peter, but he called himself Bedros, for he was an Armenian."

"Bedros?"

"Yes, Bedros."

"And what about the fisherman?"

"Nothing special. He just said: 'Can you hear the fish talking to each other?'

'No,' I said.

'They all speak Armenian,' said the fisherman.

'Then they must be Armenian fish,' I said.

'So they are,' said the fisherman."'

"" 'The Turks say they're Turkish fish,' said the fisherman, 'but I know they're Armenian because I can understand what they're saying.'

I said: 'Yes.'

And the fisherman said: 'Even the flowers in this part of the world speak Armenian, and the grass, and even the wind that rocks the treetops sings Armenian lullabies to the tops of the trees.'

'Do the Turks know that?' I asked.

And the fisherman said: 'They know it, but they don't admit it.'"''

'"And what about that fat fish?" asked the woman.

"It was a fat fish," said the man.

"What fat fish was that then?"

"The one the fisherman caught for me later on."

"Tell me something about the fish? Was it really so fat?"

"Yes," said the man.'

'And the man said: "The fisherman told me a story. It was the story of the fat fish."

"Tell me the story."

"Yes," said the man. "I'll tell you the story the fisherman told me."'

'"There was once an Armenian goddess. She was called Anahit. She sat on a rock in the Euphrates and combed her silken hair. And every time a hair fell out, the wind blew it away."

"Where did the wind blow it?"

"It blew it a long way away, but yet not so far, for the hair never blew over the borders of Armenia."

"Did the hair stop somewhere, in the air perhaps?"

"No," said the man. "After a time the hair would fall, and it always fell into water, either into a river or into a pool or into a brook or into a lake. Often into the sea."

"And what did the hair want?"

"It wanted to feed the fish in the water."'

'The man said: "Do you know what the fisherman said to me?"

"No," said the woman.

"He said: 'That is why the fish in this region are so fat, and so abundant. For Anahit is the goddess of fertility.'"''

'"'How many children have you got?' Bedros the fisherman asked me.

'Eleven children,' I said, 'and soon I shall have twelve, for my wife is pregnant again.'-

'Will it be a son?' asked the fisherman.

'I hope it will be a son,' I said.

'What will you call him?'

'I shall call my son Vartan.'"'

"'Vartan was an Armenian hero,' said the fisherman. 'He fought with his sixty thousand Armenians against the Persian empire, in AD 401. And do you know what his battle-cry was?'

'No,' I said. 'How should I know that?'

'For Hayastan and Christ, that was his battle-cry,' said the fisherman.

'So he was an Armenian hero?'

'One that Christ had chosen.'"'

"'Do you want your son to become a hero?' asked the fisherman.

'No,' I said. 'Heroes die young, and I want my son to grow old.'

'Then he mustn't become a hero.'

'Very well,' I said, 'he is not to be a hero.'"'

"'He ought to be a fisherman,' said the fisherman. 'Like me. If he becomes a fisherman he'll never be hungry.'

'I would rather he became a farmer,' I said.

'He ought to become a fisherman,' said the fisherman."'

"'An Armenian farmer has troubles,' said the fisherman. 'He is dependent on the sun and the rain. And on the Turkish tax-collectors, and the Kurdish Beys who demand taxes for themselves, and whose horsemen drive his cattle off or abduct his women or even burn his house down over his head.'

'Burn the house down,' I said. 'That's true.'

'They might drive him off his fields.'

'They might, too.'

'Believe me, it's better to be a fisherman.'

'A fisherman, then.'

'Yes,' said the fisherman."'

"'And the fisherman caught me the fattest fish I've ever seen. He cut its head off and said to me: 'We'll roast it on the spit and eat it right away. You should always eat fish fresh.'

'Yes,' I said. And I said: 'It's a pity my son Vartan can't eat this fish.'

'He'll catch other fish and eat them,' said the fisherman.

'I should have liked to keep this fat fish for Vartan,' I said, 'but I can see that it would be no use.'

'It would be no use,' said the fisherman. 'For a dead fish stinks after three days like a Kurdish woman's cunt, because the Kurds only wash in the summer, when they can bathe in the river.'

'That's true,' I said.

And the fisherman said: 'Your son Vartan will catch other fish and eat them.'"'

'The woman said: "Then let him be a fisherman."

"Yes," said the man.

"After his baptism," said the woman, "we'll put a fishing-rod in his cradle with him."

"That's a good idea," said the man. "He'll soon get used to the rod."'

CHAPTER TWO

'It's true,' said the story-teller to the last thought. 'Immediately after the priest Kapriel Hamadian had baptized your father, his mother put a child's fishing-rod in his cradle. Shall I just describe that cradle, the cradle in which your father slept, when he wasn't sleeping between his mother's big breasts?'

'Yes, Meddah.'

'At first sight the cradle looked perfectly normal, my little dove, a sort of box with a little hole in the bottom, because little children aren't always clean in their cradles, not even children called Vartan and named after a hero, even if they aren't going to be heroes themselves. Your grandfather had made the cradle himself, for his first son. All the children slept in the cradle afterwards, for each child bequeathed his little bed to the next one.'

'So is there nothing special about the cradle?'

'Yes, there is, my little lamb. Your grandfather had carved a dove in the wood of the cradle, a dove with an olive-branch.'

'What is that intended to mean?'

'It was a picture of the dove from Noah's Ark, the one that flew up from Mount Ararat to bring back the olive-branch from the country which later became Hayastan – the land at the foot of the mountain – as a sign that the Flood was over.'

'It was a custom with the Khatisians that the grandmother rocked the cradle of the newborn baby during the day, because the mother might have been kept awake by the baby during the night or because she was simply tired after feeding it so much. The grandmother was used to that cradle. And because she didn't want to be sitting by the cradle all the time, she tied a long string round her leg and fastened the other end to the cradle. That way she could

168

get around the house or the garden, even sit in front of the house chatting, and she only needed to pull the string a bit or give a tug with her foot to lull the baby when it cried.'

'Did my father have a grandmother?'

'What a silly question, my little lamb. All small children have grandmothers.'

'There was really nothing special about this cradle,' said the story-teller. 'It was filled with soft sand, which the grandmother changed when it got wet. The cradle also had a hole in the bottom, as I've told you before, so as to save sand; just a proper Armenian farmer's cradle, which had been made with love and care. There was nothing special about the cradle or about your father, who cried or screamed or kicked or lay quiet and peaceful like all little children. Your father was basically a friendly child. He slept through the first days of his life, smiled in his sleep and dreamt of his mother's big breasts, and often too of his grandmother's long string, the string she rocked him with. Perhaps he also dreamed about the dove with the olive-branch, about Mount Ararat and the land of Hayastan, although I doubt it.'

'When your great-grandfather fathered the grandmother – your father's grandmother, I mean, he said to his wife: "If it's a son – and I hope it will be – we'll call him Tigran, for he was an Armenian king, but if it's a girl we'll call her Satenig, who was an Armenian princess."

But the great-grandmother said: "I feel sure it will be a girl. But she mustn't be a princess. The best thing will be to call her Hamest."

"Why Hamest particularly?"

"Because I just feel that she can only be called Hamest," said the great-grandmother.'

'*Hamest* means modesty,' said the story-teller. 'And since she actually had a girl, they called her Hamest.'

'And was she a modest girl?' asked the last thought.

'No,' said the story-teller. 'That's just it. She was the reverse of modest. She was actually a real dragon, who ordered everybody about. They ought to have called her *Zovinar*, a name that actually means nymph but is also used to mean summer lightning.'

'Was she like summer lightning?'

'Yes,' said the story-teller. 'There was no thunder-clap after her bursts of temper. No one was upset when she lost her temper, for she meant well.'

'Was she good to my father?'

'She was good to your father.'

'And because she had that wrong name,' said the story-teller, 'she said one day – when she herself should have been made pregnant, on her wedding night – yes, she said to her husband: "I really ought to have been called Zovinar. But that isn't my name."

And her husband said: "If God punishes us and we have a daughter and not a son, we'll call her Zovinar."'

'But it turned out differently,' said the story-teller. 'None of their children were called Zovinar, for the more they thought about the name the less they liked it. Only when the good God blessed one of their sons – Hagob, it was – with a wife who was called Zovinar, Hamest said to her husband: "Now after all, and in spite of everything, we've got a Zovinar in our family. Do you remember, that's what I ought to have been called?"'

'That's how it was,' said the story-teller. 'Hamest got a daughter-in-law called Zovinar. And Hamest said to her husband: "That really must be the right name. Certainly Hagob's wife is like summer lightning." But Hamest was mistaken. For Zovinar had the wrong name. She was a modest woman and really ought to have been called Hamest.'

'In spite of her temper – or perhaps because of it – your father's grandmother had an unattractive body. She was no taller than a dwarf, thin as a Kurd's black mountain-goat, awkward in her movements and tough as the indigestible *pasderma*, that dried meat that farmers keep in their larders. She always carried a couple of cloves of garlic round her neck as protection against evil spirits and against the evil eye, so she smelt of garlic, which put many people off, but which other people found attractive, for garlic is a favourite herb. Your father often began to bawl when his grandmother came up to the cradle, bent over him and said: "Now, my fearless pasha, you must be brave or the Kurds will get you." And she added craftily: "Or the big bear."'

'Your father was still too small, just after his baptism, to know the difference between good and bad, or to know why his grandmother wore cloves of garlic round her neck. All he knew was that one of the women who looked after him smelt of garlic and the other smelt of sweet milk, and so it was understandable that it was to his mother that he stretched out his arms most eagerly.'

'His mother not only smelt of milk, she even looked like a milch cow. And in that she was the opposite of his grandmother. Fat and fleshy, with flabby breasts, she walked up and down beside the cradle. Her movements when she bent over the cradle were like flowing milk, and the soft words she whispered in little Vartan's ears gurgled like the stream of milk into the wooden bucket at milking time. Sweet were her words and sweet was her smell. No wonder he got so excited when his mother approached the cradle and gently took him in her arms to feed him.'

The story-teller's voice was serious. He said: 'Every Armenian child is in great danger during the first forty days of its life. During those first forty days the mother must never leave the child alone. It's true that his grandmother was there to rock the cradle, as I've told you, with the aid of a long string. But his mother was always sitting somewhere near. Mother and child must not leave the house during the first forty days. That was allowed only on the day of the baptism, when of course both of them had to go to church.'

'Why is an Armenian child in such danger, I wonder, during the first forty days of its life?'

'Because of the evil spirits, my little lamb. The Armenians know many different spirits. There are *vishaps*, and *devs*, and *alks*, and many others. And of course the *djinn*, in which the Turks believe too. Many of these spirits hanker after the livers of little children, which they eat at once if the mother isn't there. There was a case in the village once that was talked about for years.'

171

'What sort of case, Meddah?'
'Shall I really tell you?'
'Yes, Meddah.'

'In those days,' said the story-teller, 'when the Armenians were the first of all people in the world to adopt the Christian faith, Saint Gregory had the Persian fire-worshippers' temple in the town of Echmiadzin torn down and built in its place the first state church in the world, so splendid that even the architects of the royal palace were green with envy. The town and the church still exist. And it's from there too that the holy *meron* oil comes, with which all Armenian children are anointed at their baptism. Well, my little lamb,' said the story-teller, 'it so happened that the neighbours of the Khatisians had a child, a little girl, and she was christened *Takouhi*, which means queen. The little girl's mother had been warned. She had been told: "Don't let your child out of your sight for the first forty days. Don't forget that the spirits live in the dark and will certainly be angry because you've had such a pretty child, one that's called Takouhi." – But the child's mother had laughed and said: "Nothing can happen to my little girl, for the priest Kapriel Hamadian has anointed her with the holy *meron* oil."

And when they asked her: "Have you washed the child since then?" she laughed and said: "Of course I've washed the child."

"And was the water oily?"

"Of course it was oily, for there were traces of the *meron* oil in the water."

"It was holy water."

"Of course it was holy water."

"And what did you do with the holy water? Did you throw it away?"

"I sprinkled it all round the house."

"Because of the *djinn*?"

"Of course, because of the *djinn*."

"And you believe the *djinn* are afraid of holy water?"

"Of course they're afraid of it."'

'And so it happened,' said the story-teller, 'that the child's mother often left her alone. She had put a bible in the cradle and also hung some cloves of garlic outside the door and some horseshoes in the doorway, upside down with the points pointing to the ground, as everyone in the village did, to protect the rooms in the house from spirits. She had even put a broom by the cradle, because the *djinn* are afraid of brooms and sticks, but it was no use.'

'No use? How was that?'

'Well, now, my little lamb,' said the story-teller. 'One day . . . the woman came straight back from the well, where she had stopped for a time to chat with the old women . . . so she came back, and behold . . .'

'Behold – what?'

'The child had disappeared.'

'Disappeared?'

'Simply disappeared. It was never seen again.'

'I imagine myself,' said the story-teller, 'sitting beside your father, many years ago. He's three weeks old, and he looks at me with his big, dark Armenian eyes. "Now, you messy little kid," I say to him, "are you frightened?"

And your father, who can't talk yet, says to me: "What should I be frightened of, Meddah? My grandmother rocks me with that long string. And my mother has just gone out to the shed to pee, but she'll come straight back to feed me."

"That's true," I told him. "You've got it absolutely right. But don't you know that mothers shouldn't leave their children alone for a moment during the first forty days of their life? One single second is enough, and the child will have disappeared for ever."

And your father asks: "Because of the *djinn*?"

And I say: "Yes. The *djinn* are after your liver. And look out. Your mother's in the shed having a pee. And when she comes back you won't be there any more, because the *djinn* will have taken you."

And your father laughs and says: "No, the *djinn* can't do that, because the priest Hamadian has anointed me with holy *meron* oil – it was at my baptism – and because grandmother washed me afterwards and sprinkled the bath water with the remains of the oil all round the house. The *djinn* can't break through that magic circle. And do you know why?"

173

"No," I say. "I don't know why."

"Because Jesus Christ protects me."

"Well, I don't know," I say. "Christ isn't always there when he's wanted. Many Armenian mothers have tried that with the oil and the *djinn* have still taken their children."'

'I tell your father about the time his mother became pregnant for the twelfth time.

"There's a donkey track out of the village," I tell him, "and if you follow the sun in the early morning for an hour or two, you come to a hut, where old Bulbul lives."

"Bulbul?" your father asks.

And I say: "Yes. That's her name, just like the nightingale. Simply Bulbul, and do you know why?"

"No," says your father.

"Because she's a midwife, and she sings while the mother screams. She sings so loud that the mother thinks it's her own voice . . . and she goes on and on until the child is born."

"Does she sing like a nightingale?"

"No, my little lamb," I say. "Her voice is as ugly as the braying of a donkey, whose voice, the Prophet said, is the ugliest of all Allah's creatures."'

'"Many people get gooseflesh, as they call it," I tell your father, "and many people think of crossing themselves, when the shabby old donkey, that didn't even have a name, appears with the bow-legged Bulbul. But you needn't be afraid of her, even if people say she's bewitched by the *djinn*, turned into a walking mystery on two twisted legs, with a harsh voice like a man's and a grey goatee beard on her chin."'

'"One way or the other, no one really knows who she is or where she came from. They do say she comes from the wild mountain country called Hakkari, and is the daughter of a Kurd sheikh and one of his concubines. Her father, the sheikh, so they say, could neither read nor write but had a great thirst for knowledge, so from time to time he had a *hafiz* abducted. They are Muslims who can teach the Koran. Also, his people often carried off story-tellers from the bazaars in the big towns and brought them to his tent in chains. The sheikh made the *hafiz* recite the wisest speeches from the Koran until he had had enough, and the story-tellers had to tell him all the stories they knew. They say that Bulbul always listened when she was a young girl, so that she soon knew the most important parts of the Koran by heart and knew all the stories and fairy-tales that the *meddahs* told. Once, they say, the Kurd sheikh had captured an old story-teller, one whose long life had reached a hundred years. And because he was so old he often went to sleep as he told his tales, and Bulbul, the little girl, sat beside him and simply went on with them just as well as the old man, in fact often better. She told the stories right up to the end."

"And why isn't Bulbul still with her tribe?"

"Because one day the tribe had expelled her mother, and Bulbul left with her. Bulbul had cursed her father. And she had cursed the tribe too. They went on and on, a long way. Later Bulbul's mother died of cholera. They say that Bulbul, who was then ten years old, was picked up by some Gypsies and travelled through the country with them for a long time, until she broke away from them too. After that she wandered around the villages and towns – no one knows where – and when one day she turned up in Yedi Su she was bow-legged and hump-backed and the first grey hairs of an old woman's beard were beginning to sprout on her chin, although she still wasn't very old. She came on a shabby grey donkey, had a bag and a stick with her and – so they say – all sorts of jewels and gold. And she built herself a hut in the mountains. She has lived there ever since, with the domestic animals that she had picked up in the course of time. Bulbul is afraid of no one. No one ever does her any harm, for even the Kurds in the mountains are afraid of her spells." '

And the Meddah said: 'I tell your father: "When your mother became pregnant with you, Bulbul came riding into the village on her shabby donkey. And she said to your mother: 'You mustn't look in a mirror for nine months.'

'I never have looked in a mirror when I was pregnant,' said your mother. 'It was the same in all my pregnancies.'

'That's good,' said Bulbul.

'My mother had always warned me,' said your mother. 'In every

pregnancy she had said: "Don't look in a mirror for nine months."'
    'She was right to warn you,' said Bulbul.
    'Only my mother never explained why it was so.'
    'Well now, why indeed,' said Bulbul. 'I suppose, because the
unborn child is curious . . . but also mistrustful . . . and because
in his mother's womb he watches everything his mother does.'
    'Everything I do?'
    'Everything you do.'"'

'"And Bulbul said: 'If you look in the mirror, then your unborn
child will take your mirror image for its true mother. And since the
mirror image is reversed, it will turn around in your belly and lie
the wrong way. When that happens, the mother and her child . . .
they die during the birth. The child dies without a sound, but the
mother dies with a cry on her lips. I have known it before. There
was one mother whose child lay the wrong way who screamed as
loud as the swine of the infidels when they are slaughtered.'"'

'And so it was,' said the story-teller. 'Your father's mother didn't
look in the mirror for nine months. And when the time came and
little Vartan wanted to slip out to see his mother from outside, she
didn't even know what she looked like any more.'

'So I sit by your father's cradle,' said the story-teller, 'and I say to
him: "Don't be afraid. The spirits won't take you. They're only
stories. The real danger comes from the Turks and the Kurds.
When you're grown up, dip your little penis, which will be a real
prick by then, in holy *meron* oil, for the Turks and the Kurds have
the bad habit of cutting off Armenian men's pricks, especially when
the great *tebk* begins."
    And your father asks: "What is the great *tebk*?"
    And I say: "A *tebk* is a *tebk*. It means a special event, but what
it really means is a massacre."'

'"Don't be frightened,"' I say to your father, and I caress little
Vartan, who is only three weeks old, with my fairy-tale voice. I tell
him: "There is no *tebk* at the moment, not in this region anyway.
At the moment the only danger to you is the superstition of the

villagers." And I say to him, laughing: "Look, my little lamb. Someone has just died in the house next door. And soon your mother will come back from the shed, and will take you in her arms."

"And then?"

"Then she'll go up on the roof with you, for all Armenian houses have flat roofs."

"But why should I go on to the roof with her?"

"Because the dead take little children with them when they are taken to the graveyard. But they can only take them if the children's little legs are near the ground. It is quite different on a roof. The dead man has no power there."'

'And I say to little Vartan: "There is only one coffin in the village, and it's already over a hundred years old. Soon they will be carrying the dead man past. And soon your mother will come back from the cowshed and take you up to the roof."'

'"You may like to know why there's only one coffin in the village," I say, "and one that is over a hundred years old at that."

"Yes," says little Vartan. "What is there about the coffin?"

"Everyone that lives in the village will get the same coffin," I say. "For the coffin is only used to carry the dead man to the graveyard. Then the coffin is taken back empty."'

'"How are dead people buried, then?"

"They are buried without a coffin, my little lamb, just wrapped in their shroud. That's how all your ancestors were buried."

"And what happens to the empty coffin when the villagers take it back without the dead man in it?"

"Then it's got ready for the next one, my little lamb. For your grandfather, perhaps, who's already very old, or for one of your neighbours."

"And how will it be with me?"

"You've got plenty of time, my little lamb. You're only three weeks old. Unless the Turks or the Kurds kill you first, or you die of some serious illness, you will get very old. Perhaps as much as a hundred years, or even more. And then, when they close your eyes, people will say: 'This coffin is over two hundred years old, for it was more than a hundred years old when the dead man was born.' But don't worry about that; the coffin will last all right, for Armenian craftsmen are the best in the world. Everything they make is sound."'

'"Sometimes your mother will lay you on the floor, to let you have a good kick unhindered by the cradle, but she will take good care that no one treads on you. And she will remember what everyone has told her, even Bulbul: the first forty days are dangerous. Be careful, Zovinar, not to step over him, for that will retard his growth. And if by some chance you do do that, then you must take the same step backwards to break the spell. Then he'll grow properly."'

'"Listen, my little lamb," I say to your father. "You will catch a lot of illnesses, like all little children, but don't worry. Your grandmother will press the goat's horns on your skin; they are sawn through and heated in the *tonir*, and the cup-shaped piece sawn off is put on the skin until it goes blood-red. Then your grandmother will scratch all the red places with a sewing-needle and put leeches on them, and they will suck out all the bad blood, and with it all the things that make you ill. If the leeches get so full that it looks as if they will burst, your grandmother will take them off and throw them in a jug of salt water, so that they spit the blood out again. To make certain, your grandmother will rub them and squeeze them afterwards until the leeches have spat all the blood out into the salt-water jug. And then they'll be put on again where the drops of blood are on your skin. They will go on sucking until you're better."'

'"And if that doesn't help?" asks Vartan.
"Then your grandmother will take all the clothes that have touched your sick body in any way, and she'll hang the clothes on the holy tree that grows by itself by the village square. If the holy tree doesn't shake the clothes off, all the illnesses taken out of the house with the clothes will disappear."
"Is there really a holy tree . . . here in Yedi Su?"
"Of course, my little lamb. Every village in this region has a holy tree."

"Why is the tree holy, Meddah?"

"Nobody knows, my little lamb . . . or nobody can really remember who first declared that the tree was holy, or when that was, because generally it was a long time ago. It is enough that a dervish once slept under the tree, or Saint Sarkis."

"Was he in this neighbourhood?"

"Of course he was in this neighbourhood."'

'"When you've got teeth, and one day you get toothache, your grandmother will treat you with *raki*, or she may use the Armenian *oghi* schnapps, which comes from the country of the grapevines. She'll rub your gums with the schnapps and say: 'He shall have teeth until he's a hundred and twenty.' What do you say to that?"'

'I say to your father: "Now, you little brat, have you ever been to the Armenian graveyard at Yedi Su? Not yet, of course. It's best there," I tell him, "on Easter Monday. Then the whole village gathers at the graveyard. And Kurds and Turks and Gypsies all come down into the valley from the mountains and take their place by the graveyard. Yes, indeed, my little lamb. It looks like a bazaar, and they do actually call it the Easter Monday bazaar. There's a lot of praying in the graveyard, and then there's a feast. Since it's the custom on that day that the priest can take home all the *baklava* that's left, they also call the day the Priest's *Baklava* Day."'

'"Shall I tell you some more, my little lamb? For instance, about your great-grandfather's burial?"

And your father, who was three weeks old, said: "Please tell me."

"They had just laid your great-grandfather in a fresh grave," I, the story-teller, say, "but they hadn't filled it in yet. When they were just going to start work with their shovels, your great-grandfather's son – your grandfather, that is – quickly put a bottle of schnapps into the grave – *raki* or *oghi*, I don't know which, but anyway a good reputable brand – for he believed that the soul of an Armenian takes three days to leave the grave. The white soul goes straight to heaven, but the black soul can't overcome the wave of pure thought outside the gates of Paradise. And so he thought the schnapps might perhaps help the soul of his father, who had been a boozer and a glutton and a whoremonger, to manage the leap over the pure thoughts."'

'"Yes," I say, "and then your grandfather took another bottle of schnapps out of his pocket, and a silver goblet, filled it full and drank it off. And the bystanders said: 'Well done.' And they said: 'May the days that he never saw be added to your days.' But your grandfather said: 'No . . . not to mine, but to the days of my grandson Vartan, whom Hagob and Zovinar have not yet produced but who will be born some time.'

'Had Hagob and Zovinar planned him . . . this little Vartan?'

'Of course,' said your grandfather . . . 'but only after I'd given them a good talking-to.'

And so they all tasted some of your grandfather's schnapps, and they said: 'Here's to little Vartan, who hasn't been born yet.'"'

'"Had I really not been born then?" asks Vartan.

"Not at that time," say I, the story-teller.'

'"You have no idea where you are," I say to Vartan, who has just pissed in his nappy and begun to cry a bit. "Now, just guess where you are?"

"I'm lying in my cradle," Vartan tells me, "the cradle with the dove and the olive-branch. I've just pissed in my nappy and I'm waiting for my mother."

"You're laying in your cradle," I say. "That's true. But you don't know where the cradle is."

"I don't know that," says Vartan.

"The cradle is standing on its legs three long paces from the *tonir*. And the *tonir* is in the middle of the living-room."

"I didn't know that," says Vartan.

"The farmers in Yedi Su call their living-room *oda*, and only the Mukhtar calls his *selamlik*."

"Do all living-rooms smell as funny as this one?"

"They all smell the same," I say. "They smell of cowsheds, for the cowshed is part of the house and the animals have to go through the living-room if they want to get to the cowshed."

"Why is that?"

"I don't really know, my little lamb. But I expect the Armenians used to keep their animals in the *oda* because the fire in the *tonir* wasn't warm enough, especially in winter." And I say: "It doesn't only smell of cowshed. It also smells of smoke, for the house has no chimney. And it smells of herbs, and of *pasderma* . . . you know, that dried meat that gives little children hiccups . . . and it smells of butter and cheese too, and of the remains of the honey-cakes your mother has just baked."'

'"When Hayk, the first of the Armenians, and his followers moved to Mount Ararat – it was a long time ago, my little lamb, before we began to count the years – he came to this village, though it wasn't a village in those days, just an uninhabited valley. On the spot where your *tonir* stands today, Hayk stopped and said: 'One of my descendants will settle here, and he will dig a fireplace, and he will call that fireplace *tonir*.'

And so it was. One day a man came through this valley on his donkey, a man who was also called Hayk. He was too tired to go any further, and he was hungry and thirsty and he was getting cold, so he stopped. The donkey took him to one of the seven wells, whose refreshing water he had long been smelling. After both of them had slaked their thirst, the man came back to the place he had come to before, where your *oda* now stands. He dug a fireplace. And he lit a fire and said: 'I call this fireplace *tonir*.' Then he heard a voice that came out of the clouds, and it said: 'The *tonir* is holy. Build a house round the *tonir*. And take a woman and marry her before the *tonir*.'"

And I point at the *tonir* with my fairy-tale voice and say: "Look, my little lamb. It was in front of this *tonir* that Hayk was married. And over this *tonir* Hayk built a house."'

'"When Hayk's family was still limited to father, mother and children, he called them *endanig*. Later, when there was an extended family, they called themselves *kertastan*. At first there was just the one room in which Hayk lived with his wife, his children and his animals. But at some time Hayk built a partition along the middle of the big room, which had no windows – a strong wall supported by crossbeams, which from then on would separate humans and animals. And because, even with two rooms, it became more and more uncomfortable, more and more cramped, his descendants built rooms of their own, with their own walls and their own roofs, on to the patriarch's house. That was all a long, long time ago. But all the villagers know about it. And so many a man, when he goes past here today, points at the house of Hayk's descendants and says: 'That's where the Khatisians live . . . the whole clan . . . or all the ones that stayed here and haven't yet left.' "'

"'My little lamb," I say, "you don't know yet what your village looks like." And I say: "It looks like most Armenian villages, which are cleaner than Kurdish and Turkish villages. The houses are built of clay, undressed stone and rock, with white tiles, and they have flat roofs made of branches of poplar. The biggest house belongs to the Mukhtar, Ephrem Abovian, who has been mayor of Yedi Su for many years. Of course the streets are only mud – what else should they be? But the village has a holy spring in which the blessed Sarkis bathed many years ago. And it has seven wells, one of which is called *gatnachpiur*. That one is a milk well."

And I say: "My little lamb. There isn't really milk in the well called *gatnachpiur*, but mothers whose breasts have dried need only to pray at the *gatnachpiur* well, and then to cross themselves and dip their breasts in the water, and their dried breasts will swell again.

Perhaps you would like to know, my little lamb, what your mother did when her long, flabby breasts wobbled to and fro whenever she moved? Well, my little lamb, she prayed earnestly . . . and crossed herself . . . before the *gatnachpiur* well of course, and then she dipped her breasts in the good water, and soon they swelled up again and became fat and milky."'

"'A stranger who rides along the caravan road between Bakir and Erzurum and comes to the crossing with the roads to Van, Bakir, Mush, Kayseri, Konya and Diyarbekir will know nothing about this village, which lies half a day's ride away in one of the valleys of the plateau, hidden between the bare mountains and a short distance from the Kurdish camp of Suleyman Agha, who is also called Suleyman Bey. And if a stranger should venture to leave the caravan road and ride across country through the trackless highlands for half a day, even then he wouldn't see the village, even if he came quite close to it. For the first houses in the village hang like eagles' nests on the face of the rocks, and wouldn't be visible to the stranger if he was riding steadily over the zigzags of donkey and mule tracks."

"Can't you see the roofs of our houses?"

"No, my little lamb. Or you don't see them until you're right above the roofs."

"How can anyone be above the roofs?"

"The last stretch of the donkey track winds into the valley above the roofs. And the stranger would have to look down to see the roofs on the rock face. But he'll generally be looking straight ahead."

"Isn't it right to look straight ahead?"

"Yes, it is, my little lamb, but not always."'

'"When your mother was in her third month with you, a Kurd came riding into the village. He was riding towards the morning sun. At the beginning of the village his horse stumbled, slipped off the winding track and fell – but not very far and not so as to be killed – and it so happened that the Kurdish rider and his horse landed on the roof of your house."

"Just like that?"

"Yes, my little lamb,"

"Wasn't my mother frightened?"

"You bet she was frightened! The poplar-branch roof gave way and the Kurd and his horse fell straight into your living-room – into the *selamlik* or the *oda* . . . That's what happened, my little lamb. Your mother was just taking a nap. Suddenly she heard a terrific crash, woke up and saw the Kurd and his horse where he had fallen through the living-room ceiling, right next to the *tonir*."

"What did my mother do?"

"She did absolutely nothing, my little lamb. She just stared at the Kurd and his horse in terror."

"And what did I do, Meddah?"

"You nearly tumbled out of your mother's womb with fright."

"A miscarriage, you mean?"

"Almost, my little lamb. Your mother nearly lost you. And then there would have been no Vartan. And Vartan, who didn't exist, wouldn't have been able later on to take a wife so as to have a son by her and call him Thovma."

"Shall I have a son, Meddah?"

"Of course you'll have a son."

"And shall I call him Thovma?"

"Thovma!"'

'"What about the Kurd and his horse?"

"I've told you."

"So the Kurd was riding towards the morning sun?"

"Yes."

"And his horse stumbled? Off the track? Fell over the edge of the cliff? And landed on the roof of our house?"

"That's it."

"And he fell into our living-room, which can also be called *selamlik* or *oda*, with his horse? And horse and rider landed by the *tonir*, in which all the cowdung burns and flickers and glows?"

"Yes, my little lamb."

"And my mother was terribly frightened, so that she nearly lost me?"

"That's right."

"Which could have meant that I should never be a father . . . because there would have been no me."

"Yes, my little lamb."

"And no son Thovma either, who I was going to have?"

"That's how it is, my little lamb. He would never have existed."

I chuckle to myself. Then I say: "But, as you see, nothing serious happened. Your grandmother just came in from the next room, saw the Kurd, saw his horse, picked up the poker that was lying by the *tonir* – it wasn't a real poker, just a long piece of iron for poking the cowdung. She picked it up and beat the Kurd up with it, and his horse too. And, believe it or not, the Kurd was terrified and galloped out of the living-room. And suddenly disappeared."

"My word!" says little Vartan, who is three weeks old and can't

184

talk yet. "My grandmother really has guts. Who'd have thought it?"

"Yes, my little lamb, your grandmother has her heart in the right place."

"Is she the first Armenian woman who ever dared to hit a wild Kurd with a poker?"

"You mean . . . in all the thousands of years of the history of the Armenian people?"

"Yes, Meddah."

"I don't know, my little lamb. We'll have to ask the historians. But I, the story-teller, I've never heard of anything of the kind."'

'And I, the story-teller, say to little Vartan: "Your grandmother wasn't always such a dragon, my little lamb. But when you first see her, you'd never think she'd ever been any different."

"Different in what way, Meddah?"

"Well, just different, my little lamb. Many, many years ago, when she married your grandfather and came to live in this house, your grandmother was a nervous little bride. She was twelve, she had no breasts, no hair between her legs, but she had big ears, and no mouth at all."

"But, Meddah, that can't be true."

"Yes it is, my little lamb. It is true. For her mother-in-law said to her after her wedding night: '*Gelin*' – that's the Turkish word for a young bride, though there's also an Armenian word. She might equally well have said *hars*, for instance . . . bride, that means . . . but the Turkish word comes off the tongue better . . . it's a bit shrill, inspires respect, and fear too perhaps, sounds more progressive, more effective in talks between two woman of different standing. Do you see, my little lamb? So her mother-in-law said: '*Gelin! Gelin*,' she said, 'you've only got ears now, no mouth. You may only talk to little children and only to your husband when you're alone with him, and even then only if he says something to you first, do you see? You mustn't talk to anyone else, especially not to your father-in-law or your husband's brothers, otherwise people will say you've torn your veil.'

'And when will I be allowed to talk to other people?' asked your grandmother.

'Not before your first child is born,' said her mother-in-law. And when that happens, I shall say: '*Gelin*, now you've got a mouth again.'"

"'The Armenians call this trial period of their young daughters-in-law *harsnutian*, and the rule of silence is called *munj*. I, the story-teller, I really do wonder why the good God gave young brides tongues at all if their mothers-in-law forbid them to speak. And the mother-in-law's mother, too, even she said to your young twelve-year-old grandmother: '*Gelin*, hold your tongue!'"

"'Verily, my little lamb, it's easy enough to get round the law when it's in writing . . . but there's no way to rebel against the unwritten law of the family. Your young grandmother knew that. It wasn't until she'd had her first child that she began to talk again.'"

"'As the youngest woman in the house, your grandmother had to take on all the petty jobs. It was even part of her daily work to make everyone's bed in the morning, even her sister-in-law's bed. For in the *kertastan* none of the women made their own beds. The youngest *gelin* had to make them. And the neighbours used to stand outside and look in to see if she did it."

"And suppose she hadn't done it?" asks little Vartan.

"Then people would have said: 'Look, in that *kertastan* everybody makes their own bed. That family is pregnant. That means, it's falling apart.'"

"'The more children your grandmother had, the more her position in the family improved. She brought fourteen children into the world. Your father, my little lamb, was the youngest. She was already nearly forty when he was born. And you likewise, my little Vartan, you're your mother's last child, though you're only the twelfth. So that's how it is, my little lamb, that your grandmother has already got pretty old. And during that time she has become the patriarch."

"Does everyone in the family obey her?"

"Oh, yes."

"Then is she the oldest woman in the house?"

"No, my little lamb. Your great-grandmother is the oldest. But

186

no one takes any notice of her now, because with old age she's become feeble-minded. She just sits by the *tonir* and dozes – you can see her if you lift your head."'

"'My little lamb, your grandmother's breasts are as wrinkled as her hands and her face. But the fire in her eyes is still as bright as the flames in the *tonir*. And her tongue is just as sharp, and it always says what her heart dictates. It's as if she talks so much to make up for the long time when she had to keep silent. No one can swear like your grandmother."'

"'Guess what your grandmother said to that Kurd, my little lamb, when she chased him out of the room with the poker.'
    "How should I know that, Meddah?"
    "'You bastard,' she said. 'You grandson of a rabid sheep. You stinking Kurdish ball-bag. Tell your *Bey* I'll send him and his whole tribe to hell. I hope all your men's cocks rot, and the Padisha in Constantinople hangs the lot of you, and your children die of cholera and your men of the Frankish disease you get in brothels – I'm an old woman and forget what it's called. I hope the *djinn* and the *alks* eat your kids' livers, and the flood drowns you all.'"'

"'But tell me, Meddah. Why does my grandmother hate the Kurds so much?'
    "Well, there are reasons, my little lamb."'

"'Armenian women are more frightened of the Kurds than they are of the Turks, although the Kurds are a harmless people compared with the Turks. As I said, they're frightened of them. And even unborn children sense their mothers' fear. The mothers know that, that's why they tell their children: 'Be careful! If you aren't good the big bear will get you. Or else the Kurds will get you.'"
    "What Kurds do they mean?"
    "Not the town Kurds, my little lamb, and not the ones in the semi-nomads' villages. It's the wild Kurd mountain tribes the women are afraid of. Sometimes they carry off women, massacre their menfolk, plunder the village and burn the houses down."
    "Why do they do that, Meddah?"

"I really don't know, my little lamb."'

'"Well, my little lamb, it's all very complicated. But I'll try to explain it to you. There's the question of taxes, for instance."
"What are taxes, Meddah?"
"Well, my little lamb, taxes are taxes."'

'"It's like this, my little lamb. The Kurds don't pay any taxes to the Turks, because they don't believe in it. Only a little time ago the Padisha sent five thousand mounted men into the Kurdish mountains from Constantinople to collect the taxes, but, believe it or not, the five thousand horsemen were never seen again. It was quite simple. The Kurds let the soldiers pass until they got to the ravines, then they shot the riders down one by one, stole their horses and their boots and uniforms as well, and threw the naked bodies into the gorge. The Padisha isn't anxious to lose so many horses and men again, so he leaves the Kurds in peace. And for that reason he collects double and triple taxes from the Armenians."
"But I don't understand, Meddah."'

'"Well, that's how it is, my little lamb. The Turkish tax-collectors really pillage the Armenians. They not only have to pay the unbelievers' tax, called the *raya* tax, but they also have to pay the poll-tax, as well as other taxes and levies that I won't bother you with; but above all they have to pay the military service exemption tax, called the *bedel*. No Armenian is excused from the *bedel*, not even you, my little lamb."
"Why is that, Meddah?"
"Because Armenians are not allowed to carry weapons, and consequently can't do military service."
"But still have to pay the *bedel*?"
"That's right."'

'"And what has that got to do with the Kurds? – I find it very funny that the Kurds won't pay taxes and refuse as a matter of principle to do national service. I find that really funny. For I think nothing of taxes myself, although I'm only three weeks old and have no idea what taxes really are."'

      ★   ★   ★

'"Well, that's how it is, my little lamb. The Kurds pay no taxes to the Turks, but they collect taxes themselves from the Armenians."

"I thought it was the Turks the Armenians paid their taxes to."

"They have to pay taxes to the Kurds as well."

"Then they pay twice over?"

"They pay more than twice, my little lamb. And if they can't pay their houses are burnt down, they're driven off their fields and locked up in prison."

"And what about the Kurds?"

"It's like this, my little lamb. In this district there is a bey, who is a sheikh, called Suleyman. This sheikh is convinced that the whole country as far as the Euphrates belongs to him. He doesn't recognize the Padisha in Constantinople, nor any other ruler. He thinks everything belongs to him, even the villages in this valley and everything their inhabitants possess. But the sheikh isn't stupid. He lets the Armenians till the fields and doesn't mind if they breed cattle or things like that. He just comes down now and then to the Armenian *milets* – that's the Armenian districts – and helps himself to whatever he needs. He has the cattle driven off, takes the grain out of the granaries and anything else he takes a fancy to, often pretty girls too. He has a thousand mounted men, and anyone who resists him is made a head shorter."'

'"The other day your father said to your mother: 'The Kurds are the stupidest people in the world; they can only count up to ten.'

'But I know a Kurd who can count up to twenty,' said your mother.

'Then he must count on his toes as well as his fingers.'

'That's it,' your mother said."'

'"Well, my little lamb," I, the story-teller, say, "it doesn't matter whether the Kurds are clever or stupid. One thing is certain: you don't want to play games with them. You either give them what they want, or you wake up next morning with no roof over your head, and if you're unlucky with no head either."

"Meddah, you're making fun of me. How can anyone wake up without a head?"'

★　　★　　★

'"The Kurds also collect the bride-tax from the Armenians."

"What is that, Meddah?"

"Well, just the bride-tax. When an Armenian marries, he has to give half the bride-price to the Kurd chief Suleyman."

"Will I have to do that, if I get married some day?"

"Of course, my little lamb."

"And suppose I don't?"

"Then they'll chop your head off, my little lamb. Or something worse than that could happen."

"What, Meddah?"

"The Kurds will take your bride away before you've slept with her."

"Is that worse than death?"

"That is worse than death, my little lamb."'

'"And now you must sleep, my little lamb. Tomorrow is also a day. Your grandmother will come in a moment and rock you with her long string. And your mother will come back from the cowshed, where she has evidently not only been peeing but must have been doing some other job she hadn't expected. And surely she must have been taking time to give back to the Lord some of the good things he has sent her. Why else would she have stayed so long? – And soon, my little lamb, your father will come back from the fields. Shall I sing you to sleep?"

"Yes, Meddah."'

'But I said to Vartan: "Before I sing you a lullaby, I'll tell you how you came into the world."

"But I know that, Meddah."

"How was it then, my little lamb?"

"Under the grapevine, of course, Meddah."

But I, the Meddah, say: "No, my little lamb. That's only fairy-tales that people tell to children. Do you want to know how it really happened?"

And I say: "Yesterday Bulbul came riding into the village on her shabby old donkey. And she rode into this living-room, left her donkey by the *tonir* and squatted down by your cradle. She said to

190

you: 'Now, my little lamb. Do you want to know properly how you came into the world?'

You said: 'Bulbul, I know how I came into the world. It was under the grapevine.'

But Bulbul laughed and said: 'No, my little lamb. I know better, because I am Bulbul, the midwife.'"'

'"And Bulbul tells you. She says: 'It was three weeks ago, my little Vartan. I rode into the village on my shabby little donkey. And I heard your mother moaning. That came from the cowshed, I said to myself, the shed in the Khatisian house. So I rode to your house. And I rode through the open doorway into your *oda*. I left the donkey by the *tonir* and went on into the shed. And guess what I saw?'

'I don't know, Bulbul,' said Vartan.

'Your mother was squatting down beside the cow and whimpering. "What's the matter, chubbykins?" I said. "Has the cow bewitched you during milking? Has it got the devil in its udder? Have you drunk any of its milk? And have you got the devil in your belly now?"

"I've got little Vartan in my belly," said your mother. "I think he wants to slip out."

I said: "That wouldn't be too bad."

And your mother said: "No, that wouldn't be too bad."'"'

'"And suddenly your mother's pain began again. But I held her tight, stroked her neck and stroked her back and smoothed her hair.

"Shall I lie on my back, Bulbul?"

"No, Zovinar. Only Frankish women lie on their backs when they bear their children."

"Shall I stay squatting here by the cow?"

"Yes, Zovinar. Hold on to its teats."

"And what else should I do, Bulbul?"

"You must push, Zovinar. Just push."

"Push, Bulbul?"

"Yes, Zovinar. Imagine you'd just pissed and now you have to lay an egg . . . And you're pushing a bit, do you see?"

"Yes, Bulbul."

"And I'll strike your back and strike your neck. And I'll hold you

tight and smooth your hair. And you'll just push a little, chubbykins."
"Yes, Bulbul."''''

''"And I stroked your mother and calmed her down. And I hummed
a song with my nightingale's voice, which sounded like the bray of
a donkey. And your mother whimpered and pushed until you had
slipped out.

And suddenly there you were lying in the straw by the cow. Your
mother gave a great sigh, and I said: "That's that, then."''''

''"When you gave your first cry your grandmother came out into
the shed. She watched me bite through the umbilical cord, and
asked me: "How do you do that, Bulbul, when you haven't got any
teeth left?"
"I do it with my lips," I said.
"Why haven't you got any teeth, Bulbul?"
"Because my husband knocked them all out . . . that's why."
"And why did he do that, Bulbul?"
"Because I showed my face to strange men."
"Did you show them your teeth too?"
"Yes, those too."''''

''"And your grandmother bathed you in salt water. And while she
was doing that she sang an old Armenian song. The song was about
the good salt that strengthens the limbs, and it tells of the good God
who gave Armenian children big, dark, velvety eyes.'''

''"Later your father came, and he saw the umbilical cord that I'd
bitten off. It was lying in the hay by the cow's legs. And he saw the
afterbirth, which was also lying in the hay, also near the cow's legs.
"What's the matter with the afterbirth?" asked your father.
"Nothing at all, Hagob Efendi. What should be the matter with it?"
"And what's the matter with the umbilical cord?"
"Nothing at all, Hagob Efendi. What should be the matter with it?"
"Tell me, Bulbul . . . have you at least smeared my son's cheek
with the blood from the umbilical cord, as my mother did to me and
my grandmother did to my father?"
"Yes, Hagob Efendi," I said. "I've done that. So that later on

he'll have rosy cheeks. But look at the child now. Are its cheeks at all pale?"

"No, Bulbul. They're all red with the good blood."''''

'''''What do we do with the umbilical cord?" asked your father.

"We should bury it in the churchyard," said your mother, "but deep, so that the dogs can't eat it."

"In the churchyard?" asked your father.

"Yes," said your mother, "in the churchyard."

I asked your mother: "Why in the churchyard?" And she said: "So that he'll grow up a good Christian."''''

''''Afterwards it occurred to me that the cow might have been possessed of a devil or even have the evil eye, and because I wasn't certain whether that was so I went into the village and went into seven houses, and from the seven houses I took seven different needles, came back, went into the cowshed and stuck the seven needles seven times into the afterbirth to kill the evil, then took the needles out again, spat on the needles and then buried the afterbirth with the needles behind the house.'''"

'"Bulbul said: 'You needn't be afraid, little Vartan. The *djinn* can't take you. You should only be afraid before your first teeth, for it hurts when they grow.'

'Why is that, Bulbul?'

'Well, it just is so, little Vartan. Sooner or later everyone gets their first tooth.'

'Why, Bulbul?'

'Mainly because Allah wants to show us that we can be pierced as much from within as from without.'

'I don't understand that, Bulbul.'

'Well, just look here, Vartan. The human being is made of flesh and blood. And what consists of flesh and blood can be pierced. As your tooth grows, it pierces you from within. Never mind if it hurts. Whether you like it or not, the tooth grows and grows, and pierces your flesh.'

'And if I pray to Christ?'

'That doesn't help. Not even Christ can stop the tooth from

193

growing and piercing you.'

'So I shall be pierced from inside?'

'That's right.'

'And how are people pierced from outside?'

'There are various possibilities.'

'What possibilities?'

'A Kurd's knife, for example. Or a Turk's knife. Or of course a rifle bullet.'

'Are there other ways too?'

'Many more, little Vartan. Many more.'"'

"'And Bulbul said: 'I have been pierced too. But that was a long time ago.'

'How was that, Bulbul?'

'Well, it was like this,' said Bulbul.'"

"'And Bulbul said: 'Like this, little Vartan. I was eleven, and I had thorns between my legs. And where the thornbush was, there was the gate of promise.'

Bulbul smiled. She said: 'The gate of promise lay between two lobes that listened and watched and asked, and whose task it was to listen to every possible intruder, to learn his intentions and to ask him whether he knew that, behind the closed gate of promise, all dreams and desires were hidden. They were dainty, those listening, watching and asking lobes, though far from mature, and verily, they were no bigger than the lobes of an unborn sheep. And hidden between those lobes was my apparent guardian . . . a thin skin that was as tender as the petal of a young rose but seemed as tough and impenetrable as the goatskin stretched on the Munadi of Bakir's drum, who was a loudmouthed drummer, and town-crier.'

'A drummer and town-crier?'

'Yes, little Vartan, a drummer and town-crier.'"'

"'And one day,' said Bulbul, 'there came a prince on his white horse to carry off a poor little orphan girl. I was that orphan. The time came when we were married before the Imam. And I remember that the Imam said: "Marry your virgin. Peace be to our Prophet Mohammed, who loves the poor and the orphans."'""

* ★ * ★ * ★

"'And Bulbul said: 'The prince took me into his tent and there he showed me what he had between his legs, and it was terrible to look at. For it looked like death that suddenly comes to life.'"'

"''When that living death was forced in between my legs, I cried out to my Father in Heaven, but my Father laughed and said: "Look, it is not death, but the pain from which all life springs. You should have smeared beeswax between your legs, my little dove, or mutton fat, so that the thorns lose their points and the fearful, shrinking lobes open . . . and the skin that is as tender as the petal of a young rose and seems as tough as the drumskin on the drum of the *Munadi* of Bakir . . . now . . . that too becomes soft, to let in the pain."'"'

"''And so,' said Bulbul to little Vartan, 'that is how I was pierced and knew that man is only flesh and blood and so can be pierced.'
    'What cannot be pierced?' asked Vartan.
    'The soul,' said Bulbul. 'And thoughts.'
    'What does that mean?' asked Vartan.
    'That is how things are,' said Bulbul.'"'

"''And how will it be with my tooth?' asked Vartan. 'Is that the living death that stabs my flesh from inside?'
    'Yes, my little lamb,' said Bulbul. 'Later on your little teeth will crush everything that comes between them. They will finally kill so that you may live.'
    'I'm frightened, Bulbul.'
    'Don't be frightened,' said Bulbul.'"'

Here the story-teller's voice grew lighter. The pictures disappeared somewhere in the past.
    'We are alone,' said the story-teller. 'You and I, the Meddah and the last thought.'
    'Does the story end there?'
    'What story?' asked the story-teller.
    'The story of my father?'
    'Of course it goes on. It's hardly started.'

CHAPTER THREE

'When your father's first tooth came through and was suddenly there, and his mother realized that he wasn't a toothless creature any more but a man that could bite and crunch . . . and so kill too . . . she said to him: "Soon you won't need my milk any more. I'll sprinkle pepper on my nipples to get you out of the way of it, to spoil the pleasure you get from your endless sucking. And I'll spoonfeed you with the right sorts of food, fill your mouth with it, and I'll tell you, you're not a sucker any more, you're a biter." And your father's mother laughed, put a finger in his mouth and felt his tooth and said: "We must have a party."'

'The Armenians love parties,' said the story-teller. 'They have much more fun at their parties than the Turks do at theirs. But your father's "first tooth party" was the first party in his life given in his honour. When he was born Hagob had dished out raisins, nuts and schnapps to all the people, while Zovinar and old Hamest served sweet rice pudding and fresh well-water with mulberry syrup to everyone who looked into the *oda* through the open doorway. But now they boiled *hadig* all day, and their neighbours joined in to help. *Hadig* was made from chick-peas and bulgur, with cinnamon of course and sugar and nuts and other delicious ingredients that Zovinar and Hamest wouldn't tell about. Hayk, the first of the Armenians, had loved *hadig*, and he had known that *hadig* was a puddingy sort of food which, cooled and rinsed with cold water, turns into a wobbly cake which is surely the best cake in the world. And so at that time, on Mount Ararat, he said to his wife: "If *harissa*, that gristly, fat, overcooked stew of meat and wheat grains, is to become the Armenians' first national dish, then sweet *hadig* – my favourite dish – must at any rate become the second." And

Hayk said: "When my descendants get their first teeth, their mothers must give a *hadig* party. And they must invite to the party everyone who could become a mother or who has already done so."

'And so it was,' said the story-teller. 'When they learned that it was true about your father's first tooth, the village women streamed in from all the neighbouring huts and houses to celebrate the Khatisians' *hadig* party.'

'So you can picture it: there is little Vartan in his cradle, gnashing the teeth he hasn't really got yet – he's just got one! – and clamping his lips together because he doesn't want to show his little tooth. He's going to have to show it, though, because anyone who sees his first tooth will never lose their own teeth in all their lives.

"Why doesn't he open his mouth?" asks his grandmother. "He really must let us see his tooth."

"I don't know," says Vartan's mother.

"Somebody must make him laugh!"

"But he's such a serious child, he never laughs."

"It would be ridiculous, it seems to me, if he didn't laugh. We must do what my mother used to do to me."

"What was that?"

"Hold a *hadig* cake under his nose and put another one on his little head."

"Will that make him open his mouth?"

"Naturally. He'll laugh and let people see his first tooth."'

'So that's what happened,' said the story-teller. 'Vartan's mother waved a round *hadig* cake to and fro under the baby's nose and put another one on top of his little head. And Vartan, who was such a serious child, suddenly began to laugh and let everybody see his first tooth.

"He shall have teeth until he's a hundred and twenty," said his grandmother. And all the guests murmured "A hundred and twenty!" And they went over to the cradle and said to him: "*Achket louis*", which means light in your eyes. And they said the same to Vartan's parents. Many of them cried as they kissed Zovinar and said the same thing to her, "*Achket louis*".'

'What does light in your eyes mean?' asked the last thought.

And the story-teller said: 'It really ought to be: may your eyes shine.'

'Yes. Can't you wish people anything better than that?'

'No,' said the story-teller. 'If anyone has dull eyes, things aren't going well for him. But anyone whose eyes shine has overcome the darkness. It's as if there was bright day in his heart.'

'When a child first tries to walk the Armenians celebrate the *shekerli* party, the "first-step party", for they say the direction he takes with his first step shows the way of his life.'

'On Vartan's first-step day the whole village seemed to have gathered in the Khatisians' *oda*, though there wasn't really room for everybody. But anyone who wasn't there was there in thought, or they would say to some relative or neighbour who was going to be there: "Tell me what it was like, and then I can tell people afterwards that I was there."

'It was like this,' said the story-teller. 'Vartan's mother had cooked a lot of *baklava* in the *tonir* and put it on copper *sofras*, handy little trays that were passed round by the grandmother and the father's elder brothers and sisters. The last little bit of *baklava* out of the pan, a nicely done little bit, she had tied round Vartan's right foot, with a red ribbon. Vartan sat in the middle of the room crying and hung on to his mother's legs with his hands, as if he wanted to say to his mother: "What is all this silly party? And what is it they all want me to do?"

"Today you will determine what is to become of you later on," said his mother. And with that she lifted him up and put him down on both feet. "Now, off you go, my brave little pasha," she said. And she winked at him, looked round and winked at the guests, and said: "Look, now you'll see what will become of him." But she didn't let go of him.'

'"Why don't you let him go, Zovinar?" asked one of the guests.

"I don't know," said Zovinar.

"I had a dream the other day," said Hagob, who was standing next to Zovinar. "I dreamed that our Vartan would become a fisherman."

"Rubbish," said his grandmother. "Dreams can't determine what's to become of him."

"So who is going to decide it?"

"His little legs will decide it."

"Why his legs?"

"Because his little head decides where his legs are going."

"Well, we'll soon see," said Hagob. And he said to his wife: "Let the little pasha go!"'

'But Zovinar still didn't let him go.

"What's the matter?" asked his grandmother.

"There's nothing the matter," said Zovinar.

Hagob, his father, burst out laughing. He turned to the guests. "Now look," he said. "The *shekerli* game is just starting."

Hagob gulped with excitement and stopped laughing. He said softly to the guests: "We've put the water-bucket behind the *tonir*. If our Vartan goes to the water-bucket and catches hold of it, or even puts his hands in the water, then he'll become a fisherman."

"And if not?" asked one of the guests.

"Well, then of course he won't," said Hagob. Hagob said: "But if he goes past the bucket and comes up to the fire – the fire in the *tonir*, where Zovinar cooked the *baklava* – and if he stays there, then he'll be a workman."

"Yes, a workman," said Zovinar. "And that isn't bad either."

"And if he touches the Bible that's lying by his cradle," said his grandmother, "he'll become a religious man, perhaps even a priest."

"Yes, a priest," said Vartan's father. Some of the people clapped their hands and shouted: "A priest! A priest!"

Hagob seemed not to be joining in any more. He looked round him uncertainly and scratched his head.

"If he goes to the cowshed, he'll be a farmer," said Zovinar.

"Right," said Hagob.

"He'll till his fields and he'll watch for the rain and the sun."

"That's right," said Hagob.

"But if he goes to the door and trips out into the open air, then he'll be an adventurer."

"An adventurer?"

"Yes."

"What's an adventurer?"

"I don't exactly know."

One of the guests said: "An adventurer is a man who risks something in life, like a businessman."

"A businessman?"

"Yes."

"You mean a real businessman?"

"Of course."

And now the great-grandmother, who was already feeble-minded and just sat by the *tonir* staring, burst out laughing. She suddenly woke up. "A businessman," she giggled. "He'll be a millionaire."

Hagob nodded slowly. "A millionaire?"

"Why not?" said Zovinar. "She may be right. Perhaps he really will become a businessman . . . and make millions . . . and make us all happy."'

'Zovinar was still holding her son, though little Vartan was now beginning to cry and starting to wave his arms about and stamp his feet because he wanted to run about.

"Well, what do you think?" asked Hagob. And now he asked them all. "What do you all think? Is he going to be a farmer or a workman or a fisherman or a priest or a businessman?"'

'The people looked eagerly at little Vartan, whom his mother had now let go. Vartan stopped crying. Suddenly he was standing all alone by himself on his two unsteady legs; he looked round and tripped over to the water-bucket where it stood by the *tonir*. Somebody must have given the bucket a little kick, for the water was making pretty ripples, and as the morning sun, looking warmly into the room, had made the rippling water smile, it looked to Vartan as if the water was smiling at him, so it was no wonder that Vartan went over to look at the smiling, shining water-bucket more closely. But the bucket was close by the *tonir*, and his grandmother had put a lot of *tezek* into the fire so that it was burning brightly and crackling. That distracted Vartan's attention.

"He's going to be a fisherman," said his mother. "Look, he's going up to the water-bucket, and I bet he'll put his hands in it."

"Then a fisherman he shall be," said Hagob, his father.

But then someone called out from the crowd. "No. He didn't stay by the bucket. He's going to the *tonir*. He's attracted by the fire."

And another cried: "He'll be a workman." And everybody called out "A workman! A workman!" The people clapped their hands, some of them whistled, others laughed or giggled. "Then he'll always make a living," cried somebody.

But Vartan didn't stay either by the bucket or by the *tonir*, nor yet by the Bible that lay by his cradle. He went over towards the cowshed, and heard the voices of the animals coming from it.

"He's going to be a farmer," said his grandmother. "I knew it all the time. A true Khatisian has to be a farmer."

"That's true," said Hagob. "He's got my blood in his veins."

"Mine too," said Zovinar.

But Vartan didn't run into the cowshed, although the animals' voices lured him. He turned round and ran to the open doorway, for that was where the early morning sunlight was coming over the threshold. And the early morning brought the scent of meadows, flowers and trees with it, and the warbling of birds, which was prettier and more seductive than the dull voices of the animals in the cowshed.

"He'll fall over," cried someone. And another cried: "No, he's not the kind to fall on his nose before he knows what he wants."

"Look, he's going to the doorway!"

"He's going to be an adventurer."

"A businessman!"

"A businessman!"

Even his great-grandmother came to life again. "Yes, a businessman. He'll make millions." And she stretched out her wrinkled hands towards Vartan and called: "*Achket louis*! Light in your eyes, my little lamb."'

'And in fact,' said the story-teller, 'your father toddled over to the doorway and for a moment it really looked as if he were going outside. But that didn't happen.'

'What did happen, Meddah?'

'Your father stopped on the threshold,' said the Meddah. 'He stood there and looked out into the open with his big, velvety eyes, and didn't take another step.'

'The people were disappointed,' said the Meddah. 'They tried to egg your father on, but he wouldn't go any further. He just stood there in the doorway as if he were scared of the great world outside. And as the priest was among the guests, Hagob asked him what it could mean. And the priest thought for a little while, then he said: "He won't be a businessman or any other sort of adventurer, because he doesn't trust himself in real life."

"But he is looking out," said Hagob.

"True," said the priest. "He's one that looks, but doesn't take anything on."

"And he didn't go into the cowshed either. And he didn't want to know anything about the fire or the Bible or the water-bucket."

And the feeble-witted great-grandmother called out: "My Vartan looks!"

And the people laughed and said: "He just stops on the threshold and looks out. The bets are that he won't do anything."

One of the guests spat in his hand, rubbed the spit in his eyes, laughed and said: "He'll just be a spectator."

And another said: "A dreamer."

And the priest said: "Perhaps he'll be a poet?"'

'When the priest said that, Vartan's mother began to tear her hair and swayed towards the *tonir* in distress. It looked as if she wanted to sprinkle hot ashes on her head. Hagob quickly brought her back. It was over. The good mood was quite dissipated. The guests were upset. Hagob couldn't hear what they were muttering to each other, nor the words of comfort that some called out to Zovinar.

"It's not as bad as all that," he said soothingly to Zovinar. "Better a poet than nothing at all."

"But he won't be able to feed his family."

"Then we'll feed them," said Hagob.

"His descendants will starve."

"They won't starve," said Hagob.'

'The mayor of Yedi Su was among the guests,' said the story-teller, 'the Mukhtar Ephrem Abovian, easily recognizable by his monstrous moustache, which he wore in the Kurdish style, and the spotless red fez that hid his totally bald head.'

'Why did he cover his bald head with his fez?'

'Because any man who thinks anything of himself always keeps his fez on. But also because of all the flies and the way their legs tickled him. For the Mukhtar Ephrem Abovian is a very sensitive man.'

'And what about the spotlessness of the fez?'

'It's the only clean fez in the village.'

'So he's a very particular man?'

'Yes, you can really say that.'

'Is there anything else that's special about the fez?'

'Yes, my little lamb. It's quite a famous fez.'

'Famous for what?'

'Well, it's like this,' said the story-teller. 'When a new mayor is elected in the village, all the candidates put their fezes upside down on a copper *sofra*. The oldest man in the village and every member of his household puts a nut in the fez of the man of the choice. And whoever gets the most nuts in his fez becomes mayor.'

'Did Ephrem Abovian get the most nuts at the last election?'

'Certainly,' said the story-teller. 'For Ephrem Abovian is the richest man in the village, and nobody wants to be at odds with him.'

'Is the richest man always elected mayor?'

'Yes,' said the story-teller. 'It's always the richest man who is most powerful.'

'If you want to see things with my eyes,' said the story-teller to the last thought, 'and if you use your imagination a bit, you will now see that Vartan's mother takes fresh *baklava* out of the *tonir*, fills the copper *sofras* and passes them round among the guests. As you see, my little lamb, she offers something to the mayor and his wife first of all, then goes from one guest to another. The last one she offers anything to is the water-carrier Hovhannes. He's the poorest man in the village, has neither wife nor children, is dressed in rags, smells like his donkey's farts in the unventilated stable, stutters, squints slightly, has a facial twitch, and is altogether a creature to be pitied. I never understood why the children jeered at him and the dogs worried him.'

'Is he the village idiot, then?'

'Yes, he's also the village idiot.'

'The mayor's wife is pregnant, and, as you see, at this moment she nudges her husband, whispers something into his ear and points at the water-carrier.

"It can't be true," says the mayor.

"But it is," says his wife. "The water-carrier has the evil eye."

"What about it?" says the mayor.

"He keeps looking at my stomach," says his wife. "I bet there's going to be an accident."

"What sort of accident?"

"Our child might be a daughter instead of a son."

"So what?" says the mayor. "Haven't we got seven boys already? The eighth one really ought to be a girl."'

'Now Vartan's mother comes up with the *sofra*.

"Another piece of *baklava*?" she asks the mayor's wife.

"I've suddenly lost my appetite," says the mayor's wife. "Couldn't you turn that water-carrier out of the house?"

"He's our guest today," says Vartan's mother. "I can't do that."

"Do you think, Zovinar, that old devil's got the evil eye?"

"No," says Vartan's mother.

"He keeps on looking at my stomach."

"He's looked at my stomach too," says Vartan's mother, "and as you see, my little Vartan has turned out a perfectly normal child. He's a handsome boy and although he's only one and a half he can run like a boy of two."

"Yes, he's a handsome child, and strong. But do you think it's normal that he's going to be a poet?"

"No, I certainly don't."

"Do you think that's perhaps got something to do with the evil eye?"

"You mean, the water-carrier . . ."

"Everything's possible."

"I must ask my husband about it first."'

★ ★ ★

'And Vartan's mother asks Hagob: "Do you think the water-carrier has got the evil eye?"

"We must ask the priest," says Hagob.'

'And Hagob asks the priest. And the priest is not quite sure, and says: "Everything is possible, Hagob Efendi. For the water-carrier has no wife. And as far as I know, as a priest, he never has had one. And the other day I caught him out."

"Caught him out?"

"In the stable behind the church. He had mounted my donkey."

"Mounted it – how do you mean?"

"Well, I'm sure you know what I mean, Hagob Efendi. He was fornicating with the donkey, which is actually not a donkey but a jennet."

"You don't say, Vartapad."

"And it is possible that he's got the evil eye, for no human being should fornicate with a donkey."'

CHAPTER FOUR

'The night after the first-step party Hagob and his wife slept badly and had extraordinary dreams. When they woke in the morning Hagob said to his wife:

"I dreamed that the water-carrier's evil eye had turned the boy in the mayor's wife's belly into a little girl."

"I dreamed the same thing," says Zovinar.

"Now it's the custom," says Hagob, "for girls to be affianced while they're still in the cradle; at any rate I was engaged to you before you knew your name."

"On the day after my baptism."

"The day after your baptism."

"You were older than me, my Hagob, you were already three and even knew how to count."

"I could count up to three," says Hagob.

"Yes," says Zovinar.'

'Zovinar says: "Then your father came to my father and asked for my hand in your name. And the two men exchanged coins, threw them in the *tonir* and finally sealed the engagement with a handshake."

"That's it," says Hagob.'

'And Hagob says: "I didn't know the water-carrier had the evil eye, but as we both dreamt about it, it must be the case."

"Yes," says Zovinar.

And Hagob says: "So there we are."

And Zovinar says: "If the water-carrier's evil eye turns the little boy in the mayor's wife's belly into a little girl, perhaps it wouldn't be too bad, for the mayor's a rich man and he could affiance his little girl to our Vartan, who was also bewitched in my belly, or else he would never have decided to be a poet."

"You're quite right," says Hagob. And he adds: "I'll talk to the mayor about it tomorrow."'

'As it happened, the pregnant lady brought a boy into the world. It wasn't until Vartan was three that the grapevine blessed the mayor and his wife with a little girl.'

'On the very day after the baptism – and that was the ninth day – Hagob went to the Mukhtar's house to ask in Vartan's name for his daughter's hand. The mayor broke in that he had no desire to give his daughter to a good-for-nothing who was going to be a poet, but Hagob calmed him down and pointed out the Khatisians' land marched with that of the mayor and Mukhtar, and since it was so and not otherwise, there would in the future be no disagreements about grazing rights and so on. What's more, said Hagob, he had a cock called Abdul Hamid which was definitely the best cock in Yedi Su, and if the mayor and Mukhtar would like it, then it went without saying that he, Hagob, as Vartan's father, would without question lend that self-same cock called Abdul Hamid, should that be the wish of the Mukhtar and, naturally, of his wife.'

'And so it was,' said the story-teller. 'The two men exchanged two coins, threw them in the *tonir* and shook hands. Then they drank schnapps and drank to Vartan's health and to the health of his bride, who had been christened the day before by the name of *Arpine* – the Armenian name for the rising sun.

Everyone in the house congratulated your three-year-old father on his engagement. And the neighbours came into the *oda*, took your father in their arms and said: "*Achket louis*". Some of the neighbours said: "May Jesus Christ protect your bride from the Kurds."'

'Were they afraid the Kurds would rape her before my father had known her?"

'That's it, my little lamb.'

'Naturally your three-year-old father didn't understand what was going on around him, why people were congratulating him and what all this was about the maidenhood that his bride had to preserve for him. He didn't even know that his father had said, as he was exchanging coins with the mayor: "Look after my daughter-in-law, Mukhtar Bey, don't let anyone rape her."

And the mayor had said: "Hagob Efendi, your son will wed a virgin. That I promise you. No Kurd will carry her off and have his way with her. I'm on good terms with the Kurd sheikh Suleyman, and I pay him his taxes promptly, and give him cattle and grain, and I'll also pay him the bride-tax, half the bride-price that you'll be giving me for my daughter in due course."'

'But what does that mean, Meddah? Are the Kurds really keen on little girls still in the cradle?'

'No, my little lamb. Not until the girls reach puberty, about ten or eleven, often not till twelve.'

'I've told you already, my little lamb, that it's not the town Kurds the Armenians are afraid of, not even the semi-nomads in those dirty Kurd villages. It's the wild, rapacious mountain tribes. They have their spies everywhere. They know exactly what's going on in the Armenian villages, who's wealthy and who isn't, who has a son and who has a daughter. They know how old the girls are and when they become pubescent.'

'And then they just carry them off. Believe me. That's true. That's why the girls are married as soon as possible, for it's only virgins they're after.'

'To Christian virgins in the remote, undefended villages of the plateaux, the wild Kurd is every inch of him the symbol of a thrusting, flashy, irresistible penis. Everything about him is male. Even the dark, piercing gaze. When the Kurds gallop through the village after the harvest to collect the taxes for the sheikh, the girls piss themselves in their laced-up trousers with fright and excitement. But with many of them the piss only drips a bit on to the inside of the naked thigh, because the lobes between the virgin's legs cling together from sheer fright; they listen, test and ask no more and remain desperately folded; sometimes they can't be separated, as if the holy Virgin Mary had sewn them up for safety.'

'I see the question in your eyes, my little lamb. And I'm telling you: it is so. The Armenians can't protect their womenfolk, because they're not allowed to carry weapons.'

'Because they're Christians?'

'That's it.'

'And the Kurds?'

'The Kurds are Muslims. Every Muslim has a right to a weapon.'

'And what about the Turkish authorities? Why don't they protect the Armenians from the Kurds?'

'Because they just aren't interested, my little lamb. They're afraid that unbelievers may be rebellious, and therefore they find it only right that the Kurds should terrorize them, hold them in check, so to speak, as the long arm of the Sultan.'

'And what about the courts?'

'What courts?'

'I mean, if a Kurd is brought before the court?'

'That does sometimes happen in the towns, but not in remote villages. For look, my little lamb: the few saptiehs there are in the villages are afraid of the Kurds themselves. So who's going to arrest the Kurds and bring them before the court? And even the brave saptiehs – if there were any – could they wage war against a whole tribe of Kurds? Or even track the Kurds down? In the ravines and gorges in the mountains, anywhere between the two seas?'

'So it's hopeless?'

'It's hopeless, my little lamb. And even if anyone succeeded in bringing a Kurd before the court, it wouldn't do any good; Christians and unbelievers never get justice before the Kadi, even if they have two Muslim witnesses.'

'And they don't have, anyway?'

'Usually not, even if they pay a couple of false witnesses.'

'Can that be done?'

'It can. But in the case of a girl who's been carried off and raped, it wouldn't give the plaintiff much comfort, neither the girl nor her father.'

'Why, Meddah?'

'Well, why indeed my little lamb? Can even a successful case restore lost innocence, or the hymen lost without trace? And what Armenian man who thinks anything of himself would ever marry such a girl? To carry out the holy act with her later and father Christian children who would bear his name?

So you see, even if you win your case, it's pretty pointless.'

'So the mayor promised to give your father a virgin, to take care of her and protect her from the Kurds. And also the only saptieh in the village, the flat-footed, pockmarked Shekir Efendi, promised to do his best to protect the child. Later, after the betrothal, he drank *raki* with the mayor in the coffee-house.

"You can never know, Mukhtar Bey," he said to the mayor. "They say those Kurds won't touch babies, that they don't prod them with their fingers or stick other things into them, like the thin bones of a young lamb, say, or sticks from the dwarf oak or just flower stalks or something like that, but I have heard recently that they've been carrying off babies."

"What for?" asked the mayor.

"To feed them up until they're big enough and bleed by themselves."

"What do you mean, bleed?"

"Every month, the way they do."

"And then?"

"Then they are deflowered without using any sticks or young lambs' bones or flower stalks or anything like that."

"How then, efendi?"

"Well, the usual way, Mukhtar Bey. With what the Kurds have between their thighs, and that's generally pretty impressive."'

'They drank *raki* and then sweet coffee in little bowls. The mayor knew that he was only saying these things to scare him, so as to get his usual tip. Together with his *baksheesh* you also give him meat and wheat flour and fruit from the garden.

"And you'll really look after her, Shekir Efendi?"

"Like the apple of my eye," said the saptieh. "Allah be my witness. And next time the Kurds come to drive off the cattle, I'll

210

stand outside your door and keep guard so that they won't take the child as well." And the saptieh tapped his old rifle with his knuckle and said: "I'll guard her like my own daughter."

"But you haven't got any children, Shekir Efendi. So you haven't got a daughter."

"Unfortunately not," said the saptieh. "My wife has run away, and no one knows where she's got to."

"Why did she run away, Saptieh Agah?"

"Because she couldn't get any children," said the saptieh, "and because I threatened to kill her if she didn't produce some."

The mayor nodded. He said: "Yes, Shekir Efendi." And he thought: "I hope he won't lay hands on the child when he's looking after her, for he's got no wife and he has it off with donkeys and mounts them from behind, just like the water-carrier, who is possessed of a devil and has the evil eye.'"

'There was one other man in the village who was said to have the evil eye. That was the red-headed village smith, Kevork Hacobian. Now it was the case that many women dyed their hair with henna and consequently had red hair under their veils. The smith's hair, however, was not dyed with henna or with any artificial colouring from Frankistan. It was God-given. But it was most unusual, and therefore suspicious. What normal man of Armenian parentage ever had genuine red hair? Had the good God already punished the child in its mother's womb, so that it would be born with red hair? Or was the devil in it somehow? Had the smith's mother perhaps got mixed up with the devil-worshippers, or with Gypsies, who all have the evil eye, as everybody knows? Or was the priest Kapriel Hamadian right when he said once in the graveyard: "Yes, it's true. I know the cause of his red hair, for the mother of the red-headed smith has confessed everything to me."

"But she never goes to confession, Vartapad."

"True. But I dreamed about her confession."

"And what did you dream, Vartapad?"

"I dreamed," said the priest, "that that red-headed devil's mother had come to confession."

"And what did she confess?"

"She said to me: 'Vartapad, do you remember that red-headed

Irish missionary who was here in the village once, just before my son, the red-headed smith, was born?'

'Of course,' I said. 'I remember.'

'That false saint wanted at that time to convert all your lambs to Catholicism, although everyone knows that our Saviour Jesus Christ can't have two natures, as the Catholics believe, but logically only one, the divine and that our faith, the Gregorian, is the only true faith.'

'Quite right,' I said. 'And what do you wish to confess, my daughter?'

'I dreamt,' said the mother of the red-headed smith, 'that that red-headed Irish missionary had had me in my sleep at that time, though I'm not quite sure, for I was young then and slept very deeply, so deeply that I hardly noticed anything.'

'Then it's possible that that false saint had you, or could have done?'

'Yes, Vartapad.'

'And that could explain your son's red hair?'

'Yes, Vartapad.'"'

'However it may have been,' said the story-teller, 'to Vartan that red-headed smith was the most important man outside his own family.'

'How was that, then?'

'He was Vartan's godfather.'

'His godfather?'

'Yes, my little lamb. The red-headed smith was your father's godfather, for at the time of the baptism Hagob couldn't find anyone else to be godfather.'

'Wasn't Hagob afraid of his evil eye?'

'No,' said the story-teller. 'For little Vartan's grandmother, who they used to say could see through everyone, had said: "Hagob, the smith is just the right man to be godfather, for he has kind eyes. There's nothing of the devil in them." And if she said that, then it was sure to be true.'

'Everybody in the village knew that Armenian smiths are the real saviours of the world, although the smith's enemies, and people who were jealous of him, would not agree with that.'

'How can Armenian smiths be the saviours of the world?'

'The Armenian legends tell us so, especially those about Mount Ararat.'

'How is that, Meddah?'

'Well, here's how it is, my little lamb.'

'Imprisoned in Mount Ararat there is a giant . . . the Persian giant Meher. He is chained to the rock wall inside the mountain. He has horns growing on his forehead. Savage dogs, black ravens and poisonous snakes guard him. And they say that one day, on the eve of Ascension Day, he will break the chains and emerge from the mountain to destroy the world.'

'How will he do that, Meddah?'

'Well, now, my little lamb, the earth is a *sofra* made of clay, a semicircular tray on which the good God has laid out all his treasures, all the things he loves. The *sofra* is held up by angels, who are changed regularly. All the heavenly bodies revolve round this clay *sofra* that we men call the earth. When the giant breaks his chains and comes raging and roaring out of the mountain, then he will simply overturn the *sofra* with his huge, frightful hands, and all that God loves will fall into the abyss and die.'

'Even the flowers?'

'Those too.'

'And the trees?'

'Those too.'

'But they are growing on the earth.'

'That's true, my little lamb. But that's how it will be.'

'I thought that only things that are not growing can fall, I mean things that aren't fixed and can move about?'

'No, my little lamb. When the giant overturns the *sofra*, nothing more will remain on it.'

'Nothing more of the things that God loves?'

'Nothing more, my little lamb. Everything that God loves will perish. And the whole world will perish, for what sense would there be in a world if everything that God loves had ceased to exist?'

'There would simply be nothing more?'

'That's right.'

* * *

'And what has that got to do with the Armenian smiths?'

'It has a great deal to do with them. From Easter Monday till Ascension Day the smiths in this region beat with their hammer on the anvil three times, early every morning. That gives new strength to the giant's chains, which by Easter are beginning to grow thin. So the giant cannot break loose, and the world will not be destroyed.'

'Are the Armenian smiths the true saviours of the world?'

'They are.'

'Even the red-headed smith Kevork Hacobian, who is my father's godfather?'

'He above all, for he strikes three times on his anvil in the early morning not only between Easter and Ascension Day, but all the year round.'

'Every morning?'

'Yes, my little lamb. Just to make sure. Every morning. And since we're just talking about the time between Easter and Ascension Day, I must quickly tell you a little story.'

'On Ascension Day the Armenians in the village of Yedi Su celebrate a special holiday, a feast of heathen origin, which has little to do with the ascension of our Saviour to Heaven. And yet it does have something to do with it, for I'm sure that Christ would be glad if he knew that on the very day of his ascension the children in the village of Yedi Su count the stars in heaven.'

'How is that, Meddah?'

'Well, it's like this,' said the Meddah. 'On Ascension Day, early in the morning, all the children gather on the village square. Then they go off in groups to the meadows and fields, pluck flowers and adorn themselves with them, This feast is called *vijak*, and it has something to do with the sun-god Mir.'

'Is it a flower festival?'

'No, my little lamb. Actually, not. It's the feast of chances, of drawing lots, and of counting the stars.'

'What is that, Meddah?'

'Well, it's just so,' said the Meddah. 'After all the children have adorned themselves with flowers, the little girls fetch earthen jugs.

214

With those they go to the seven wells. On the way there they may
not look either sideways or backwards. But in the village of Yedi
Su they take the water-carrier with them, for it isn't easy for little
girls to draw water out of the seven wells.'

'What does the water-carrier do?'

'He lowers the heavy water-buckets down to the bottom of the
seven wells, brings them up to the daylight again filled to the brim,
and puts them down at the feet of the little girls, who may not look
sideways or backwards. As soon as that is done, the little girls, all
festooned in flowers, bend down, hold their hands clasped behind
their backs, and in their turn draw water – from the buckets, of
course, but they draw it with their mouths.'

'With their mouths?'

'Yes, my little lamb. The little girls act as if they were going to
drink the fresh water. But they don't drink it, they spit the water
into the brown clay jugs they have brought with them to the seven
wells. So they fill the clay jugs, put a pebble or some object in them
and go off to the church. There the priest Kapriel Hamadian is
waiting for them; his task is to bless the water in the little girls'
jugs on Ascension Day. And that he does. And after that he leads
the little girls with their jugs seven times round the church.'

'And then, Meddah?'

'Then the little girls go home and hide their jugs full of holy water.
When the evening comes they take their jug up to the roof, put it
down by the smoke outlet and leave it there, so that the holy *vijak*-
water in the jug can count the stars.'

'Does the holy water really count the stars?'

'Yes, my little lamb. Just like the sun-god Mir, who counts the
stars in the heavens every night to see whether all the sun's children
are still there.'

CHAPTER FIVE

'When Vartan was three years old the older boys in the village took
him to the meadows and fields on Ascension Day. They decorated
him with flowers and carried him on their shoulders. Then they
went along behind the girls, followed them to the seven wells, teased
them and pelted them with birds' eggs, which the boys had collected
in advance. One of the boys said to Vartan: "Listen, young 'un.
The girls will hide the jugs with the holy water. We'll try to find the
hiding-place before the girls can take them up to the roof so that
they can count the stars. Listen, young 'un. You steal a jug and
then ask one of the girls to pay a forfeit, or else you won't give it
back."

And your three-year-old father, who had no idea what a forfeit
was, asked: "A forfeit?"

And the older boy laughed and said: "Yes, young 'un, a forfeit.
The girl must give you a kiss, or else you don't give the jug back,
see?"

And your father laughed, although he didn't understand a thing.'

'At the *vijak* feast, when the boys in the village asked your three-
year-old father to get a kiss as a forfeit, something else happened
that your father was still able to remember later.'

'What was that, Meddah?'

'It was an incident with that silly water-carrier.'

'What happened to him?'

'The boys were looking all day for the little girls' hidden clay pots.
During the search they came on the water-carrier, who had just
mounted the Khatisians' donkey. It was towards evening.'

'The donkey?'

'Yes.'

'Was it a shabby old beast like Bulbul's donkey?'

'No. It was called Ceyda.'

'How did the water-carrier get into the cowshed to mount Ceyda, when you have to go through the living-room to get to the shed?'

'The donkey Ceyda wasn't in the shed, because the grandmother had left it in the yard, tethered of course.'

'And what about the water-carrier?'

'The boys jeered at him, pulled him off the donkey, tied him up and dragged him up to the flat roof of the Khatisians' house. Your three-year-old father saw it all.'

'Even the water-carrier copulating with the donkey?'

'Even that.'

'And how they tied the water-carrier up and took him up to the roof?'

'Yes, my little lamb. He saw it all. And he even saw the howling water-carrier's dripping penis, which they took hold of to pull him by – sadistic as only boys can be – he saw how they pushed it back under the messy trousers before they dragged him up to the roof. As you see, a poor, crazy village idiot. One of the boys said to your father: "We'll leave the water-carrier Hovhannes on the roof all night as a punishment, so that he can count the stars."'

'Did the water-carrier really spend the whole night on the roof? And did he really count the stars?'

'No, my little lamb,' said the Meddah. 'It's not a good thing for a man with the evil eye to count the stars beside the holy water. So Vartan's grandfather fetched the poor chap down again.'

'Your father's grandfather – I haven't told you anything about him yet, because he was completely overshadowed by the grandmother. He was a quiet man, quite the opposite of his wife Hamest. He was said to have been quite jolly once, full of amusing ideas, but things had changed.'

'Did something happen in the life of my great-grandfather, who would have been my father's grandfather, that turned him into such a quiet person?'

'Yes, my little lamb,' said the Meddah.'

*   *   *

And the Meddah said: 'In the winter the wild Kurds, high up in the mountains, send their old and sick down to the Armenian villages to pass the winter. Those old and sick Kurds are uninvited guests, but no one dares to turn them away. For the most part they live in the cowshed, taking the food they need of course from the Armenians' store-rooms and then going back to the shed. When the spring comes they disappear again.'

'Why does no one dare turn them away?'

'Because if they did they'd have the whole Kurdish tribe on their backs, not to pass the winter in the cowshed but to avenge the old and sick members of their tribe. The Kurd sheikh would send his horsemen into the village to cut off the men's pricks and rape the women and burn the house down.

Well, in the year 1846 your father's grandfather had refused to let the old and sick Kurds sleep in his cowshed. But that did him no good at all. On the very next day a hundred armed Kurd horsemen came galloping into the town. They dragged Vartan's grandfather to the market-place, stripped him naked and were just going to cut off his prick when his wife, Hamest, ran up howling and begged the Kurds for mercy. The Kurds were mollified and didn't cut his prick off, but they cut off the lobes of his ears and then had him whipped. That was a lesson the grandfather never forgot.'

'Didn't the villagers resist?'

'They never resist, my little lamb. The village's one saptieh was shivering with fright, gnawing his dirty fingernails and grinning stupidly when one of the Kurds took his rifle away from him. The Kurd said to him: "Don't make a fuss about it. The rifle is older than you are. The government will give you a new one."'

'And the Armenian men in the village?'

'They just stood round the village square in silence.'

'My little lamb, it really is no wonder that the Turks and the Kurds regard the Armenians as the most cowardly people in the world. It's as if they were only born to bare their backs to the whip and their pricks to the scimitar, just as their women's cunts only seem to be there so that the circumcised pricks of the faithful can have a good time.'

* * *

'After the affair with the Kurds, the public shame and the fear that he had suffered, this grandfather acquired a piping voice . . . and it really seemed as if the Kurds had not stopped short at the threat of emasculation, but had actually cut off the still youthful grandfather's male pride with the scimitar. Now it is a fact, my little lamb, that a man's dignity, and also his pride, dangle between his legs. But dignity and pride dwell also in the head, for there is a secret bond between a man's head and the swinging pride between his thighs. So it is no wonder that many a man who has accepted the humiliation of his male dignity without resistance sometimes believes he has actually lost his male organ.

As I told you, that grandfather was a quiet man, kept himself in the background, had no bass voice and twittered like a sick bird if he wanted to complain about the grandmother's domineering nature and stormy temper; he began to drink, and finally became a drunkard. But I don't want to dwell on that sort of thing, my little lamb, on the grandfather's imagined loss of his sexual organ or his treble voice. I'd rather talk about his kindheartedness . . . and the remakable blanket he gave your father one day.'

'Vartan was his youngest grandchild, and that may have been the reason the grandfather was particularly fond of him. One day he gave Vartan a brightly coloured hand-knitted blanket, and told him: "This *yorgan* comes from the time of Sultan Ibrahim, from the year 1642. You shall have it, my little lamb. And your firstborn son must have it." And your father, who was only just four, asked: "My firstborn son?" And the grandfather said: "Yes, your son, my little lamb. You'll call him Thovma . . . the same name as mine, just Thovma."

And the grandfather said: "This *yorgan* really does come from the time of Sultan Ibrahim. Do you know who he was, my little lamb?" And because your father didn't know, he said: "Sultan Ibrahim was a man with a tired tool beween his legs, for he had too many wives in his harem. Like all men, the Sultan carried everything that gave him guts in two little sacks under his trousers, jolly little bags they were too, which had once been firm and well-filled but had now become flabby. And his tool was flabby too, and so was everything else that had once been bony and gristly and had stuck out lustfully from those sacks. His wives were beginning to bore him, for not only were there too many of them, but all of them were too willing. However, the Sultan was jealous, for he regarded every one of his wives as his personal property. Now it came to the Sultan's ears one day that one of his wives had been sleeping with a eunuch, although that sounds incredible, for as you know eunuchs don't have any eggs. Do you know what I mean when I say 'eggs', my little dove?"

And your four-year-old father said: "Yes, the cock Abdul Hamid lays an egg every day."

And his grandfather, who didn't often laugh, grinned broadly and said: "Not the cock Abdul Hamid, my little dove, it's the hens that lay the eggs."

And then he said: "So that was how it was with the Sultan Ibrahim's wives: one of them was sleeping with an eggless eunuch. The Sultan tried to learn which one of them it was that had committed adultery, but he simply couldn't find out anything, because the women in the harem backed each other up and gave nothing away. So just guess what the Sultan did?" And because your father couldn't guess, his grandfather said: "This is what happened. One day he had all the women in the harem tied up, all two hundred and eighty of them – that's how many there were – had them stuffed into big sacks loaded with heavy stones, had the sacks taken to the harbour at Constantinople and ordered them all to be thrown into the water so that they were all drowned. And that is what was done."'

'"Is that really true, grandfather?"

"That is true, my little lamb. Turkish history is full of that sort of cruelty, so it's no wonder that the Franks from Frankistan, who in their own way are even more cruel, think the Turks are the cruellest people in the world."'

'"This *yorgan* is home to generations of dead fleas," said the grandfather, "but dead fleas won't bite you, my little dove."'

'And what about live fleas, Meddah?'

'You get used to them,' said the Meddah. 'The Khatisians' house was alive with fleas. They hopped over the carpets and rugs, over the clay pots and oil lamps and pretty well everything. And they were living in your father's new *yorgan* too, which really was very old. As a child your father used to snap at the fleas with his mouth and was delighted when he caught one. Of course by now your father wasn't sleeping in the cradle with the dove and the olive-branch any more, but had his own bed of lambskin. When your grandfather gave him the *yorgan*, he said: "The cradle with the dove and the olive-branch is still empty. But one day your son will sleep in it."

"My son?" asked your father.

And his grandfather said: "Yes, your son Thovma."'

'Your father often played with his little penis, as all small babies do, without realizing how dangerous it was. When the grandfather caught him at it one day, he said: "You must never do that again, or else your son Thovma will never see the light." And he added: "And you'll be as crazy as Hovhannes the water-carrier, for he played with his prick as a little boy too."

Your father said: "But I'm not a water-carrier."

"That's not what I said," said the grandfather. And he said: "Your prick is a tricky toy. Not only can you go mad if you play with it, but it can also turn the most sensible people into *parvanas*." And because your father, barely four years old, didn't know what *parvanas* might be, his grandfather explained: "Well, my little lamb, a *parvana* is a moth from the east which is very common in this district, because it's a district with a lot of sun and flies and mosquitoes. And if anyone plays with that little leg between his thighs too often, then love can go to his head. Then he treats every girl as his sweetheart. And often he can't tell her from the flames in the *tonir*."

"And what happens then?" asked your father.

"Then the lover behaves like a *parvana* and dives blindly into the flames that he mistakes for his sweetheart."

"And what happens then?" asked your father.

"Then there's nothing left of him." said the grandfather.'

*   *   *

'And the grandfather laughed and said: "But never fear, my little lamb, my little pasha, my little dove, progenitor of my great-grandson Thovma. You won't need to play with your little tail later on, when it's really serious and you really feel a longing for a woman in your balls. You won't want to mount a donkey like Hovhannes the water-carrier. And you won't have to become a *parvana* and dive into the flames of the *tonir* for sheer love. We've already picked a bride for you. She's still peeing in her nappies, but she'll wait for you, my little lamb. Her father, who is our mayor, will take care of her. And she'll have a fat bottom, but a decent one. And you will be decent too and enter into the holy bonds of marriage with her. And she'll give you a son, and you will call him Thovma."'

'Yet that was a good time ago,' said the story-teller. 'The begetting of his son Thovma was still in the stars. Even as your father celebrated his fourth birthday, he still didn't know anything about the serious side of engendering children, of the duties of an Armenian man, his responsibility for the extended family, and all the worries. Moreover, at the age of four, your father didn't know anything about Abdul Hamid, who had ascended the Sultan's throne two years before he was born, in 1876. All he knew was that his father had a cock called Abdul Hamid and that from then on all cocks would be called Abdul Hamid. For the cock was destined to have its head chopped off. All Armenians wished that Abdul Hamid would lose his head, for there were so many rumours about him. People were saying that Abdul Hamid wanted to exterminate the Armenians.'

'Your father was still living in a fairy-tale world. And they really were wonderful tales that his grandfather told him. For example, there was the story of Noah's Ark, the angel and the Saviour's sweatband. Shall I tell it to you, my little lamb?'

'Yes, Meddah.'

'Well, this is how it goes,' said the Meddah.

'One day,' said the Meddah, 'the Armenian King Abgar fell sick of leprosy. Then in a dream he heard a voice, which told him: "Only

222

the sun-god Mir can cure you of your leprosy, O Abgar. So you must climb Mount Ararat, up to its highest peak. There you will be near to the sun, and so to the god Mir."

'And it was so,' said the story-teller. 'The king climbed the Armenian mountain. But when he had reached the very top the sky grew dark and the sun was nowhere to be seen. The king staggered here and there, and suddenly he came across the wreck of a ship, which looked like the Ark. And since he'd never heard of Noah's Ark, for he knew neither the Bible, which did already exist, nor the Koran, which didn't . . . anyway, when he saw the wreck, he asked himself in wonder: "How did a ship get on to this mountain?" And behold, when he asked that question, an angel appeared and said: "It was from here the dove once flew down to the country, which would later be called Hayastan, and brought back an olive-branch."

"An olive-branch?" asked the king.

"A sign from the Lord," said the angel, "that the world would once more be saved."'

'And the angel said: "There is no sun-god Mir. And it is in vain that you stand on the highest peak of the Armenian mountain to be near the sun. The sun cannot cure any sickness."

"Who can cure leprosy?" asked the king.

And the angel said: "Jesus of Nazareth."

"Jesus of Nazareth?"

"Yes."

"Where can I find this man?"

"In the land of the Jews," said the angel. "He goes about there fishing for souls."

"So he's a soul-fisher?"

"Yes."

"And a magic doctor?"

"That too."

"Will he make me well if I find him?"

"Only if you truly find him," said the angel.

"And how do I truly find him."

"Only if you believe in him."

"Will I be made well if I believe in him?"

"Yes," said the angel.'

'But the king was suspicious, and first he sent his spies into the land of the Jews to find out if it was true that a man called Jesus of Nazareth could really cure leprosy.

'Well, it so happened,' said the story-teller, 'that the Armenian king's spies arrived in the Holy Land at the very moment that Jesus was preparing to preach the Sermon on the Mount. The king's spies followed the people who were flocking to the mount. And so it happened that they heard the Sermon on the Mount.'

'When Jesus finished his sermon, one of the spies said to the other: "This is an unusual holy man, who blesses the meek and the poor and the simple and even promises them the Kingdom of Heaven. How would such a man heal our king, when our king is neither meek nor poor nor at all simple, and we know anyway that he is going to the gods in heaven?" And they wanted to turn back and leave. But one of the spies said: "That false Saviour has just come down from the mount. And we have a letter for him from our king. We must give it to him."'

'And they gave Jesus the letter from the Armenian king. And Jesus read the letter, and said: "Your king wants to believe in me, and he asks me to go to Hayastan to cure him of leprosy. But I haven't time to make such a long journey on my donkey. I have much to do in the land of the Jews. And I must also go to the city of David, which they call Jerusalem, to drive the traders and money-changers out of the temple." And Jesus said: "And I must go to the Cross that has already been prepared for me."'

'That was a strange speech, and the spies didn't know what to make of it. When Jesus of Nazareth saw the confusion of the king's spies, he took off the sweatband that he had bound round his head before the Sermon on the Mount. Jesus said: "I have sweated a little during the sermon, for it is not easy to persuade the stubborn people that the meek and the poor and the simple are going to the Kingdom of Heaven. Take this cloth with my sweat and give it to your king. And your king will be well again."'

224

*   *   *

'The spies took the sweatband and rode back with it. When they had left the land of the Jews and were riding back to Hayastan through the cedar woods and mountain slopes of the Lebanon, they were suddenly attacked by robbers. Those were the forebears of the wild mountain Kurds. They beat the spies of the Armenian king to death, threw their bodies in the gorge and stole their clothes, their shoes and their horses. They took everything, in fact, except the Saviour's sweatband, dirty and sweaty as it was. They threw that down into one of the deep mountain gorges of the Lebanon, and it lies there to this day.'

The Lord's sweatband . . . pondered the last thought. So it is still lying in one of the gorges of the Lebanon? Why didn't the good God save the king's spies from being killed? Why did they have to die, and the sweatband be lost?

'Tell me, Meddah. What happened to the Armenian king?'

'He died a painful death, my little lamb.'

'And what would have happened to him if he had had the sweatband?'

'He would have been cured of leprosy, my little lamb, and would have adopted the faith of Christianity during the Saviour's lifetime, he and probably also the whole of his people. But it happened just as I've told it to you. He never received the sweatband. And so Armenia remained heathen. It wasn't until AD 301 that Armenia, or Hayastan, became the first Christian state.'

'And that was so,' said the story-teller. 'In Armenia there reigned King Tiridates III, called Tiridates the Great. One day he heard about the apostle Gregory, whom the people called Gregory the Illuminator. He was going about Hayastan preaching Christianity. Some said he was the son of the escaped regicide, who had killed the father of the present king, and that he would have to pay the penalty for the crimes of the murderer. King Tiridates III was afraid that the murderer's son would also kill him, so he had Saint Gregory arrested, put in chains and thrown into a den of lions.'

'That should have been the end of Saint Gregory. But, behold . . .

when the king's soldiers threw Saint Gregory into the cave, the good God turned the hearts of the lions into lambs' hearts. Gregory lived in the lions' cave for many years. Secret Christians supplied him with food and drink. But King Tiridates went mad. Soon he began to walk on all fours like the wild animals with lambs' hearts in Gregory's cave.'

'One day, when King Tiridates had a lucid moment – which happened now and again – his sister Chosroviducht said to him: "Gregory is still alive. He has changed the hearts of the wild animals into lambs' hearts. He is a magician, and he could surely conjure your madness away."'

'And so the king's soldiers fetched Saint Gregory out of the lions' den and brought him before the king and his sister. She said to Gregory: "Can you cure my brother, the King of the Armenians, of his madness?"
    "Yes," said Gregory. "For the king is only possessed by the devil."
    "How can you cure him, Gregory?"
    "With the Bible," said Gregory.'

'And Gregory swung the Holy Scriptures three times round the head of the mad king, and spoke words like those the Saviour spoke when he healed the sick and the lame. And he asked the sick king, before he became confused in his mind again, "Do you believe in the Son of God, who has healed the sick and the lame?"
    And the king said: "Yes. I believe." And from that moment he was cured.'

'When the Armenian King Tiridates adopted Christianity, he also converted the whole royal family. And the whole of his people. And that is how it happened that in AD 301 the Armenians were the first people in the world to declare Christianity the state religion.'

'The Armenians were fated to suffer for Christianity like no other people on earth,' said the story-teller. 'Among the many stories that his grandfather told to your four-year-old father about the suffering of the first Armenian Christians, there were the stories of Yezdegird and Shapur.'

'Who was Shapur?'

'A Persian king, my little lamb. A fire-worshipper, a real devil in human form. An Armenian slave girl, a Christian, had once tried to convert him to Christianity in bed, but that did little good, because her heathen rival, who shared King Shapur's bed the next night, had whispered something else in his ear.'

'What was that, then, Meddah?'

'"If you adopt Christianity," she had told Shapur, "your war elephants will change like the lions in Gregory the Illuminator's cave. He changed all the lions' hearts into lambs' hearts."

"But that will not be good," Shapur had said, "for how am I to wage war against my enemies if my elephants have lambs' hearts?" And because the king was afraid the Christians could overcome him through their faith, he decided to kill them all.'

'Only a week after he had heard the Christian slave's whispers of conversion in bed, and listened to her rival's malicious words the next night, his troops invaded neighbouring Armenia. In the occupied territory the king initiated a bloodbath. He had thousands of men killed, the Armenian cities were razed to the ground and the heads of the priests and notables hacked off and planted on the city walls. In the Armenian capital he had all the women driven to the market-place, raped in the open streets and then trampled by elephants.'

'A terrible story.'

'Yes, my little lamb.'

'Shapur?'

'Yes, King Shapur.'

'And who was Yezdegird?'

'Another Persian king, also a fire-worshipper and a thoroughly evil man.'

'This Yezdegird was just as cruel as Shapur,' said the story-teller, 'but he was cleverer. Yezdegird knew that he could only permanently impose obedience on the Armenians in the provinces occupied by the Persians if he destroyed their religion. So he told the drivers of his elephants: "This people's religion can't be destroyed with the help of war elephants."

"So how will you destroy it, great Yezdegird?" asked the elephant drivers.

"I'll convert their priests," said Yezdegird, "and make fire-worshippers of them."'

'And so it happened,' said the story-teller, 'that Yezdegird decided to write a letter to the Armenian priesthood in the following terms: "If you adopt my religion, then we will make you rich and honour you, but if not, then we will erect fire altars in the whole land of Armenia and our Magus and Mobeds will rule the land. And any who rebel against us will be killed, with all their followers." And do you know, my little lamb, what the Armenian priests replied?'

'No, Meddah.'

'They wrote to King Yezdegird: "No one can take our faith from us. Take from us all you desire, great Yezdegird. Our earthly goods we give you, and we are ready to honour you as the only king on earth. But our Lord in heaven is Jesus Christ."'

'The bigger children in the village often played at being King Yezdegird and King Shapur. And they also played at being the Armenian kings Tiridates and Abgar. The game of King Abgar and the Saviour's sweatband was particularly exciting, with one of the king's spies defending it against the marauding ancestors of the Kurds until he fell dead in one of the gorges in the Lebanon, beside the Lord's sweatband.'

'In the dry season the children played the rain game, with the puppet Nuri, which actually was only a Christian cross dressed up as a puppet. They went from house to house with it. Everyone there had to give the children something, often eggs and oil but most commonly *hadig*; also *pokhint*, a similar sort of sweetmeat made of nuts, honey and flour. Then the children sang the old Armenian rain-song, which their parents and their parents' parents had sung: "Dear God . . . dear God . . . Thou hast given thy faith to the thirst of our souls, give water to the thirsty flowers. Send us rain, dear

God . . . rain . . . rain." And the children prayed to the puppet-cross, collected their *hadig* and *pokhint*, oil and eggs, pulled and shoved the puppet-cross and sang: "Dear God . . . dear God, send us rain."'

'Of course the wilder kids liked to play at Turks, Kurds and Armenians. The brave ones were always the Armenians, the less pretentious and cowardly ones always Turks and Kurds. But the Kurds and Turks were armed, while the Armenians had only their bare hands and legs, and of course their heads too, to defend themselves with. But in the end the cowards always defeated the brave ones, for even the strongest arm and the wisest head avails nothing if the other side has weapons. At the end of the game the brave Armenians lay dead on the ground, while the Turks and Kurds waved their wooden swords and danced a dance of joy.'

'Your father was only four, but he already played with them. Once the boys got hold of the red-headed son of the village smith, who was even younger than your father, and sent him off to the pastures to steal a lamb. You're a Kurd now, they told him. You go to the pasture and steal a lamb. You bring it to us here. The smith's son, who was called Avetik, did what they told him. Since all the sheepdogs in the nearby fields knew the little red-headed Avetik, they didn't bark much when Avetik took a lamb away with him. They growled and whined, even began to howl, but they didn't do anything.'

'Avetik brought the kids a lamb. One of the kids was pretending to be the elderly saptieh Shekir Efendi, another a Turkish captain and a third the Kadi. The saptieh arrested the Kurdish thief, although all the kids knew that the saptieh Shekir Efendi would have been much too frightened to dare to arrest a Kurd. The saptieh grabbed the little redhead by the collar, throttled him a bit and dragged him before the Turkish captain.

"Where is the owner of this lamb?" asked the captain. All the kids pointed at your four-year-old father. He knew the game, and laughed. He'd learnt his role from the older kids, so he knew what he had to do and say. First your father gave the saptieh a tip, his *baksheesh*, then he gave a bigger one to the captain, and the biggest one of all he only showed to the kids, but kept it, for that was the one for the Kadi, who was a Muslim judge.'

'They hauled your four-year-old father before the Kadi. And your father had to say what the kids had taught him. "Kadi," he said and pointed at the red-headed Avetik, "this Muslim Kurd has stolen my lamb, and all the Armenians in the village saw it and are witnesses."

"The Armenians are Christians," said the Kadi, "and the evidence of a Christian has no validity. You must produce two Muslim witnesses."

"But there weren't any Muslim witnesses."

"Well, you've had bad luck, you son of an unbelieving whore who has bred a bastard with an infidel blasphemer."

Your father now slipped the Kadi the big tip, at the same time whispering something in the Kadi's ear. And the Kadi nodded and said softly, but loud enough for everyone to hear: "The Muslim false witnesses are in front of the *hukumet*. Buy a couple of them. And by the truth of Allah, who is great, I have seen nothing and know nothing. And that will cost you two more silver piastres."

Your father handed the Kadi the two piastres. Then he went to the *hukumet*, which the children had made out of two cases, one on top of the other.'

'That's where the false witnesses were hanging about, pathetic figures played by barefooted children. Your father had a look at the false witnesses, picked out one of them and said to him: "Efendi, will you come to the Kadi with me and tell him what you've seen?"

"What am I meant to have seen, *chelebi*?"

"I'll tell you what," said your father, without showing that he felt flattered, for to be called *chelebi* meant honoured and noble sir. "I'll tell you what, efendi. You've seen a dirty Kurd stealing my lamb. You saw it with your own eyes."

"With my own eyes, *chelebi*?"

"Of course, silly! But not with my eyes."

"And what sort of lamb is it meant to have been, *chelebi*? One with a black patch on its neck? Or several patches? And how old

230

was the lamb? When did its mother throw it?"

"I must just have a look, efendi."

"But the lamb must be locked in the police station?"

"Then I'll go to the police station."'

'And then your father came back and said to the false witness: "Actually the lamb has got two black patches, one on its neck and one on its face. And its mother had it two weeks ago."

"Have I got to have seen its mother throw it?"

"No, silly!"

"What am I meant to have seen, then?"

"What I told you, silly! You saw that dirty Kurd steal the lamb, the one with the two black patches that its mother had two weeks ago."

"And what did the Kurd look like, *chelebi*?"

"It doesn't matter what he looked like. The Kadi will show him to you, and you'll say 'That's him!'"

"I must have seen his face when he stole the lamb, the one with two black patches that its mother had two weeks ago?"

"Of course you saw the Kurd's face."

"While he was stealing the lamb?"

"Of course, silly!"

"And what will you pay, *chelebi*?"

"Half a piastre."

"But, *chelebi*, I can't swear a false oath and sell my soul for half a piastre."

"Then I'll give you a few more paras."

"But, *chelebi*, must I sell my soul for half a piastre and a few paras?"

"Then I'll give you a silver piastre. Now, what about it?"

"That's different, *chelebi*. I'll do the lot for a bit of silver. But you've forgotten that Allah requires me to give alms."

"What sort of alms?"

"Well, *chelebi*, if I'm going to give sinful false evidence, then I must either fast for seven days or give alms to the poor, or Allah won't forgive my sins."

"Then fast for seven days."

"But, *chelebi*, how could I fast for seven days? Can't you see how

231

skinny I am? Am I to get even thinner and have my wife and thirteen children laughing at me?"

"Then you must give alms, as Allah requires."

"But, *chelebi*, how am I going to give alms out of one silver piastre? You must give me another silver piastre, one for me and one for Allah."

"All right, then. Two silver piastres."'

'"But, *chelebi*, for two silver piastres I've only seen the Kurd's back. But not his face. How could I have seen his face as well for only two silver piastres?"

"How much do you want to tell the Kadi you saw his face too?"

"Three silver piastres, *chelebi*. That's a mere nothing to a *chelebi* like you, an educated and rich man. Are you trying to laugh at my poverty? Isn't it bad enough that a faithful Muslim like me has to give evidence for an uncircumcised *giaour* and *raya* like you? And all for three lousy piastres?"'

'Now your father began to tear at his hair, to howl and scream. The children laughed and whispered something in his ear. Your father shouted at the false witness: "Efendi! You're ruining me! I'm ruined! I shall have to give the same amount to the other witness. And I've given the Kadi a bribe too. And the captain, and the saptieh. And it will all cost me more than the lamb is worth. I'm ruined. Is there no pity in the world for the uncircumcised?"'

'Among the boys who were playing was one older boy, christened by the name of Garabed but later just called Garo. He was ten, the youngest son of Kupelian the saddler, a man who had once had all his cattle driven out of his cowshed by the Kurds.'

'Now this son of the saddler Kupelian, this Garo, was a very odd character, a grouser and a spoil-sport. In the war games he always managed to get the role of the brave, unarmed Armenian; he refused ever to play for a change as a cowardly but armed Kurd. And he would never let himself be killed by the cowardly Kurds and Turks, although that was in the rules of the game, but just pretended to play and waited till the Kurds and Turks attacked him with their wooden swords. Then he began to defend himself furiously, with punches and kicks, grabbed the wooden swords away from the enemy and then laid into them so hard that they cried and ran away. People said that Garo wasn't just a spoil-sport but a future Armenian freedom fighter, probably one of those who would finish up on a Turkish gallows: a nationalist!'

'The nationalists!

There was a lot of talk about them in the eighties. One of them actually came to the village once, to talk with the priest, the mayor, the smith and some other men, of whom Vartan's father Hagob was one. But he didn't stay long and rode off again on his mule.'

'Vartan didn't know who the nationalists were and what the man on the mule wanted. His grandfather explained it to him: "He wanted his people to bring weapons into the village, which the mayor could have hidden somewhere, probably in the graveyard."

"Where dead people are buried?"

"Yes, my little lamb."

"Are they hiding weapons on the graves?"

"No, my little lamb. They're putting them in the graves. They put them on top of the dead bodies."

"Can the dead sleep if they put weapons in their graves?"

"Of course, my little lamb. They sleep all the better, because they know we need the weapons to defend ourselves from the Kurds."

"Are the dead frightened of the Kurds?"

"They have been frightened of them, my little lamb. And they're glad when they see that we who are living aren't frightened any more."

"Did the man with the mule bring the weapons?"

"No, my little lamb."

"Why not?"

"Well, he just didn't. Anyway, it's forbidden. Do you think we all want to go to the gallows?"'

'People in the village said that the nationalists had hidden weapons in many villages. The red-headed smith said: "The Armenians should prepare for defence."

And Garo said: "Next time the saptiehs come with the tax-collectors, and then the Kurdish horsemen from the Sheikh Suleyman, we ought to shoot their heads off."

But the priest Kapriel Hamadian, who was present at these talks, he said: "No, no, that would be a mistake."

And the mayor said: "The Turks would send troops here, and then there'd be another *tebk*."

"That's right," said the mayor's wife. "Another *tebk*. God save us from that."

"The nationalists are a disaster to us," said the mayor. "The Turks and the Kurds are only waiting till they find weapons in our hands. That will be an excuse to kill the lot of us."

The priest said: "The great *tebk*! I can see all those gallows. And I see fire and smoke."'

'Once a hundred saptiehs rode into the village with a *yusbashi* to search for weapons. They ransacked the Armenians' houses, dug up the fields and the yards and even went to the graveyard, to knock down the gravestones on the graves. But they didn't find weapons anywhere.'

CHAPTER SIX

'The older you get,' said the story-teller, 'the quicker the time passes. The great-grandmother, for instance, had long since given up counting the years. The other day she said: "Ah, our young Vartan will soon be skipping like a young foal, he jumps about in the yard like a flea on the kilim, and I reckon he rides like a grown-up on Ceyda, that shameless jennet that lets itself be mounted by the water-carrier. And yet it's barely a year ago that he was peeing in his nappies. That little grandson of mine, Zovinar . . . do you remember how my daughter Hamest bathed him in salt water the other day?"

"But, grandmother," Vartan's mother said, "that was years ago."'

'Even Vartan, as he grew up, found that time didn't stand still, and that his third pair of trousers, given him by his father on his seventh birthday, were always getting shorter.

"The trousers aren't getting any shorter," his father had said, "your legs are getting longer."

The same thing was happening to the other children, especially Avetik, the red-headed son of the red-headed village smith, who seemed to grow all too fast and was taller than all the children of his age in the village. By the time he was nine Avetik was already wearing his father's trousers, and not worrying about the things people whispered in the village, that he must have drunk a Gypsy woman's milk as a child, and that she must have been nursed by a long-legged bitch. But never mind about all that, one thing is clear: the good God doesn't share his time equally, and what raced past the great-grandmother passed more slowly to Vartan, like the lumbering footsteps of Ceyda when Vartan led

235

her through the nearby mountain gorges.'

'Not much happened in the village. On and off, visitors came from neighbouring villages, from small towns, often even from the bigger towns like Mush, Erzurum, Diyarbakir, Van or Bakir. Once a man actually came from Constantinople, dressed in the latest fashion and wearing a Frankish suit. Vartan's grandfather said: "Some day your uncle from America will come, my son Nahapeth, who's a rag-and-bone man over there, and a rich man."

"How many uncles have I got in America?"

"A whole lot, my little lamb. But I can only remember two of them."

"Who's the other one?"

"My son Krikor, the coachman."

"But one of my uncles is a coachman in Bakir."

"That's right, my little lamb. One is a coachman in Bakir and one in New York."

"Has my uncle who's a coachman in New York got a mule on his coach?"

"No, my little lamb. He's got a real horse, an American mustang."

"What sort of horse is that?"

"An Indian horse, my little lamb."

"And what sort of coach has he got?"

"One with wheels that go round the axles."

"But, grandfather, the wheels of a coach don't go round the axles. I've nailed wheels on myself, on our coach, and I nailed them to the axle."

"We're in Hayastan here, my little lamb. Our coaches are just like our ancestors'."

"And in America?"

"Everything's different there, my little lamb. All wheels in America go round the axles. And, believe it or not, the coachmen over there don't powder the parts of the coach that squeak with dry flour, the way we do here, but smear them with oil, an extraordinary sort of oil that they dig out of the ground."

"Does Uncle Krikor do that?"

"Yes. Just as I said."

"And what does Uncle Krikor look like?"

"I don't know now, my little lamb. I've only got a picture of your other uncle, Nahapeth, the rag-and-bone man."

"And what does he look like?"

"The picture isn't very clear. All you can see on it is a big hat – a hat with a broad brim."

Vartan laughed. "I've heard about those funny hats, but I've never seen one."

"No hurry," said his grandfather. "When your uncle comes from America you'll see one of those hats."'

'Naturally enough, the people from the village sometimes went off themselves, mostly to the neighbouring villages but often enough to the big towns. Then they told astonishing stories about big bazaars, beggars, brothels, ramparts, horse-coaches with springs and beautiful women scented with roses and lilies. People who ventured to travel were admired and envied. Not always, though; no one envied the ones who were robbed or even murdered by the Kurds on their way through the narrow, deserted mountain passes.'

Now the story-teller said to the last thought: 'Do you see that white, bare chalk slope on the way out of the village? The people call it *Ak Bayir*, the white slope. And only three donkey's farts away from the slope – and that's barely a stone's throw – so far and no farther, there is the *Göbekli Tepe*, the round hill, where the children play their war games . . . a splendid place. And between the *Ak Bayir* and the *Göbekli Tepe* there's an old hut. You can see it.'

'I can see it,' said the last thought, 'because I see everything you see. And I can also see the white slope that people call *Ak Bayir* and also the round hill called *Göbekli Tepe*. And I can hear the children's battle-cries as they play. And I can see the old hut and the smoke from the *tonir* coming out of the open doorway.'

'There isn't a *tonir* there,' said the story-teller, 'but only a Turkish stove, that looks just like an Armenian *tonir*, though the Turks have a different name for it.'

'Different?'

'They call it a *tandir*.'

'Who lives in that hut?'

'The only Turkish family in the village.'

'You haven't told me anything about them yet.'

'I forgot, my little lamb. Simply forgot.'

'Why, Meddah?'

'I don't know, my little lamb. The very word Turk is like a bad sickness, and people only talk about bad sicknesses if they're threatened by one. But those Turks in Yedi Su are no threat to anyone; they've been living among the Armenians as peaceful neighbours for many years. People in the village are so used to them that they hardly notice them.'

'Do the Turkish children play with the Armenians on the big playground on the round hill that they call *Göbekli Tepe*?'

'Naturally, my little lamb.'

'And do they dance at Armenian weddings?'

'Yes, my little lamb.'

'And no one thinks anything of it?'

'No one thinks anything of it.'

'The only thing that bothered people about those friendly Turks,' said the story-teller, 'was the names of the men and the kids, because they were the same as the names of the Turkish tax-collectors, saptiehs and officials and of the Kurdish brigands, all those that made the village insecure and that people didn't want to be reminded of. So the villagers just gave the owners of those unpopular names nicknames. Turkish names of course, but more attractive than the real names, names that got rid of the embarrassing equivalents, and that emphasized the personality of the individuals' nicknames. For instance, the head of the Turkish family was named Suleyman, the same as Suleyman the terrifying leader of the Kurds, but they called him *Tashak*.'

'*Tashak*?'

'That's right.'

'What does that mean?'

'It's a description of what the man has got in his scrotum.'

'And what has Suleyman got in his scrotum?'

'The same as any other man, my little lamb. Only in his case it's all a bit more noticeable. This Suleyman had once lifted a heavy sack of grain on to his back, and had got a hernia. Believe it or not, people used to say that his scrotum hung down below his knees, though nobody had actually seen it, for Suleyman never took his trousers down in front of other people, not even when he was working in the fields and had to answer the call of nature in a hurry. And since there's no *hamam* in Yedi Su where you can have a steam bath with other people, you get no chance to see for yourself.'

'So how did people know that Suleyman's scrotum hung down below his knees?'

'They worked it out from the way he walked. He walked as if he had the eggs of whole henhouse hidden in his trousers.'

'You don't say so!'

'I do.'

'But that must be pretty painful.'

'Of course, my little lamb. Especially when the tax-collectors came to the village. Then poor Suleyman didn't dare show himself on the street, for fear that the tax-collectors might think he had something hidden in his trousers.'

'Hidden in his trousers?'

'Yes.'

'A secret sack of eggs on legs?'

'That's it.'

'Tashak?'

'Tashak.'

'Tashak's eldest son was called *Bodur*, or Short-legs. He waddled too, like his father, but for quite different reasons. His legs were rather bandy, positively O-shaped, and too short. Bodur was already fifteen and wanted to get married soon. The people used to laugh at him and say he must make sure his future wife didn't step over his future son without taking the same step backwards, otherwise he'd be as short-legged as his father, whose mother had stopped his Turkish legs growing because, before he was forty days old and had played on the prayer mat, she had stepped over him without carefully taking the same step backwards.

Bodur's younger brother was called *Tiryaki*, the Addict, a name generally given to chain-smokers. The little children ran after him in the street shouting *fosur-fosur*, which means more or less *puff*,

puff. Fosur-Fosur Tiryaki couldn't afford proper tobacco, so he smoked everything he could find, especially the hairy pistils of the corncobs dried in the sun, but also hay, dead grass and sometimes dried cabbage leaves, the same cabbage leaves used – in their fresh, undried condition, of course – by the women in this village to make a tasty stuffed cabbage, filled with meat and rice, with a rich sauce poured over it. The Armenians call it *patat*, the Turks call it *sarma*.'

'Yes,' said the story-teller, 'that makes your mouth water. Shall I tell you some more about those Turks? Well, yes: there were some small girls in the Turkish family, and they all wobbled their behinds as they walked, a dangerous thing, for none of the Armenian boys dared to pinch them, well knowing that there's always a knife ready in a Turk's pocket, especially in the pockets of small girls' brothers. The ten-year-old girl was called *Hulya*, the Dreamer, the nine-year-old *Shirin*, the Cutie, and the seven-year-old *Meral*, the Fawn. Tashak's wife was called *Neshee* – Happiness. Just that. Probably because she was always so good-tempered and had never forgotten how to laugh, or because she was said to have come into the world with a cry of joy. Tashak's youngest son, who looked after the chickens, was nicknamed *Gög-Gög*. He was three years older than your father.'

'Gög-Gög: That's what you say to call the chickens to feed. When the sun rose, Tashak knelt on his prayer mat in front of the house door, his Turkish head turned towards Mecca. While Tashak was saying the morning prayer with the usual bodily contortions of the faithful Muslim, Gög-Gög ran round the house and called the chickens: "Gög-Gög-Gög". Anyone who went past the Turkish house knew it was early morning; the cock had just crowed, Tashak was praying to Allah and Gög-Gög was calling the chickens.'

Now just imagine this: the boys are on the *Göbekli Tepe* and are all having a pee. Your father is four, and standing next to Gög-Gög. For the first time in his life he sees a circumcised prick. He is so shocked and horrified that he pees against his own knee. He runs home crying.'

*   *   *

'"What's he crying about?" asks Hamest.

"He's seen a carved piece of meat."

"What sort of piece of meat?"

"Oh, just a piece of meat."'

'"Many years ago I saw a circumcision in a Turkish village," says the grandfather. "It was just like a wedding."

"Like a wedding?"

"Like a wedding."

'"Well, I can't remember it so very clearly," says the grandfather. "But I know the men of the village and the kid whose little sausage was going to be carved were assembled in the Mukhtar's house. There was a lot of talking and smoking. Then I saw the boy's father come out of the Mukhtar's stable with a white horse. He took the little boy by the hand and put him on the horse. The boy rode from house to house, and everyone wished him good luck. A little prince on a white horse, a prince in white clothes with red stripes and gold embroidery. And an embroidered blue cap on his head."

"What happened then?" said Hamest.

"The boy's father led the horse by the reins. He led it to his home. There they waited for the *sunechi*."

"Who's he?"

"The one who does the cutting."

"And what happened then?"

"Nothing at all," said the grandfather. "Suddenly I saw some other men. They seized the little prince and pulled his trousers down. And the cutter seized his prize between the prince's skinny thighs, simply grabbed it, pulled it right out into the open, and suddenly he had a sharp knife in his hand."

"And then?"

"Then he cut the foreskin off."

"Is that all?"

"Yes, that's all."'

'"Of course the *sunechi* powdered the wound with flour. And the father took the howling boy in his arms and put him down on a big cushion in the doorway, so that everybody in the village could see the boy. And there were drums and flutes playing outside. Some of the people started to dance. And then the whole village danced."'

"'Our Vartan seems to have been upset when he saw Gög-Gög's little stump."

"Yes," said the grandfather.

"He must have thought it was a bird's beak with no skin?"

"But, Hamest, a bird's beak doesn't have any skin."

"Then maybe he thought it was a frog's head."

"A frog's head with no skin? Scalped, perhaps?"

"Well, there it is."'

CHAPTER SEVEN

'There are some things that are beneath a man's dignity. Gathering cowpats is one. That's a job that was left to the women, or most often to the small children. In summer the *tezek* was dried in the sun on the flat roofs of the houses; in winter the cowpats were just slapped on the wall of the living-room and left to dry in the heat of the *tonir*. When they were dry they just fell off by themselves, and you just needed to pick them up. Vartan went around with the children when he was four, picking up *tezek*, copying what they were doing and crying when they pushed him out of the way. Later, as he grew older, he pushed back and fought with the boys and girls who wanted to get in front of him. Generally the red-headed Avetik helped him. They got together and divided their spoils fairly. Avetik thought the *tezek* shouldn't always be taken home but could actually be sold; but that would be something for a smart businessman who knew about trading. Once he said to Vartan: "Well, what about it? You want to be a poet. Can't you think of something? Where should we sell the *tezek*?"

"In the town," said Vartan. "The people in the villages have got all they want."

"And how are we going to get to the town?"

"With the donkey," said Vartan.

"Then we shall want another sack."

"I'll pinch one from my father," said Vartan, "he'll never notice."

"And suppose the Kurds pinch the sack from us?"

"You mean, when we're riding through the mountains?"

"Yes, of course."

"The Kurds never pinch *tezek*."

"How do you know?"

"I just know."'

*   *   *

'But the boys didn't trust themselves alone outside the village.

"When we're older," said Avetik, "we'll be strong enough to take on the Kurds if they think they can pinch the *tezek* from us."

"Then we might take Garo with us," said Vartan. "In no time he's going to have muscles as big as the village smith's."

"You mean as big as my father's?"

"Yes."

"That's not a bad idea."

"Or we can wait until I'm officially engaged. Then I shall be grown up and can go on business trips whenever I want. But until then my father won't let me go to the town alone."

"That's a point," said Avetik. "Mine wouldn't let me either."

"So, you see," said Vartan.

"And what about this engagement? I thought you'd been engaged for years?"

"Of course I've been engaged for years," said Vartan, "but we don't have the official engagement celebrations until my bride begins to bleed between her legs."

"How do you know that?"

"My father told me."

"How old is your bride?"

"She's three years younger than me. She's five now."

"When will she start to bleed between her legs?"

"Not until she's old."

"How old?"

"About ten or eleven, I think."

"But we can't wait all that time with the *tezek*."

"You're right there."'

'Once Vartan's father took him in the donkey-cart to the mill. That was the first journey he'd made in his life. The mill was in the Armenian neighbouring village of Piredyik, which in Turkish means no more or less than Fleas' Nest. And Piredyik lay in the Valley of Flies called Sinek-Dere. It wasn't far to Piredyik, an hour or two perhaps if there had been a straight caravan road, but you needed several hours before you'd got through the mountain passes and steep ravines. The Armenians' mill, at the entrance to the cwm, only worked during the flood season, in the spring when the snow melted in the mountains, or on days of heavy rain. And since on the day Vartan drove to the mill with his father it was neither the flood season nor raining, the miller said to Hagob: "Hagob Efendi, how can the mill be working when there's no snow in the mountains and not a cloud in the sky? Do you want me to piss in the stream to make enough water in it?"

"Where is the stream, anyway?" asked Hagob.

"The earth has swallowed it up," said the miller.

"And when will the earth spit it out again?"

"When it rains," said the miller. "Or next spring, when the snow melts in the mountains."

"How would it be," asked Hagob, "if we all three of us pissed in the stream, you and I and my son Vartan. Perhaps the stream would come to life again and the earth would spit out what it's just swallowed up."'

'On the way back from the mill they met Bulbul, riding home to her hut, high up in the mountains, on her shabby old donkey. She sat on her donkey looking glum. Bulbul had tied a beheaded cock to her donkey's tail, and blood was still dripping out of the place where the head had been cut off with every pace of the donkey, staining the narrow mountain path.

"Why have you cut the cock's head off already?" asked Hagob.

"Because the donkey was frightened of the cock," said Bulbul, "and it got stubborn and wanted to throw me off with the cock. It was a restless cock and kept squawking and fluttering where I'd tied it to the donkey's tail."

"Who gave you the cock?"

"Your mother, old Hamest," said Bulbul.

"Is it our cock Abdul Hamid?"

"No," said Bulbul. "You can see it isn't. It's a stray cock that flew into your chicken-run the other day and caused a lot of fuss, for Abdul Hamid can't stand having another cock anywhere near him."

"But this cock might have been stronger than Abdul Hamid. Maybe we ought to have kept it?"

"It wasn't stronger," said Bulbul. "Abdul Hamid would have

pecked it to death if old Hamest had let him. Believe me, Hagob Efendi, two cocks in one chicken-run get on worse together than two women at the same stove."

When Bulbul had gone on, Vartan asked: "Is it true that Bulbul is a midwife, and is it true that she helped to bring me into the world?"

"Yes, that's true."

"Did she breast-feed me too?"

"No. She's not a wet-nurse."

"She's a Kurdish woman. What are they like? Do Kurdish women feed their own babies?"

"Of course."

"And what is their milk like?"

"As sweet as any mother's milk."

"As sweet as my own mother's milk?"

"Yes," said Hagob.'

'They talked a long time about Bulbul. They talked about the lonely hut up in the mountains where she lived, alone with her donkey and her chickens, and they wondered who she ever talked to when it grew dark and the evening by the *tonir* grew dull. Finally Hagob said: "She talks with her animals, and I'll bet you, my son, that isn't so boring, for animals know how to listen better than people."

"Why hasn't she got a husband?"

"They say she did have one," said Hagob, "before she came down this way, but her husband threw her out of the house."

"Just threw her out?"

"Yes."

"Do only Muslims do that?"

"No," said Hagob. "It sometimes happens with Christians too."

"And with Armenians?"

"I don't really know," said Hagob. "But I don't know of anything of the kind among my friends or in the family. Quite certainly not in Yedi Su. However much the husband and wife may quarrel. Those whom God has joined together, let no man put asunder."'

'There was once a case in the village of Yedi Su which Vartan remembered, during his lifetime. There was an Armenian trader who lived near the Khatisians. He had a hook-nosed wife, of whom people said that she needed it every night. The trader and his wife already had thirteen children, and one night the husband said to his wife: "That's enough."

The trader was seldom at home, because he carried on his business in the big bazaars in Bakir. He generally brought rich presents when he came home in his mule-cart.

Nobody knew exactly what sort of business it was he did. He was said to go around the Bakir bazaars with a Greek and a Jew. The Jew had a grey horse at his home, the Greek had a grey donkey. When it was getting dark and people could no longer tell the grey of one animal from the grey of the other, the Armenian would swiftly sell the Jew's grey horse to some credulous Turk, but in the gloomy evening light smartly exchange it for the Greek's donkey while distracting the Turk's attention or tricking the Turk in some other way. The Jew and the Greek helped in that manoeuvre. As soon as the negotiation was concluded and they had put the Turk on the donkey, the three of them made themselves scarce, spent the night in the Greek's house, bought a similar donkey that cost less than what the Turk had paid for the horse and then shared the profits – let's call it the surplus value – honestly between them. But, as always happens, the jug goes so often to the well that at last it is broken. One day the three of them were caught and arrested.'

'Of course there was a trial. The only school teacher in Yedi Su, who was consumptive, but an educated man, actually engaged a lawyer from Van, who was a relation of his. This lawyer, or so the school teacher told the Yedi Su farmers – this lawyer had tried to show by legal arguments that the surplus value that the three crooks had ended up with had nothing to do with the surplus value theory of a certain Karl Marx, and that the three were loyal Ottoman citizens who had nothing to do with the new-fangled ideas of that infidel Frank of German-Jewish descent, which were brought over the Turkish border from wretched Frankistan by rogues, conspirators, bunglers, loonies and left-wing students. However, the Armenian lawyer's pleading had done little good, since the crooks could not produce the money to bribe the judges. So it worked out as it was bound to work out. The three went to gaol, but only for one year plus the additional time between Ramadan and the feast of Bairam.'

'Now the hook-nosed wife of the Armenian trader, who really did need it every night, waited impatiently for her husband. But one day her patience was exhausted, and that was something to do with her hooked nose, for they say that hook-nosed people never can wait, especially when there's really too much of an itch between their legs.'

'In 1889 the wife suddenly became pregnant, although the husband had been in gaol for months. The priest Kapriel Hamadian said that adultery never occurred among Armenians, and so it could be that the hook-nosed wife – because she never could wait – had been overshadowed by the compassion of the Holy Ghost, for only the Jews' God was a god of vengeance, whereas the God of the Christians was a compassionate god, not so different from Allah, of whose compassion Tashak, the Turk, had so often told them.'

'Now when the child came into the world and proved to be a little red-headed girl, the priest said that it could not have been conceived by the Holy Ghost, because the Holy Ghost never conceived redheads, which were possessed by the devil. Some people in the village suspected that the red-headed smith had bewitched the wife, but others said that it might well be that the smith's eldest son, although he actually had black hair but still had his father's blood in him, had fathered a red-headed girl with the trader's wife, because the smith's eldest son was always after all the girls, and even looked up the bottom of the trader's hook-nosed wife every time she went to the well to draw water, although she'd already had thirteen children and wasn't a girl any more. In short, the smith's eldest son was accused of having fathered the little red-headed bastard with the trader's wife.'

'Rightly or wrongly, the Mukhtar Ephrem Abovian condemned the wife, had her hair cut off and put her on a donkey facing backwards, holding the bastard. The donkey was led through the village very slowly, from house to house. The woman sat on the donkey weeping, with the little bastard in her arms. The people spat at her, smeared mud on her face and didn't even spare the little bastard, which was also spat at and smeared with mud. Vartan remembered later on that it was mostly the quarrelsome old women who behaved most furiously. Their poisonous spittle seemed to come from spiritual sources that were particularly fertile. At the end of the show Vartan's father said: "The old women are the worst. They're jealous because they'd like to have tasted the smith's son's prick themselves."'

'True enough, the men in the village didn't make much of a fuss about it, only the old women. They were the true guardians of morality. And it is also true that the trader, when he came home again, didn't throw his wife out. They say she sleeps alone now in a corner of the *oda*. They say she screams at night and swears aloud in her sleep. And they say the red-headed little bastard doesn't sleep in her cradle, but with her mother, and creeps around under the *yorgan*, her little hands playing with the corncob between the thighs of her screaming, swearing mother.'

'Your father's childhood . . . the village of Yedi Su . . . the furtive eyes of the Kurds up in the mountains . . . the death in the files of the Turkish authorities, that sooner or later emerges from the files to clean up forgotten provinces . . . the Sultan in Constantinople who doesn't like Christians, especially Armenians . . . rumours . . . somewhere at the arse of the world. And still nobody notices the first signs of a storm that was to come like the Flood.'

'So,' the story-teller said, 'everything possible occurs to me and I say just what comes into my head. I don't even know why I haven't told you anything about your father's brothers and sisters. It's because of the airy way I talk.'
  'My father's brothers and sisters?'
  'All older than him, for he was the youngest – but you know that already.'
  'I know that already, Meddah.'
  'One was three years older than your father. He was called

Dikran, like the one the Turks hanged on the Gate of Happiness years afterwards.'

'Dikran, the shoemaker? The one with the yellow boots, the most beautiful boots in all Bakir?'

'Yes, that one.'

'Is it the same Dikran?'

'The same one. When he was only seven he said to your father: "When I'm grown up I'm going to be a shoemaker." And he added: "I shall move to Bakir, the big city, and I'll make myself a pair of yellow boots that will be the finest in all Bakir."

"Bakir?" your father asked.

"Bakir," said Dikran. "We've got lots of uncles living there, and one of them is a shoemaker. The shoemaker will teach me the trade."

"Is that uncle Levon?"

"No, he's the *arabachi*. The shoemaker is Uncle Dro."'

'Was that right?'

'That was right, my little lamb. Uncle Dro was a shoemaker in Bakir. And Dikran went to him later to learn. He became a good shoemaker, married, became independent, had many children and one day made a pair of yellow kidskin boots, of the most beautiful genuine kid, which looked so handsome that peoople said they were the finest in all Bakir.

The Gypsies particularly admired the yellow boots. One of them wanted to exchange a young foal for the yellow boots, but Dikran wouldn't part with them.'

'I remember,' said the story-teller, 'the Gypsies came from the horse market and trotted through the Armenian craftsmen's quarter. They stopped in front of Dikran's house. Dikran was sitting behind his last and polishing the yellow boots.

"I'll give you a foal for those boots," said one of the Gypsies.

"These boots are not for sale," said Dikran.

"Everything that people need is for sale," said the Gypsy. "It's just a matter of finding the right price. I'll give you a goat as well."

"I'm not selling them," said Dikran.

The Gypsy said: "What's so special about those yellow boots? Can you do magic with them like Aladdin and his magic lamp?"

"Something like that," said Dikran. "The very look of the boots strengthens my faith. And if my faith is strengthened, then I enjoy my work and everything goes on better."

"What faith are you talking about, efendi?"

"My faith in my art, and my faith in myself."'

'"Look," said Dikran. "The boots have brought me luck, for the idea that one day I should make a pair of good boots spurred me on, and so it's thanks to these boots that I've become a good shoemaker."

"Did you say they'd brought you luck?"

"Yes."

"Then let me read your hand, so that we can see whether they're really lucky boots."

"You want to read my hand?"

"Yes," said the Gypsy.'

'But the Gypsy couldn't ready anything from the hand. So he called his old mother. And she came and read Dikran's future from his hand.

"I see a hanged man," said the old Gypsy woman. "He's wearing boots the same as these."

"What else do you see?" asked Dikran.

"I see a blind beggar," said the Gypsy woman, "and he's putting your boots in his old sack."

But Dikran only laughed and snatched his hand away. He said to the Gypsy woman: "You just want to frighten me because I don't want to let the boots go for a foal and a goat."'

The story-teller said: 'The story of the hanged man wearing Dikran's yellow boots, and the story of the blind beggar and his old sack – those stories soon spread. Even the priest Kapriel Hamadian heard them. And he said: "That's just Gypsy rubbish. A good Christian should cross himself three times before he lets a Gypsy tell his fortune."

"And what should my brother Dikran do?" Hagob asked the priest.

"He should cross himself if the Gypsies appear before his house again."

"And if they don't?"

"Then he should rub the boots with garlic," said the priest. "Then he shouldn't wear the boots for a week, seven days exactly, and then he should lay his hand on the Bible, his right hand, while he pulls the boots on again with his left."'

'Many years later,' said the story-teller, 'your father was coming back from visiting a relative in Bakir. As he went through the Gate of Happiness in his donkey-cart he saw a sick, blind beggar lying beside the road. The traffic seemed quite ready to drive over him, and the animals and vehicles would have trampled and crushed him to death if your father hadn't rescued him. He simply put him on the cart and took him to Yedi Su. There the Khatisian family cared for him until he was better. Weeks later your father brought the blind beggar back to the Gate of Happiness. The blind beggar's name was Mechmed Efendi.

Mechmed Efendi said to your father then: "You have saved my life. One day I will save your life." And then he said: "I know your brother Dikran, who often comes past the Gate of Happiness to give me half a piastre and have a chat with me. Your brother Dikran is a good man, and so I always give him bits of good advice."

"Then you must know the story of the old Gypsy telling his fortune?"

"You mean all about that hanged man . . . some time in the distant future . . . the hanged man wearing Dikran's boots?"

"Yes, Mechmed Efendi."

"And the thing about the blind beggar and his old sack in which the hanged man's boots disappear?"

"Yes, Mechmed Efendi."

"What sort of old sack?"

"It could be your sack, Mechmed Efendi," said your father, and laid the blind man's hand on the old sack that he always carted around with him. But Mechmed Efendi had only shaken his head in astonishment and said: "But, Vartan Efendi, there are many blind beggars and many old sacks. And anyway I've heard that your brother Dikran protected his boots with garlic and the Bible."

"Do you believe in our Bible, Mechmed Efendi?"

"I believe in the words of the Prophet," Mechmed Efendi said to him, "of which they say that he has only explained the Bible in a different way."'

And the story-teller said: 'Don't expect me to tell you the history of all your father's brothers and sisters, let alone the stories of his aunts and uncles and other relatives. Some of them lived in the *kertastan* of Yedi Su, most of them in Bakir and other towns in Turkey and its former provinces like Greece and Bulgaria, Romania and Hungary or even in Serbia and Bosnia and in towns like Sarajevo, which was a Turkish town. And some have travelled overseas, like so many Armenians, of whom the Turks say that they infiltrate the people like the Jews and so turn up everywhere in camouflage hats and masks in order to make trouble. Where should we get to if I were to tell you about them all? And how should I even bring my story to an end in time? For Thovma Khatisian is at his last gasp, and his time is short. But he would still like to know whether I will, or whether I could, tell it all to his last thought. And because I say this to you, I the story-teller, the time is short. But if you like, I'll tell you quickly about two sisters and three brothers, because your father specially loved them.'

And the story-teller said: 'The one sister was fourteen years older than your father and already married before he was born. She was called *Makrouhi*, the cleanly one. Although she was the very reverse of being cleanly. People used to say that she only washed in the summer, like the Kurdish women, but that she had a heart of gold. Makrouhi called in every day, for she lived on this side of the village, the Khatisians' side, only five minutes away; she helped her mother and grandmother about the house and played with your father. She really did have a heart of gold, for she gave your father sweets when he was still lying in his cradle, bathed him in salt water when his grandmother wasn't there and later, when he was a boy, washed his wounds if he had fallen over and hurt himself in the rough game of Kurds, Turks and Armenians. This Makrouhi was married to the master-saddler Armenag, though he was called Armen; just that, Armen. And this Armen had big, wrinkled, strong hands . . . honest hands . . . for the hands beat Makrouhi every day, until she began to wash regularly and get herself in line with her name Makrouhi.'

'Another sister was called *Aghavni*, which means dove. She lived up to her name, for she really was as gentle as a dove. And one day off she flew, to marry Pesak, the son of a rich carpet merchant from Bakir. This Pesak was an inconspicuous sort of man, although he wore glasses and had studied for a time in Stamboul. Who would ever have thought that this Pesak would become a Dashnak at the turn of the century, and at one time actually one of their most wanted leaders?'

'How did she come to marry Pesak? You'd like to know that? Well, my little lamb, it was arranged with the help of the marriage-broker Manoushag, whom they called in the village Michnort Manoushag, which means more or less Violet the go-between.'

'No, my little lamb, Manoushag, the Violet, was neither young nor beautiful. She was what Armenians call *duhne menatzaz*, which means left at home, an old maid.'

'I know what it is you want to ask, my little lamb. You'd like to know whether your father's engagement with the mayor's daughter had been negotiated by Manoushag. Well, my little lamb, you know very well that that was not the case, because Hagob had arranged the union himself – unusual, true, but that's how it was. And that was why Manoushag, the marriage-broker, got a bit cross with Hagob when she learned that he and the mayor had exchanged the engagement coins before the holy *tonir* without her knowledge.'

'One of your father's brothers was called *Sarkis*. He became a goldsmith in Bakir. This Sarkis married a hook-nosed woman, who was every bit as randy as the wife of the Armenian trader in Yedi Su. That was also the reason that Sarkis was always pale and hollow-cheeked, for his wife simply couldn't get enough of the bone that Sarkis had between his thighs and which – so people used to say – the good God had given him for pissing rather than for the engendering of offspring. But the goldsmith had to have it off with her every night if he wanted peace and quiet round the family *tonir*. He definitely didn't want his wife to get round to doing it with other people, which would inevitably have led to a haircut, or, as Hagob said, to the woman's having her head shaved and being put on a donkey facing backwards, like the hook-nosed wife of the Armenian trader from Yedi Su. But the goldsmith's wife didn't have a red-headed bastard like the trader's wife, a bastard that liked to play with the corncob between its mother's legs, which really ought not to be there are all, for it had not grown as bone but as God's fruit from the field.

The goldsmith's wife was not only randy, she was also avaricious. And so she often used to say to Sarkis: "Why do you wear yourself out behind your bench from morning to night? Why don't you do the same as the money-changers in the alleys between the bazaars? They just count money. They toil not, neither do they spin, but the Heavenly Father feeds them all right."'

'There was another brother called *Boghos*. This Boghos was a ne'er-do-well, who pretended to be working with his sister Aghavni and his brother-in-law Pesak in the carpet shop, but actually hung around in Bakir, and in very bad company. His companions were failed students from Constantinople, Erzurum and Van, who had come back to Bakir at some time or other to live on their relations. Evil geniuses, they were, spreading left-wing ideas of equality and fraternity, which Boghos got madly enthusiastic about. Once when Boghos came to Yedi Su, he said to his father Hagob: "Do you know what the Hinchakists are?"

"Yes," Hagob had said. "They're madmen."

"They are Marxist-trained Armenian nationalists," Boghos had answered. And then he had asked his father: "Do you know what the Dashnakzagan are?"

"They're madmen too," Hagob had said. "Only they're mad in a different sort of way."

"They're right-wing radical Armenian nationalists," Boghos had said.

But Hagob had only shaken his head and said: "I don't understand any of it."

"And do you know what Marxists are?"

"No," Hagob had said.

"They're levellers," Boghos had said. "Think of that! All men are equal!"

"But they aren't equal," Hagob had said.

A really odd character, Boghos was. Whenever he felt like some of his mother's and grandmother's good cooking, he came back to Yedi Su for a longish visit. He often sat by the *tonir* with Hagob, smoking a *chibouk* with him. Once he said to him: "You're a lot of reactionaries."

"What does that mean?" asked Hagob.

"You just want everything to stay as it always has been."

"What we want doesn't matter," said Hagob. "All that matters is what the good God wants."

"And what does the good God want?"

"That everything should stay as it always has been."

And Hagob had said: "Has the cock got to crow at midnight instead of in the morning? Have the poor got to eat good food and the rich starve? And have the Armenians got to thrash the Turks and the Kurds instead of the other way round? Everything has its right order and man must go along with it."'

'There was one other brother, whom your father loved nearly as much as Dikran, the shoemaker. This brother was twenty years older than your father; his name was *Haygaz* and he was the eldest of Hagob's children. Haygaz was short and bald, rosy-cheeked and chubby, a bit asthmatic, short-legged and plump. He had thick fingers, fingers with little pads of fat, fingers adorned with gold rings, rings with emeralds and diamonds. When, in 1858, Haygaz tumbled out of his mother's womb on to the *yorgan* – grandfather's *yorgan*, the one that Vartan was later to inherit and over which Zovinar had squatted, that same *yorgan*, filled with straw and sheep's wool, inhabited by lively fleas and also by many generations of dead fleas, surrounded by swarms of bluebottles and mosquitoes – as I was saying, when Haygaz tumbled on to this *yorgan*, this Haygaz had become the only asthmatic scion of the Khatisians. His first cry came coughing and wheezing out of his toothless little mouth. However, he wasn't ill. A few minutes later, when his grandmother bathed him in salt water and scrubbed him thoroughly, while Haygaz coughed and cried, she said to Zovinar: "Your firstborn isn't ill. He's just coughing with impatience."

"What do you mean by that?" asked Zovinar.

"Well, just that," said the grandmother. "This little creature, and we'll call him Haygaz after my father, who is still alive and whose days count towards your Haygaz's; well, my little dove, this little creature is simply coughing out of impatience."

"Impatience for what?"

"Well, it's like this," said the grandmother. "Your Haygaz simply can't wait to make big business deals."

"What sort of big deals?"

"Well, just big deals. It's written on his forehead that he's going to be a rich man."

"How can you see that?"

"From the way he puffs himself up so that it wrinkles his forehead."

"So he's going to be a rich man?"

"Not a doubt of it."'

'Of course the grandmother was right, for at the *shekerli* party, the first-step party, it was obvious right away that Haygaz was an impatient and lively child, for with his first steps he toddled, not straight to the *tonir* or the water jug or the cowshed or even to the cradle with the Bible that his mother had put there . . . no; he dashed straight out into the open air, through the doorway of the *oda*, out into the sunlit village street.'

'Haygaz also began dealing in *tezek* as a boy, just ordinary cowshit, just as Vartan did later, and many other small children. But when he was no more than seven, when Haygaz went to the neighbouring villages he brought back things which were not available here, to sell at a profit. When he was ten he ran away from home, went to his uncle, the *arabachi* in Bakir, hung around the bazaars in the big city doing little deals with people, trading with no matter who, and he finally moved into big business with watermelons from Diyarbakir.'

'When he was thirteen Haygaz took over one of the big melon stalls in the Bakir melon bazaar. People coming back to the village from Bakir reported that Haygaz still coughed and wheezed like a thirsty camel, but all the same he was still as rosy-cheeked as ever and had cheeks like the bottom of a baby that a naughty mother had overfed. They said Haygaz also had a pot-belly and pads of fat on his fingers, but still wore no jewels, because he didn't want to buy those until his brother Sarkis could get them for him cheap – though Sarkis, they said, was not yet a qualified goldsmith, but was still learning. In brief, Haygaz was well on the way to becoming a successful man, and his melons, so people said, actually came from the area of Diyarbakir and were so big and heavy that one could only wish they would fall on the heads of the Armenians' enemies.'

'There was a lot of talk about Haygaz, and his melon stall was the subject of many rumours. In the village café, next to the tobacco shop, people swapped jokes about Hagob's short, fat, asthmatic son who was making his fortune in Bakir. The story got about that Haygaz, who was only thirteen, had married an old woman, a dim old lady of thirty-five who was at his heels every evening when Haygaz closed his stall and made his way home with the donkey and cart.'

'And it was so: one day Haygaz announced his engagement, and a year later he married the widow Warthouhi, a name that meant she was as lovely as a rose.'

'"How can a woman of over thirty-five be as lovely as a rose," said Hagob to his wife. "And what does a woman who's older than a lot of grandmothers in Yedi Su – what does she want with my son, who's so short and has a pot-belly and who coughs and wheezes when he speaks . . . and even when he isn't speaking . . . because that's how it is . . . although he was duly bathed in salt . . . and scrubbed, too . . . with salt water, I mean . . . what does a woman like that want from my Haygaz, whose sperm is still young and hardly ever discharged."

"What is she after?" asked Zovinar. "Yes, that's what I'd like to know too."'

* * *

'And the priest Kapriel Hamadian, who was sitting beside the two of them, said: "The question, Hagob Efendi, is not what she wants from him, but what he wants from her."

"Yes, that's the question," said Hagob.

"That's the question," said Zovinar.

"I've heard that she might be very rich," said the priest.

"I've heard that too," said Hagob.

"Her late husband was the richest money-changer in Bakir."

"I've heard that too."

"And the asthmatic Haygaz is a businessman!"

"At any rate he's no fool," said Zovinar.

"And he's my son," said Hagob.

"That's so," said the priest.'

'It was foreseeable. After his marriage with the widow Warthouhi, Haygaz went into business on a big scale. But not as a money-changer, like Warthouhi's first husband; because he was chubby, rosy-cheeked and fond of good food, and by nature a gourmet and a *bon vivant*, for those reasons, or maybe for some other reason, Haygaz went into the business of so many gourmets. He became a restaurateur. And because of all that, or, as the Muslims say, because it was in his *kismet*, where all that is predestined is written, it was no wonder that his new luxury restaurant, called the Restaurant Hayastan, soon became the most famous in all Bakir. People said that at the Hayastan even the Turkish customers became friendly with the Armenians, for Warthouhi enchanted every customer with her Armenian delicacies, a sign that even the wisest of maxims, such as "Love grows through the stomach", have their validity in Turkish-occupied Hayastan.'

'But now, back to your father,' said the story-teller. 'He was already selling *tezek* as a boy. When he and Avetik were a bit older and more mature, they went to Bakir more often to sell the dried cowpats they'd collected. Often they took Garo with them, but usually it was the Turkish boy Gög-Gög, because he was such a good donkey-driver. He could make the most obstinate donkey get a move on. Since Ceyda, the jennet, was a feminine creature, Gög-Gög didn't only tempt her with the sweet-smelling hay that he waved playfully to and fro in front of the donkey's mouth, but Gög-Gög also talked to the animal, whispered gentle words into Ceyda's ear and fondled her sexual organs. Often Gög-Gög would pinch a certain spot on Ceyda's hindquarters where she was specially sensititive, and burst out laughing when she suddenly sprang forward.

"At least I suppose you know the right people in Bakir who will buy *tezek*," asked Gög-Gög once, when Ceyda was being stubborn again.

"Of course," said Vartan.

"He even knows somebody who pays good prices," said Avetik.

"An Armenian?"

"An Armenian."

"And he doesn't tell you a lot of lies like saying the *tezek*'s made from goat's dung?"

"No, that chap doesn't."'

'"Who is this Armenian in Bakir who takes your *tezek*?"

"It's my eldest brother, Haygaz."

"The one . . . the one they say is so rich?"

"Yes."

"And he doesn't have any wood for heating?"

"Of course he does. But dried cowshit is cheaper."'

CHAPTER EIGHT

'In the late eighties,' said the story-teller, 'some curious schools were opened all over Hayastan by the Franks, run by nuns and priests. Missionary schools, they were called, and the object of them was to teach the true Christianity to the Gregorian Armenians. Later the Americans came too, and they were really Franks too but lived on the other side of the pond. You could learn all sorts of things there and even go on to study at the big universities in Stamboul or in Frankistan. Many Armenians sent their sons and daughters to those schools. But not from the village of Yedi Su.'

'In Yedi Su everything stayed as it always had been. The boys went to the village school, the girls stayed at home. The former mayor of Yedi Su – who was still more respected than the present mayor Ephrem Abovian – and of whom it was said that he had personally deflowered all his servant girls, had said: "An educated wife is the ruin of the family." That's what he said. And how right the Mukhtar was. The priest himself had recently said to the virgins in the village: "Just look at the educated women in Bakir. Education goes to their heads, and pride between their legs. The fire goes out in their *tonirs* and domestic peace leaves their *odas*. Their husbands lose their desire and become tame, and they're frightened, for verily, a woman's airs will shrink a man's erection."

And the priest had added: "I knew a man in Bakir who had an educated wife. And guess what he said to me in confession?"

"What, Vartapad?"

"Vartapad," he said, "my wife isn't a woman. Her well has dried up. There are *djinn* living in her pubic hair. Her withered chalice is like a scarecrow and her warm and slippery tunnel of joy a silently constricting vice."'

*　　*　　*

'Your father went to the village school,' said the story-teller. 'He could read and write, but no more. However, he knew how to play the little wooden flute that Gög-Gög the Turk had cut for him. When your father was looking after the sheep and had driven them too far into the mountains, he only needed to play his flute and the sheep came back again.'

'No, nothing much happened in the village of Yedi Su,' said the story-teller. 'The only happening of any importance was the affair of the box full of books.'

'Box full of books?'

'Yes, just a box full of books.'

'It was like this,' said the story-teller. 'There was a consumptive school teacher, who died when your father was nine years old. Soon afterwards another teacher came to Yedi Su. He was consumptive too, and he also wore rimless spectacles, like the one who had died. The people told the teacher: "If you ride into the mountains on your donkey, Hodja Efendi, you'd better leave your glasses at home, for the Kurds think everyone who wears glasses is a spy. They've already killed a lot of men who wear glasses."

But the new teacher didn't listen to the people. He often rode into the mountains, and one day he didn't come back again. The people said: "He was consumptive, and probably he felt weak and slid off his donkey and lay down somewhere." But others said: "No, he was wearing glasses. Didn't the Kurds kill a man who wore glasses in the year 1874, because they thought the Sultan had sent him to spy out the Kurds' district for the saptiehs and tax-collectors? They must have killed him, his body is down there in some ravine and his teacher's soul is somewhere with Christ."

"And where will his donkey be?" the people asked.

"The Kurds have taken it."

"But a proud mountain Kurd doesn't ride on a donkey."

"True enough."

"Perhaps the Kurds have slaughtered it and eaten it?"

"Or they've just killed it and it's lying in a ravine with the teacher."

"Then the donkey's soul will be with Christ too."
"That is possible."'

'Yes, it really was a puzzle. The teacher was still missing. He'd left nothing behind, at least nothing worth anything. The only thing was the box full of books.'

'It was like this. When he arrived in this village, the teacher had brought a box of books with him that was so heavy that only the red-headed smith and Garo, the saddler's son, could manage to carry it between them. Since the teacher lived as a lodger with the smith, and there wasn't much space in his room, for that reason and that reason only the box was kept in the big smithy, behind the foot-operated bellows. It was just left there. Now . . . after the death of the teacher, the smith wanted to burn all the books as fuel, which would save him a lot of good, carefully dried cowshit. In other words, it saved him capital. But things turned out otherwise.'

'And it was like this,' said the story-teller. 'When the smith was on the point of burning the books . . . at that very moment . . . his godson Vartan came through the smith's doorway. Vartan said: "I'll give you three sacks of *tezek* for those books."
"What do you want the books for?"
"I want to read them," said Vartan.
"They say you're going to be a poet?"
"Yes," said Vartan.
"Does that mean you've got to read all those books?"
"Not really."
"So why do you want to read them?"
"I just do," said Vartan.'

'And they fetched Garo, the saddler's son, and carried the box – this time it took three of them – into the Khatisians' *oda*. Hagob had no objection, nor had Zovinar, for there was plenty of room in the *oda* now that the children had grown up and many of the older ones had left home. That was how Vartan, who could play the flute and call the sheep out of the mountain pastures, began to read books. There were a lot of good books in the box. The teacher had said: "Many of them are written in Armenian, many are translated. And they all try to explain the world."

"All those books will muddle the boy's head," said Hagob to Zovinar. "Do you remember? The water-carrier had a muddled head too."

"But not from reading books," said Zovinar.'

'The consumptive teacher had once said to Vartan: "If ever I die, you can have all those books in my box."

"Must I read them all, to be a poet?"

"No," the consumptive teacher had said.'

'And the consumptive had said: "I've seen how you manage the sheep with your flute. Every time you play the flute, they stop in front of the ravine and go back into the safety of the valley."

"Is that a sign that I'll be a poet one day?" Vartan had asked.

"No," the consumptive had said.'

'And the consumptive said: "If you want to be a poet, you'll have to play a different flute."

"But, Hodja Efendi . . . what sort of different flute?"

"An invisible flute, my little Vartan, one that is not of this world."

"And how can I hold it in my hands, Hodja Efendi, or blow it with my mouth, if it isn't really there?"

"Who said it wouldn't be there? Look, my little lamb, even things that are not of this world exist."

"And how do you recognize them, Hodja Efendi?"

"You recognize them without eyes, my little lamb."

"How, then?"

"Well, how indeed, my little lamb? With our mind, of course. One day you will see this flute, which you can't touch, without your eyes and hold it without your hands, and you will never let it go."'

'An old shepherd had told him that he had once known a cripple who couldn't find a wife. And because he was alone, and lonely, he began to sing of love and became a poet.

"Can you only be a poet if you're a cripple?"

"Yes," the old shepherd had said.'

*   *   *

'But the consumptive teacher had said that wasn't true. Poets are not cripples. Poets, said the consumptive, are really Gypsies, only they don't read the secret signs on the brow and the hand, only the handwriting of the soul, which they then set down as verbal melodies.

"When will I read the handwriting of the soul?"

"When the time comes for the invisible flute."

"And when will that be?"

"Any time," the consumptive had said. And he had stroked Vartan's curly mop, smiled, and then said to him: "The time will come when the flute sends its heralds."'

'When Vartan was pubescent, he thought the heralds of the invisible flute had come to him in a dream. And a great sadness grew up in his heart, and also a great fear, but at the same time also an itching joy, a feverish expectation. The heralds of the invisible flute played to him, and in his dream he heard a thousand and one melodies. What he had suspected became certainty. It seemed to him as if torrents rose out of hidden sources and swelled into rivers, lakes and seas. The angels sounded their trumpets with their red lips. In his dream Vartan saw the wrinkled breasts of Bulbul, the Kurdish woman. They hung like sacks over the back of her shabby old donkey. The further Bulbul rode, the more her breasts changed, and when the donkey reached the outskirts of the village her breasts were like the warm, soft, milky breasts of his mother, and finally even those changed. And now Vartan saw the breasts of his bride, which he had never seen before. They were small, but firm as pomegranates, with fleshy, tempting nipples. "Come, touch me, my bridegroom," said the breasts. And the breasts laughed, because his hands hesitated, and they said: "You may."

And Vartan touched them.

"Don't press," said the breasts. "You must do it gently. And softly, very softly."

"Shall I only do it with my hands?"

"No, my bridegroom."

"How then, *gelin*, my little bride?"

"With your lips, my bridegroom. With your lips."'

265

★   ★   ★

'And Vartan began to suck, as he had sucked as a baby. Sobbing, craving, he clung to his bride's breasts. The more he sucked, the tinier her breasts became, until at last they disappeared.

"They are not there any more," he said to his bride.

"You have swallowed them up," said his bride.

"What shall I do now?"

"You must go on sucking, my little bridegroom."

"But what shall I suck?"

"Everything your lips can taste, my little bridegroom."

"Even your hands?"

"My hands too."

"And your feet?"

"My feet too."

"And what else?"

"Everything, my little bridegroom. Everything."

"Do you have lips between your thighs too?"

"Yes, my little bridegroom."

"Are they really as narrow as the ear-lobes of an unborn sheep?"

"Yes, my bridegroom."

"Or are they as big and floppy as a donkey's ears?"

"You can find out."

"May I really?"

"Yes, you may."

"Are we married already?"

"I don't know."

"It couldn't be our wedding night?"

"Yes, it could be."'

'But the itching joy drove out the fear and the sorrow and the shame and a new freedom released him from them as he awoke with a shout.'

'"It's nothing," said Hagob, when Zovinar showed him her son's wet mattress, the mattress, stuffed with straw and sheep's wool, which was not nearly as old as his grandfather's *yorgan*.

"What do you mean by nothing?" said Zovinar.

"He's become a man," said Hagob.

"And what about the mattress?"

"It's wet," said Hagob.

"Your son produces expensive semen," said Zovinar. "He just squirts it out anywhere instead of giving it to his wife."

"But he hasn't got a wife."

"That can be changed."

"We ought to get him married."

"Yes."

"When are you going to speak to the mayor?"

"Soon."'

'But it was not time yet,' said the story-teller. 'It was not until the following year that the mayor's daughter stained the straw and wool mattress. She stained it with blood, blood that came from no wound."

"It's time," said the mayor's wife, when she saw the blood on the mattress next morning. "Now we must announce her engagement to the Khatisians' youngest son officially."

"But she's only eleven," said the mayor.

"Eleven isn't ten," said his wife. "What do you want to wait for? Is she to become an old maid?"

"It's the custom," said the mayor, "for the wedding to take place a year after the first period. But we can't do that."

"Why can't we?"

"Because we haven't fattened her up yet. Do you think the Khatisians' youngest son wants to marry a bag of bones, just because his father and I exchanged two coins that time?"

"How long does it take to fatten her up?"

"Two years generally."

"We ought to have started earlier."

"Yes."

"Two years, did you say?"

"That's what I said."

"Well, we shall just have to manage it in a year."''

'And it was so,' said the story-teller. 'The first engagement, many years ago, on the day they exchanged coins, when the bride was still in nappies and didn't know what was happening to her, that first engagement, which had been rather discreet, just a promise and a matter of honour between the two men, Hagob and the mayor, would now, on the day after the bride's puberty, be confirmed publicly by the mayor and Hagob. It was definite now; Hagob's son and the daughter of the mayor were becoming an engaged couple. It was unchangeable. The mayor told everybody that his daughter had started bleeding without any wound, and was a woman. And the matter of feeding up the bride was no secret. That meant that this skinny little girl, who was already bleeding with no wound, this framework of fragile bones, had to be fattened up to make a handsome woman of her. It meant the mayor's wife had sworn that by all the saints. It meant that Vartan's mother had told the mayor's wife: "I'll send your daughter forty *sofras* of *baklava* on the day my son Sarkis, the goldsmith, completes the engagement ring and it's on the way here." And she had added: "It must be forty *sofras*, so that people will say: 'The bride has had forty, as is the custom when children of respected people are engaged.'"

It meant that the mayor's wife had replied: "Forty let it be. That's right. Forty *sofras* of *baklava*. And every time my daughter has eaten them empty I'll fill the *sofras* up again."

"In God's name," Zovinar had said. "She's going to be fat enough and handsome enough. Feed up my daughter-in-law, and then my son won't be laughed at."'

'Vartan hadn't set eyes on his betrothed all that often. They had often played together as children, of course, but it wasn't proper to be seen with his fiancée, to look at her too boldly or even to touch her in games. "Be careful you never stand too close to her," his mother had told him. "Otherwise you'll get talked about."

"What does that mean?"

"People will say: 'His bride is one who doesn't respect the veil.'"

"But she doesn't wear a veil."

"But she will wear one, silly boy!" And his mother said: "You must be careful. Never go too near her before she has the ring on her finger. Her good name is your good name too, and the good name of your children and grandchildren."'

★　　★　　★

'The bride's fattening-up time offered the villagers plenty of material for old wives' gossip and malicious tittle-tattle. There were many who said that the mayor's daughter never would put on fat, because as a child she had never seen salt, since they don't use salt for washing in the village, but natron from Lake Van, which itinerant Armenian traders sold to the farmers from time to time, and which the mayor possessed in great quantities. They also said that the mayor's daughter had not been bathed in cooking salt, as she should have been but in a soapy water substitute, in water with Lake Van natron, and that that weakened the body during the first forty days of life, which, as everybody knows, was not the case with cooking salt. But the mayor just laughed at the people. He said: "Just take care. Lake Van natron or cooking salt, there's no difference. I'll bet anyone thirty sheep, if anyone wants to take it on . . . I'll bet my daughter Arpine will be so fat the day she goes to church to marry the Khatisians' youngest son that she couldn't fall down the *gatnachpiur* milk well if she wanted to."

"And what do you mean by that, Mukhtar Bey? Anyone who wants to fall into the *gatnachpiur* well will fall into it. Or do you mean they would land at the side of the well if they jumped into it?"

"Oh, come on, you ass. Why should my daughter land at the side of the well if she jumped into it? Why can't you understand? What I'm saying is this: her bottom will be so fat that the shaft of the good milk well will be too narrow for her bottom to go down it. That's what I mean."

"But no one has a bottom like that, Mukhtar Bey. We simply don't believe anyone could have a bottom like that."

"I'll show you," said the mayor.

"And how do you expect to do that, when your daughter has never seen salt and has been washed in that washing mixture from Lake Van?"

"Never mind, I'll show you."

"And how much *baklava* will she have to eat before her bottom, which can't get fat anyway because she's never seen salt, becomes as fat as you say?"

"Well, if you want to know, efendiler, she's going to eat forty pieces of *baklava* every day, for it has to be *forty*. And do you know how many pieces of *baklava* that means my poor wife, God preserve her for me, will have to bake to make my daughter a respectable woman?"

"No, Mukhtar Bey. Only a consumptive could work that sort of thing out, like the late school teacher. But he's dead and disappeared in the mountains with his donkey. God rest his soul."'

'Yes, that's how it was,' said the story-teller. 'Everybody followed the fattening-up time with excitement, especially those in the families concerned, for it was a matter of honour to the mayor and Hagob. So much *baklava* was baked in the mayor's house over the year that the smell of the little sweet cakes hung over the whole village. Even the Kurds up in the mountains finally noticed it. And so it happened that the Kurd sheikh Suleyman said to his sons: "There's going to be a wedding there soon. Unless my spies have lied to me, it will be the daughter of the bald-headed Mukhtar Ephrem Abovian and the youngest son of the farmer Hagob. It would be a pity if the two of them refused to pay the bride-tax to me and my family."'

CHAPTER NINE

'Vartan could hardly wait for the wedding-day. The fatter his bride grew, the more urgent grew his longing for her bottom, which got stuck in the top of the *gatnachpiur* milk well and was bigger and more handsome than the watermelons from Diyarbakir. In a dream he heard the voices of the costers in the melon bazaar of a distant city. "Melons of flesh and blood. Bigger and fatter and juicier than the biggest and fattest and juiciest melons from Diyarbakir. Can't fall into the *gatnachpiur* well. Ah, Allah, thou who madest the walls of the well and the flesh of the melon. Why can the melon not fall into the wall?"

In his dream Vartan saw the people by the melon stall. One of the eager ones was a rich Turk with a gold pocket-watch visible under his waistcoat.

"Hey, you . . . melon-seller! Why can't that melon fall into the well?"

"I don't know, efendi. But I suppose it's because Allah made the well too narrow for such a fat melon."

"But Allah doesn't make wells, you perfect fool. Allah only sends us the water. It's men who make the wells."

"Yes, efendi. Allah be my witness, that is so. You have spoken the truth."

"So who made the well that's too narrow for the fattest melon?"

"The Armenians, efendi."

"Those unbelieving dogs."

"Yes, efendi. They deliberately built the well so narrow that the melon sticks in it."

"Why did they do that?"

"I don't know, efendi. But I suppose it was so that people should see how big the melon was, and how fat, for it can't fall into the

271

well, that damned well the Armenians call *gatnachpiur* that's too narrow for those Armenian melons."

"So, an Armenian melon?"

"Yes indeed."

"And why does that sort of melon grow in Turkey?"

"Because the Armenians say there is no Turkey, at least not in this region. This country is called Hayastan. Everything is Hayastan. And everything that grows belongs to the Armenians. Even the melons."

"And how about selling me this particular melon for my gold pocket-watch?"

"I'm afraid not, efendi."

"I want to slice it open. And stick my tongue into it. And I bet you, you dumb dog, that I can lick the honey out with my tongue."

"But, efendi, there's no honey in the melon."

"Yes there is, you bloody fool. There is honey in it. And I bet you there's something more in it."

"But, efendi, I can't sell it."

"And why not, you stupid bastard? I'll give you the gold pocket-watch."

"Because the melon is already sold."

"I suppose you've sold it to some Armenian?"

"Yes, efendi."

"Those dogs buy everything before we can get at them."

"Yes, efendi."

"Do you know what this dog of an Armenian is called?"

"He's called Vartan Khatisian, efendi, and he's the fourteen-year-old son of Hagob Khatisian."

"This Hagob and his son will have to be whipped. May Allah bring these unbelievers to reason with fire and sword. Don't you see, they take everything from us, even the best melons."

In his dream Vartan heard the coster's voice and the voice of the rich Turk with his gold watch, and he heard the murmur of the great bazaar and breathed the scent of a thousand and one delicacies. Suddenly he saw that the big melon, which was nothing else but the backside of his bride, had risen into the air and flown on a flying carpet to Yedi Su, straight under his *yorgan*. And the fat melon said to him: "I belong to you. Soon we shall be married. But don't forget to pay the bride-tax, exactly half the bride-price."

"And if I forget?"

"Then the Kurds will ravish me."

"That is impossible."

"No, it's quite possible."'

'Vartan seized the melon in his dream, and although he was not married yet and actually should not do it, he stroked the rounded flesh and felt that there was a thorn bush beneath the melon, which opened and divided like the Red Sea before the patriarch's staff.

"I can feel a mouth behind the thorns, opening its lips."

"The lips are just the sea, my bridegroom. Have you got your staff?"

"Yes, *gelin*, my bride."

"The sea has vanished, my bridegroom, do you see?"

"Yes, *gelin*, my bride."

"There are just the lips now, that open themselves to you."

"Yes, *gelin*, my bride."

"They are as dainty as the earlobes of an unborn lamb."

"No, *gelin*, you lie, they are as big as the ears of a fully grown donkey."

"It's all one, my bridegroom. What could I do about it, when all the *baklava* made them so big and fat?"

"I don't know, little *gelin*, my bride."

"Or would you rather have had a skinny little dolly?"

"No, little *gelin*."'

'No man will ever confess how often he has come all over the *yorgan* in his dreams,' said the story-teller. 'But I reckon that the good semen your father wasted during the bride's fattening-up period would have completely filled the clay pots by the walls of the *oda*, provided the pots were empty and not full of whey or cheese, pickled green tomatoes, paprika and other sorts of food. Of course his grandmother observed it, and so did his mother.

"Haven't I told you not to play with your thing? Do you want to grow up like the water-carrier?"

"But I don't touch it, mother. It all happens in my dreams. Can I help it, if that big melon of flesh and blood and honey follows me into my sleep?"

273

"Do you dream about her?"

"Yes, mother."

"And who rubs your man's tool – it's not a child's tool any more – when you dream?"

"Nobody, mother."

"The good God, perhaps?"

"I don't know, mother."'

'Weddings in the village of Yedi Su were held immediately after the harvest. It had always been so. When the wind from the Hayastan mountains blew the chaff at the threshing far out into the Armenian countryside, the old women used to say: "There will soon be a *harsanik-pilav* again", and what they meant was the Armenian wedding rice, which the Turks knew too, though they called it *zerde-pilav*. It was obvious that the old women knew something. For that's how it is: when it's autumn, the goddess Anahit comes on silent feet into every village and town of Hayastan, to tempt the bride out of her parents' house into the house of the bridegroom. And so it was in 1893, when Anahit appeared to Hagob in a dream and said to him: "The time has come, Hagob, for you to lead your youngest son to the altar, for look, Hagob, the bride is fattened up, she will be a fruitful cushion for your youngest son, on which he can sow and reap."'

'Everyone in the village was talking about the coming marriage. The old men cracked jokes by the seven wells, and the old women giggled coyly.

"Hagob wanted him to be a fisherman," said the old women. "But he's just become a farmer and a shepherd who also pretends he's a poet."

"He is a fisherman," said the old men, "for he's hooked a fat bride." And the old men laughed and said: "A fisherman needs a strong rod to catch a fish as fat as that. Do you think the Khatisians' youngest son has a strong enough rod to hold such a fat fish on the hook?"

Then the old women blushed under their head-scarves and said: "We don't know. But his rod is young. God send him many children."'

* * *

'Seven days before the wedding Bulbul rode into the nearby town of Gökli on her shabby old donkey, to bring a message to the town-crier, Nazim Efendi. The town-crier, Nazim Efendi, a Turk lame in one leg and deaf in one ear, was responsible for seven Armenian and two Turkish villages in this area.

"I come on behalf of Hagob Khatisian," said Bulbul to the town-crier. "His son Vartan is getting married next week in Yedi Su, to the daughter of the mayor, Ephrem Abovian. Can you spread the news to the seven Armenian villages and tell them that everybody is invited unless they've got cholera or the French disease?"

"Why didn't Hagob Khatisian come himself?" said the town-crier.

"Because he sent me," said Bulbul.

"And what does that Armenian reckon this will cost?"

"A new pair of boots, which his son Dikran will make for you."

"And how am I to know whether it's true?"

"How long have you known me?" asked Bulbul.

"Over twenty years," said the town-crier.

"And how often have I brought you news?"

"Often enough," said the town-crier.

"And have I ever lied?"

"No," said the town-crier.'

'The town-crier knew all the people in the seven villages,' said the story-teller. 'And naturally everyone knew the town-crier. Every time he hobbled through the streets, with his fur hat sliding off his head, his dilapidated clothes and shoes and the goatskin drum and two drumsticks dangling over his cummerbund, to proclaim the Sultan's latest pronouncements to such people as were in the village square at the time, the children all shouted: "The Munadi's coming! The Munadi's coming!" Many of them bellowed insults and obscene swearwords in his deaf ear. Since the town-crier could neither read nor write, he always took a literate Armenian with him who could read the Turkish text in the Arabic script. Then the literate Armenian whispered what he'd read in the good ear of the lame town-crier, deaf in the other ear, and the town-crier held the paper in front of his nose to make it look as if he had no trouble in reading it, and then bawled the Sultan's notices loud into the crowd. The Munadi had such a powerful voice that people were scared even when it was good news. People said that the Munadi shouted so loud that the echo of his voice reached the Kurds in the mountains, though of course the Munadi knew that the Kurds didn't care a damn for the Sultan's orders.

The last time Hagob's wife had become pregnant, when the Munadi came to the village with his Armenian, Hagob had gone up to him and asked: "Well, Nazim Efendi, what's the news?"

"You'll hear it in a minute," the Munadi had said.

"Can't you just let me hear a bit of it in advance, Nazim Efendi?"

"No, Hagob Efendi."

"Not even for a little tip . . . a little *baksheesh*?"

"I should have to think about that, Hagob Efendi." And he thoughtfully added: "Hagob Agah."

"Suppose I gave you a big *baksheesh*?"

"A big *baksheesh*, did you say, Hagob Agah? Did I hear you aright, Hagob Bey?"

"You did hear me aright."

"Well now, Hagob Pasha. For a big *baksheesh* let me just have a word with myself, and I'll tell you more than I know myself."'

'"Hagob Pasha," the Munadi had said, "the Russo-Turkish war is over. The Russians are withdrawing. What do you say to that?"

"What war is that, Nazim Efendi?"

"Well, the war, Hagob Pasha, the war of 1877, I think, and the 1878 war . . . which I think we lost, although the Russians suddenly withdrew."

"Was there really such a war?"

"Of course, Hagob Pasha."

"But we didn't see any soldiers here."

"Not even Russians?"

"No, no Russians either."'

'"Have you got any other news, Nazim Efendi?"

"Yes, Hagob Pasha. But I'm afraid it's bad news."

"Can't you keep the bad news to yourself?"

"No, Hagob Pasha, I'm afraid I can't. You Armenians are now going to have to pay the military service exemption tax again, the *bedel*, I mean, because you're such cowardly dogs, too feeble to bear arms for the Sultan."

"But we're not as feeble as all that, Nazim Efendi."

"Have you got some weapons hidden away somewhere?"

"God forbid, Nazim Efendi."'

'"Tell me, Nazim Efendi, couldn't you read the people something from your paper that isn't really there? I mean, read out that the Sultan had said he congratulated me on my son Vartan?"

"And where is your son Vartan, Hagob Pasha?"

"He hasn't been born yet, but he'll soon be with us. My wife is pregnant with him."

"When will your son be with us, Hagob Pasha?"

"When the first leaves fall from the trees, Nazim Efendi."'

'"All right, Hagob Pasha. That can be done. The Sultan can certainly have said what he hasn't said. By Allah, everything is possible. Perhaps the Sultan really has congratulated you and doesn't even know it."

"That's right, Nazim Efendi."

"And after all, Hagob Pasha, come to think of it, why should the news about the withdrawal of the Russians be any more important than the imminent arrival of your son Vartan?"

"That's it, Nazim Efendi."

"And how big is the *baksheesh*?"

"Well, Nazim Efendi, that depends on how you say it."

"How do you mean, Hagob Pasha? Do you mean the bit about the withdrawal of the Russians and the bit about the war and the bit about the *bedel*?"

"No, Nazim Efendi, I mean the bit about my son."

"That bit, then?"

"Yes, just that bit."'

'That was a long time ago,' said the story-teller. 'And now that same town-carrier went out to the villages to tell the people that Vartan, son of Hagob, whom years ago he had congratulated in the name of the Sultan, had not only been born a long time ago but was going to be married, and moreover to the daughter of the mayor, Ephrem Abovian from Yedi Su.'

CHAPTER TEN

'Exactly two days before the wedding, Uncle Nahapeth arrived from America. He brought his son Howard with him, who was actually called Hovhannes, like the crazy water-carrier, and who – believe it or not – was still a bachelor, although he was five years older than Vartan. The arrival of the two Americans in Yedi Su was such a notable event that even the sparrows on the roofs lost their voices in surprise, but only temporarily, for as soon as the two of them got out of their *arabas* outside the Khatisians' house, the sparrows on the flat roof began to twitter again, more excited than before and absolutely confused.

"That's Hagob's brother," the people said. "He's a rag-and-bone man in America, and a millionaire."

"And the son?"

"He's his successor."

"Why does the rag-and-bone man wear a hat with a brim?"

"We don't know."

"And his son's got the same sort of hat."

"Yes, so we saw."

"The Turks will strike them dead if they go about the streets wearing hats with such big brims."

"But not in this village."

"Do you think they went about in Bakir like that?"

"We'll have to ask them."

"They have been in Bakir, haven't they?"

"Yes, they spent a couple of days with Hagob's eldest son Haygaz."

"The owner of the Hayastan?"

"Yes."'

*   *   *

'"I've heard that Hagob's eldest son sent the rag-and-bone man a telegram about the wedding."

"Yes, I've heard that."

"The rag-and-bone man must have given the telegraph boy in America a big tip. Or else he'd never have got the telegram."

"Yes, that's true."

"Apparently those telegraphs boys in America get huge tips. Just think what a chap like that must get if he takes telegrams to all those millionaires."

"We'd better become telegraph boys in America."

"I bet you even the telegraph boys are millionaires over there."''

'While the women had gathered at the seven wells to exchange the latest news, and talked most of all about the two Americans with their checked jackets and creased trousers and broad-brimmed hats, but also about the bride, who was going to be taken to the *hamam* in Gökli next day to be bathed and cleaned on the day before the wedding in the famous steam bath in the nearest county town, the two Americans sat in the circle of men in the village café to let people have a good look at them.

"Do all men in America go about the streets in big hats like those?" asked the Mukhtar.

"Yes," said the rag-and-bone man.

"And nobody strikes them dead for it?"

"No, nobody."

"Tell us this thing about your hats again," said Hagob. "I mean, what it was like in Bakir when you two took your big broad-brimmed hats out on the street."

"But I've just told you."

"But not everybody heard."

"OK, then I'll tell you once more."''

'But Uncle Nahapeth clearly seemed to be in no hurry to tell them about the hats, but talked about America, the land of freedom, where Kurds, Turks and Armenians lived together in peace, where there was no military exemption tax, where even common words like *bedel* and *teskeré* were unknown, where the Muslims didn't get indignant if Christian men refused to be circumcised. All men were

equal there, and everyone had equal rights. It was only different for
the niggers, for they weren't real men but tame apes, as a man from
the Southern States had told him once. How that man could talk!
Imagine: the Southerner told him that one of those tame black apes
in his city had smiled at a white woman. And, understandably,
white men in black hoods had come and taken the ape out of bed
at night, and just hanged him. Just like that. But otherwise
everything was great over there. There was money lying in the
streets, but it could only be seen and picked up by capable men.
And of course by people with brains in their heads. The others
remained poor, and it was their own fault. Everyone could get rich
quickly if he had the right stuff in him and God was on his side.

"And what about those big American hats?"

"What big American hats?"

"The ones you and your son went out in in Bakir."

"Oh, you mean those hats?"

"Yes, that's it."

"Well, let's see," said the uncle. "Just let me think."'

'The uncle from America sat chubby-cheeked among the men. His
red drinker's nose seemed to be laughing like his little, black,
mischievous eyes. "I was born in Hayastan," said the uncle, "but
that one, my son Hovhannes, whom we call Howard, he was born
in America," and he pointed derisively at his son, sitting between
Hagob and Vartan, thin and pale and a little shy, and sucking now
and then at the water-pipe that Hagob had put beside his cushion.
"This American oaf," said the uncle, still pointing at his son as if
he were accusing him of something, "doesn't understand Kurdish
or Turkish and can only speak a few words of Armenian, and that
so pathetically that you have to laugh to stop yourself crying."

"And what can he speak?"

"He can only speak *ingilizce*."

"And why can't he speak Turkish and Kurdish, and not even
proper Armenian?"

"Because he's a real American," said his uncle, "and because he
thinks that everybody in the whole world only speaks *ingilizce*, a
language that sounds as if people had their mouths full of pebbles
and shit."'

* * *

'"Well, we wore our big hats when we went out in Bakir," said the uncle. "I was really afraid the Turks would strike us dead, but, as you see, we're still alive."

"So you are," said Hagob.

"So we went for a walk in our hats," said the uncle, "and I was afraid the Turks would kill us, but we're still alive."

"You've just said that," said Hagob.

"So I have," said the uncle.'

'"So we took our hats for a walk in Bakir," said the uncle, "and the people just stared at us stupidly, especially the Turks, but the other Muslims too."

"I can imagine," said Hagob.

"*Sinek kagidi*, some of the people said, and they said it loud enough for us to hear.

'What does that mean?' my son asked, the American oaf.

'It means flytraps,' I told him. 'What else would it mean?'

'And why do people say flytraps to us?'

'I'll show you,' I said."'

'"We went through the alley with the grocers' shops," said the uncle. "Among all those Armenian grocers there was also a Turk. He sat fast asleep in front of his shop catching flies."

"How can he catch flies if he's asleep?" asked Hagob.'

'"So we stood there in front of the grocer's shop and the sleeping Turk. 'Do you see all those bluebottles?' I said to my son in *ingilizce*. 'Do you know where they come from?'

'No, father,' he said.

'I don't know either,' I said."'

'"Well, that's how things are,' I said. 'There's a town here called Turhkal. It's the dirtiest town in Turkey. In summer there are so many bluebottles that the Turks actually pick them out of their wedding soup.'

'Wedding soup?' he asked, that American oaf.

'Yes, wedding soup,' I said. 'The Turks call it *dudun chorbassy*.'"'

*　　*　　*

'"'So why are there so many bluebottles there?' he asked.

'Because the old streets are three metres under the present streets.'

'And what's under the old streets?'

'Just filth, my boy,' I said. 'Because for hundreds of years these people have been chucking their garbage, even their shit and everything, into the street. There were dead cats and dead dogs lying there, and many a beggar has actually died and rotted on the street. And it's all been trodden flat or rolled flat by the traffic and the people's filthy feet for hundreds of years.'

'And what's it like here in Bakir?'

'Even worse,' I told him.

'Then is Bakir the dirtiest town in Turkey?'

'The dirtiest, and the most beautiful,' I said.'"'

'"And then I pointed at the sleeping Turk. 'Look, my son,' I said, 'every time a bluebottle tickles him, he wakes up.'

'Yes, father,' he said. 'So I see.'

'And he watches it with half-closed eyes.'

'Yes, father.'

'And he waits until the fly crawls a bit higher, up his nose, up his forehead, as far as the edge of his fez.'

'Yes, father.'

'And he doesn't kill it till then. Did you notice?'

'Yes, father.'

'So that he won't get any blood or dirt from squashed flies on his skin. He squashes them slowly on his red fez, almost as if he enjoyed it, and then he flicks the dead fly on to the street with his finger.'

'Yes, father, I saw him.'

'That's why Turks won't wear hats with brims,' I told my son. 'How could a Turk flick a dead fly off the edge of his fez on to the street with one finger, if that fez was a hat with a brim? It would be impossible. The fly would stick to the brim.'

'So is that why hats with brims are flytraps?'

'That's why, my boy.'"'

'"But the Muslims got pretty worked up when we first went past their mosques wearing our hats," said the uncle. "The faithful there didn't say *sinek kagidi*, they said *sapkaci*. My son asked me what it meant. And I told him: 'That's a Turkish word, and it means the Hatter. It's a dangerous word, my son.'

'Why is it dangerous, father?'

'Well, why indeed, my son. I don't know. It's just dangerous.' And I told him: 'When I was a boy I often walked about Bakir, I hung around the bazaars and looked at the women, the women in their black *charshafs* and their double veils. And there was an Englishman once, with a hat like the ones we're wearing. And the people swore at him and said "*sapkaci*". And next day they found the Englishman outside the city. His head had been cut off. And lying by his head was the big hat. And the hat had no brim. And I suppose that whoever it was who cut his head off had also cut the brim off, because it particularly infuriated him.'

'Why?' my son asked.

And I said: 'You oaf. Never mind why. Isn't it enough that the brim of the hat had infuriated him?'"'

'Now the priest intervened. He had been sitting and listening to the rag-and-bone man in silence all the time. "There is a reason," said the priest.

And the priest said: "When the people say 'Flytrap' to the broad-brimmed hats, that's harmless, they're just using the hat as an excuse to say something rude. They don't strike the man with the hat dead and cut off his head, not even the brim of his hat. But when they say 'Hatter', that's different. '*Sapkaci*!' That word isn't a joke. What they mean by it is that the man wearing the hat with the brim has come there deliberately to challenge the faithful, and above all to poke fun at the Mahdi."'

'And the priest said: "The Mahdi lives in the Paradise of the faithful and was already a saint in his lifetime. Often, the Muslims believe, Allah sends the Mahdi down to earth for few seconds to reveal one of the many secrets of Paradise to the true believers. The Mahdi always appears to the believer after he has fasted and washed, but only when he is praying, specifically just when he has touched the dust with his forehead as he pronounces the name of Allah. If the

Mahdi appears, the believer, kneeling before Allah, need not stand but only turn his eyes and look upwards. Then he sees the Mahdi."

"What's that got to do with the brim of a hat?" asked Hagob.

"It has a great deal to do with it," said the priest. "For how can the believer, as he prays kneeling on his prayer mat, his forehead in the dust, turn his eyes upwards . . . how is he to see the Mahdi if the brim of his hat blocks his view? The brim isn't made of glass."

"Not made of glass," said Hagob.

"That's it," said the priest.

"Is that why Muslims never wear hats with brims?"

"For that very reason," said the priest.

"Those big hats are really dangerous," said Hagob. "My eldest son Haygaz is coming to the village tomorrow. I'll ask him to find something more suitable for my brother and his son to wear on their heads."

"That's a good idea," said the priest. "There's a wide choice of decent hats without brims in Bakir. Your eldest son ought to get them straight after the wedding, when he's back in Bakir I mean, and send them here the quickest way with an *arabachi*. A turban wouldn't be bad, it's very attractive, but I think such fine gentlemen as your brother from America and his son really ought to wear a red fez. Don't you think, Hagob Efendi, that you ought to tell your eldest son that a red fez would be best for the gentlemen?"

"Yes," said Hagob.'

'The men drank a lot of *raki* in the coffee-house, also the Armenian *oghi* schnapps, and they ate sweetmeats and drank spiced tea and sweet coffee. The uncle had put his arm round Vartan and whispered something in his ear. Vartan blushed, and the uncle repeated it, very softly, so that no one but Vartan could hear it.

"Tell me, nephew, have you ever had a woman before?"

"No, Uncle Nahapeth."

"And do you know what you have to do on your wedding day?"

"No, Uncle Nahapeth."

"And your bride? Does she know?"

"I don't think so."

"Then I must have a talk with you later."''

*   *   *

284

'No one had ever seen the bride's naked behind, not even the water-carrier, who spied on the women of the village when they relieved themselves in the cowshed. Even Vartan couldn't imagine anything reasonable that would correspond in any way with reality. The only way of finding out anything more about her behind, and other things as well, was from the reports of the women who accompanied the bride to the steam bath on the day before the festivities. So it was understandable that the visit to the *hamam* was awaited with great excitement not only by Vartan but also by all the others who ought not to have been interested. The men spread wild rumours round the village, and even some of the women who hadn't gone into the steam bath as companions nattered excitedly to one another. When the bride's escort finally came home from the *hamam* in the evening, they were bombarded with questions.

"Did you see her behind?"

"No. She'd wrapped towels round it."

"But the bath attendant, the *hamamji*, must surely have seen the bride's behind when she helped her to wrap the towels round it?"

"Oh yes, she saw it."

"And what did she say?"

"She said it was a good behind, her hips were strong and supple. The *hamamji* said the girl would have many children."

"And what does her behind look like?"

"The *hamamji* said, just like her face. A fat lump of flesh."

"But that's impossible. A behind doesn't have eyes and ears and a nose."

"True. But it looks like her face if you can think of it without the ears and the eyes and the nose."

"And what about her mouth?"

"A behind has got a mouth, only it's shaped like a long slit and runs up and down, the other way round."

"The other way round?"

"Yes, just the other way round."'

'"And what about her breasts? Are they really like pomegranates? Or are they great cheese bags that you could get whey out of?"

"Her breasts are neither pomegranates nor cheese bags," said the women who had seen the bride in the *hamam*. "Her breasts are like doves without feathers, but with red beaks, and, believe it or not, although the doves have no feathers they look as if they would fly away at any moment."

"Then it's high time the wedding was celebrated," said the men, "and Hagob's youngest son got hold of those breasts before they do fly away."

"You're right," said the women.

"But Hagob's youngest son wants to be a poet," said the men. "His hands are soft and can't catch hold of them properly."

"He'll have to be trained," said the women.

And the men said: "Yes, you're right."'

The story-teller said: 'God created the world in six days, and on the seventh he crowned his creation with the Sabbath. So it was no wonder that Vartan's wedding lasted seven whole days, and that the church ceremony took place on the seventh day, the day that the creation was crowned, and in fact on a Sunday, because the Christians had shifted the holy Sabbath to Sunday.

Already, the day before the wedding, when the bride was taken to the *hamam*, relatives of the Khatisians were arriving in their *arabas*. Many of them had come a very long way, from such towns as Belgrade and Sarajevo, towns that had once belonged to the Ottoman Empire. Among them was Ghazar Khatisian, the coffee-house proprietor from Sarajevo, with his wife and six children and his brother-in-law, Khachatur Babaian, who had a textile works in Belgrade. I can't tell you about all the Khatisians' relatives who came from the neighbouring villages and the little towns and the big towns, many of them in donkey-carts, many in *arabas* drawn by oxen, mules or horses, for the time – as we both know – is short. So it will have to be enough if I assure you that all those whom your father loved best were there.'

The story-teller said: 'Some of the guests were robbed by the Kurds on the road, and they came with no presents, almost naked and barefoot. The relatives from Bakir came all together, under escort, for Haygaz had good connections with official circles, and, for a big *baksheesh*, they had made twenty armed saptiehs available for the proprietor of the Hayastan and his caravan of relatives, to

286

escort the caravan through the Kurdish area.'

'Yes, that's how things were,' said the story-teller. 'On the day the festivities began the village was so crowded that all the priest Kapriel Hamadian could do was to put up in his church all those of the visitors who couldn't find anywhere to stay in the houses, cowsheds or barns. All the Armenians from the seven villages had come, and even a few Turks from the nearby Turkish village of Keferi Köi, relatives of the Turkish family befriended by the villagers of Yedi Su. Persian, Russian and Arab merchants suddenly bobbed up in the village, not to mention semi-nomad Kurds and a few Chaldean Nestorians, remnants of an early Christian sect who lived in caves near the Armenian villages. Suddenly the village was swarming with uninvited guests, not least the devil-worshippers, Gypsies, beggars and down-and-outs who were always around when there was a free supply of food and drink. People said that the announcement of Vartan's wedding, with the Munadi's drum roll, had been heard far beyond the borders of the seven villages, carried by the echoes and the wind. Among the beggars came the blind man from the Gate of Happiness, Mechmed Efendi. Dikran, the shoemaker, had brought him.'

'People in Yedi Su always said, if you have a daughter you lose her on her wedding-day, but it's different if you have a son. For the bride leaves her parents' house to go and live under the bridegroom's roof. But the bridegroom's parents don't lose anyone. They gain a daughter.

No wonder, then, that there was rejoicing in the Khatisians' house, while in the Mukhtar's house there was weeping and wailing.

"The bride there is packing all her things," said the people. "She's breaking her mother's heart."

'But I'm not so sure,' said the story-teller, 'that the bride was really breaking her mother's heart, for why had the Abovians been in such a hurry to fatten up their daughter and get her under the veil so quickly? The fact is that loud weeping and wailing at the packing of the trousseau and the farewell preparations are all part of the customary etiquette, for the bride's parents have to let the whole village know how sad it makes them to lose their beloved daughter. Two ballad singers from Bakir, whom Haygaz had brought with him at the Mukhtar's request, were therefore standing outside the Mukhtar's house, sometimes in front of the windows, sometimes in front of the open doorway, singing their satirical songs. *Go with God, my daughter*, sang one of them, imitating the voice of the bride's mother . . . *Go with God, my daughter, and never forget us.*

How should I forget you, mother? sang the other in the high piping voice of the fat girl . . . *how could I forget you, whose sweet milk I have drunk?*

Go with God, sang the first . . . *Go with God, my daughter, to whom I have given my milk.*'

'Yes, that's how it was,' said the story-teller. 'Hagob had paid a thousand piastres for the milk rights, the customary sum among respected families besides the money for the trousseau, which they call *ojid*. On the day before the festivities Zovinar had taken her daughter-in-law a bowl of henna, a clay bowl standing on a wooden dish, richly decorated with fruit. Henna and fruit were symbols of the goddess Anahit, and the bride, who ate some of her mother-in-law's fruit the day before the wedding and painted her fingernails and toenails with henna straight afterwards, would be fruitful and give her mother-in-law many grandchildren. As Zovinar gave her daughter-in-law the bowl, she said to her: "A fat behind is no guarantee. You must eat my fuit, *gelin*, my daughter-in-law . . . and paint every nail the good God gave you on those little fingers and toes with this magic red colour. And don't forget: when my son, who is healthy and has good blood in his veins . . . when he has made you pregnant . . . with the help of God and the Saviour . . . don't forget to lay the Bible beside your bed and hang garlic outside the door."'

'Hagob had slaughtered more sheep and lambs than his herds could really spare, and the Mukhtar too had contributed enormously from his own flocks.

"There are no beasts left to pay the bride-tax to the Kurdish sheikh," Hagob had said to the Mukhtar.

And the Mukhtar had said: "To hell with the Kurdish sheikh and his bride-tax."

"Let's hope the Kurdish sheikh has forgotten all about the bride-tax."

"One can only hope," the Mukhtar had said.'

'There was a sweet, spicy smell in the village. Sometimes the smell from the spits was carried by the wind over the flat roofs of the houses up into the mountains.

"That smell might get up the sheikh's nose," said Hagob.

"Let's hope the wind drops in time," said the Mukhtar.'

'It was customary for the bridegroom to be shaved and have his hair cut by an approved barber the day before the church ceremony. This was regarded as a sign that the bridegroom took the wedding seriously and was ready to lead a modest domestic life. The greater the barber's reputation, the more serious the intentions of the bridegroom. It was usually the godfather's responsibility to engage an approved barber, if possible one who could sing ballads as he shaved and cut the hair, old Armenian songs about weddings, big families, modesty, good fortune, money and happiness. Since the red-headed smith who was Vartan's godfather didn't know any barbers who met with the approval of the Khatisian family, Hagob was obliged to ask his eldest son Haygaz to bring a really good barber with him from Bakir, for everybody knew that there were fine singing barbers in a town as big as Bakir. The proprietor of the Hayastan had actually brought one with him in his *araba*, not just any one but the famous Armenian barber Wagharshak Bahadurian, a real wedding barber, who mixed freely with rich people and knew their sons' hair and beards better than their mothers and wives did. This famous barber was the one who attended to Haygaz when he wedded the elderly Warthouhi, but – and this was the real sensation – a few years earlier he himself, with his razor and scissors, had prepared the former Armenian Mukhtar of Bakir (a widower, marrying for the second time) for his marriage bed – no small task, when you come to think of it, for the former Mukhtar was as bald as Ephrem Abovian, the Mukhtar of Yedi Su. He had an untidy, stubbly beard, he suffered from flatulence and hiccups, especially during the haircut and shave, when he broke wind anxiously whenever his skin and hair were touched with the sharp implements; but the famous master barber Wagharshak Bahadurian had not only clipped and trimmed the grey locks above his ears and on his temples in expert manner, but had even pressed and oiled them with oil of roses. A masterpiece, it was, a real work of art. Even in shaving him, people said, he had managed to shave him without leaving any marks. This barber, so people said, could sing like the decoy birds in the early morning, and his voice brought everyone good luck, good health and great potency, a proven fact, for all his wedding clients were vigorous and bore male offspring, even the former Mukhtar of Bakir, even though, as everyone knew, he was no longer young when he remarried and already had suspicious flatulence, did frightful farts and suffered from hiccups.'

'I haunted the village streets of Yedi Su, unseen, for seven days and seven nights,' said the story-teller. 'No one had perceived me, and yet it seemed to me as if I had eaten and drunk with the wedding guests and sung and danced in the narrow alleys and on the village square. We were lucky with the weather, for the good God had driven the threatening clouds back over the mountains. And so it was not surprising that the yellow sun, which the Kurds, high up in the mountains, hid away every evening in a black goats'-hair tent, smiled unhindered over the land of Hayastan day after day in the most friendly way, it seemed to me, here in this district where the village of Yedi Su stood with its little Gregorian Apostolic church, its market-place and its coffee-house, the village smithy, the few, narrow, dusty alleys, the white-tiled clay huts and occasional brick and stone houses - the village of Yedi Su with its flat roofs open to the sky, the roofs where they slept during the summer, where there was washing hanging and cowpats drying – *tezek* – and where the women spread mulberry and grape juice on thin metal sheets in the rays of the sun and the swarms of flies and mosquitoes. Gaily coloured were the women's dresses, dainty their soft slippers, gleaming the jewellery on their arms and their ears and round their necks and on their double veils. The men's strong boots looked all the rougher, their sleeveless jackets, white, grey and brown baggy trousers and black fur caps all the more awkward. What would have happened, I wondered, if it had actually rained during the festivities? Where would all this outdoor gaiety have disappeared to? What room would there be for the dancers under the roofs of the houses? How would they have danced in those gloomy rooms? Would they perhaps have stayed on the streets to get wet and sink in the mud? And where would the musicians have played? In the rain, possibly?'

'On the sixth day of the festivities, exhausted, I rested on the eastern arch of the church. Next to me sat my seeming shadow, or one who might well be my shadow.

"How do you like the weather?" I asked.

"It's very pleasant," said my shadow.

"The Kurds might well have kept the sun shut up, just to annoy the Armenians."

"But they didn't."

"True."

"True," said my shadow.

"Or the good God might have got out of breath, and in that sad case he wouldn't have been able to blow the clouds away. Then the clouds would have hidden the sun, and its rays wouldn't have helped much in rainy weather."

"That could have happened."

"But it can't rain at Armenian weddings."

"Why not?"

"Because Christ is among the wedding guests."

"How do you know that?"

"Everybody knows that," I said.

"Are the Armenians the Christians He loves most?"

"Yes, my little lamb," said I, the story-teller. "He loves the Armenians best among Christians, because they are in such great danger here in the land of the Muslims."

"In great danger?"

"In great danger."

"For His sake?"

"For His sake."'

'"Hagob is beaming all over his face," I said to my own shadow, "for everything seems to be going right at this wedding of his youngest son. I don't mean only the weather, but the music too."

"I've never seen so many musicians at a country wedding before."

"The *saz* instruments and drums come from Yedi Su," I said, "and the young chaps who can play them . . . the others, with the Anatolian wind instruments and strings, come from the nearby villages, but there are also some from Gökli, the Munadi's town, and even some from Bakir. Haygaz engaged those together with the wedding barber."

"I've seen some Gypsies, too, ragged-looking people."

"And have you seen their fiddles too?"

"Yes."

"They come from Russia," I said. "They're smugglers, who bring Armenian schnapps from Yerevan to Van. We often see them in these parts. They never go anywhere without their fiddles, and although they can't read music, even without notes they know how to express longings and dreams in melodies. Fiddles have a language of their own, and when they tell stories of dreams and longings the women's eyes grow moist, but the men look wilder."

And I said: "The wind carries the sound of the music up to the ears of the Kurds in their tents. And because I have ears that can also hear what the Kurds hear, I must tell you now that the Kurds are lying in wait. Their spies have been active for a long time."

"Will the Kurds raid the village?"

"I don't know."'

'And I could hear what the Kurdish sheikh's mother was saying to her son: "Those Armenians, my son, are making such a din that your blessed father will turn in his grave."

"But my father must rest in peace," said the sheikh.

"Those unbelievers won't let him rest."

"You're right."

"They're celebrating a wedding again. It's Hagob's youngest son and the daughter of the bald-headed Mukhtar, Ephrem Abovian."

"I know."

"Have Hagob and the Mukhtar paid the bride-tax?"

"No, not yet."

"Then you ought to go and collect the bride-tax."

"I shall do."

"When?"

"On the seventh day of their festivities."

"Will you carry off the bride?"

"Of course."

"And who will deflower her."

"One of my sons will deflower her."

"Which one will that be?"

"I don't know."

The old woman nodded. Then she laughed and said: "We'll give those Armenians a warning that people in the seven villages will remember, to remind them what happens to an Armenian who doesn't pay the bride-tax."'

'"Hagob has been pretty generous with both schnapps and wine," I said to my shadow. "Have you noticed, even the Turkish guests have had a skinful?"

"Why not?" said my shadow. "There's nothing in the Koran about Armenian schnapps and Armenian wine. Why shouldn't the Muslims enjoy themselves?"'

'We talked for a while, my shadow and I, then my fairy-tale voice had a little nap, but soon woke up and rubbed its imaginary eyes. Towards noon on the sixth day of the festivities I, the story-teller, flew from the arch of the church, together with the one I thought of as my shadow, hovering over the village until we finally landed at the market-place, in front of the coffee-house, just as the smith was drinking the health of his godson.

"We must break up now," the smith said, "for Vartan will soon be having his public shave and haircut."

"Will they shave him and cut his hair in the market-place?"

"No, in front of the Khatisians' *oda*, outside the door."

"Then we must be quick if we want to get a place where we can see."'

'And so I went off after the men. And behind us came the women. Everyone wanted to be there to see the ceremony, and of course to applaud the famous barber, Wagharshak Bahadurian, whom they'd all heard so much about.'

*   *   *

'Hagob had laid two sacks of grain in front of the open door of the house and put a thick carpet over them. Vartan sat there like a young king on his throne. There was a huge crowd of people round him, all chattering to one another. People kept on saying: "Where's the barber, then? Where is Wagharshak Bahadurian . . . Wagharshak Bahadurian?"'

'My shadow and I pushed through the crowd and sat next to Vartan. We noticed that Vartan was nervous, a bit embarrassed even and confused, for he was not used to so much honour and attention. Possibly in his modesty he had not expected to become the central figure, the one with all the people round him. Vartan looked for his bride, but couldn't see her; dazzled by the bright light of the midday sun, all he could see were the bright clothes of the wedding guests all round him, and could smell their sweat and the scent of schnapps and wine on their breath. Probably he was thinking: "The barber's coming soon to get you all ready for the marriage bed, and tomorrow you will be married in church, and later . . . yes, later you have to deflower the bride, and hang the bloody bed-sheet in front of the door so that everyone can see that she was still a virgin." And that, of course, that she should still be a virgin, was a matter of honour.

"We Armenians call honour *badiv*," he had said once to Gög-Gög, the Turk. "Honour is everything. And the honour of the bride is also the honour of the bridegroom."

And Gög-Gög, the Turk, had said: "It's just the same with us Turks."

My shadow and I sat there, unseen, beside Vartan. When at last the barber came and began clipping, we both darted off and joined Vartan's relatives.

"Where is the bride?" asked my shadow.

I said: "The bride is hidden by her relatives. But she's sure to come soon, when the priest blesses the clothes of the bride and bridegroom. It's true that the church wedding is not till tomorrow, the seventh day, but the sixth day is the day of the blessing of the clothes."

"So the priest will bless the clothes today?"

"Of course," I said. "Today . . . by the holy *tonir*."

"After the haircut and shave?"

"Immediately after," I said.'

'"Have you seen those Gypsy women?" asked my shadow. "One of them has put a spell on the barber's scissors. And his razor."

"She spat on the razor and the scissors," I said. "But that just means good luck."

"Good luck?"

"And good, friendly thoughts."'

'"The Gypsies know everything," I said. "We ought to ask them when the great *tebk* is coming."

"The great massacre?"

"Yes. Or just whether the Kurds are going to carry off the bride. The Kurds do that on the seventh day of the festivities, just after the church wedding . . . but only if the bride-tax hasn't been paid."

"Why don't the Kurds carry off the bride before the wedding?"

"Because the deflowering is more effective, and the shock to the bridegroom is greater, if the bride is already wearing the ring, and with the ring has taken his name."

"The Kurds will carry the bride off, then?"

"Actually they have to do that," I said. "It's a matter of honour. But maybe the Kurd sheikh has other things to worry him and has just forgotten the wedding. Anything is possible."

"We can only hope," said my shadow.

"That's right," I said.'

'Going back to the Gypsies, I said: "They have slept for five nights in the open air under the holy tree, because they believe it has magic powers."

"For five nights?"

"Yes. And today is the sixth day."'

'Now we watched the barber, who was dealing with the bridegroom's head with professional skill. Soon he would begin work with the razor. The barber deliberately worked slowly. Now and then he put down the scissors to pick up all the tips that the guests, in accordance with custom, had thrown to him. It rained copper, silver and gold coins. The barber swept up the money with no sort of expression. And offered no thanks for it.'

'It wasn't until the barber began shaving – lathering Vartan with genuine scented, foaming Frankish soap – that he started to sing, and his voice really was like the voice of the decoy birds in the early morning. And the musicians picked up their instruments and accompanied the barber.

"Where are the Gypsies?"

"They're here, my little lamb," I said.

"Why don't they play their fiddles?"

"They're still waiting, my little lamb," I said.'

'When the Russian Gypsies began to play, all the other musicians stopped, and the barber's voice grew lighter. The sobbing of the fiddles carried us both away, my shadow and me. And with the magic sounds from the souls of the fiddles and the souls of the Gypsies, the whole village seemed to rise in the air, the market-place and the dusty alleys, the crooked houses with the *tezek* on the roofs. And below us Christ was waiting, for He was there the whole time. We rose up into the sky, and then we came down, and suddenly, as the fiddles fell silent, we were all there again.'

'"I can see a lot of people among the gapers," said my shadow, "whom the priest Kapriel Hamadian has said belong to the sect of devil-worshippers. The men are a wild-looking lot, wearing turbans, and the women are wearing bright dresses like Kurdish women."

"I can see them too."

"They sleep at nights on the roof of the village smithy."

"Where else are they to sleep," I said, "when everywhere else is so overcrowded?"

"Did the priest let them into the church?"

"I don't know."

"I'm terrified of those devil-worshippers," said my shadow.

"They're harmless people," I said.

"Do they really believe in the devil?"

"They believe in God," I said, "but they also believe that the struggle between good and evil is not yet over."

"Do they pray to God?"

"No," I said. "They don't pray to God, because they believe that God is so good that he can never punish people. And so, because he doesn't punish, he needn't be propitiated."

"So whom do they try to propitiate?"

"The devil. For he is evil. And they're very frightened of him."'

'"Though they do also worship the *Melek Taus*," I said. "That's a bronze bird. There's only a few of them in the country. The *kavals* carry this bird from village to village, for it embodies the spirit of God on earth."

"Who are the *kavals*?"

"They're the devil-worshippers' priests."'

'I said to my shadow: "Those *kavals* don't live an easy life. They really are harassed creatures, for not only do they take the bronze bird from one village to another, but they also have to mount the wives of their followers, for every devil-worshipper feels particularly honoured if his wife receives the spirit of God through intercourse with the *kaval*."

I said to my shadow: "The devil-worshippers have their children baptized as Christians, but they have the boys circumcised like Jews and Muslims."

"It seems to me, they're a scared people."

"What do you mean?"

"Well," said my shadow, "it looks as if the devil-worshippers didn't want to disagree with any of the three religions, didn't want to quarrel either with the God of the Christians or with the Gods of the Jews and the Muslims."

"That could be it, my little lamb."

"How are these Turkish subjects treated by the Sultan?"

"Well," I said, "a little time ago the Sultan was still hunting them down, and had the men publicly speared. But at the moment he leaves them in peace."'

'We chatted about this and that for a time, my shadow and I . . . and we hadn't even noticed that the famous barber had finished his job and that we two were alone, sitting beside the grain sacks with the carpet over them.

"Where are all the people?" asked my shadow. "And where is that famous barber? And, above all, where is Vartan? He was sitting there like a king just now, on those grain sacks."

"His family has taken Vartan into the *oda*," I said. "While we were chatting, the bride arrived with the whole procession of her relatives, and of course her godmother, the *ginka mair*. And the priest has gone in too."

"Is the priest going to bless the clothes now?"

"Yes," I said.'

"It struck me," said my shadow, "just now, when Vartan was being clipped and trimmed and brushed, sung to, soaped, shaved and scented – I mean, when he was sitting there on those stuffed grain sacks with a carpet under his bottom – I did notice that he had his oldest clothes on."

"There's a reason for that," I said. "The bride, too, who's just been taken into the bridegroom's *oda* by her family procession, she's also got her oldest clothes on."

"But why?"

"That's how it's done," I said. "Vartan is now sitting by the *tonir*, with the bride standing behind him. She is silent – she mustn't say a word. Then, soon, Boghos will come in bringing in two packages. They're wrapped in sackcloth, and there's a secret hidden in them."

"What secret?"

"Under the sackcloth are their new clothes . . . in one package the bridegroom's, in the other the bride's, with her new veil. The priest will bless the new clothes and the new veil. And he will pray for a time and then join the right hands of the bridal pair. Then the bride and bridegroom will withdraw, take a bath in the shed – not both in the same shed, Vartan in the Khatisians' shed and the bride in the Mukhtar's. Then they'll put on their new clothes and show themselves off to the wedding guests." And I said to my shadow: "I can tell you something now. The bride wears red. The wedding-dress is red. And her outer veil is red, and it will cover the inner one, the only one she has on up till now, so as to hide her mouth and chin. And her shoes are red, I mean those soft leather slippers that are so delicate that one can hardly believe it."

"What is it you can hardly believe about them?"

"That they can stand up to all that fat that the bride has put on during the fattening-up period."

"And Vartan?"

"Vartan won't be wearing those baggy trousers," I said, "nor boots nor a sleeveless waistcoat. Not even the usual fur cap."

"What will he wear?"

"Fashionable gear that his eldest brother Haygaz has bought for him in Bakir: a suit from Stamboul, a red tie from Van, the Armenian garden and fortress city, shoes from Erzurum and a real Bakir fez, stiff and strong and red."

"He'll look a real dandy!"

"He's no dandy."'

When Zovinar and Hamest and Zovinar's daughters went round the guests with their *sofras* full of sweets, pretending to be hurt if anyone said: "No, my stomach is full already" . . . as the women went round with their *sofras*, as I was saying . . . it seemed to the two of us, me and my shadow, as if we too were tasting their sweets, especially the *baklava* that Zovinar had cooked, and as if Hagob, and Vartan's grandfather too, were pouring out schnapps and wine for us, and later we really thought we were dead drunk. Seemingly drunk, we fell into a deep sleep. By the time we woke up, the sixth day was over.'

'And it was the seventh day, the day of the church wedding. During the ceremony my shadow and I kept watch over the little Gregorian village church.

"If the Kurds come to carry off the bride, we ought to do something," said my shadow.

"Yes," said I, the story-teller.

"But what?" said my shadow. "We don't really exist, do we, you and I, story-teller and shadow?"

"Are you really right there?" I said. "I don't think you are. Perhaps we do exist. Only we exist in a different way."

"What could we do, then?"

"Go on keeping watch," I said. "And go on recording what

happens for the world."

"For Thovma Khatisian?"

"That's right."

"Very well," said my shadow. And while he was saying that, we both looked hard at the winding track that led up into the mountains, above the roof of the Khatisians' house . . . up to the black tent of the Kurd sheikh Suleyman.'

'"Once there was a Kurdish horseman coming down that zigzag path above Hagob's roof," I told my shadow, "and his horse slipped, and horse and rider fell through the roof and landed just by the *tonir*."

"I know that story," said my shadow.

"If they come to ravish the bride," I said, "we ought to pray the good God to make them all fall through the roof. Maybe they'd break their necks."

"Or fall straight into the *tonir*," said my shadow.'

'While we talked to each other as we kept watch, we could hear the liturgical chanting of the priest and the congregation through the church door, which was standing ajar. And among all the voices we head Zovinar crying for joy. And we heard also the sad sobbing of the Mukhtar's wife, who was losing her daughter. "The bride and bridegroom are now standing opposite each other," I told my shadow. "Soon the priest will touch their heads and press their foreheads together, and, as the custom is, he will wind a pearl charm – the *narod* – round the brows of the bridal couple, which they will wear for a week. It's a charm against evil spirits, and it's much more effective than garlic or horseshoes hanging upside down."

"And what about the crosses?" asked my shadow.

"Everyone there carries a little cross," I said. "Only the smith, Vartan's godfather, carries a big one. And he holds that big cross protectively over the young couple's heads."

"And what about the wedding-rings?"

"Well, what about them?" I said. "The priest will present the rings to them on a plate, and Zovinar will sob louder and so will the Mukhtar's wife, and the hands of the bridal pair will shake, for putting on the ring is a conclusive act. After that, only death can part them."

"Will even the ring finger shake?"

"That one most of all, my little lamb."'

'So while we two, my shadow and I, were watching for the Kurds, the marriage service in the little church came to an end. The church door burst open and the laughing newly-wed couple came out into the street. We saw Vartan's eldest brother Haygaz lay a fragile plate in front of the couple as they stood in front of the church door, and Vartan tread on the plate. And we heard some people weep, and some laugh. Hagob laughed especially loud. Even the grandfather laughed, and in his piping voice quoted the old Armenian saying: "Break the crockery . . . and the bride and bridegroom will live long!"

Then the two of us, my shadow and I, simply flew away.'

'But we soon came back, to join the merry wedding procession on its way through the village.'

'I nearly pinched the bride's bottom,' said the story-teller. 'You don't see such a lovely young bottom every day. Looking like a wine-skin on short legs, the fat bride waddled through the village streets between her parents and her godmother. Everyone admired the costly red wedding-dress with its gold embroidery, the little red woman's fez with the white and red veil, the gold jewellery and the necklace of silver coins. Here too the women's procession followed after the men. When the married couple came out of the church the musicians had struck up again. The wives of the devil-worshippers, Muslims and Gypsies began a loud *talil*, that trilling of the tongue that goes right through any faithful Christian. Especially the devil-worshippers' women, who preferred to stay up on the roof of the village smithy and just follow the procession with their eyes, trilled louder and more shrilly than the Gypsy and Muslim women, as if they wanted to appease the devil at the same time. Often the wedding procession stopped at the houses to talk with the old women sitting in the doorways, joke with them or accept presents from them. Many of the old women had spread dough on gold, silver or copper coins, to make them stick to the bride's forehead. She let them stay there while she thanked them, then took them off and threw them to her godmother, who soon made them disappear under her apron. Yes, it was a real joy. It went on half the afternoon, until at last the wedding procession reached Hagob's house.'

'The year before, Hagob had built another room behind the cowshed. That was where Vartan and his young wife were to live. The room actually had its own *tonir* and even a window, which was unusual, but Hagob had said: "A window, just like rich people in the towns have in their *odas* and other rooms. I'm told," said Hagob, "that in Frankistan even the poor have windows in their *odas*. So now, when my son wakes up early in the morning . . . God willing . . . he can go over to the window to take a breath of fresh air and see what the weather's like."

When the wedding procession finally reached Hagob's house, there was a tethered lamb outside the door. Vartan's eldest brother Haygaz was standing by the lamb, and he had a knife in his hand.'

'And it all happened just as it had happened at Hagob's wedding, and Hagob's father had told him: "Yes, it was the same with me and your mother and the same with their parents, and the parents of their parents. It always has been like this. Why should it ever be different?"'

'The wedding guests threw ears of wheat over the heads of the bridal couple, and some clapped when Vartan took the knife from Haygaz and stroked the lamb's throat with his left hand at the point where he could make the swift cut. Then Vartan spat on the knife and cut the lamb's throat, jumped aside as the jet of blood hit the door, pulled the kicking lamb away from the door, put his index finger in the open, bleeding wound, pressed a few drops of blood on his bride's forehead and a few on his own, drew out an old sword that he had hidden under his jacket and raised it – symbol of his protection – over his young wife's head. And under the protection of the sword, she slipped into her new home

The musicians had stopped playing for a second, but now they

egan again, louder and more merrily. The wedding guests were all
alking at once, many of them clapped rhythmically in time with
he music. Even the *talil* got louder, for some of the devil-
vorshippers' women had climbed down from the roof of the smithy
nd run to Hagob's house, their tongues trilling, and two Gypsy
vomen followed and imitated them. Now the mayor came too, at
 run. He brought the holy fire from his own *tonir* and handed it
ver to his daughter, now standing before the house door again.
And so it was that the bride put on the kettle with the holy fire from
er parents' *tonir*. She cried when her father gave her the kettle with
he fire, and kissed his hand, and, still crying, she went into the
ridal room. There, in the new *tonir*, she lit her own fire.'

Vartan and his bride had gone round the *tonir* three times when
Hagob and Zovinar entered the new room. Zovinar had a white
heet over her arm.

"Your mother has brought you the white sheet," said Hagob to
Vartan. "Now we'll leave you alone, so that you can do your duty
s a man. Don't waste time thinking about it, the people outside
he house are waiting impatiently."

"What are the people waiting for?"

"For the blood-stained sheet," said Hagob, "that you'll be
anging up outside the door, so that they can all see that your wife
vas a virgin."

"Does it have to be now?"

"It must be now," said Hagob. "Once it's dark the people won't
e able to see the blood."

"Can't it wait till tomorrow morning?"

"No," said Hagob.

"For God's sake," said Zovinar, "don't waste time, and disgrace
he family."

"She's right," said Hagob. "Do it now. Tomorrow morning, when
he cock crows, it might already be too late."'

But Vartan was much too confused to deflower his wife now. So he
ook her by the hand and led her out of the Khatisians' house again.
And he took her as far as the market-place, to gain time.

Later, he thought, I'll do it later.'

*   *   *

'Hagob and Zovinar had been right, for there are some things that
never ought to be put off until the cock crows next day. Just as
Vartan and his wife were coming back from the market-place, a
hundred armed Kurdish horsemen came galloping into the village.
Their shrieks were even louder and shriller than the women's *talil*.
The Kurds fired at random into the air, scattering the people; they
rode to Hagob's house, then to the market-place and back again,
suddenly saw Vartan and his bride, surrounded them, struck
Vartan on the head, seized the screaming bride and pulled her up
on to one of their horses and galloped away with her.'

CHAPTER ELEVEN

'The village elders had assembled in the Mukhtar's house, with one or two other men, members of the bride's and bridegroom's families and the godfather and godmother. The priest was also there. The men sat in the *selamlik*, round the *tonir*, smoking.

"Why didn't you pay the bride-tax?" asked the red-headed smith.

"I don't know," said Hagob.

"I don't know either," said the Mukhtar.

"I suppose you thought the Kurdish sheikh would forget the wedding," said the priest.

"That's what we thought," said the Mukhtar.'

'"The Kurds won't rape the bride if we pay the ransom right away," said Hagob. "The only problem is, the ransom will be much bigger than half the bride-price."

"The bride-tax," said the smith.

"The bride-tax would have been cheaper," said the priest.'

'"We'd better saddle our three best horses," said the Mukhtar, "and ride after the Kurds. If we catch up with them and offer them a reasonable ransom, we may be able to buy my daughter back."

"Unless we can catch up with the Kurds, she's as good as deflowered," said Hagob.

"That could be," said the Mukhtar.

"And what about my son's honour then?"

"I don't know," said the Mukhtar.'

The story-teller said: 'There were three riders who saddled the three best horses in the village and rode after the Kurds. One of the riders was Vartan's brother-in-law Pesak, the second was his brother

Dikran, the third was Avetik, the smith's son.

When the three riders returned to the village it was almost dusk.

"Did you catch up with the Kurds?" asked the Mukhtar.

"Yes," said Pesak. "They were waiting for us in one of the mountain gorges, because they knew we should offer a ransom."

"And is my daughter still a virgin?"

"She's still a virgin."

"How do you know?"

"The Kurds assured us of it."'

'"Do the Kurds want the bride-tax?"

"No. They just want the ransom."

"How much do they want?"

"They want twenty sheep for the bride, ravished but alive."

"But we want the bride as a virgin."

"That will cost a hundred sheep."

"A hundred sheep is too much. Where could we get a hundred sheep?"

"Then just give them twenty, Mukhtar Bey. Twenty sheep for your daughter's life."

"Twenty sheep I can afford. And since I'm sure Hagob will contribute ten, it will be only ten."

"That's right," said the priest. "Twenty sheep from the two families won't ruin you."

"True enough," said the Mukhtar. "But what will my daughter's life be worth if she isn't a virgin? Her children will be despised, and her children's children. And how is my son-in-law going to go on living? Is he going to be the laughing-stock of the village? And who will ever speak to my daughter? The old women will spit in her face and the young ones will turn their heads away. And how can I continue as Mukhtar? This disgrace will stain both families."

"You're right, Mukhtar Bey," said the priest. "You give them fifty sheep and Hagob will give them another fifty."

"But what will become of our flocks?" said the Mukhtar, and Hagob said: "Yes, what will become of our flocks?"'

'Yet on that same evening the men of the two families drove a hundred sheep into the mountain country of the Kurds. Only one woman rode with them, and that was Bulbul, the Kurdish woman. She sat on her shabby old donkey and urged the men and beasts on.

"Hey, Bulbul," said Hagob, "why do you always want to turn up everywhere?"

"Why shouldn't I turn up?" said Bulbul.

"Well, actually, why not?" said Hagob.

"And why shouldn't I be here now?" said Bulbul. "Are you going to examine your daughter-in-law yourself to see if she's still a virgin?"

"Will you examine her?"

"Who else?" said Bulbul. "Or are you just going to give your hundred sheep to the Kurds without making certain that she is still a virgin?"

"Of course not," said Hagob.

"Because if she isn't," said Bulbul, "a hundred is too many."

"Yes, a hundred would be too many."

"Then you'll only pay twenty," said Bulbul.'

'Late in the night Bulbul and the men came back with the bride. Vartan and the rest of the Khatisian family were standing in the doorway as that strange, ghostly procession arrived. The oil lamps were still alight in the village.

"Hey, Bulbul," said Vartan.

"Well, my little bridegroom," said Bulbul.

"How is it, Bulbul?"

"All right."''

'It was already late, but the villagers still hadn't gone to sleep, even the visitors on the roofs of the houses were still awake. By a piece of luck the Turkish town-crier and drummer, the Munadi, lame in one leg and deaf in one ear, was among the wedding guests.

"Go and get your drum," said Hagob to him, "and let everybody know that she's still a virgin and that the honour of both families is saved."

"*Badiv?*" said the Turk.

"*Badiv,*" said Hagob.

"Shall I tell the people anything else?"

"Yes," said Hagob. "Tell them that tomorrow morning, just after

the first cock-crow, they'll see the bloodstained sheet hanging
outside my door."

"Do you think the cock will crow tomorrow?"

"The cock always crows at daybreak," said Hagob. "It was
already crowing when God created the first day."

"Then there was a cock before that day?"

"That's right," said Hagob.'

'The bride was so exhausted and so frightened that she went to sleep
at once on the bridal bed, before her lawful wedded husband had
been able to perform what was his most sacred duty. Vartan
wouldn't have done it anyway, for he was greatly distressed; he was
in shock and had a severe headache from the blow he had had on
the head. So he lay down by the bride and went to sleep at once.'

'Vartan only woke up once. It was in the middle of the night. What
are people going to say if the sheet isn't bloody, he thought. He felt
his wife's fat bottom. You ought to wake her up, he thought, but
he didn't dare to.

Vartan tried to imagine how many pieces of *baklava* she must
have eaten to put on so much fat. Forty every day, he thought. And
for a whole year. He tried to work it out. How many pieces of
baklava was that in a year? But because he was a poet and not a
mathematician, he got no answer. He was trying to count all those
pieces of *baklava* in the way people count sheep, and it made him
so sleepy that he didn't get very far. Later, when the figures had
sent him to sleep, he dreamed about a mountain of cakes.'

'There was no end of trouble the next morning when Zovinar found
that the sheet was unstained. And Hagob was on the spot at once.

"People will think the Kurds have done it instead of my son," he
said.

"We're disgraced!" said Zovinar.

"Disgraced," said Hagob.

"What's the matter with you?" Hagob asked his son. "Is she still
a virgin or not."

"She is one," said Vartan.

"Can you prove it?" said Hagob.

"No," said Vartan.'

'"Have I given you a sound male organ or haven't I?" asked Hagob.

"You have, father," said Vartan.

"Then why isn't the sheet bloody?"

"Because she was asleep," said Vartan.

"And what sort of a man are you if you daren't even wake your wife up?"

"I don't know," said Vartan.'

'Just after the cock had crowed seven times Bulbul came and knocked on the door, as if she knew where good advice – which they say is so dear – was most urgently needed.

"The sheet is as white as snow," said Hagob. "What will people think of us?"

"Hasn't your son got a hard-on?"

"Yes, of course he has," said Hagob.'

'"You helped to bring my Vartan into the world," said Hagob. "In the cowshed, that time? Do you remember?"

"I remember, Hagob."

"And that's why I thought, Bulbul, that you might have some idea of how to restore his honour."

"I might think of something, Hagob. I always manage to think of something."

"Have you got any ideas?"

"Just let me think, Hagob."'

'And Bulbul thought it over, and said to Hagob: "You will now kill the cock Abdul Hamid. And you will redden the sheet with the cock's blood. And then you can hang the sheet, all white and red, outside the door."

"Shall I do that?"

"Yes, Hagob."

"And what will people say?"

"They will rejoice," said Bulbul. "They'll say: 'The Kurds actually didn't deflower her. Vartan has done it. And there is the proof. The bed-sheet is stained with blood. And that Vartan is a real man. He has a good, strong tool. God bless him. And his parents, who gave him that tool. And the parents-in-law too, who took care that the hymen was intact.'"

"Right, Bulbul."

"So let's have the cock Abdul Hamid," said Bulbul.

"You can have the cock, Bulbul," said Hagob.'

'Bulbul cut the cock's throat, but not before it had crowed a few more times. Then she sprinkled and dripped the fresh red blood on the white sheet, and held the sheet over the fire in the *tonir* to dry the blood. Then she said: "There, Hagob Efendi. Now we'll hang the sheet outside the door."'

'In the afternoon of the eighth day Vartan took the blood-stained sheet to his mother-in-law. His grandfather had told him that, when he married his grandmother, he had driven two days in the donkey-cart to take the blood-stained sheet to his mother-in-law, who lived a long way away. It was the proper thing to do, a sign of respect and gratitude. "Here is the sheet," he had told her, "and here is the proof that your daughter was properly brought up by you. It was clean and unstained before our marriage." And his mother-in-law had said: "How should it be any different, my son-in-law? After all, she comes from a reputable family, doesn't she?"

"There's no girl from any better, more respected family," he had said, "who would have deserved to marry a Khatisian."

And the mother-in-law had cried a little, sniffed the sheet and said: "*Achket louis*, may your eyes be bright, my son-in-law, and may God bless you."

"That's what you'll say to the Mukhtar's wife, the same as grandfather said to his mother-in-law," thought Vartan. "And if she sniffs the sheet and says it smells of chicken a bit, you'll just deny it."'

'On the way to his mother-in-law he met his uncle from America and his son, the one who knew neither Turkish nor Kurdish and who only spoke a few scraps of Armenian.

"This oaf," said the uncle, pointing at his son, "this oaf refuses to marry a girl from this village, though I've told him they're the best and the most dependable."'

'It was seven days and seven nights before Vartan managed to know his wife.

"She has a dry well between her thighs," he told his father.

And his father had said: "Her well isn't dry. It's up to you, my son, to bore down to the ground water, thoughtfully, with patience and a lot of tenderness, and you'll see how quickly the spring will bubble again."

"But it doesn't work," Vartan had said.

"Then you must use some mutton fat, my son, for where the ground is resistant and the tool too hard, good fat will smooth the way in."'

'And Vartan listened to his father. And he knew his wife. And she became pregnant.

"If she has a son," said his grandfather, "you'll call him Thovma."'

'But as things turned out, Thovma was to be born by another woman, not by Vartan's first wife. For her lifeline was short, so short that the Gypsy women were shocked when they read her hand.'

'The grandmother had warned Vartan's wife: "Never look in the mirror while you're pregnant." But Arpine had just laughed at the old woman; she didn't like the grandmother and was jealous of the privileged position she held in the *kertastan*. And because she was by nature vain, troublesome and lazy, and with increasing pregnancy neglected her housework and daily duties, she found more time to look in the mirror than she should have done. Consequently the unborn child in her womb took the mirror-image of her mother for real mother, and lay the wrong way round.

"Be careful," the grandmother warned her. "You don't know what you're doing."

"But nothing can happen to me," said Arpine, "I've not only hung double horseshoes outside the door of the bedroom, and put the Bible by my bed, and hung garlic in every corner and over the entrance, even round my neck, as you do, Grandmother, but I've also smeared the edge of the well in front of the house with butter. How can the *djinn* possible bewitch my child?"

"At least hang your little golden cross in front of the mirror."

"But I like to wear it between my breasts."

"Your blubbery udders, which aren't even full yet?"

"Yes," said Arpine.'

'And so it happened, as it was bound to happen. Arpine died in childbirth, after nine months of pregnancy.'

'She died at a time when the trees in the land of Hayastan had already started to bud and the good God had decorated the whole *vilayet* with a bright carpet of flowers in honour of the Ascension of Christ, so that everyone was happy, even the Muslims and the Jews, the Gypsies and the devil-worshippers. The sparrows on the flat roofs of Yedi Su were already welcoming the summer.'

'"You might almost think the *yezidis* were right," Vartan said to the priest, "those stupid devil-worshippers who believe that the struggle between good and evil is not yet over. For how can I believe it, when the will of the *djinn* in my blessed wife's cursed mirror was stronger than the will of God?"

"You do yourself wrong," the priest had said. "Certainly it was God's will that she died. Otherwise she would have survived the birth."

"And why did my Thovma have to die with her?"

"That was not your son Thovma," said the priest. "It was a nameless stillborn child. And it is certainly God's will that you take another wife and have another son by her, and name him Thovma."

"Thovma?"

"Yes," said the priest. "Thovma."'

'A week after the burial, the great-grandmother died too. Since the mentally deficient old woman had spent hours sitting motionless by the *tonir*, no one had noticed it. She had simply nodded off. It wasn't

312

till the evening, when the animals came in from the fields and tramped past the *tonir* on the way to the cowshed, and one of them hit the drooping grandmother with its tail so that the dead woman fell down, that Hagob noticed it.'

'Her death was long overdue, said the people. After all, she was over a hundred.

"I'm sure she was grieving because my grandson Thovma was born dead," said Hagob. "Someone must have told her."

"But the priest said it wasn't Thovma," said Zovinar. "It was a nameless child. And Thovma still has to be conceived."'

CHAPTER TWELVE

And there was the voice of the story-teller, and he said: 'It was the year 1894, the year in which all the drummers and town-criers in the land of Hayastan announced in the public squares, in the name of the Sultan, reforms and tax cuts and other concessions for *rayas* and *giaours*, in fact for all unbelievers, whom Allah, praised be his name, has cursed for all time. The Munadis much enjoyed announcing those promises over the heads of the crowds. The Armenians would continue to pay the military tax – the *bedel* for the Sultan – as they always had. And they still could not carry weapons, apart from a few Armenian saptiehs, who together with the Muslims would be responsible for future law and order in the *milets*. The Sultan promised the Armenians a share in the government, and required all Armenian traitors from the war of 1877/8 to exchange secret Russian passports for Ottoman passports. The Munadis were experienced town-criers and sometimes made their promises sound as sweet as if their mouths were full of honey.

Only very few people in the village of Yedi Su understood what the Sultan meant, so after the announcement, Hagob asked the Munadi: "What does the Sultan really mean?"

"I don't know either," said the Munadi.

So Hagob asked the literate Armenian who still went round with the Munadi.

"It means nothing at all, Hagob Efendi," said the Munadi's Armenian. "Absolutely nothing, Hagob Efendi."

"But surely it must mean something?"

"Well, yes," said the Armenian. "There is something there. Have you ever heard of the Congress of Berlin, Hagob Efendi? The 1878 Congress, I mean?"

"No, *chelebi*," said Hagob.

"The Sultan made certain promises there to the Christian powers, especially on the question of reforms, and he promised more freedom for the Christians in the Ottoman Empire and protection from the Kurds and from any arbitrariness by the Turkish authorities."

"We haven't seen much of that yet," said Hagob.

"True enough," said the Munadi's Armenian.

"And what good does it do the Christian powers if things are better for us here?"

"None at all," said the literate Armenian.

"So why do they bother about us?"

"It's just a pretext," said the literate Armenian, "an excuse to justify their interest in this part of the world. It serves their political interests. Do you understand that?"

"No, *chelebi*," said Hagob. "I don't understand."'

'Later, in the coffee-house, the literate Armenian told Hagob: "The great powers use the Christians as an excuse to provide the sick man on the Bosphorus with their own crutches. They'd like to hobble along with him, if possible in their own direction. Do you understand that?"

"No, *chelebi*," said Hagob, "I don't understand it. Who is this sick man on the Bosphorus?"

"Ask the Munadi," said the literate Armenian. "He knows."

But the Munadi didn't know either.'

'In one of his sermons, the priest said: "Every time the Sultan announces reforms he plans a little massacre."

"Why, priest?" asked one of the congregation.

"Because he's irritated by his own generosity," said the priest. "Or because he wants to annoy the Christian powers whom he has just soothed with his plan for reform."

"And who will be massacred?"

"Well, now, who indeed?" said the priest.'

'At the end of 1894 massacres took place in some remote Anatolian villages, but not in the seven villages or in the near surroundings of Yedi Su. Itinerant Armenian traders spoke of them. One of them said: "The Kurds cut the Armenians' throats, and burnt many of them alive."

"Which Kurds?" asked the priest.

"Those 150,000 Kurds that the Sultan has recruited. *Hamidiye*, they're called. Haven't you heard about them?"

"No," said the priest.

"The Sultan pays the Kurdish Beys a lot of money for their warriors."

"The Beys need money, do they?"

"That's right, Vartapad."

"And what does the Sultan use his *hamidiye* regiments for?"

"I don't know exactly," said the Armenian trader. "I presume it's to keep the minorities in check, and maybe to frighten the great powers."'

'Nothing much really happened in Yedi Su and the neighbouring Armenian villages,' said the story-teller. 'Even in 1895, when the massacres increased, there was nothing to see here. The old Turkish saptieh sat in the coffee-house as usual, gossiping, or took a nap out in the sun while the children examined his rifle, which was older than he was. Suleyman's armed horsemen only appeared when taxes were due, but behaved peacefully if they were given what they asked for. And the Turkish officials only came when they wanted money. Once one of the traders brought an English newspaper but no one could read it.

"And what's in this paper?" asked the priest.

"It says these *hamidiye* have massacred 300,000 Armenians," said the trader. "In the towns, too. In Constantinople there are dead Armenians lying in the middle of the road. And in Urfa they burnt 1,000 Armenian women and children in the cathedral."

"But that can't be true," said the priest. "Do you believe what it says in the paper?"

"Yes," said the trader.

"And have you seen anything yourself, with your own eyes?"

"Yes," said the trader. "I saw a slaughter in a little town. There were Kurdish *hamidiye* there, but some Turkish civilians too."

"Were they killing sheep?"

"No, they were killing Armenians."''

* * *

'But no one in the village really believed the terrible news brought by the Armenian trader. The few Turks in the village were friends, and their relatives who came to visit them had been known for a long time. They were no better and no worse than the Armenians, even though they didn't believe in Christ; none of them was a murderer or would tolerate a massacre or just look on quietly if the Christians' throats were being cut or women and children burnt in a church. Even the one Turkish saptieh in the village was no exception. He played cards in the coffee-house like the other men, or sometimes *tavala*, the game of dice, he drank no more and no less, smoked the same tobacco and often farted when he'd eaten too much or too quickly. Life in the village went on as usual in spite of the bad news.'

'Shortly after Christmas, a feast that the Armenians observe at the beginning of January, Hagob said to his youngest son: "You really ought to be thinking of marrying again. What about it, my son? Shall I have a word with Manoushag? She's a good marriage broker. She got your sister fixed up with that rich carpet-dealer in Bakir."

But Vartan didn't want to ask for advice from the marriage broker.'

'Saint Sarkis' day falls on 21 January. He is the patron saint of lovers and on this day the bachelors used to go to the *gatnachpiur* well and scatter food for the birds. You only had to throw a few breadcrumbs down in front of the well, wait till a hungry bird came and snapped up the crumbs in its beak . . . and then watch it. The bird flew off in the direction of the bride. You only had to follow the bird in flight and you were sure to meet the right girl, the one you'd been waiting for all your life.'

'On Saint Sarkis' day Vartan also went to the *gatnachpiur* well to scatter bird food. But he arranged it more ingeniously than the others; he built a bird trap in front of the well, caught a little sparrow with its crumbs already in its beak, threw a cloth over its head, picked the bird up carefully, tied a little ring round its foot

and then let it fly away. That made it quite certain. He would
follow in the direction – and find – the bird with the ring, somewhere
near his bride-to-be.'

'On that day Vartan ran for some hours in the snow-covered
mountains, following the direction in which the bird had flown. In
the afternoon he reached the outskirts of Yazidye, and its fields
covered with snow. It was the smallest of the seven villages, just a
hamlet of a few houses.'

'The village was burnt down. Two Kurdish women in bright
headcloths were poking about in the ashes. Their horses whinnied
as Vartan approached.'

'"The *hamidiye* were here," said one of the two women. "We saw
the smoke up in the mountains."
   "Are there any survivors?" asked Vartan.'

'There were none. Or at least it looked as if the Kurds had done
the whole job for the Sultan. It was hard to make out whether the
Kurds had shot the villagers, beaten them to death or killed them
in some other bestial way, for they had piled up the dead, women,
men and children, on a funeral pyre and burnt them. Not all the
bodies were completely burnt. Vartan could see that some of the
men had no heads, others no genitals.
   "Did you see how they did it?" asked Vartan.
   "No," said one of the women. "We only saw the smoke."'

'Vartan hunted through the ashes of the burnt-out houses, but
found no sign of life anywhere. The two Kurdish women followed
him. Their faces were red from the icy cold. They held their bright
headcloths on with their hands as they walked. They evidently came
from one of the semi-nomadic villages on the plateau, and neither
they nor their menfolk had anything to do with the *hamidiye*. Vartan
often turned and looked at them, but it seemed to him that they
had nothing evil in mind. When they reached the last of the
seven houses he saw a dark, dead bird in the snow. It was his Saint
Sarkis bird. It was frozen. The ring he had tied on one foot to

recognize it was still there.'

'And suddenly Vartan heard something. And the Kurdish women heard it too. A soft whimpering. It came from the burnt-out house before which the bird was lying.

"One of the women had a baby yesterday," said one of the Kurdish women. "I was up here yesterday, selling a cock to her husband."

"Life is a miracle," thought Vartan.'

'The Kurdish women rubbed the baby with snow and then dried it. Then they massaged it again and again. One of them gave her breast to the child, and the other fetched a horse-blanket and wrapped the child in it.

"It's a little girl," said the one who had given it her breast. "We'll take it with us."

But Vartan said: "No. I'll take it."'

'And that was how it happened,' said the story-teller, 'that the dark grey bird of Saint Sarkis led Vartan the right way to save Anahit's life. For she would be called Anahit, she who one day was to bear his son Thovma in her womb.'

'Vartan's story, and the appearance of the burnt baby – only its eyes seemed to be alive – spread fear and horror through the whole village. The people shut themselves up in their houses.

Vartan handed the baby over to the priest Kapriel Hamadian, who – strange though it may have been – sent for Bulbul, the Kurdish woman, for the priest said she had healing plants in her hut, could work magic and, even though she was a Kurd, had good hands to which this little Armenian girl could safely be entrusted.'

'Then the villagers bolted their doors, for if there was a massacre there would be nowhere for them to run away to except the trackless mountain tops where they would all starve and freeze in the snow and ice. There was nothing else to do but wait. But everybody knew that bolted doors were no fortress that couldn't be conquered by the *hamidiye* or the *djinn*, so the people soon opened their doors again,

319

came out snuffling into the open air and got on with their usual lives. Whatever was going to happen, well, let it happen. Nobody could do anything to change it.

"Trust in God and Jesus Christ," said the priest.

"I'll defend myself and my people with my hatchet," said Garo, the saddler's son, who later on became a Dashnak like Pesak, Vartan's brother-in-law.

"I'll chase those buggers away with my hammer," said Avetik, son of the smith.

And Vartan said: "I'll use my marriage sword."

Even the Turks in the village promised their help. "We're Muslims," said Tashak, "and we're allowed to carry weapons. And I've still got an old rifle in my shed. Those swine of *hamidiye* are nothing but wild mercenaries, no better than the *bashibazouks*, and I don't know why Sultan Abdul Hamid has lent his name to such cowardly swine."'

'And they didn't come. The only threat to the village was the whirlwind from the mountains which threatened to blow the poplar roofs down, and then, as the spring began, the torrents from the melting snow in the mountains, which could almost have washed the crooked little houses away. Everything remained calm. The itinerant traders, who came back to the village with the better weather with beautiful silk fabrics, rare jewellery and fruits from foreign countries, said that the world press had been full of criticism and condemnation. On account of the Armenians, of course.

Hagob asked one of the traders why the world press didn't help the Armenians, but the trader said that the newspapers were nothing but paper and printing ink, and the characters they printed were miserable soldiers who helped no one but the great and powerful in whose name they were printed, and what the papers proclaimed to the world was no better than the boastful, hypocritical singsong of the costermongers in Bakir.'

'A lot of those itinerant traders came to Yedi Su, and each said something different. In the season when the mulberries were ripening, the traders said that nobody heard anything more about the *hamidiye* because the Sultan had sent them to Arabia. The

Russians, the traders said, saw the *hamidiye* as Kurdish Cossacks and were just waiting for them to come over to their side as mercenaries in a future war. The Czar was said to have promised the Aghas and Beys on this side of the frontier mountains of gold or, among other things, better arms for the horsemen, better horses, bigger fur caps, gold roubles, women and other loot. The traders laughed and soothed the villagers and advised them not to make any trouble but rather to buy in stores, for the time of the massacres was definitely over. The traders assured the peasants that it would be wiser to take their gold coins out of their boots, their padded jackets, their clay pots, even the holes in the sheds and the hiding-places in the fields, and invest them in silks, beautiful jewels and certain rare fruits for bottling. One of the traders asked Hagob: "Is it true that your youngest son is going to America?"

"Who told you that?" asked Hagob.

"The postman told me, when I took him some of the way in my *araba*."

"And where did the postman hear it?"

"Well, I suppose he must have read one of the letters in his post-bag."

"Do you mean that letter from America from my brother Nahapeth?"

"That must be the one."

"He was here quite recently, at the time of the wedding. He was here with his eldest son, an oaf who can't even speak Armenian properly."

"And this brother wants to take your son Vartan to America? Is that what it said in the letter?"

"That's what it said," said Hagob. And he added: "I gave that postman a big *baksheesh* only a little while ago, not to open my letters."

"But the postman told me you only gave him the *baksheesh* to have the letters delivered punctually. He didn't mention opening the letters."

"That may be," said Hagob. And he said: "To hell with the postman. It's really all the same to me whether he knows what my brother writes. There aren't any secrets there. And I reckon it's all the same to the Sultan whether or not my brother turns my youngest son's head with this journey to America."'

'And so it was,' said the story-teller. 'The uncle from America wa serious about his suggestion that he should take Vartan to America and Vartan himself had nothing against it, for since the massacr in the village of Yazidye he didn't want to stay in Hayastan an longer.'

'In the autumn of 1897 a man with an odd big hat with a brim cam to the village again. He said he'd come from America and ha brought some money from Hagob's brother Nahapeth, and th money was actually for Hagob's youngest son Vartan. And he reall did bring the money, hidden under the brim of his big hat.

'I remember,' said the story-teller, 'that Hagob had counted th money and said: "But this isn't enough for such an expensiv journey."

"It's exactly half," said the American.

"What do you mean?" said Hagob.

"Well, what do you think I mean?" said the American, wh certainly wore a hat with a brim, but came from Hayastan and sti talked as the people here do; even his expressions and his gesture looked familiar. "What do you think I mean, Hagob Efendi? It' enough for half of a ticket on the ship."

"Can you go to America with half a ticket?" asked Hagob.

"No," said the American.

"Has my son got to go half-way and then disembark, though know of course you can't disembark in the middle of that grea ocean?"

"No," said the American. "Vartan is to take the money, and yo have to find the rest for him. Your brother said: 'You must dig th gold coins out of the *pag*.'" And the American, who wasn't a tru American, pointed at the farmyard, with all the hens, ducks an geese.

"So I've got to dig it out of there?"

"Yes," said the American.'

'And so Hagob dug up a couple of gold coins and gave them to hi son, and in the spring of 1898 he travelled to America. Hagob too him as far as Bakir in the donkey-cart. From there he went with the caravan of Greek, Jewish and Armenian traders, whose *arabas* were escorted by saptiehs. When Vartan arrived in Constantinople some of his uncles and aunts, whom he hardly knew, were waiting for him. The big city scared him, and it was a good thing that, being an Armenian, he had aunts and uncles everywhere who could take care of him. He stayed with his relatives, and on his departure date they took him to the harbour, a harbour that scared him even more than the big city.'

Vartan didn't know that the story-teller was standing beside him at the rail. And he didn't notice that the story-teller jumped off again when the ship's great funnels, with deep, steamy hoots, gave the signal for sailing. As the story-teller jumped off, the ship immediately started to shake in every joint, driven on impatiently by its glowing furnaces, with all those sweating stokers shovelling coal in the boiler-room. When the ship finally sailed, the story-teller simply remained behind and disappeared in time. But now and then he bobbed up again, as he did towards the end of 1899, ready to jump into the new century.

BOOK THREE

CHAPTER ONE

No one knows why story-tellers are so often in a hurry to blow away the calendar years and only retain what is important to them. So I needn't explain why I passed over the first few years of the new century with no great interest. There was the fall of Abdul Hamid in 1908, the breaking up of the *hamidiye* regiments and the seizure of power by the Young Turks. There were the Russians who cast an eye on the Bosphorus, the British who dreamed of the shortest route to India, which would pass through the middle of Turkey, and there were lesser and greater powers that looked greedily at the 'rotten cake' that Abdul Hamid had left behind him. Everybody wanted to cut themselves a slice, including the Germans; but the Germans were the cleverest, for they knew how to hide their insatiable eyes behind cold monocles. Opaque monocles, of thick grey glass. The Germans supplied the Turks with arms and sent military advisers to train them, and their diplomats lived in Pera, the smartest part of Constantinople, with fashionable shops and high-class hotels. They also built the Turks a fabulous railway, which they called the Baghdad line; they smilingly built this road with iron, steel and fire, to demonstrate their efficiency as well as their progress and their goodwill. So, as it worked out, among all the crutches so zealously showered on the sick man on the Bosphorus by the greater and lesser powers, the Germans' crutches were the most useful.

During the Balkan War I flew to Bulgaria for a little while, but soon turned back to accompany the German officers to Bakir after the shooting in Sarajevo. There I circled for a time to have a look at the town, and finally came down on the Gate of Happiness.

'I heard shots a couple of days ago,' said my shadow.

327

I said: 'Those were the shots in Sarajevo.'

'Oh, those,' said my shadow.

'Yes,' said I.

'Why weren't we there?'

'Because I didn't want to see the Austrian Crown Prince and his wife bleeding to death in front of the crowd.'

'And what difference would that have made?'

'It would have made no difference.'

The period of the hanged men hadn't come yet. The black hooks on the Gate of Happiness were still unoccupied, and apparently useless. And they remained so, even in the next weeks.

'The period of the hanged men hasn't come yet,' I told my shadow, late in the summer.

'Who's going to be hanged?'

'Armenians.'

'When?'

'Some time,' I said. 'Some time. I don't know yet. The Turks mobilized today. It's the 3 August 1914.'

'How did Vartan's trip to America go, back in 1898?' my shadow asked.

'So-so.'

'And what about Anahit?'

I said: 'The priest and Bulbul looked after the burnt little girl. She had no face – nothing but eyes – eyes which shone as if she had seen Christ. And because her eyes shone in that way, it wasn't hard for the priest to find adoptive parents who would bring her up in the Christian faith. Not that the priest didn't trust Bulbul, but Bulbul was not a Christian.

So new parents were found for the little girl, a childless couple living on the edge of the village.'

'The little girl's foster-parents were the silkworm-breeder Yeremian and his wife, who was barren and had had dry breasts all her life. Therefore it was necessary to find a wet-nurse for the little girl, and godparents who would take her to be baptized.'

* * *

'And the priest Kapriel Hamadian had a word with Hagob: "Christ has preserved this child. And it was His will that the little girl Anahit should have been found by someone whose heart is pure."

"You mean my son Vartan?"

"Your son Vartan."

"My son wants to marry this girl when the time comes," said Hagob, "for it seems to be the will of the Saviour that the two should be together."

"Then let him marry her, when the time comes," said the priest.

"But the child ought not to be suckled by the same wet-nurse who suckled my son, for that is forbidden if they're going to be married some day."

"Then find another wet-nurse."

"And the red-headed smith can't be her godfather, nor his wife her godmother, for the two of them were my son's godparents."

"It is forbidden to have the same godparents," said the priest, "if the two are going to be man and wife."

"Then I'll arrange for Anahit to have different godparents," said Hagob. "And I'll talk to the smith, who's already told people that he'd like to be the godfather."

"Do that," said the priest. "And explain to the smith why he can't be the godfather."'

'And they found another wet-nurse and different godparents. When the child was christened they called her Anahit, for Anahit was the goddess of fertility. Anything that survives should be fruitful, to let the devil see that God did not sow in vain.'

'Hagob exchanged symbolic coins with the silkworm-breeder. And they threw the coins in the sacred fire of the *tonir*, fished them out again, blew on their hands, spat on hands and coins and threw the coins in again.'

'When Vartan went to America, Anahit's foster-father said to Hagob: "Your son is engaged to my daughter. What does he want in America?"

"I don't know," said Hagob. "He says he wants to be a poet."

329

"Does he have to go to America for that?"

"Not really," said Hagob.

And Hagob said: "Perhaps he's just afraid of the *tebk* that's coming some time, a great massacre that none of us will survive. Or he just wants to travel because he's young and doesn't know yet that the roots are more important than the fruit that hangs up there on the trees."

"Maybe he'll become a millionaire?"

"He's sure to become a millionaire," said Hagob, "for everybody who goes to America becomes a millionaire. And then he'll come back for Anahit."

"But he'll have to wait some years before the first blood flows between her legs without any wound, to tell us that she has become a woman."

"He'll wait," said Hagob.

"But there're a lot of women over there," said the silkworm-breeder, "and they show more than their legs."

"True," said Hagob. "But I know my son. He'll come back."

"And it won't worry him that his bride has got no face, just eyes?"

"He knows that," said Hagob. "It won't worry him."

"Will he take Anahit to America?" asked the silkworm-breeder. "Or will he come back to Hayastan with his millions and settle here with Anahit?"

"Unless the great *tebk* comes," said Hagob, "it may well be that my youngest son with all his millions won't go back to America. He'll marry Anahit and buy himself a villa here."

"But there isn't a villa anywhere near here," said the silkworm-breeder.

"Then he'll have one built," said Hagob. "Or he'll buy one in Van, maybe in the Armenian garden quarter, or right on Lake Van, where a rich relation of mine lives."

"That's a beautiful lake," said the silkworm-breeder. "Isn't it the place we get soap from?"

"Yes, from there," said Hagob. "If you live on the lake, you only need to draw some water, let it dry in the sun, and the salt that's left is the purest soap."

"So he'll never need to buy soap, but could just fish it out of the lake for nothing?"

"Yes," said Hagob.'

'The night before he left Vartan dreamt he saw the priest Kapriel Hamadian. The priest said to him: "If it's true, my son, that the wheat over there is pure gold, then take a sickle and go out into the fields in that great country and harvest the fat golden grains before the locusts eat them. And if it's true, my son, that there's money lying in the streets in the great American cities, then get a broom and sweep it up quickly, before the rats get at it. But if you find, my son, that there's nothing in the golden grains of wheat and the piles of money in the street but leeches, which will suck the warmth from your heart and the treasures from your soul, then break the handles off the sickle and the broom and throw the worthless tools away. And go into your little room, where no one can see you. And take up the poet's quill and turn it into a fishing-rod."

"What should I be fishing for, Vartapad?"

"The songs from your heart, my son, and its treasures that can't be consumed by locusts, by rats or by leeches."'

'The feeble-minded water-carrier had heard from the villagers how Vartan had saved the life of the girl Anahit. But he had also heard the words of the priest, when he said: "Our Saviour Jesus Christ has saved the little girl." And since the water-carrier was one of those people *who are poor in spirit*, as well as being a bit confused in the head, he believed that Vartan and Jesus Christ were one and the same person. And as a result of that, every time Vartan appeared he began to gabble loudly, and crept along behind Vartan making wild gestures. Once he followed Vartan to the *gatnachpiur* well, and because he had heard that the bird on Saint Sarkis' day had flown from that well to lead Christ to Anahit, he fell down before Vartan and kissed his feet, stammering. By chance, the priest appeared. And several other people came. They laughed at the water-carrier, beat him and made as if they would throw him in the well. Hagob also ran up, but he only saw the priest driving the people away and comforting the water-carrier.

Later Hagob asked the priest: "Did you understand, Vartapad, what the water-carrier was gabbling about, after you'd calmed him down?"

"Yes," said the priest.

"What was he trying to say?"

"He stammered something about Christ. And then he pointed at your youngest son and asked me whether he would soon walk on the Sea of Galilee."

"And what did you tell him?"

"I said: 'That boy there is going to walk over the big pond. To America.'"

'Hagob didn't cry like the others when he parted from his son. He just said to him: "Don't forget that you come from Hayastan."

"I shall never forget that," said Vartan.

"And that a good tree should never be transplanted."

"I'll always remember that, father."

"The real tree can't be transplanted," said Hagob, "and even the most fertile earth abroad can't make any difference."'

'At first the people in the village talked a lot about Vartan, but after a time it died down, and a while later they only talked about him if a letter had come from him. Vartan wrote often at first. His letters were long and detailed. As time passed they grew shorter, and finally they stopped altogether. Whenever Hagob complained about his son, people said: "When people get rich they forget their loved ones. The more millions anyone has, the more forgetful he becomes."'

'While Hagob and his wife waited for the post and discussed between themselves what could be the reason for his silence, while one year gave way to another and they grew older and more tired, they had hardly noticed that Anahit, the faceless one, had blossomed into a young woman. The silkworm-breeder had sent his adopted daughter to a relative in Bakir for a time, so that she could go to school in Bakir, for there were American and Frankish missionary schools there that also took girls, even girls of the Gregorian faith. When Anahit came back, the Young Turks were just seizing power. It was 1908, and Anahit had been bleeding between the thighs without a wound for some time.

"Vartan really must come home now," said the silkworm-breeder. "Anahit is nearly thirteen, and she's been bleeding so long that I've been afraid she'd soon be too old to find a decent husband."

"She hasn't got her engagement ring yet," said his wife.

At first no one had found it difficult to look at Anahit with her burnt face, but now people looked away and whispered unkind things behind her back.'

'So it wasn't altogether unexpected when Manoushag, the marriage-broker, said to the silkworm-breeder and his wife: "Shall I start looking for a husband for her?"

"No," said the silkworm-breeder. "I've promised her to Hagob's son."

"But he never gets in touch."

"No . . . but I'm sure he will."

"The longer she has to wait, the worse she'll look," said the marriage-broker. "Who will want to marry an old maid – an old maid with no face?"'

'In 1909 an American with a big hat came to the village again. He brought a gold ring for Anahit and a few lines from Vartan.

"He didn't want to send the ring by post," said the American.

"How is my son?" asked Hagob.

"Not so bad," said the American.

"I get letters from my brother Nahapeth," said Hagob, "and from another of my brothers and from other relatives in America, but no one ever mentions my youngest son."

"Because he hasn't made a million," said the American.

"Will my son come back?"

"Yes, he told me he'd be coming back."' .

'I don't know,' said the story-teller to his shadow. 'I mean, I don't know why Vartan kept putting off his return, but I suppose he didn't have the fare and he'd have to save up for that first. Or maybe he had the fare and wanted to save a bit so that he wouldn't come back to his home village a beggar. However it was, it went on till 1914, when, on a day in early summer, Vartan decided to book a passage on the *Graf Schwerin*, a German ship that would bring him safely to Europe.'

'And that's how it happened,' said I, the story-teller, to my shadow, who was sitting uncomfortably on the Gate of Happiness, just beside me. 'In the early summer of 1914, there was Vartan standing at the rail of this German ship and looking back at New York harbour. The ship sailed past the Statue of Liberty, which neither smiled nor waved. The torch in the statue's hand looked like a naked sword, and on it stood the last New Year's message: "Happy New Year 1914".'

'Happy New Year 1914?' – my shadow began to giggle, but it didn't sound malicious. 'Is that meant to be a bad joke, Meddah?'

'No,' I said. 'It's just a New Year's greeting.'

'Could Vartan perhaps have foreseen something?'

'Foreseen what?'

'About the storm of fire that would change the world within a few weeks?'

'How could he have foreseen that? He was thinking of Anahit and his forthcoming marriage. Perhaps he also thought about his son Thovma, whom he would father. And certainly,' said I, the story-teller, 'he was thinking at that moment, as he passed the Statue of Liberty, about the faceless, numbered streets of the great city, streets that, it seemed to him, after a long time had faces that he could recognize again. But his heart yearned for Hayastan.'

'Sixteen years Vartan was in America,' said my shadow. 'That's a damned long time.'

'Yes,' I said.

'And yet . . . why did he have to go home just then, of all times, just before the outbreak of the Great War? He simply couldn't have picked a worse time.'

'That's true,' I said. 'All the same, it was lucky he didn't wait longer. If Vartan had put off his return journey a bit more he might never have got home at all. A few weeks later the war had started, and soon the great massacre began.'

'Which massacre are you talking about?'

'The coming one . . . the one I call the holocaust.'

'Holocaust?'
'Holocaust.'

There can be good luck in bad,' I said to my shadow. 'Let's take
t that it was unwise of Vartan – or even crazy – I mean simply
crazy, to leave a safe haven like America and go back to Turkey,
only to get involved in a war, and together with that war in the
holocaust that he could perfectly well have escaped. So let's call
that bad luck. But isn't there a lucky side to this bad luck? For if
Vartan had put off his return by only a few months, he would never
have seen his family again, neither his father nor his mother, his
brothers and sisters and all his other relatives and friends. He would
never have seen Anahit again, and the wedding would never have
taken place. For everyone he had deep in his heart, everyone who
meant anything to him, was to disappear in the holocaust. And then
he would never have fathered Thovma, to whom I'm telling this
story.'

'Thovma?'
'Thovma.'
'The good luck in the bad?'
'Yes.'
'So it was intended that he should be the eyewitness?'
'It was intended.'
'And you call that good luck?'
'I call it good luck.'

Vartan was astonished how much times had changed during his
absence. All over Hayastan he was assured that things were better
for the Armenians than ever before. Even the Armenian businessman he gave a lift to in his *araba* from the terminus of the Baghdad
line to Bakir assured him that it was so. After the fall of Abdul
Hamid, the businessman said, the new government of the Young
Turks, led by Enver Pasha, Talaat Bey and Jemal Pasha, had
solemnly promised that from then on all Ottoman citizens, Muslim
or not, would have equal rights. Those rights, the businessman said,
were at present mostly still on paper, and, in the remote provinces
especially, they hadn't been easy to put into practice. But all the
same, Armenians were now allowed to carry arms and served as

soldiers and officers in the Turkish army, something that in earlie
times would have been unthinkable. The authorities, said th
businessman, had even distributed weapons in the remote pro
vinces, for the protection of the villagers from the Kurds. "And thi
I heard with my own ears," said the businessman, "a Turkish tax
collector saying to an Armenian cattle-dealer: 'It's quite true
efendi. You Armenian rogues have always paid the highest taxes
We must admit that, efendi. And since you fill the exchequer witl
the money you cheat out of people, then you ought to be given you
rights.'

'We ought to be given our rights,' said the cattle-dealer.

And the tax-collector said: 'That's the truth. Allah be my witness
that is the truth.'"

"Did he say anything else?" asked Vartan.

"Yes. He said: 'I've heard, efendi, that the Russians treat you
people badly over the other side. They persecute your priests an
shut your churches. And they've even banned your language in th
schools.'

'That's been so for a long time,' said the cattle-dealer. 'It reall
was so, I'll be damned if it wasn't. But recently the Russians hav
promised their Armenians a whole lot of improvements.'

'Well, you know very well, efendi,' the tax-collector said, 'tha
all Russians are liars. Are there any greater liars than th
Russians?'"

'"The two of them whispered to each other for a bit," said th
businessman, "and I couldn't hear any more. But then they talke
a bit louder, and I heard the tax-collector say to the cattle-dealer
'Well now, efendi. The new government treats you well, you hav
to admit it. And if the Russians see that we treat the Armenian
better than they do, they'll get really scared, for they'll be afrai
that their Armenians will come over to our side in the coming war.

'Yes, that's true,' said the cattle-dealer.

'Our triumvirate isn't stupid. Especially Talaat Bey, who's reall
smart, and so in their own ways are Enver Pasha and Jemal Pasha
They knew very well why it's wise to treat the Armenians well an
even give you dogs weapons.'

'Yes,' said the cattle-dealer.'"

*   *   *

'"So are things going well for the Armenians now?" asked Vartan. "Really better than with the Armenians on the Russian side?"

"Oh, yes," said the businessman. "The bad days under Abdul Hamid are over. The new government is well disposed towards the Armenians, and its policy really is better than anyone expected. There is hope everywhere. It's no wonder that even the Dashnaks are getting together with the Young Turks and offering to support the new government."

"And what about the Dashnaks' dream of setting up an Armenian state again?"

"The Dashnaks seem to be prepared to swap their dreams for citizens' rights."

"Are you quite sure of that, efendi?"

"Everyone says so."

"And suppose there's a war on the Russian front now? Will the Turks trust us? Won't they prefer to believe that the Dashnaks aren't serious about their equal rights in a great Ottoman state? Won't they rather think that the Dashnaks will go on dreaming their secret dreams, the dream of independence . . . and that the Russians might help them in it?"

"Nonsense. The Turks know very well that the Czar wouldn't hand over the areas they seized to the Armenians, because he'll want to keep them for himself. So the Czar will never agree to the Armenians setting up an independent state in the liberated areas. And if the Turks know that, the Dashnaks know it too. Everybody knows it. No Armenian has ever trusted the Russians." And the businessman laughed. "Do you know, efendi," he said, "I used to know an Armenian fishmonger who wanted to go to Russia to buy salt fish in the Arctic Ocean area. And do you know what I said to him?"

"No," said Vartan.

"I told him: 'Don't trust a Russian, efendi. Hasn't their Czar promised us everything already! You want to buy fish there? Don't you know what the Russian fish are like which they promise to the Armenians?'

'No,' the fishmonger said.

'Well, it's something that works both ways,' I told him.

'What do you mean, efendi?' asked the fishmonger.

And I said to him: 'Well, it's like this, efendi: if a Russian promises you a fish, then he only gives you the bones and hopes you choke on them.'

'Is it really like that?' the fishmonger asked me.

And I said: 'Yes, it is.''''

'It really was so,' said the story-teller. 'At the time Vartan came back to Turkey, people were saying that the Armenians on the Russian side looked on their relatives on the Turkish side with some envy. Their relatives who lived among the Turks seemed to be having things better than they were.'

CHAPTER TWO

'Vartan's second marriage took place after the harvest, just like the first, and it hardly differed from that one. There were festivities in the streets of Yedi Su for seven days and seven nights. The music was no different, and the sound of wind instruments and string instruments, the beating and rolling of drums, but most of all the magic voices of the Gypsy fiddles, rose up to the sky, where there were no rain clouds. It must never rain at Armenian weddings. Lambs and sheep were slaughtered according to custom and hung over the smoking spits by Hagob and his helpers. There was baking and boiling, and the scent of a thousand and one luxuries hung over the little church and the flat roofs of the houses. And yet this second wedding was different from the first, for people in the village weren't so frightened of the Kurds. The men in the village were armed now. And the Kurds up in the mountains knew that. Consequently there were seldom clashes between them. None the less Vartan had insisted this time that the bride-tax should be paid to the elderly sheikh Suleyman, for it would have been rash to challenge the sheikh and his sons and grandsons, whose horsemen considerably outnumbered the villagers of Yedi Su.'

'So the bride-tax was paid?'
   'Yes, it was paid.'
   'And the bride wasn't abducted?'
   'No, she wasn't abducted. Nor was she deflowered by the Kurds without the blessing of the church. The marriage went off without incident. As I told you, the festivities went on for seven days and seven nights. And the seventh day was the day of the church wedding, and the day of the bloodstained sheet, which once again had to be hung outside the house door, as it always was in the old days.'

'Did Vartan have the same difficulties in knowing his wife that he had had the last time? And did Hagob, with old Bulbul to help him, have to kill a cock to stain the sheet?'

'No,' said I, the story-teller.

And I said: 'That time, with his first wife, the fattened-up daughter of the mayor, the well that had to be tapped was dry, I should say dried out, and neither the borer's passion nor his utmost endeavours during those first days of marriage could lead the drill to the spring that lay hidden and which he had to find. And the thorn bush before the hidden well was so unmanageable that I only mention it reluctantly. But this time it was quite different.'

'No. Anahit was not fat, although they had tried to feed her up. Somehow all her foster-parents' *baklavas* and all the encouragement given her by the silkworm-breeder and his wife had no visible effect worth mentioning. Anahit wasn't thin, but since she had grown so tall the little pads of fat on the different parts and curves of her body didn't fill out very much. Anahit was taller than all the women in the village, and even a head taller than most of the men. She wasn't a beautiful woman, for she had no face, and her body was covered with burns and scars. But Anahit moved with grace and pride, and the eyes in her burnt-out face shone as they always had, as if she had seen Christ.

Vartan knew her on the first night. And there was no dried-out well, and no unmanageable thorns. There was a grateful, passionate spring that longed to be rewarded, and gave itself eagerly for it. And all that was hard and bony and ruthless, as people say, in the man became gentle. And the pleasure that was self-seeking also sought the other with true tenderness. It was as if Christ had brought man and wife together for ever, as long as they breathed.'

'When war came to the country all the able-bodied men in the village had volunteered for service, even before the drummers and town-criers came and the postmen of the slow Turkish post brought the individually written call-up papers. If you were rich you could still buy yourself out through the *bedel*, and that applied equally to the Muslims and the unbelievers, but in the village even the rich

men's sons had opted out of payment of the *bedel* and gone into
barracks in Bakir. I, the story-teller, can only be amazed when I
tell you that it was no different in other villages and towns . . . or,
let's say, much the same. There were deserters and cowards here
and there, as much among the Muslims as the Christians. But the
great majority of young Armenian men hastened to join the colours
and take up arms.'

'How did the Dashnaks react?' asked my shadow.

'They encouraged their people to fight for the Young Turks.'

'And Pesak, Vartan's brother-in-law?'

'He put on a Turkish uniform and joined up.'

'Hadn't he become one of the leaders of the Dashnaks?'

'Yes, he had.'

'And even he wanted to exchange dreams for rights?'

'Yes,' said I, the story-teller. 'The mood in the country had
completely changed, above all among the Armenians. The prospect
of becoming Ottoman citizens with equal rights was more tempting
to them than the idea of setting up a new Armenian state, which
in any case would have been too small and too weak to survive long
between two giants like Russia and Turkey. The simple people
among the Armenians wanted security, that was all. They wanted
to carry on their businesses and look after their families. What they
wanted was stability, and the Dashnaks knew that.'

'And were the Young Turks going to make this dream of a sound
and secure life come true?'

'The new government had promised it,' I said.

'And what did the Armenian priests do when war broke out?'

'They encouraged their congregations to fight for the Turks. And
they prayed for the Padisha.'

'Which Padisha?'

'I'm not sure about that, but I think it was the Turkish.'

'And the priest Kapriel Hamadian?'

'He said: "It is as it should be. The new government has given
us rights, and now we must win those rights, for many of them are
still only on paper. We have an opportunity now to show the Turks
that we are loyal citizens. There has never been a better opportunity

in all history. The Young Turks have given us arms, and our men are now Turkish soldiers like all the others.'

'Strange Munadis came into the village to drum up support. A few weeks after the outbreak of war with Russia the aging Munadi Nazim Efendi came too, lame in one leg and deaf in one ear, to tell the people, in the name of Enver Pasha, Talaat Bey and Jemal Pasha, that is, of the Triumvirate and the Committee for Unity and Progress, but also in the name of the Sultan, about the great victories in the war. Before he went to the market-place Hagob had offered him a glass of *oghi* schnapps, given him a decent *baksheesh* and whispered a secret into his sound ear. Later, in the market-place, the Munadi proclaimed that Vartan's wife was pregnant and that the Committee for Unity and Progress, the Triumvirate of Enver Pasha, Talaat Bey and Jemal Pasha, not to mention Sultan Mohammed the Third, wished good luck to Vartan and his wife and also to his future son, who would be called Thovma. The Munadi went on to announce that the Turkish army had occupied Tabriz and the Russians were beaten, that Enver Pasha, who was at the front himself at the head of his troops, would soon have liberated the Caucasus and all the Turkish people, that the German allies had for some time been outside Paris, a sinful town in Frankistan, and that Allah was on the side of the just.'

'There wasn't much to do in winter. The farmers played cards or *tavla* and spent the evenings dozing by the *tonir*. The house and the livestock had to be looked after, of course, but there was no work in the fields. And so, all winter long, they dreamt of the spring and of the fresh ploughing. They wondered if the storks would come back again next year, and whether after the war, which was sure to be over by the spring, things in Hayastan would still be the same in the season of sowing and the spring winds.'

'And one day, when the winter sleep of the marmots grew lighter and the land was waiting for the melting of the snow, a troop of saptiehs came, and halted in front of Hagob's house. The saptiehs' uniforms were bespattered with snow and mud, and their boots looked no better. They searched Hagob's house and all the

342

neighbouring houses of the Khatisian family. They didn't find much, only a few harmless photographs belonging to Vartan, and his papers, which he didn't carry on him in the village, papers with foreign stamps and visas which were lying in a box with the photos.

Later, when they rode away, they took Vartan with them. The NCO, a fattish, goodnatured-looking *choush*, said to Hagob: "It's only a formality. Your son is an American. The Mudir of Bakir just wants him to sign something."

"When will my son be back?" asked Hagob. And because he feared the worst, he added: "Tell me, Choush Agha, shall I ever see my son again."'

'The *choush* didn't answer Hagob's last question,' said I, the story-teller, to my shadow. 'How could an ordinary *choush*, a corporal, answer a question like that honestly? But the *choush* thought about Hagob's question on his way over the Taurus Mountains. And later, when the *choush* handed Vartan over to the Mudir of Bakir and asked the Mudir the same question, the Mudir said: "This Armenian is never going back to his people."

"His wife is pregnant," said the *choush*. "She told me she was expecting a son."

"He'll never see that son either," said the Mudir.

"A father ought at least to be able to listen when his son comes into the world," said the *choush*, "just once, I mean, when his son cries the first time . . . the first time of all, although he still doesn't know the world, which Allah has created for us all."

"This Armenian with his American passport," said the Mudir, "that one there . . . he'll only hear his own crying, and that will be so loud that his son will hear it in his mother's womb."

"May Allah have mercy on his soul," said the *choush*.

"Many of those traitorous people are going to cry," said the Mudir, "some louder and some not so loud. But every time they cry, the just in Paradise will close their ears. And the bones of the faithful, which smell of musk and lavender, will rest more quietly. The Prophet has cursed those unbelievers. May their mothers shudder at every cry of their sons."

"Yes," said the *choush*. And as he shut the door of the Mudir's office, he whispered: "May Allah have mercy on their souls."'

CHAPTER THREE

The first Armenians had been hanged on the Gate of Happiness three weeks before Vartan's arrest, and we, my shadow and I, were witnesses. And then there were more. Day after day the Turkish authorities hanged some Armenian, often several of them. It didn't matter how many.

'There have been more and more since Vartan was arrested,' said my shadow. 'Could that have something to do with his arrest?'

'Rather the other way round,' I said. 'His arrest had something to do with the new policy, and deterrence by hanging is one aspect of that.'

'Those hanged men look scornful.'

'That just confirms the government's fears.'

'What's happened to the promises of the Unity and Progress Party?'

'There's a war on,' I said.

'I mean the question of equal rights.'

'That was before the war,' I said.

I said: 'Franz Joseph of Austria wanted to meet the German Kaiser in Paris, but apparently that didn't come off.'

'Perhaps the Austrian emperor is too old to go such a long way,' said my shadow, 'especially as he's had trouble peeing for some time. That would be tiresome on a journey.'

'That's possible,' I said.

'And what about Enver Pasha? Didn't he want to meet the Kaiser too?'

'Certainly.'

'Where?'

'In St Petersburg.'

'And what happened to that meeting?'

'Nothing at all,' I said. 'Enver wanted to take the Caucasus first and free all Turkish people from the yoke of the Czar, before he went to St Petersburg. But nothing came of that.'

'And the German Kaiser?'

'He's put off his visit to St Petersburg too. For tactical reasons, as they say.'

'And how are things going on the Turkish-Russian front?'

'Badly for the Turks,' I said. 'Enver Pasha's army is practically beaten. And someone has to take the blame for that.'

'Who?'

'The Armenians.'

'But they were brave soldiers. And they were loyal. It said so in the Turkish papers. Enver acknowledged it.'

'That was denied long ago.'

'Were any reasons given?'

'There are always reasons.'

'Where do they find them?'

'In their own fears.'

'It can be proved that they're not responsible.'

'That makes them all the more guilty. For that would upset the historical picture of them, the picture that other peoples have sketched for them. And that is a sin. That is a crime. You see, that would call everything in question . . . all the justifications of Turkish history, and of those who write it.'

'So they just have to be guilty?'

'That's right.'

We talked for a while, my shadow and I. When we heard something flutter between us. We both heard it, my shadow and I, the story-teller.

'Something fluttered between us,' says my shadow.

'That was the last thought of Thovma Khatisian,' I say.

'Really his last thought?'

'No,' I say. 'That's still in his head, waiting for the signal to take flight.'

'Then what last thought is it?'

'Just the last thought from the story of the last thought . . . the story I'm telling him as he dies, so that he will know how it will be with his last thought, or how it might be . . . when it finally does take flight . . . anywhere in time.'

And I, the story-teller, hear the last thought sigh. And now I hear his question.

'Does my father come out of prison today?'

'Right, my little lamb,' I say. 'It's today he comes out. And there are twenty-five saptiehs waiting for him in the prison yard.'

'To take him to Constantinople?'

'That's it.'

'For the trial?'

'For the trial.'

And I show the last thought the blind beggar's sack, on the side of the road by the Gate of Happiness.

I say: 'In that sack the blind beggar has got the boots of your uncle Dikran, who was a shoemaker, the best in Bakir.'

'I know that,' says the last thought.

'I expect you'd like to know why he doesn't sell them?'

'Yes,' says the last thought.

'I don't know either,' I say. 'Let's just listen to what the blind beggar says about it.'

'"I did really want to sell the boots," says the blind beggar Mechmed Efendi to his grandson Ali. "But I've thought it over. They aren't by any means the best pair of yellow kidskin boots in the city, although I've always believed they were. I've simply believed a legend."

"Why, Dede? Why aren't they the best boots, when you always thought they were?"

"What used to be, is long past," says the blind beggar. "And what used to be valuable once is worthless today. That's how it is with the best boots in Bakir, made of good yellow kidskin. Once they were new. And today they're worn out. Just look at them. The leather is shabby and full of cracks, there are holes in the soles, the

346

heels are worn down and everything that was in good condition and supported the foot is hopelessly trodden down."

"And what about those gold coins that every Armenian hides in his heels?"

"There was no gold in these heels, my little lamb. Either Dikran was too poor to put any money aside, or else he wasn't prudent enough."

"What will you do with the boots, Dede?"

"I can't give them back to the dead man, my little lamb. But I could give them to his wife. Or to his brother! Yes . . . why not his brother? That would be the most sensible idea, because he might need them himself."

"Which brother?"

"Vartan Khatisian."'

'"He's coming out of prison today, my little lamb. I heard it from the saptiehs. They want to send him to Constantinople. For the trial."

"For the trial?"

"For the trial."'

'"Will you give him the boots today?"

"No, not today."

"When will you give them to him?"

"When he needs boots."

"Doesn't he need them today?"

"No, not today, not yet."'

And I, the story-teller, say: 'Do you see those Kurdish horsemen? They're coming from the direction of the great bazaar, and now they're riding up to the Gate of Happiness.'

'Who are they?' asks the last thought.

'They're highwaymen and robbers. They often come into town to raid the bazaars, but today it wasn't worth it, because of all the saptiehs and soldiers hanging about.'

'Do they really live from robbery?'

'Their tribe does have some sheep, but they can't live only on sheep-breeding. Their old men, women and children look after the sheep while the young men are out on the road. It's only a small tribe, living high up in the mountains. They're related to the Hartnoshi Kurds and are under the rule of Sheikh Halil the Just. A small tribe, as I said, almost wiped out.'

'How is that?'

'Well, yes, how is that?' I say: 'Three hundred years ago, the son of the sheikh of that time stabbed the son of another sheikh to death. But his brother had to avenge his death, because the law of blood vengeance is holy and demands it. The two tribes have been in a state of feud ever since. They murder each other. And of the people of Sheikh Halil, known as Halil the Just, there aren't many left.'

'How many?'

'I don't know exactly. But I do know they only have about fifty warriors and not many horses.'

'Why are you telling me this?'

'You'll see in a moment.'

And I say: 'Do you see . . . the Kurds have stopped by the blind beggar. And one of them – he's the sheikh's son – dismounts, goes up to the beggar and throws a silver *mejidiye* into his begging cloth.'

'Yes, I see.'

'They've been friendly with the blind man for years.'

'How has that happened?'

I say: 'Those wild Kurds can't read or write. And moreover they don't believe what's in the papers. The blind beggar is their most reliable source of news. Every time the Kurds come into the town they get the latest news from the beggar.'

'Can the blind man read the papers?'

'No. But he has good ears. And he keeps them open.'

'"How's the war going, Mechmed Efendi?" asks the sheikh's son.

"Very well," says the beggar. "The question is, who for?"

"For Enver Pasha's army?"

"No."

"For the Czar's army?"

"That's the one."

"When will the Czar's cavalry be in Bakir?"

"Not by this summer," says the beggar. "But they will be here.""

'"And what about those damned Armenians? Are they going to hang them all?"

"Not all of them, son of The Just."

"Why not all?"

"Because they're going to drive them out. They'll drive the women, old men and children into the desert. And any man who's still got spunk in his balls they'll shoot."

"How do you know?"

"I've heard it."

"And what will happen to the Armenians' houses, their land and their cattle and their shops?"

"Heirs will turn up, son of The Just. And the heirs will be in a hurry, for heirs always are in a hurry. And believe me, those heirs are already standing by. And they're impatient. They've forgotten the words of the Prophet, who said *All haste is from the devil.*"

"Is everything ready yet?"

"Not yet."

"What are the authorities waiting for?"

"They want proof, and a credible accusation."

"Who told you that?"

"A *yusbashi* told me."

"And why do they need that?"

"For the press. For somehow or other they must explain why there aren't any Armenians any more."

"But there are still some?"

"At the moment there are.""

'"One of those Armenians is accused of being a spy," says the beggar. "And he's been in prison a long time. But today they're letting him out."

"Releasing him?"

"No. He'll be riding through the Cannon Gate today, handcuffed, and there will be twenty-five saptiehs with him."

"How do you know all this?"

"I know the Armenian, and for weeks I've been going to the

prison every day to talk to the saptiehs, who know me."

"Do you know where they're taking him?"

"To the Baghdad line. Then to Constantinople."

"Oh, there?"

"Yes, there."'

'"They'll just ride a bit of the way along the caravan road towards Erzurum," says the blind man, "but then they'll take the short cut through the mountains."

"Which short cut, do you know?"

"There is only the one. You know that very well, son of the great bey. You Kurds call this short cut the El Buraqu road, like the Prophet's horse that flew up to heaven."

"It's a very narrow pass, very dangerous."

"Yes, it is," says the blind man.'

'"So there will be twenty-five saptiehs and just one prisoner?"

"Yes," says the blind man.

"How many horses is that?"

"If you had enough fingers and knew how to count, you'd make it twenty-six horses."

"Twenty-six horses, did you say?"

"That's what I said."'

'"We could use twenty-six good horses," says the sheikh's son. "Do you know what sort of horses they are?"

"They won't be bad horses," says the blind man.

"And what about the saptiehs' fur hats, and their boots?"

"Not at all bad fur hats, and not bad boots. And their arms are perfect, and so are their brand new uniforms, for when the Great War began they were all newly equipped."

"We don't need uniforms."

"And what about the horses?"

"We do need horses."

"And modern rifles?"

"Those too."

"And the fur hats and the boots?"'

"And the fur hats and the boots too."'

★   ★   ★

'"It will be child's play for you," says the blind man, "to shoot those cowardly saptiehs down, especially above the ravines, where they have to separate and ride along the passes in single file."

"It won't be much of a job."

"But you must spare the prisoner. He's a friend."

"A friend?"

"Yes."'

'Later, when the Kurds had ridden off and had long disappeared behind the Gate of Happiness under the hanged men, Ali asked his grandfather: "Will the Kurds steal the horses, and the caps and the boots?"

"Yes, my little lamb."

"And what will they do with the uniforms?"

"They'll throw them down into the gorges, with their wearers."

"And the prisoner? What will happen to him?"

"I don't know yet."

"Will he ever get to Constantinople?"

"No, my little lamb."'

'The Mudir had overslept, and when he finally arrived at the *hukumet*, late in the morning, the chief clerk realized that the files that had to be handed to the escort were not complete. Before everyone was ready to leave and the Khatisian Case, men and papers – and of course they belong together – could be sent off to march to the Baghdad line, costly hours had passed. It was not till nearly noon that all the papers were ready and the Mudir, who had been trotting to and fro himself between the *hukumet* and the prison yard, finally decided that everything was in order, and the column got on the move. First the saptiehs took the prisoner to the barracks, to water the horses, draw provisions and ammunition and fill their water-bottles. After that they made a stop at headquarters and picked up an important bag of mail, and then rode slowly, under the eyes of a curious crowd, to the inner rampart, towards the Cannon Gate. By the time they had finally ridden out of the city and disappeared along the dusty road outside the ramparts, it was long past the hour for the midday prayer. They rode neither fast nor slowly. They rode as they always rode when they had a long and uncomfortable journey. But they knew the road, and they rode quite confidently. As laid down, following the Mudir's instructions exactly, they would take the caravan road towards Erzurum, then branch off and take the shorter way across the Taurus defile.'

CHAPTER FOUR

'At the beginning of May the Vali of Bakir invited several important men to his office.

"Efendiler, how long does a troop of experienced saptiehs take to reach the Baghdad line?"

"Three days at most, Vali Bey."

"And if they take the short cut?"

"At most two."

"But they've already been more than two weeks on the road, and we still have no news. All we know is that the troops with the prisoner – that man Vartan Khatisian – have never arrived at the terminus of the Baghdad line."

"Not in Constantinople, then?" asked the Kaimakam.

"Of course not," said the Vali. "How could the prisoner get to Constantinople if he hasn't even got across the Taurus . . . to the terminus of the Baghdad line?"

"There are several stations on the line," said the Mudir. "And the Taurus is between them."

"But there's only one terminus you can go from to Constantinople without changing."

"Yes, that's true," said the Mudir. And the Kaimakam said: "It really is true. But I just don't understand why the Germans haven't been able to build a tunnel through the Taurus yet."

"They could do it all right," said the Vali, "but they work slowly on purpose so they can keep their technicians here for years."

"It seems," said the Mudir, "as if the German Kaiser sleeps more easily so long as he knows his technicians can go on keeping us in suspense."

"To hell with those technicians," said the Vali.'

★   ★   ★

'"I've sent several telegrams to the stationmaster of the Baghdad line," said the Vali. "And telegrams to all the police stations along the caravan road to Erzurum, and to the ones responsible for the area of the passes the troop passed through. But the answer is always the same."

"What is the answer?"

"The column with the prisoner was last seen as it left the caravan road to take the short cut through the mountains. Since then it has disappeared."

"Disappeared into the gorges in the Taurus?"

"That's it."'

'"Have search parties been sent out?"

"Yes."

"With what result?"

"None whatever."

"But if a result is not a result, maybe that is a result of sorts?"

"I don't know, efendiler."

"And who would know?"

"Allah might know."

"So Allah will have to find them?"

"Well, why not?"'

'"The column could have fallen into one of those gorges and the whole lot of them lie dead at the bottom?"

"That's possible."

"Or the Russians might have picked them up?"

"That's possible too."'

'"No," said the Mudir. "That would not be possible for the Russians. They are still much too far away. It's impossible that they should have fallen into the hands of Russian troops."

"Maybe there were Russian patrols?"

"Not even their patrols push forward so far."

"Who could it have been then?"

"Allah will know," said the Mudir.'

'"It could even have been the Kurds," said the Mudir. "When they need horses and weapons, they stick at nothing. It wouldn't be the first time they've attacked the saptiehs."

"Yes, that's true."

"And they don't leave any survivors as witnesses."

"That's true too."'

'"Even if there was just one left alive, he'd surely have turned up long ago. But there simply hasn't been a sign of anyone."

"Really, Vali Bey? Not even of the horses?"

"Not even the horses, Mudir Bey."

"And the prisoner?"

"Nor of him either."'

'"So what about the trial?"

"What trial?"

"Well, the whole business of the Khatisian case. I mean, this affair of the murder of the Austrian Crown Prince and his wife, and the affair of the Armenian world conspiracy."

"Oh, yes, that. To be quite honest, Mudir Bey, I've never really believed in that. After careful consideration, it's become clear to me that we should just be making ourselves look ridiculous in the eyes of the world."

"Then perhaps it's better that the case is sorted out by the death of the prisoner?"

"Yes. I agree."

"And I suppose there's really no doubt that the prisoner is dead?"

"No," said the Vali. "Since not a single man from the troop has appeared for nearly two weeks, they must all be dead."

"The Kurds make a good job of things when they do anything like that."

"They do," said the Vali.'

'"Let's forget the Khatisian case," said the Vali. "There are more important things."

"Such as?" said the Kaimakam.

"Such as this business of the revolt in Van."

"Do you know any details about that?"

"Yes," said the Vali. And the Vali said: "Efendiler, we've at last got a credible charge against that rabble of Armenians."

"And what would that be?"

"For some days now, Armenian bandits have been firing on Turkish troops. Up to now we didn't know any details, but since yesterday we've been able to see detailed reports from the Vali of Van. It's true. A revolt has broken out in the Armenian quarter of Van. Just behind the front!"

"Incredible."

"It's definite, efendiler. The whole world will know about it. And think: there are Armenian volunteers fighting on the Russian side and their soldiers aren't by any means all Russian citizens. They come from every country in the world and join the Russians."

"What, just to fight against us?"

"Yes."

"Are there Turkish citizens among them?"

"Some. Armenian deserters."

"That's really shocking."

"And now this revolt in Van," said the Vali. "The Dashnaks are behind it. They've got people everywhere, in every town, every village. There's a revolt being prepared all over the country."

"Is it absolutely certain that the revolt in Van is not an individual case? That the revolt really is spreading? Is there a plan behind it?"

"Efendiler," said the Vali, "nothing is certain. But it will be proved."'

'And there was the frost, and the cholera,' said the story-teller. 'And with the thaw and the spring weather came typhus and dysentery. The beaten Turkish troops were pouring back into Anatolian territory, and the attached Kurdish regiments with them. On the return march the Kurdish and Turkish soldiers plundered the Armenian villages and butchered the inhabitants. Jevdet Bey, Enver Pasha's brother-in-law, appointed commander of the Third Army in the Caucasus after the hasty return of Enver Pasha to Constantinople, made no secret of it that he was going to wipe out every single Armenian in the Vilayet of Van, for Jevdet Bey was not only the commander of the troops but at the same time Vali and provincial governor of the Vilayet of Van. The Armenians in Van, which people said was the biggest and most beautiful of all

Armenian cities, knew what they were in for. And when Jevdet's troops were just outside the city and the local police had started to arrest Armenian notables and to shoot some of them, when the word got round that women were being raped and men beaten down in the streets, the Armenians retreated to the centre of the city, shut themselves in and took up arms.'

'They didn't have many weapons,' said the story-teller. 'Most of them came from the armouries of the Young Turks, and some had been smuggled in from Persia by the Dashnaks during the persecution under Abdul Hamid. The Armenians in Van had neither planned a revolt nor had they any connection with the approaching Russian troops and the Armenian volunteers on the Russian side. They simply denied the saptiehs and Jevdet Bey's troops entry into their part of the city, a defence plan, no more . . . the only step they could take to prevent a massacre or the deportation of the whole population.'

'But nothing suited the extermination plans of the Committee for Unity and Progress better than the fact that Armenians were firing on Turkish troops. At last they had the proof of high treason that would justify in the eyes of the world press the final plans they had against the Armenians. What was actually self-defence could now be publicized by the Turkish press and the drummers and town-criers in the villages and towns as high treason, as an Armenian uprising behind the lines on the Turkish front. All that was necessary was to prove that the revolt was spreading outside the region.'

'And so,' said the story-teller, 'I imagine all the leading heads of the Committee for Unity and Progress coalescing into one giant head, and that giant head sitting on the shoulders of a uniformed man in the government quarter of Constantinople. The uniformed man is not alone, for I, the story-teller, am there too. But he doesn't see me, because I am sitting in his ear. And because he has no imagination, he thinks he's unobserved. He doesn't think that thoughts have voices.

"The Armenians don't know yet what we have in store for them," says the uniformed man . . . "I mean, they don't know anything yet about our final plans and the ultimate solution of the Armenian problem."

"Actually they must know it," I say.

"We chucked them out of the army during the winter and turned them into a labour corps behind the front."

"The Inshaat Taburi?"

"Yes, the Inshaat Taburi. Later we'll have them all shot."

"I know," I say.

"Of course we can't shoot the whole lot. A lot of those cowardly dogs have deserted and gone and hidden in the mountains, and in the villages and towns too, with their friends and relations."

"Yes," I say.

"In the little town of Zeitun, and in the surrounding villages, we've deported the whole population, and they've all seen the death columns. And they still haven't got the idea."

"Yes," I say.

"They see those deportations in Zeitun as no more than a warning."

"I understand," I say.

"We've hanged a lot of them and had thousands of notables arrested. But they still don't get the idea."

"They don't believe you can possibly wipe out a whole population?" I say.

"No," says the uniformed man. "Those blockheads think there will just be a few insignificant and harmless incidents. They don't realize that it's just a foretaste of what's actually waiting for them."

"You're talking of the final solution?"

"That's what I'm talking about."'

'"What do you make of the revolt in Van?"

"Not much," says the uniformed man. "The world press will play it down. Those bloody journalists will say it was self-defence."

"And what about the Armenian volunteer battalions on the Russian side?"

"The world press will play that down too. The journalists want to persuade the world that that is an internal Russian matter, nothing to do with the Turkish Armenians."

"But you must find that very convenient?"

"Of course," said the uniformed man. "We're already exploiting ese things for our propaganda, you see. But that isn't enough."

"What do you mean?"

"We need quite different evidence . . . for the final indictment, hich will initiate the final plans."

"And what evidence is that?"

"We've got a plan."'

'What will the final solution be like?"

"Very simple," says the uniformed man. "When the revolt in Van reads and all the Armenians in Turkey rise up against us, then e shall strike."

"But this general revolt simply doesn't exist."

"We shall provoke it."

"How will you do that?"

"Well, we have a plan."'

'What will this final solution be like?"

"We don't know ourselves precisely," says the uniformed man. But there are suggestions. As I said, we don't know anything recisely."'

'Well, it's not so complicated," says the uniformed man. "This eneral revolt that doesn't exist, and can't exist because the rmenians have no weapons and not enough manpower and are either organized nor united . . . this general revolt will be crushed efore it breaks out. Then we shall have all suspicious men shot. nd since anyone able to carry a rifle is suspicious, we shall have em all shot, just to make sure."

"And what will you do with the women and children, and the old eople?"

"We shall deport them."

"Where to?"

"Nowhere."'

nd the uniformed man, who doesn't seem quite content with the ord *nowhere*, says to me: "We must consider the Allies, and also

the world press. So we shall have to give them some destination
We shall announce that this mob is being resettled in Mesopotam
on security grounds, or simply in the Syrian desert."

"Resettlement?"

"Yes," says the uniformed man.'

'"I don't believe that man is naturally static," says the uniforme
man. "Basically he can live anywhere, provided the climate sui
him and there's enough water and food."

"Yes," I say.

"And plants can grow anywhere too, so long as they have su
and soil and water."

"It has to be the right soil," I say, "and the right sun and t!
right water."

"True enough," says the uniformed man.

"And if they don't have those conditions?"

"Well, then . . ." says the uniformed man . . . "then they die
frightful death before their time."'

'"The deportees will be driven on to the trackless passes throug
the Taurus," says the uniformed man, "and through the Ponti
Mountains and other ranges. There are enough of them in th
country . . . Others will be driven round in a circle, or taken
certain distance along the Baghdad line and then taken off an
chased off. They will be made to go on foot until they've got no fe
left, or only what's left of their feet, and mounted saptiehs will dri
them on with their whips until they drop dead. The rest . . . tho
that refuse to die and cling desperately to life, not that it will l
worth anything to them . . . we'll just drive them into the deser
on foot, with no water and no food. And some will actually arri
at their destination, the toughest ones, I suppose. And there we'
erect large-scale reception camps, so that the world press won
think we'd forgotten to provide for them, and that it may not be
genuine resettlement that we're carrying out. For a new homelan
must be the object of a resettlement scheme, mustn't it? Isn't th
right? There's got to be a new homeland for this rabble, far fro
the front, of course, on security grounds. But there won't l
anything for them to eat in those reception camps, because there

war on and we haven't got much ourselves. The press will
nderstand that . . . and the consulates of allied countries and
eutrals, they'll understand it too. By the end of the war there won't
e a single one of this mob left."

"So there won't be any Armenian question in Anatolia any
nore?"

"That's right."

"Because there won't be any Armenians there any more."

"Right."

"When is the Armenian question going to be solved?"

"By the end of September at the latest."

"End of September?"

"Yes."

"And how will you put your case to the world press?"

"Quite simple. Look: we'll ask our interior minister, Talaat Bey,
o hold a press conference to give an official account. And he'll be
nly too glad to do that. For when that time comes he'll be able to
ay: 'Gentlemen, I don't know what you're expecting from us. There
s neither an Armenian nationality problem in the disputed
natolian province of Turkey, nor is there any Armenian question
r any sort of Armenian majority. For you see, gentlemen . . .
ccording to the best of my information, there aren't any Armenians
ere any more.'"'

nd so I took one of my enormous jumps out of the uniformed man's
ar and flew back to the last thought, who was waiting for me on
e Gate of Happiness. I told him about my conversation and then
said to him: 'My little lamb, as you see, it's not so complicated.
asically it's all a question of preparedness, for the good as for the
ad, and since in some circles they see good in the bad, that makes
all much simpler. The priests and all the God-botherers hold the
ood God responsible for the great catastrophes brought about by
an. *It was God's will*, they say. But those who plan new changes
n the maps and in the state beat their breasts and talk of national
equirements, of the hurdles of conscience they had to get over, and
ey speak in a self-satisfied way of the triumph of the will, of the
ad, delayed and ineffective solutions and of the good ones carried
ut with determination, and conclusive.'

* * *

'And so in no time the Turkish bureaucracy was moving heaven and earth to translate the ideas that had cropped up in the leaders' heads into reality. The Turkish people were not consulted. It all came from the top and was passed down. I, the story-teller, was amazed when I saw the corrupt, rusty machinery of the Turkish bureaucracy carrying out all the measures demanded by the Committee for Unity and Progress with almost Prussian efficiency and precision. Such a plan, with finality as its goal, is like a work of art. Or am I wrong there? Perhaps it is only life that is a work of art, not something that leads to its extinction . . . since life is surely more complex than death, and because it is much more difficult, more skilful, to create life than to extinguish it. Can't any clown do that? I find it a real puzzle. But why should I, the story-teller, bother my head about it?'

'The fact was, the planners meant it seriously. The Special Organization, the Teshkilat-Mahsuse as it was called, originally set up for political warfare beyond the front as an organ for counter propaganda and agitation, with the aim of rousing Turkish people and other Muslims and minorities living in enemy areas, this Special Organization was now to stimulate hatred of the Armenians. With the first heat wave and the first early summer weather in 1915, representatives of the Special Organization, grey eminences in Stamboul suits and red fezzes, set out for the provinces. Their message was clear, and brooked no argument. It was all ready. The Valis were responsible for carrying out the plans in their *vilayet*. And the Valis had to pass on the orders to the commanders of the individual *sanjaks*, the *kasahs* and the local police . . . to the mutessarifs, the kaimakams, the mudirs and all the other officials whose job it was to receive orders and carry them out. It was important that the Armenians should be found to have weapons, and they must be hidden weapons, secret stores of weapons in great numbers of which the government had been unaware and which could serve now as evidence of the planned revolt. One way or the other, the shooting of every man able to bear arms must be carried out quickly. The greater the surprise, the easier it would be for the government to remain master of the situation. Deportation of the women, children and old men was also part of the plan. Everybody must be gone by the autumn, even sooner in the *vilayets* near the front, in the next few weeks even. The gentlemen from the Special Organization made it clear to the Valis that by no means all the deportees were to arrive at their destination. They explained to them that the Kurdish tribes in the mountains would be alerted to massacre women, children and old men passing through the Kurdish area, free from punishment of course. The Kurds should be encouraged, and valuables, clothes, shoes and other booty promised to them. The gentlemen also promised help. The local saptiehs would get reinforcements for their difficult, serious task. Whole regiments of gendarmerie were already on their way, both to take part in the shooting and to escort the deportees. *Chettes* would also be coming, all those criminals that Enver had personally got out of gaol to help to free the Turkish people from the Armenian pest. The *chettes* were stationed as commandos wherever it was necessary: at all crossings along the caravan road, on the mountain passes and the banks of the rivers. Their task, the travelling gentlemen of the Special Organization said, consisted of cutting down the women, children and old men, either with picks and shovels, bayonets, knives or any other deadly weapon, but also with their rifles, so long as they had enough ammunition. But the government didn't give the *chettes* much ammunition, since in those difficult times they had to be economical with it. The *chettes* were of course thieves and murderers, said the gentlemen from the Special Organization, but they were being given the opportunity to cut down their sentences in the service of their fatherland. The government, said the gentlemen, gave the *chettes* no pay, but had encouraged them to help themselves to pay from their victims, a sort of self-rationing justified by the circumstances. They would shut their eyes to any plundering by the *chettes*. For the rest, the government expected that the *chettes* would be treated with respect by the representatives of the official police and of the army. For the *chettes* wore the uniform of the war minister, Enver Pasha, and were soldiers like any others, although in fact they were mercenaries like the *hamidiyes* and the *bashibazouks*.'

CHAPTER FIVE

'Early in the summer a whole heap of telegrams in cypher had landed in the office of the Vali of Bakir and were laboriously, and with astonishment, decyphered and then burnt, for – so ran the order from Constantinople – no written matter must be retained. Then, when the first gentlemen from the Special Organization arrived in Bakir to convey personally the orders of the Committee, even those who had declared that they hadn't understood the content of the telegrams correctly were now unanimously convinced that it was inevitable.

"I really do think it's a good thing," said the Mudir to one of the gentlemen from the Special Organization, "to make an end of those rats once and for all."

"Rats, that's what they are," said the Vali.

"Well, yes," said one of the gentlemen from the Special Organization. "That's right enough."

"Only I don't understand," said the Mudir, "why we also have to deport all the old women. Old women aren't going to lead a revolt."

"When you kill rats, you have to kill them all," said the Vali. "The old women will die on the road if they're deported. And that's a good thing."

"Let's be realistic," said the Special Organization gentleman. "Rats or not, the old women are dangerous because they talk so much. If they survive they might talk about us, spread all sorts of lies and give us a bad name."

"And the dead don't talk?"

"That's right, Mudir Bey. A dead mouth can't spit poison."

"And what about the little children?"

"They're the most dangerous of all," said the Special Organization gentleman. "They'll grow up and avenge their fathers."

"And their mothers," said the Mudir.

"And their sisters and brothers," said the Vali.

"They're the most dangerous of all," said the Special Organiza-
on gentleman.

How shall we put it to the consulates?" asked the Mudir.
Especially our allies' consulates?"

"Don't worry," said the man from the Special Organization. "If
rious questions arise, we have a good case. Everything the
overnment has decided is legal."

"What about having the men shot?"

"It's perfectly normal to shoot insurgents. And we are at war. If
her countries had had the same sort of internal problems they
ouldn't have done anything different."

"And the deportations?"

"What deportations?"

"Well, I mean, the deportations."

"Oh, those?"

"Yes, those."

"Well, now, Mudir Bey. We're talking now as it were about the
acuation of a hostile population from the war zone."

"Not all the provinces are in the war zone."

"It's all a war zone, Mudir Bey. Don't forget, the internal enemy
everywhere."

"And how are we to explain to the consulates that most of the
portees never reach their destination?"

"Tell them the truth, Mudir Bey. Tell them it's the *chettes* and the
urds that are responsible for the killings, and that it's impossible
keep an eye on the *chettes* and the Kurds all the time, as the
nsulates well know. Tell them we recruited the *chettes* as
inforcements because our men are at the front. And tell them –
st to keep them quiet, you understand – that we didn't know the
ettes would exceed their authority. And as for the Kurds – well,
s as I said. They can't be fenced in. And we can't start a row with
em in wartime. If they come down out of the mountains and mow
own women and children – what can we do about it? Should the
ptiehs – generally just a small escort – should they fire on the
urds, who have hundreds of horsemen with rifles? That would be

straight suicide. You must see, we can't be responsible."

"But the saptiehs will be killing the deportees too."

"The saptiehs will just do their duty, and only kill if there's ▮ alternative."'

'The gentlemen went on discussing one thing and another. The▮ smoked a lot and drank a lot of strong, sweet coffee, served in litt▮ bowls.

"Do you know, efendiler," said the Special Organization gentl▮ man, "old Abdul Hamid was a terrible bungler. He had a fe▮ Armenians scuppered in '94, '95 and '96, but the Armenians wh▮ survived have bred like rabbits ever since and their losses have be▮ made up over and over again. Just look round. The Armenia▮ proliferate like weeds in good fields."

"I've been saying that for a long time," said the Vali. "The▮ really are more and more of them."'

'"Let's get to the point, gentlemen."

"Yes, let's get to the point."

"What about those guns?"

"The Armenians have handed them in," said the Vali.

"When was that?"

"Last winter."'

'"Just after the first step was taken against the Armenians," sa▮ the Mudir, "at the time when the Armenian soldiers were throw▮ out of the army and the prohibition of weapons for the Armenia▮ came into force again, we sent the munadis into the Armenia▮ *mahalles*. We had all the new rules announced, and we stuck poste▮ up on the houses."

"What about?"

"About handing in the guns."

"What guns?"

"They were legal guns," said the Mudir, "guns issued to t▮ people by the Committee the year they took power."

"Yes, I know," said the Special Organization gentleman.

"We told the Armenians to hand those guns in again."

"And did they do what you told them?"

"Of course," said the Mudir.

"We threatened them with the death penalty if they didn't hand in their guns," said the Vali.

"That's right," said the Mudir.

And the Vali said: "That's how it was, Allah be my witness."'

"It may be that some of those Armenians have kept their guns," said the Mudir, "but that shouldn't worry us, because there can't be many of them. We counted the guns handed in, and the number is about the same as the number of rifles we first issued."'

"And what about the Dashnaks and their hidden guns?"

"They're hard to find, efendiler."

"Too true," said the Vali. "They are hard to find."

"We've already searched all the Armenians' houses," said the Mudir.

"And the farmyards, and the barns? And the graveyards?"

"Those too."

"The graveyards especially," said the Mudir. "We took down all the gravestones. But we didn't find any weapons hidden there."

"It's certainly going to be a hell of a job to find where they've hidden them," said the Special Organization gentleman.

"Too true," said the Vali. "How right you are, efendi."'

"Well," said the Special Organization gentleman, "we know all that. And you mustn't think the Committee is stupid. We're not stupid."

"Allah be my witness," said the Vali, "I've never considered the Committee to be stupid."

"Well, now, you see," said the Special Organization gentleman, "the Committee has decided that the weapons have got to be found in the next three weeks as evidence of the planned uprising, supported by the Dashnaks and the Russians. And the Committee, in its wisdom and foresight, has also decided to help you find the weapons."

"Help us?"

"Well, yes," said the Special Organization gentleman.'

"It's all quite simple, efendiler. In the next few days you'll send your munadis on the streets again. And you'll put posters up wherever there are Armenians living, demanding that the weapons be handed in."

"But these secret stores of weapons may not exist?"

"They've got to exist, efendiler."

"Yes, they've got to exist," said the Vali. "And Allah be my witness that they exist."

The gentleman from the Special Organization said: "Vali Bey those weapons do exist. And Allah have mercy on you if they don't."

'The gentleman from the Special Organization said: "The Armenians naturally won't hand in their hidden weapons, which may well not exist. But the Committee in its foresight, its wisdom and its sense of justice, has found a solution."

"A solution?"

"Yes, a solution."

"A solution to such a difficult problem?"

"No problems are insoluble to the Committee, efendiler. Really Allah knows that well."'

'And the gentleman from the Special Organization said: "Have all the Armenian notables arrested and hold them as hostages. Threaten the community that the hostages will be shot if the weapons aren't handed in."

"And if there aren't any such weapons?"

"A few rifles will be found somehow or other."

"Is that all?"

"No, that's not all."'

'"You will then arrest a couple of hundred men and have them tortured – the notables with them, of course. Do whatever you think right."

"The usual bastinado?"

"The bastinado, if you like."

"We could tickle their balls a bit. Just slit them open, perhaps?"

"Just think of something."

"We've tried pulling out their beards. But that isn't a very effective method."

"No, it isn't specially effective."

"We've chopped the hands and feet off some of them. We made them drink their own piss and put their eyes out, but even that didn't work much. Your Armenian just won't talk if he doesn't want to talk."

"We've torn some tongues out too," said the Mudir, "but then of course they talk even less."'

'"Just think of something," said the Special Organization gentleman. "Have your prisoners tortured until they reveal the hiding-places of the weapons."

"The hiding-places of the weapons which may not exist?"

"That's right."

"What then?"

"Then you'll examine the hiding-places and check that there really are no weapons there."

"And then?"

"Then you'll make a suggestion to the prisoners."'

'And the gentleman from the Special Organization said: "The Committee, in its wisdom and justice and foresight, has decided to sell those obstinate Armenians in Bakir four thousand rifles. They can use them to fill up their empty stock of weapons."

"But, gentlemen, the Armenians will never go in for such devious horse-trading."

"You're mistaken, Vali Bey. The Armenians certainly will go in for it."'

'"Listen, Vali Bey. The ones you've tortured will be softened up. And you, Vali Bey, will say to them: 'Efendiler, the Committee for Unity and Progress has decided to release you from the pains of torture, for nothing is less acceptable to the Party than these nasty, obsolete methods, because the Committee in its wisdom, justice and foresight has decided simply to sell you the weapons which, as the Committee has ordered, you have to surrender. So we'll sell you four thousand rifles at a low price. You will put them in your hiding-places, and in the hiding-places that we shall indicate to you, so that we can then find them. Then you will let us know the names of your ring-leaders. And we, the authorities in Bakir, can then

369

report to the Committee in Constantinople that the uprising was discovered in good time, the weapons have been found and the ring-leaders arrested. And then, gentlemen, you can go home in peace.'"

"But the Armenians won't go in for that sort of horse-trading."

"Of course they won't, efendiler," said the Special Organization gentleman.'

'And he said: "The Armenians are a race of traders and speculators. They'll make you a counter-offer. And you'll think it over. So that you can make a counter-offer to them."

"Logical," said the Mudir.

"How true," said the Vali. "And what sort of counter-offer shall we make to the counter-offer of the Armenians?"'

'"Well, now," said the Special Organization gentleman. "You will say to the Armenians: 'Efendiler, it's like this. We shan't find the hidden weapons, but you'll hand them over to us yourselves. We'll sell you four thousand good rifles of Russian make, captured rifles of course. And live ammunition, naturally. You'll take delivery of them under cover of darkness, so that no unauthorized person can see. You'll take them to your hiding-places, and then we'll give you three days. During those three days our munadis will call on you to hand in the weapons the Russians have given you. For three whole days the munadis will be shouting this out at the top of their voices. And they'll also promise you a general amnesty if you hand the weapons in voluntarily. We'll also put up posters with the same demands and the same promises. When those three days are up you'll take the weapons out of the hiding-places and bring them to the barracks. We shall be waiting for you there. We'll count the weapons and make a note of the numbers, and then we shall make our report to the Committee, to the effect that the uprising has been discovered and that the Armenians have voluntarily handed in their weapons and so have to be pardoned. Only the ring-leaders will have to be arrested. But don't worry about that. We'll warn them, and they'll have time to disappear. What about that, efendiler?'"'

'"That's a marvellous idea," said the Vali.

"It's fantastic," said the Mudir.

"Just something that occurred to the Committee," said the man from the Special Organization.'

'"But in that case we shall have to let the prisoners go?"

"Naturally," said the man from the Special Organization, "but only to arrest them a couple of days later."

"And what about the promise of an amnesty?"

"There won't be any amnesty," said the man from the Special Organization.'

'"The Armenians simply won't have time to hand in the rifles they've just bought. Because all the saptiehs in the *vilayet*, the very next day after you've sold them the weapons, will be out in strength and searching all the houses, also all the known hiding-places for weapons. You'll find the weapons and seize them, and then arrest every Armenian man capable of bearing arms. And on the following day you will announce the discovery of the weapons, the great number of them and where they came from . . . and at the same time you will begin the mass shootings."'

'The Special Organization man smiled, and I, the story-teller, saw his smile and could read his thoughts: four thousand rifles and ammunition for them, at a low price still to be arranged. The Vali will have to pay in the money to the state, but this Vali is smarter than he looks. He's sure to sell the Armenians 6,000 rifles, but only deliver 4,000 of them . . . and the difference in the payment will disappear into his own pocket. But what should we do about it? It would be pointless to try to teach the ethics of the Committee to these leftovers from the time of Abdul Hamid and his corrupt regime. What do they understand of the ideals of the new leadership, its battle against corruption, its care for honesty and order, its open-mindedness and western orientation, its aims of a new order and national unity? No, there would be no point. These incorrigibles would go on cheating the state and filling their own pockets at the state's expense. Since we have to work with them, it would be best not to ask any questions.'

'"If it goes all right," said the Vali, "then the Committee can reckon we shall begin the shootings before the holidays. It will be Ramadan in a few weeks. By the time the faithful begin their fast, it should all be over."

"Certainly it should," said the Special Organization man. "It must be all over long before then."'

'"And when shall we start deporting the women and children and old men?"

"After the shooting, but still before the holidays. The Armenian quarter must be empty before the beginning of Ramadan."

"And how shall we deport them? On foot?"

"Some on foot, some in ox-carts."

"But we could never collect that number of ox-carts!"'

"Think of something."

"Why can't we drive the whole mob out of the town on foot?"

"Because of the press, and the consulates. Don't forget that we're calling it an evacuation, or rather a resettlement. They must proceed decently, in good order."

"What about supplies?"

"So long as we can't be sure whether the press and the consulates are watching the whole thing, bread and water will be issued."

"And afterwards, when the transports disappear into the ravines of the Taurus?"

"Then no more."

"And what about the Armenians' houses? Their furniture? And their clothes and personal belongings? And what about their money, and gold and jewellery?"

"Objects of value must be handed in," said the Special Organization man, "handed in under threat of the death penalty. As for personal baggage, the Armenians can take what they can carry or get on the ox-cart. We will announce that immovable property will be restored after the war, when the deportees return."

"Are any of these people ever going to come back, then?"

"We'll take good care that nobody comes back."

"Then nothing will actually be restored, none of the immovable property, I mean?"

"That's right."'

*   *   *

And I, the story-teller, say: "Whether they come back or not, their houses will still be standing. But there will be different people living in them. Turks and Kurds, especially Turkomans and *mohajirs* – yes, *mohajirs* most of all, the Muslims who fled from the Caucasus and the European provinces lost in the Balkan War."'

"Some day, when the time is ripe," the gentleman from the Special Organization had said to the Vali over a glass of *raki*, "some day we'll make real Turks out of the Kurds. But it's not the same with the Armenians. The Armenian is a foreign body in our flesh, a cynical thorn that can't be taught or absorbed or changed, who will always look in a foreign, uncomprehending way at Turkish ways, or – let's put it like this – he's stuck into us so we can't get him out, and his only aim is to poison the body that feeds him."

"The Mudir said something like that the other day," said the Vali, "and I've often thought much the same thing."

The gentleman from the Special Organization nodded, with a benevolent smile. "Abdul Hamid thought the problem could be solved simply by making Muslims of the Armenians. But we Young Turks have learnt from the Europeans that it's not only the religion of our citizens that we have to think about, but the national attitude, the race and the blood. Enver Pasha has promised to unite all the Turkish peoples of the world, and he has promised to make Turks out of all that can be made into Turks."

"Yes," said the Vali.

"Abdul Hamid didn't know anything about these new ideas, so he couldn't have known that it does no good to convert Armenians."

"It doesn't do any good," said the Vali.

"The Armenians abroad have already influenced the neutral press against us," said the Special Organization gentleman, "especially the American press, and once we start on the final steps they'll storm at us more than ever. That's what we expected. But we've warned them. And we've told them, months ago: if international Armeniandom succeeds one day in raising the whole world against us, that will mean the annihilation of the race."

"In our sphere of influence, efendi."

"Absolutely right, Vali Bey."'

CHAPTER SIX

'A few weeks before the holidays, passers-by who found
entertaining to take a walk along the prison wall near the *hukum*
could distinctly hear the screams of the prisoners being tortured. I
wasn't the first time, for there has been torture in Turkish prison
as far back as memory goes. But this time the screams sounde
different. It may be that it only seemed so to those who heard then
The screams went right through them. Often it sounded as if ther
was a singer on the rack, trying to sing to the beat of an unmusica
choirmaster, untutored, with no knowledge of scales. There wer
different kinds of scream: the gurgling, long-held ones that coul
only come from prisoners who had had something stuck in thei
mouth which could not quite smother the scream: perhaps som
saptieh was just holding the tip of the prisoner's tongue between hi
fingers and pulling on it a bit, but not too hard, because the prisone
still needed his tongue to make the confessions they expected from
him. Other screams came at regular intervals, like the blows of
whip, and then you knew that someone was being beaten on hi
naked skin, probably on the soles of his feet. Armenians' feet wer
thought to be particularly sensitive, for those people who though
they were a master-race and wanted to rule over their landlord
never went barefoot, at least not in the town. And the passers-b
knew that the owners of those feet had tender skin. They weren
hardened, callused feet protected by horny skin, like the feet of th
lower classes, the Turks and Kurds. Those feet were used t
wearing good shoes, silk stockings even, which were quite unneces
sarily washed and changed. Sissy feet, they were, and the screamer
were sissies. Of course there were yet other screams, and you didn
have to have graduated at the University of Constantinople to know
that what they were about. Screams caused by sharp objects wer

particularly easy to recognize. There were screams on every note of a lunatic scale, which seemed to come from the beyond, perhaps from the purgatory of hell . . . some short and sharp, some shrill, others that came from the depth of the tormented body, others only from the fleshless, damned soul. Many of the passers-by made bets, declaring that they knew exactly what sort of screams they were or what the saptieh in charge was doing, or was just going to do.'

'Then suddenly it fell silent, and there was nothing more to hear.'

'The gentleman from the Special Organization had got it right. After some days of torture the Armenian notables and the representatives of the community were ready for anything, even the horse-trading over the sale of weapons. They recognized that the Vali of Bakir needed evidence of the planned uprising in order to satisfy the Committee in Constantinople. The Vali had promised an end to the torture and a general amnesty, if they would voluntarily hand in the weapons they hadn't got, but could get.

And how could the representatives of the community refuse such a tremendous offer, since the weapons were to be had so cheap?'

'The important business was carried out at night. Not until most of the inhabitants of the city, the city reputed to have a thousand and one mosques, had blown out their oil-lamps, did the hectic activity begin in the armouries of Bakir. Long lines of ox-carts stood ready in the barracks. They were loaded with rifles and ammunition-boxes and then moved off towards the Armenian *mahalle*. Overtired saptiehs accompanied the transport, and even the fat, sleepy Vali rode some of the way with them, as well as the Mudir and the Mutessarif and the Kaimakam and of course the gentlemen from the Special Organization. In the Armenian quarter, only the initiated knew about the great comedy that was to end a chapter of Armenian history and open a new one. The initiated blew out their oil-lamps, but they didn't lie down to sleep. Despite the curfew they were out on the streets late at night, which clearly didn't worry the Vali and the other gentlemen . . . they took delivery of the weapons, took them into the hiding-places under the eyes of the saptiehs, met later in the house of the former Armenian Mukhtar, then went to the Hayastan restaurant, which had been closed for weeks but had been opened at this unaccustomed hour on the orders of the Vali; those of the notables that still had hands and legs that had not been cut off and who had not been wounded by excessive whipping, those in fact who could walk or limp – they met, after the weapons had been safely packed away, in the Hayastan with the government representatives, drank *raki* with them, assured the government in Constantinople of their loyalty, listened again to the complex reasons for the horse-trading in weapons and the general amnesty, showed understanding, heard the Vali express reassurance again and again but observed the faces of the other gentlemen as he did so, let themselves be calmed down, then said nothing more about the arrangement and later mentioned only casually that for their part they would keep their mouths shut and duly hand in the weapons in three days' time.'

'But the comedy was already over next morning. At least, it began all right. For in the morning, when the notables woke up with nothing to fear for the first time for a long time, when they kissed their wives and told them that everything would be all right now, an arrangement had been made with the authorities and the situation had calmed down, there were saptiehs standing outside the doors of the houses. They didn't stay outside the doors for long, for when it became known that the weapons had been found, that the Armenians' hiding-places had been discovered, when it was announced that the weapons were just being picked up, weapons that those traitors had not handed in, which they had received from the Russians and their confederates for the uprising that had long been planned and was to break out when the Russians were at the gates of the city . . . when all that news got around, the saptiehs forced their way into the houses.'

'Yes. It all went off very quickly. According to plan. On the same day the weapons were found, a wave of arrests began such as had never been seen before. It was 20 June 1915, just two weeks before Ramadan, the festival of the great fast and inner purification, which would begin on 2 July. There would actually have been plenty of time for the shooting, which need not have disturbed the faithful during the month's fast, for the first cannon shot from the citadel which had always given the signal for the fast to begin was still days off. None the less, the very next morning, at daybreak, the Vali ordered the shooting to begin. Not that the Vali was in a hurry; he wasn't. It was just that the gentlemen from the Special Organization wanted to move on, and said they couldn't leave until it was all over. The Vali put the Mudir in charge. And he had a serious talk with the Mudir and made it clear to him that everybody should be shot who was capable of bearing arms. And that meant everybody who could hold a long stick in his hand without his mother's help, even anybody who had teeth which weren't just his first teeth or a pisser that he didn't only use for pissing. Everybody was dangerous who looked dangerous or who could become dangerous within foreseeable time.'

'For three days the men who could bear arms were led out of the town in columns of fours, tied to each other with ropes. At the same time the town-criers bawled out at the top of their voices the news of the uprising in Van, of the Armenian volunteer battalions on the Russian side and of the cooperation with those scoundrels of the Armenians in Bakir. Now it must all be cleared up, the Turkish fatherland saved by Allah in its hour of need. And the imams in the mosques said the same sort of thing, and the *hodjas* spoke to the children in the Koran schools and warned them against the devil, the *djinn* and the Armenians. Screaming posters on the ramparts, the city gates and the walls of the houses denounced the Armenians, and the newspapers vied with each other in their stories of Armenian treachery. In the streets of Bakir, Turkish and German officers stood side by side, embarrassed, and the consulates of the neutral nations, deeply concerned, shut their windows.'

'In most towns in Anatolia the Armenians were shot just outside the city gates, but in Bakir they were more careful. Since there were high mountains not far from the city, they took the men for a little walk, not more than three or four hours, but certainly not less. And where the ravines were so deep that even the saptiehs were scared to look over the edge of the cliffs, where the *djinn* howled in the wind and even a strong man couldn't pee down into the depths without a pounding of the heart, where you trod carefully and kept your horse on the bridle, there they shot the men. Actually they were not all shot, for the regiments of gendarmes from outside the region that came as reinforcements for the Bakir saptiehs said they must save ammunition, for supplies were limited, and there wouldn't be too much time – as others had said before them – so those alien saptiehs simply cut the men down with their sabres. And there were the *chette* units too, which had arrived in good time. And those *chettes* had a lot of axes in their saddlebags. The slow, stupid Bakir saptiehs were amazed when they saw how skilfully the *chettes* broke open the skulls of the Armenian men, as if they'd been doing nothing else all their lives.

It was an advantage too that they didn't have to bury the dead, for the gorges made the best graves. And because they had to throw so many of them into the gorges – for they didn't all fall obediently into them but, contrary to orders, just lay on the mountain path – it was decided to leave those dead dogs to the living dogs. For there were more than enough living dogs – four-legged ones – in the country. A lot of the Franks used to call Turkey the country of abandoned dogs. Nowhere in the world, the Franks said, were there as many abandoned dogs as there were there. They were more numerous than the vultures, and ate all the dead bodies in the alleys of the villages and towns, on the country roads and the mountain passes. The whole country was their hunting-ground, and while they were not as quick as the vultures they made a better job of it, because they ate more at a time and seldom left anything behind.'

'The gentlemen from the Special Organization were astonished that the Kurdish tribes hadn't played some part in the bloodbath. The Kurds were generally on the spot at once on such occasions, when they could pick up some boots and clothing.

"The Kurds are just waiting," the Vali had said. "I suppose they don't want to clash with the *chettes* and all those strange saptiehs from Erzurum *vilayet*."

"We've already warned the tribes," said the Special Organization gentleman, "and let them know that there will soon be transports of women and children and old men passing through their area."

"There will indeed," said the Vali. "The Kurds are just waiting until the families of the men who have been shot go through their area, because they assume there won't be many saptiehs escorting them."

"Yes, I expect that's it," said the Special Organization gentleman.

"And of course the Kurds will reckon on getting more loot from the women and children and old men than from the able-bodied men, who don't carry any baggage."

"That's right, Vali Bey."

"All the same, the Kurds ought to be held in check."

"On the contrary," said the Special Organization man, "if we send the women and children and old men over the mountains, the Kurds can go ahead and slaughter them. The problem is with the foreign press and the reports of the consulates."

"What about them?"

"Well, I've explained this to you before. And the other gentlemen have heard it too: the shooting of the insurgents was forced on us by the war situation. We can accept the responsibility for that. But the cutting down of the women and children and the old men . . . we're leaving that to the Kurds. Then the government can say they had nothing to do with it."

"Yes, you explained that to us."

"So that should be clear."

"But the attacks by the saptiehs . . . and especially by the *chettes*?"

"That's another thing I've told you and your people about not so long ago. The Committee knows what it's doing, and it recognizes it responsibility. The saptiehs are only doing their duty, and if they have to use their weapons now and then to keep order, that's something that they will understand abroad. And the *chettes*? Well, we've explained that too. They're robbers and murderers. We've had to employ them because we haven't enough manpower. What else were we to do? And is it our fault if the *chettes* sometimes break the rules? They've just come out of the condemned cells. Do we have to send a lawyer along with every one of them? The eye of the law can't be everywhere. These are hard times, Vali Bey. We just have to employ the *chettes*."

"And the deportations?"

"There are no deportations. Have I got to explain that again too? Look here: it's a question of resettlement made necessary by the war on strategic grounds. Those Armenian women and children and those rickety old men are just going to be sent on a journey. Why else would we be making ox-wagons available to them and letting them take their luggage? That's all it is, a little journey, no more and no less."'

CHAPTER SEVEN

'In Bakir they called the few days before the month's fast of Ramadan the munadis' days, for never before had the drummers and town-criers had so much work bellowing the orders of the authorities at the closed windows and doors of the Armenians. Most of the town-criers knew the owners of the ears for which the messages were intended, and they knew that the Armenian was always wide awake, from birth to death; even in his sleep he heard the message of doom that would be addressed to him. But the Armenian was naturally stubborn and acted as if he was not really aware of his fate, not even of all that was predestined, that was in the book of fate from which no one on earth could escape. These Armenians acted as if they had not even heard about it, as if the day set for deportation simply didn't exist on Allah's calendar. The munadis heard the relatives of the executed men weeping and mourning behind closed doors and windows, so the munadis yelled louder than ever to make sure that the mourners didn't miss anything. Many of the munadis were good-natured men and would have liked to do something to help the Armenians, for in all the years that Allah had granted them they had done business with the Armenians, traded with them, bought things from them, had their clothes and shoes made by them, their leather money-belts, their *kühlas* and *kelims*, their copper pots and pans, their iron house-keys; they even owed their drums and drumsticks to the skill of Armenian hands – and so as it turned out many of the munadis, after making their important announcement in the name of Enver Pasha, Jemal Pasha and Talaat Bey, and especially in the name of the Committee for Unity and Progress . . . that such a munadi spoke privately to the owners of the ears, often to the little children, often to the old men, but mostly to the women. And many of them told them:

"There's no point in mourning for the men and acting as if you hadn't heard the orders. You have to give all your valuables and your money to the state. But the state is generous and allows you to take 300 piastres with you on the road. So pack your things up and take your 300 piastres for the road. And if you've still got any gold or jewels which you haven't handed in yet and don't want to hand in, don't hide it in your clothes or in your hair or in your cunts or up your arses, for they'll find it all and pinch it. Bury it somewhere where you'll be able to find it again." And many of the Armenians listened to the munadis and buried anything they didn't want to hand in to the state, but a lot of them didn't because they believed that no one should ever set out on a journey without some gold coins.'

'An extraordinary comedy was played before the eyes of the staff of the consulates in those last days before Ramadan. It started before daybreak and went on until it got dark. Thousands of women and children and old men passed through the city gates in long columns, accompanied by mounted soliders. Anyone who couldn't find room in an ox-cart went on foot. And similar columns came from the surrounding villages and small towns, all going through Bakir. There are hundreds of thousands of them on the road, wrote the heads of the consulates to their governments. They're all being resettled. The government says they're going to Syria. The statements are pretty vague. No one knows their true destination.'

'It was obvious that some craftsmen and people whose services were essential had to be excluded from the shooting and the deportation, and their families with them, for those conscripts wouldn't do their work properly if their families were exiled and they were left behind by themselves. But since in this part of the world crafts were almost exclusively in the hands of Armenians, it happened, or it chanced to happen, that the people the state found most important or most indispensable were allowed to remain. Even one or two rich people were allowed to remain, for the Vali had plans for them that the gentlemen from the Special Organization didn't need to know about.'

* * *

'At the end of June 1915, just two days before Ramadan, the Vali
sent for the owner of the Hayastan restaurant to his office.

"Haygaz Efendi," said the Vali, "I've often dined at your place,
and the Mudir has often dined there, and so have the Kaimakam
and the Mutessarif. And lower grades, too . . . even saptiehs and
munadis have eaten in the Hayastan. The cooking is outstanding.
There is no better cooking."

"Yes," said Haygaz, "my wife is a good cook, and I've always
done my best to satisfy my customers."

"Just so," said the Vali. "That's quite true. And you've never
taken a single piastre from anyone wearing government uniform."

"Why should I?" said Haygaz.

"And we've always looked after you."

"Yes," said Haygaz.

"You'll admit that?"

"Yes," said Haygaz.'

'"I have exempted your house, Haygaz Efendi," said the Vali. "But
you don't seriously think I've done that because I've dined well
there?"

"No," said Haygaz.

"I had my reasons."

"Yes," said Haygaz.'

'"The government," said the Vali, "has allowed me to exempt fifty
craftsmen and their families."

"Yes," said Haygaz.

"But I've written to the Committee that I shall need a hundred
craftsmen if the town isn't to come to a full stop. Do you
understand?"

"Yes," sais Haygaz.

"I don't really need so many," said the Vali. "Do you
understand?"

"No," said Haygaz.

"Well," said the Vali, "it's like this. I shall enter the names of
fifty of the richest Armenians in my book together with the fifty
craftsmen. And do you know what that means?"

"No," said Haygaz.

"It means that those fifty people will survive in spite of not being craftsmen. Do you understand now?"

"Yes," said Haygaz.'

'"I've put you down as a carpenter, Haygaz Efendi. From now on you're a carpenter."

"Yes," said Haygaz.

"Do you know anything about carpentry?"

"No," said Haygaz.'

'"Well, that doesn't matter," said the Vali. "What does matter is that we should understand one another."

"Why are you doing this?"

"Well, why shouldn't I?"'

'And the Vali said: "You've buried a whole lot of gold and jewels, efendi. Or shall we say, hidden them to avoid state action. But we don't know where."

"I haven't hidden anything, Vali Bey."

"Oh, yes, you have," said the Vali. "You've hidden a whole lot."'

'And the Vali said: "Every Armenian has four hiding-places. If I have him tortured he'll tell me the first hiding-place, to escape further torture. But the first hiding-place doesn't have the real treasure in it. You see?"

"Yes," said Haygaz.

"And then, if I have him tortured a bit more, maybe he'll tell me about the second hiding-place. But that won't have the real treasure in it either."

"Yes," said Haygaz.

"And he might possibly tell me about the third," said the Vali. "But even there there won't be the least bit of his valuables."

"That's possible," said Haygaz.

"The real treasure is in the fourth hiding-place," said the Vali. "But he'll never tell me about that one."

"Yes," said Haygaz.

"It doesn't matter what I do," said the Vali. "He'll never give it away."'

* * *

'And the Vali said: "So there isn't much point in having you tortured, efendi. Really, there would be very little point."

"Yes," said Haygaz.

"I've therefore thought of something else, something more effective, something we should both like better."

"What is that, Vali Bey?"

"You'll bring your treasure to me voluntarily, efendi," said the Vali. "You'll actually ask me to accept it. You'll come here every day, to the *hukumet*, on your knees, and beg me to accept your treasure."

"Why should I do that, Vali Bey?"

"Well, that's the question," said the Vali.'

'And the Vali said: "Our German allies laugh at us over our regular military service exemption tax, which at the moment stands at forty-four Turkish lira. We call it the *bedel*, and at one time every Armenian born to his mother paid that tax. So why shouldn't an Armenian like you, efendi, pay the *bedel* for exemption from deportation? Don't misunderstand me. This is not the official *bedel*, for where should we be if every Armenian we want to shoot or send off into the desert could go free by paying a whopping *bedel*? No, that wouldn't do at all."

"So it wouldn't work?"

"If the matter remains between us two – and that's my advice – then something could be arranged."

"Something could be arranged?"

"Yes, efendi. As Allah is my witness, something could actually be done."

And the Vali said: "Every day you'll pay me forty-four lira – the *bedel*, in fact – in gold and silver coins. Precious stones would have to be valued and counted in towards the forty-four lira."

"What about paper money?"

"No paper money," said the Vali. "On account of depreciation."

"I see," said Haygaz.

"So long as nobody knows about it – only you and I, you understand – then you, and naturally your immediate family, will be exempted from deportation."

"I see, Vali Bey."

"You're a craftsman now, efendi, a carpenter, essential to the state. A carpenter, fancy that!"

"Yes, Vali Bey."

"It's regrettable that we've had to confiscate all Armenian houses, but as a craftsman you may stay in your house as long as the state needs you."

"Yes, Vali Bey."

"Every day, efendi, you will open your vault and take out the gold and silver or the necessary valuables. In the course of time you'll rediscover all that hidden treasure you've buried to swindle the state. Bit by bit you'll dig it all out, without my having to torture you or anything else so barbarous. I won't even have you whipped or anything. We won't pull out any of your teeth, or cut off your greedy fingers, or even your prick, which can beget more of the mob, as you Armenians are vulgarly called. We won't even slit your balls. It won't be necessary. Every day you'll bring in your money or your jewels, for each consignment will mean one day's postponement or one day's freedom from deportation. And you'll bring it all to me voluntarily."

"Yes, Vali Bey."

"If the war lasts a long time, sooner or later you'll get round to the fourth hiding-place, the one with the real treasure, and bring that to me."

"Yes, Vali Bey."

"So that's that," said the Vali.

And Haygaz said: "Thank you, Vali Bey."

"It's only a pity," said the Vali, "that we had to hang your brother Dikran a little while ago."

"Yes, Vali Bey."

"He was a good shoemaker. And we need good shoes nowadays. All the dead Turkish soldiers' boots have to be hurriedly patched up so that the live soliders can wear them. And even the live soldiers' boots – especially after long marches – are generally in a pathetic state. You understand, efendi. Materials are short. And a good shoemaker can work wonders. But where can we find all the shoemakers we need so urgently now? That sort of work was mostly in the hands of the Armenians."

"Nearly all shoemakers are Armenians."

"As you say, efendi."

"Yes," said Haygaz.

"It's a pity," said the Vali.'

'"That Armenian mob had golden hands," said the Vali. "Everything they touched turned out successfully. Satan must have helped them, for how else could you explain the way they do everything so perfectly. How, eh? Look here, efendi. Even I, the Vali of Bakir, have my boots made by an Armenian. And my civilian suits too, as well as my uniform. Everything made by Armenians has style. What I mean is, a conspicuous and suspicious quality. But what's the difference? I've always liked wearing my Armenian boots and suits and uniforms. The man who cut my uniforms was an artist in his line. This uniform I'm wearing now makes me look ten years younger and ten okka thinner."

"Yes, Vali Bey."

"But I still had him shot, because it turned out that there were already too many tailors on the list of craftsmen to be saved."

"I see, Vali Bey."

"Pity, though," said the Vali.'

'"How is your brother Sarkis?" said the Vali. "A goldsmith, wasn't he?"

"A goldsmith," said Haygaz.

"I must have a look and see if he's on the craftsmen's list," said the Vali.

"He isn't," said Haygaz.

"How do you know?"

"He was shot with the others," said Haygaz.

"That's a pity," said the Vali. "A clever goldsmith."

"Yes," said Haygaz.

"It would have been different if he'd been a blacksmith," said the Vali. "We don't need any goldsmiths in wartime, not in the cavalry anyway. What they need is blacksmiths."

"Yes, Vali Bey."

"The best blacksmiths were Armenians," said the Vali. "And there are so few of them left now. It's a pity."'

*　　*　　*

'The Vali offered Haygaz a cigarette, an Amroian cigarette. "These are the last of the Amroians," he said, "inexpensive cigarettes, but exquisite, genuine Armenian quality. Do you know, efendi, I've laid in quite a store of them, because that Armenian Amroian's cigarette factory has been closed."

"They're good cigarettes," said Haygaz.'

'"Do you have any news of my brother Vartan?" said Haygaz. "Vartan Khatisian?"

"No," said the Vali. "We think he must be dead, and we've already written him off."

"Isn't there going to be a trial, then?"

"No, there won't be any trial." And the Vali said: "The Vartan Khatisian case was an idea of the Mudir's. He was obsessed by it. And I'm glad the case is over with. Do you know, efendi, if those press windbags ask me any questions to try and find out about that case, I'll say: 'What case is that, then? You mean the Khatisian case?' And I'll laugh in their faces and say: 'Gentlemen, that case was a Turkish fairy-tale, one of those once-there-was-once-there-wasn't stories. But there's no such case now, and there wasn't one and never has been.'"'

'The case of Vartan Khatisian, called the Khatisian case for short, doesn't exist any more, my little lamb.' And I, the story-teller, I say that too to my shadow. 'And if later on, after the war – in better times, which maybe won't be any better – you leaf through the history books, I'm pretty sure you won't find anything there about the Khatisian case, or about one Vartan Khatisian, said by a distorter of world history, that obsessed Mudir of Bakir, to have shot the heir to the Austrian throne and his bride, that day in Sarajevo. And I'll bet you, my little lamb, that the historical snoopers will shake their heavy heads now and then, especially when I, the story-teller, happen to be sitting in their ear. They'll tell me: "No, we've never heard of the Khatisian case before. The Turks blamed the Armenians for so much, there's nothing left now to blame them for. An Armenian shot the Archduke? And with that fatal shot unleashed the Great War? We don't believe that. It's absolute rubbish!"

But I shall say: "Of course it's rubbish. But listen, ladies and gentlemen. Will it really be very significant if we add one more to the thousand false charges brought against the Armenians . . . so that we can say, once there were a thousand and one charges . . .'''

'I hear an embarrassed silence. The thought-voices of the budding historians are chattering excitedly to each other. One of the thoughts speaks to me: "Listen, Meddah. Everything in my books – the history books – is basically just a concatenation."

"A concatenation of what?"

"Well, Meddah, a string of lesser and greater mass murders from the beginning of time on. And there's a reason for every one. There's a pretext for every one of them. And there's some accusation for every pretext. I understand now, Meddah, why more or less nothing matters in those accusations."

"You're right," I say.

"Was there a Khatisian case, or wasn't there?"

"It doesn't make any difference," I say.

"And what about the world conspiracy, and what about Satan, who is responsible for it all?"

"I don't know."

"There's nothing about it in the textbooks."

"No," I say. "It doesn't matter."

And I turn to the ladies and gentlemen present.

"Ladies and gentlemen," I say, "you'll find nothing in your textbooks about Satan and the world conspiracy, but just have a look in your heads. And just think it over. Or, better, just don't think about it.'''

CHAPTER EIGHT

'You see that queer German, the one that keeps on coming to the men's toilet at the *hukumet* and showing his bottom to the saptiehs – can you see him, my little lamb? And can you also see that other German, the one with glasses? Do you see their field-grey uniforms?'

'I can see both of them,' says my shadow.

'The one with glasses has just written something down,' I say. 'Do you see how he's grinning? Now he says to the queer: "According to our calendar, our allies' Ramadan in 1915 falls on 2 July. And it will be over on 1 August."

"A long time to fast," says the queer.

"It's only half as bad as that," says the one in glasses. "The fast begins with a cannon shot and ends with a cannon shot. The same thing happens each day. By day these Muslims tighten their belts, and after sunset they let them right out again. Then they stuff their bellies full and drink like their horses."

"And what about love?"

"It says in the Koran: 'Wives are your field, go to your field how and when you will.'"

"Even during the fast?"

"No, actually not."

"So, is love forbidden during Ramadan?"

"It's forbidden in daytime, but it's allowed at night."

"Between sunset and sunrise?"

"Yes."

"Is that in the Koran?"

"It says in the Koran: 'It is permitted to have relations with your wives at night during the fast.'"

"Is that all?"

"No. The Prophet also said: 'Lie with them now and desire what

390

Allah allows you.'"

"And what about the other sort of love during Ramadan?"

"What other sort of love?"

"I just mean . . . what about the sort of lovemaking that doesn't involve women? If a faithful Muslim happens to be homosexual, may he have a man in Ramadan?"

"You'd have to ask the imam that," said the man in glasses.

"Or one of the *hodjas*?"

"Yes, or one of them. They'll know the answer too."'

'Never before had the authorities worked so quickly and thoroughly as they did in the last days before Ramadan. It was as if all those ubiquitous soldiers of the German Kaiser had blown a little of the Prussian wind into the chaotic offices of the Turkish allies. As a result, the city of Bakir was free from Armenians in the week before the fast days. Only the few craftsmen were still there, and the few rich men the Vali had been able to exclude from the shooting and deportation orders. It made the German officers swear, because there was nothing left for them to buy for their wives, since the Armenian jewellers' shops had been closed. Closed too were the tailors' shops, the stalls where they sold fabrics and silks, the spice stores, in fact all the Armenian shops where they offered those goods that looked so fabulous to western eyes. Everything seemed to have changed in the city since the Armenians disappeared. The bazaars were almost empty, the streets and the alleys had fallen silent. They even smelt different, for that legendary scent that the Germans loved to sniff on their romantic walks, although it not only smelt of sweet and strange and delicious things but also of rubbish and filth – that had suddenly gone. The city had become dreary, and the sun too was dreary as it shone on the caps of the foreign soldiers.

"It's interesting," says the queer German to his companion. "Since the Armenians disappeared, there's nobody hanging under the Gate of Happiness any more."

"Yes, that is interesting," says the other.'

'Because for the moment there's nobody left to hang,' say I, the story-teller, to my shadow, 'I suggest you hang yourself under the Gate of Happiness.'

'But I haven't got a neck,' says my shadow.

'I know,' I say. 'I didn't really mean you to be hanged, only the black hooks under the Gate of Happiness happen to be empty. I should just like you to wait for me here so that I can find you again.'

'Are you going to fly away without me?'

'Yes. I'm flying a long way away.'

And so I flew behind the column of women and children and old men, to see why the ox-carts on which, according to orders, they had left the city with their baggage had all come back empty.

'I soon found out that the women and their families had not immediately been shot. Nor the old men. It just happened that the *arabachis* responsible for the ox-carts had only taken their passengers as far as the crossing of the caravan roads, of which one led to the swampy district of Konya. I heard how one of the *arabachis*, an old town Kurd, had told one of the saptiehs: "We're not going any further. The Mudir told us, only as far as the road crossing to Konya."

"Bloody crossing," said the saptieh.

"But we're not going to drive to Konya," the old Kurdish *arabachi* had said. "We've got to take the empty ox-carts back to Bakir to be re-loaded."

And then the leader of the saptiehs came up and said: "Yes, that's right. Just chuck all that mob out on to the road. This gang of Armenians can go on foot."

"Are they really going to Konya?" asked the *arabachi*.

"I don't know," said the leader of the saptiehs. "They're going somewhere or other. To Mesopotamia, I believe."

"Then you'll have to go some other way."

"I've got to take these people to Konya first," said the leader of the saptiehs. "And I have to leave them there. And then I suppose they'll be going on."

"To Mesopotamia?"

"Maybe," said the leader of the saptiehs. "Or maybe not. The devil can take this lot that's got to be taken somewhere though nobody knows where that somewhere is." And the leader of the saptiehs spat out his chewing tobacco in a wide arc, and gave a signal to the saptiehs with his riding-whip.'

* * *

'It was all done very humanely. Even the saptiehs, who had been present a few days before when these women's husbands had been shot or beaten to death, were surprised that the *choush* in command of the section didn't give the order just to kill the women with all the kids – not even the old men, who some said were really women, for they were no longer real men with pricks that would stand up. Yes. It would have been more practical to make short work of these unbelievers, for what was the sense of sending the gang on further with all that baggage and all hidden valuables which those bloodsuckers had got hold of and hoarded and which belonged to the Turkish people and not to anyone else? To Konya? Why Konya, when there were shorter ways to Mesopotamia by way of Malatya and over the Euphrates?

When the saptiehs started to drive the people off the ox-carts with their whips and to hurl their baggage on the road, the Turkish and Kurdish *arabachis* laughed. But after a time they didn't laugh any more.'

'It was all done very humanely. And Allah was witness, that it was no fault of the saptiehs that the Armenians had so much baggage, more than they could carry. Most of it was left lying on the road after the saptiehs had begun to drive the people on with curses and insults, tickling them up a bit with their riding-whips. Since many of the Armenians, especially the very old ones, couldn't walk fast enough, the whips didn't just tickle them but beat them. But that was unavoidable, for how else could the order to continue marching be carried out? And later, when the very old and weak ones collapsed and had to be shot, because no one was allowed to stay behind, at any rate not alive, it was clear to the saptiehs that they really had dealt with them humanely.'

'It was a hot June day when I, the story-teller, flew up behind the first of all the columns of five thousand Armenians. I wasn't thirsty, for I had no body, but I heard the shouting of the victims; early in the afternoon, after a march of several hours, they were already beginning to call for water. The longer I flew behind that column, the more it struck me how the lines of the victims were thinning out.

More and more of the old and weak, the sick and crippled, the exhausted and depressed, had fallen out and had been shot by the saptiehs. What was it I said, that it was a hot June day? It surely was hot. And the dead lay far too long on the road. But Allah, in his wisdom and foresight, had made provision for that. He had arranged for the vultures in the air and the abandoned dogs on the ground to follow close behind the column, so they were on the spot ready to tear the clothes off the dead and gnaw the flesh off their bones before they began to decay. For it really was hot. It's like that in this part of the country. In the winter it's desperately cold in the summer it's hot. And behind the snarling, growling, starving dogs and the croaking birds, gulping down whole mouthfuls, came the rabble from the slums of Bakir and from the surrounding villages. They kept their distance, for they didn't want any trouble with the saptiehs. But they found the baggage on the road, and they found what was left of the dead women's clothes, especially headcloths and anything else that hadn't been eaten, such as boots and shoes. But the rabble didn't have it easy either, for they were nearly all on foot, and many of them found the going hard, and they had to defend themselves against the others in the gang when it was a matter of who got the best loot. They had to struggle with people with the same idea as themselves, and there were some wounded, even some dead, among them. Yes, really, that's how it was: the poorest of the Muslims had come out to claim from the Armenians what Allah had withheld from them for centuries in the state of the Sultan and his corrupt officials . . . but they came too late, for the saptiehs had already gone through the baggage and appropriated the hidden valuables. The mob was furious, and tore up the dead people's bitten and chewed clothes even more looking for the gold coins that the Armenians were said to have sewn in them. They even tore the heels off the boots, and often they found something and often they didn't.'

'The Armenians' houses were surrounded until the columns were clear of the town. Then the looting began. The authorities had announced that the houses and furniture of the unbelievers would be returned after the war, and for a time they acted as if they would take care of them. But in practice there were no inventories made:

and anything that wasn't grabbed by the mob was kept by the officials. Anything that looked valuable disappeared somewhere where the eyes of the Committee weren't looking.

The looters were confused. A lot of them said: "They've buried their gold," while others said: "No, they've taken it with them. We must follow them along the road. They've sewn it up in their clothes and hidden it in their shoes." But others said: "No. The Armenian is a smart chap. Surely he'll have swallowed his gold. We'll have to slit their bellies open."'

'No. Not all the Muslims had plundered the houses. The distinguished ones among them had already been on the spot when the drummers went through the streets, and they all of them knew whose hour had struck. They bought up all they could for as little as they could. Many Armenians handed a whole lot to the distinguished Muslims for nothing and asked them to look after it until they came back. Together with the distinguished Muslims there were also a few unbelievers, whom I had mistakenly counted as Muslims, so greedy were their eyes behind their feigned sympathy. Some of them were Greeks, and some were Jews. One Greek bought a piano for seven piastres, a ridiculous price. And a Jew, who was standing beside him and was jealous of his bargain, asked the former owner of the piano if he hadn't got another one, and said he would pay eight piastres for that; but he hadn't got another. The Greek tinkled on his piano, which annoyed the Jew, who could play better than the Greek because he was musical. There was a time, said the Jew to the Armenian, when Jews were treated like this, but thank God those times are over. And he told the Armenian about the pogroms under the Czar of Russia and also about the bloodbaths of the crusaders and about the Spanish Inquisition.'

For some weeks I, the story-teller, flew about Anatolia, then I went back to Bakir. I prised my shadow loose from the hangman's hooks – the ones under the Gate of Happiness – and comforted him and took him on my lap.

'I am the story-teller,' I said. 'Call me Meddah.' And I said: 'The story I'm telling you is not a fairy-tale. It's true history.' And then

I told my shadow what I'd seen.

'So there were piles of dead on the highway?' asked my shadow
'And those who could still walk lived on?'

'For two days,' I said, 'they went along the caravan road toward
Konya. There were fewer and fewer of them. Or, to put i
differently, the country road became more and more colourful, with
all the dead on the roadside in their bright clothes and yellow
brown, red, black and blue shoes. And the dead women'
headcloths and veils, often of the highest quality, are unforgettable
and of course the dead old men's hats, hats with no brims, and the
headwear given to the children to keep the sun off their heads. The
dead looked like milestones and signposts, and that is how they
appeared to the regiments of saptiehs and *chettes*, showing them
which way to go, where the deportation route went and which
particular road they had to take.

Four reserve regiments clattered behind the funeral procession on
their Anatolian horses. But most of them were already waiting in
the mountain gorges of the Taurus. For after marching for two
days, still on foot, along the caravan road, the escorting saptiehs
turned on to the shorter road through the mountains. On the
mountain passes, and in the valleys too, the special units of *chettes*
were waiting.'

'Yes. It's true. The *chettes* are famous for getting down to thing
right away without wasting any time. But they wanted to enjoy the
young women first . . . and what would be the sense in killing the
women and then mounting and penetrating something that couldn'
wriggle and scream any more? So they only killed the little children
and the old men. They tore the clothes off the young women and
threw them on the furrowed, sun-warmed earth, which in spite of
the sun and the wind and the lack of rain was not dry, but wet and
sticky from the fear of the women, who had soiled themselves. The
chettes didn't care about the piss and shit. They stuck their hand
in it and had great fun with it. And they showed the women their
penises, crowned with knobs of flesh and peeled and circumcised
so strong and threatening to behold. Often the *chettes* used their
bayonets to help, if the organ between their thighs didn't, or

couldn't, find the opening between the thighs of their victims because fear had caused that opening to close. And the saptiehs had a lot of fun too, took off their uniforms and, because they didn't want any trouble with the *chettes*, shared out what they had left over among themselves as brothers should.'

'You will hardly believe it if I tell you how rampant the saptiehs and *chettes* were. Even the oldest of them became young again. It was as if the screams of the woman, and their terror, made the blood surge through their veins. Yes. It was hot and wet, although the yellow sun was still not to be seen.'

'And where were the Kurdish tribes? Well, I don't know. The authorities had tipped them off long before, for they wanted to be able to blame them for the massacre. They turned up later, when the remainder of the five thousand got further into the Kurd area. Suddenly, there they were. They had a free hand, for the authorities had promised them rich booty, and the escort knew that. They came out of their mountain hideouts, on horse and on foot, howling and screaming. They fired off their rifles in the air, as if they wanted to frighten the escort as much as the victims. And they were frightened. None of them wanted a fight with the Kurds. The Kurds only appeared during the day, before the sun was imprisoned in its great black tent. They raped every woman that had survived. And they rode over the women like the waves of the sea over the sandbanks. Many of them carried women off, others left the women lying down and cut their throats, either because they were dead already or because they looked so old that they were ashamed to have done it with them.'

'The Kurds had stripped the victims of their clothes and shoes, but that didn't worry the escort, for they thought that, after all, it was summertime and the victims wouldn't get cold if they drove them on naked and barefoot. And they'd have to be driven on, for in Konya they had to be handed over so that the Konya saptiehs could take them on to Mesopotamia. And it was understood that some of them had actually got to arrive in Mesopotamia, for this was just a matter of resettlement. And what sort of resettlement would it be if none of the people being resettled arrived at the prescribed destination?'

'At some time,' said I, the story-teller, who also call myself Meddah, to the shadow on my lap, 'at some time, my little lamb, it occurred to the leader of the saptiehs that the naked women might have concealed some gold and valuables. But where could they hide anything, if they were naked?

'So first,' said I, the story-teller, 'the saptiehs looked in the victims' hair, especially in the thick knots of hair of the women. And since they didn't find much gold, they forced their victims' mouths open and tried to stick their fingers down their throats, because they believed that an Armenian's stomach was just the place to hide gold from the state. They also cut open the victims' stomachs and felt in their intestines. And they searched in their back-passages as well as in their vaginas, and the saptiehs and *chettes* stuck their hands in them. Often they actually found some gold.'

'The leader of the saptiehs, who held the rank of *choush*, said to one of the *chettes*: "Armenian mothers especially have the bad habit of swallowing good Turkish gold so that they can buy bread for their bastards some time, somewhere, if they can shit the gold out again without anybody seeing."

"But where is there any bread for them to buy, Choush Agah?" said the *chette*. "And where could they shit it out unobserved, if we examine the shit every time? And what's the point of buying bread for the bastards when all the bastards are dead?"

"Not all of them," said the *choush*. "There're still a few."'

'But the *choush* was still suspicious. "You don't know the Armenians," he said to the *chette*. "They're tricky. Not even their shit tells us the real hiding-place."

"That's true," said the *chette*. "They keep their secrets even when they're dead."

"That's true," said the *choush*. "And it's also true that the vultures and the dogs know more than we do."

"How do you mean, Choush Agah?" said the *chette*.

"I'll bet you," said the *choush*, "that the vultures and the dogs have not only eaten up the dead people's bellies, but everything that was in them . . . even the gold coins."

"Do you really believe that, Choush Agah?"

"Yes," said the *choush*.

"Then we shall have to shoot all the vultures and dogs and have a look."

"So we shall," said the *choush*.'

I talked with my shadow for a long time, and told him about the hundreds of thousands of people who were on the road, about the columns from Kayseri and Mush, Trebizond and Erzincan and other places. 'There's a whole nation on the road,' I said. 'They're simply being led astray by the saptiehs. Many of them don't have far to go, because as soon as they're clear of the city they're shot or cut down with axes or bayonets, but some others have to go further.'

'So they're coming from all directions?'

'From all directions,' I say, 'though I don't really know how many directions there are in the world.'

'And which way are they being taken?'

'No way,' I say. 'That's just it. The roads don't go anywhere, there's no firm destination, they're not going anywhere.'

'And yet there had to be some destination, for I was flying over them for a long time, and my eyes can see further than a golden eagle's. And so I saw that some survivors crossed the Euphrates. They were staggering along, whipped by the saptiehs, across flat desert country as smooth as the pate of the Mukhtar of Yedi Su. The land seemed to have swallowed up everything that God created and hidden it under the flat sand. There were some tents and some huts. The few that did arrive there were all crammed in together, and left without any food or drink.'

said: 'I heard the crying of the hungry and thirsty. And I heard the yellow sun laugh as it hung pitilessly over the land, in a cloudless blue sky. And I heard the screams. And I saw dead babies sucking at their mothers' breasts.'

'But dead children can't suck.'

'That's what it looked like,' I said. And I said: 'I saw mothers whose madness shone out of their eyes. And I saw many who ate their dead children to still their hunger, and drank their blood to quench their thirst.'

And while I was telling him all this, something fluttered between me and my shadow, and I thought: 'That is the last thought of Thovma Khatisian. Something has disturbed him.'

CHAPTER NINE

'I see a saptieh in Bakir,' said the last thought, '. . . a saptieh who looks different from the others. His eyes are different.'

'I see him too,' said I. 'He has an Armenian's eyes, and any Turk who looks him in the eyes could recognize him.'

'He's walking through the Armenian quarter,' said the last thought, 'past the abandoned houses and closed shops. His eyes are half-shut, but sometimes he opens them wide. He's trying not to attract attention, walking slowly as if he was just out for a stroll.'

'People who try not to attract attention generally do just that,' I said. 'There's something unnatural about this curious saptieh's movements. He mustn't try too hard to be inconspicuous. That just makes people look at him.'

'Who is that man?'

'We'll see in a moment; he's coming towards the Gate of Happiness. He'll soon be here.'

'The saptieh with Armenian eyes walks more and more slowly. He seems to be tired, and looks as if he wants to sit down and rest. But he doesn't stop anywhere, for it's Ramadan, and the coffee shops don't open until the cannon shot from the citadel suspends the fast. There is a *kahveji* sitting on a cushion in front of the door of his shop. And he calls to the saptieh: "Hey, Saptieh Agha. Allah has sent me some fresh green coffee-beans, and I've just roasted them. They're brown and fragrant, and they smile in my sack like the eyes of a bride under her veil. But it's Ramadan, Saptieh Agha. Come back when the sun is down and I'll make you some coffee that will cheer anyone up however tired they are." But the saptieh just smiles and says nothing.

'Meanwhile the muezzins have begun to call the faithful to the mosques. Today is 27 July, by the Franks' calendar. These are the last of the fast-days and, and as is always the way, more of the faithful crowd in to pray together on the last days of Ramadan than ever before. The calls of the muezzins are more insistent, even if they do repeat what everybody knows: *Allahu akbar.* God is great. I bear witness that there is no god but Allah. I bear witness that Mohammed is God's Prophet. Up to prayer! Up to salvation! *Allahu akbar. La ilah illa 'llah.* God is great. There is no god but Allah. And since these are fast-days, the days of Ramadan, I, the story-teller, hear that the muezzin is going on with his chanting. I hear him say: Feed, ye faithful, feed the orphans, the needy, the homeless and the lowly, for his sake, and say: "We feed you for the sake of Allah and we ask no word of thanks from you and nothing in return."'

'The saptieh with Armenian eyes has reached the Gate of Happiness. There's a crowd of people under the arch of the gate, not because the authorities have just hanged three people – that hadn't happened for quite a time - and the crowd wanted to enjoy the spectacle, but because the poor are coming in from their huts and their caves outside the city wall to make their evening prayers. The saptieh stops by the blind beggar, who sits there like a statue, one hand on his lap, the other open beneath his begging cloth. The saptieh stands before the blind man for a time without a word, until at last the blind man notices him and anxiously feels the saptieh's boots with his hands, and then his uniform trousers, as if he wants to find out who he is.'

'"It's me," says the saptieh. "Vartan Khatisian."
   "Vartan Khatisian?"
   "Yes," says the saptieh.
   "Vartan Efendi," says the blind man. "Thanks be to Allah. You're alive."'

'It's already getting dark. I, the story-teller, see the beggar give a sign to the saptieh, and I hear them whispering to each other, and I too whisper something in the ear of the last thought. "Look out," I say softly. "Your father must be careful, for under the Gate of

402

Happiness there are informers and cut-throats and talebearers, and in any case it's not advisable to hang about here long, especially when you have an Armenian's eyes." And we three, my shadow and I and the last thought of Thovma Khatisian, we see that strange saptieh turn his back on the beggar and let himself be carried off by the stream of the faithful.

"He's going into one of the mosques with them," I say, "because at this time he'll attract less attention there, for as you see, my little lamb, your father isn't the only one in uniform."

"I can see that," says the last thought. "My father isn't the only one. There are a lot of saptiehs and men in uniform among the faithful."

"I suppose your father has made some arrangement with the beggar," I say. "They'll certainly meet soon in the mosque or outside in the courtyard where the faithful wash themselves."

'We three watch your father, the bogus saptieh, in the forecourt of the Mosque of the Holy Mantle, and we see him perform the prescribed ablutions as if he'd always done it, and we presume that he learned it from Gög-Gög and the Turks in Yedi Su. He doesn't attract any attention. Nor does he later, at prayer in the mosque. Your father recites the evening prayer by heart, like the others, and he kneels like the others and calls on Allah, though I'm sure he's really thinking of Christ. And, like the others, he stares fixedly for a time at the back of the imam as he stands before the Kibla, giving sharp cries and calling on the name of Allah. The imam presses his thumbs behind the lobes of his ears and spreads his other fingers, and he sobs and calls his God and falls on his knees and puts his hands on his stomach, and later he lays them on his knees and twists his body, and during that time he keeps looking sideways as if at that moment he could see the holy Khidr or the Mahdi, who would tell him something of the secrets of paradise.

'After the service your father stands, rather lost, in the forecourt of the mosque. One or two pious Turks speak to him, thinking he's one that doesn't have a family and doesn't want to sleep in the barracks tonight, perhaps one of those saptiehs from other areas, of whom there are so many in the town. One of these Turks, a very old man, says: "My son, a man shouldn't be alone on Ramadan. My house is open to all believers." But your father shakes his head.

He says: "I know you will be offended if I refuse your invitation.
But I've already been asked somewhere else. And I mustn't offend
them."

'Then . . . suddenly your father sees the beggar.'

'Our eyes follow your father, who walks slowly over to the beggar
in the dusk. The blind man with his stick follows him as far as the
Gate of Happiness and then on, out of the city, to the huts and
caves where the poor live.'

'The beggar's dwelling consisted of one big room, with no windows.
In the *tonir*, which the Turks call the *tandir*, there was a good fire
burning. There were several women and children in the room,
members of the beggar's family, all of whom he maintained. Even
his grandson Ali was there.

"This man has returned from the dead," said the beggar. "He is
my guest."'

'With every mouthful the Turks take after the long day's fast, they
say *Bismillah*. It was no different with the beggar and his family.
And your father also said *Bismillah*, though he was really thinking
of Christ. Your father ate a lot, and rather too fast, for he had had
nothing in his stomach for a long time. He particularly enjoyed the
spicy titbits with which they started. The beggar kept on filling his
wooden plate. One of the women passed the *sofras* round, and your
father didn't hesitate to eat plenty. Later they sat down on the flat
earth round the *tandir*, the beggar had the oil lamps blown out and
they could only see one another's faces by the light from the *tandir*.
Even the blind man could see the faces, although he saw nothing,
but it seemed to your father as if the blind man saw more than all
the others.'

'"It was absolutely unexpected," said your father. "We were riding
in single file over the pass. Suddenly the Kurds opened fire."

"Did you know it was the Kurds?"

"No, I didn't know."

"I had sent the Kurds," said the blind man.

"I know," said your father. "I found out later."

"From the sheikh's son?"

"Yes," said your father.'

'"It all happened very quickly. Before the saptiehs could pick up their rifles, they were all shot dead. Yes, it really did happen quickly."'

'"The Kurds took me to the next village, a village where there was still an Armenian, a blacksmith whom the saptiehs had allowed to live because he was useful to them. The Kurds killed the saptiehs in the village too – there were only a few of them – and then they sent for the Armenian smith and told him to take off my chains."

"Chains?"

"Yes."

"Did the peasants see you?"

"No," said your father. "It was the middle of the night."

"And the Armenian? He must have seen you."

"The Armenian won't give me away," said your father.'

'"Later I wandered about the district. The Kurds gave me the uniform off a dead saptieh. And a pair of boots, and a cap. But they didn't give me the dead saptieh's papers."

"That was a mistake."

"Yes," said your father. "But it was bound to happen, because the sheikh's son hates anything to do with paper and printing. The sheikh's son had all the papers burnt."

"Even the papers of the village saptiehs?"

"Those too."

"That's a pity," said the blind man.

"Yes," said your father.

"What did the Kurds do with the bodies?"

"They undressed them and slung the naked bodies down in the gorge."

"Was it a deep gorge?"

"It was, very deep."

"And the bodies of the village saptiehs?"

"The Armenian had to bury those."

"The blacksmith?"

"Yes, that chap."'

'"How will you get on without papers?"
"I don't know yet."
"You'll have to get some new papers."
"Yes, I'll have to."'

'"There is an Armenian in Bakir who can forge papers," said the beggar. "He's called Kevork Hacobian, and he's an artist at his craft. And I know where he lives, in the Street of the Felt-makers just behind the *hamam*. But I can't be sure whether you'd find him for they've shot all the men and only a handful of craftsmen and a few of the Vali's favourites are left. And some are hiding."
"Perhaps he's still there," said your father. "Perhaps he's on the list of craftsmen and favourites."
"He was a printer," said the blind man. "And printers are often wanted. Perhaps he really is still there."'

'"Have you been to Yedi Su?"
"No," said your father. "If the authorities look for me anywhere that's where it will be. I expect they're waiting for me there."
"Nobody's looking for you," said the blind man.
"How do you know that?"
"I know it," said the blind man.'

'"You're on their list of dead men," said the blind man. "They're not looking for you any more."
"Is that in the newspapers?"
"The papers conceal anything they want to conceal. But the saptiehs in the *hukumet* and the prison are chatterboxes."
"Have you talked with them?"
"Yes, Vartan Efendi."
"And they told you that?"
"They told me a whole lot."'

'"I've really come to Bakir to get my wife out of the women's prison," said your father. "I don't know how I'm going to do it, but I thought something might occur to Mechmed Efendi."

"Something has already occurred to me," said the blind man. And as he said that he looked straight into your father's face, as if those lifeless eyes could really see the excitement in the other's face and the sparkling in the Armenian eyes of the bogus saptieh.

"I knew your wife was in the women's prison," said the blind man. "They're holding your wife as a hostage, the saptiehs said."

"Yes," said your father. "My wife and the unborn child in her womb."

"That's it," said Mechmed Efendi.

"Yes," said your father.'

'"But you've come back to Bakir for nothing," said the blind man, "for everybody thinks you're dead. Even the Mudir thinks so. And the Mudir can't put pressure on a dead man with a hostage, not even when it's the dead man's wife and she has his child in her womb."

"How do you mean?"

"The prisons were overcrowded," said the blind man, "so they sent most of them back home, including your wife, who was no more use to them as a hostage. That made things more practical for them, do you see, since the Armenians are being deported anyway. So why not send them all back to the villages and towns, where they can pick them up together, instead of having to feed them at the state's expense?"

"So my wife isn't still there?"

"They've released her," said the blind man. "I was with the saptiehs at the gate of the women's prison. And although I'm a blind old man, they still talk to me. Especially when Ramadan began and the saptiehs' consciences began to nudge them and they suddenly started giving alms to the beggars, for the sake of Allah's mercy, then they began to talk. And when I asked about your wife, they told me."

"Then she's back in Yedi Su," said your father.

And the blind man said: "Yes. She went back to Yedi Su. And if the village hasn't been evacuated, she'll be there still."'

'"You know the village," said your father. "It's a long way off, remote, and it was overlooked when Abdul Hamid's *hamidiyes* began with the massacre."

"I know," said the blind man. "And if it is the will of Allah, it will be overlooked again. Sooner or later you'll go back to Yedi Su as a free man, and you'll find your wife there and your son, who may have been born by then."

"That's a wonderful thought," said your father, and he sighed and shut his eyes. For one moment his face looked happy, and only I, the story-teller, knew that he didn't believe it.'

'They talked about so much during the evening, even about the Hayastan restaurant, which had been shut for months. Your father tried carefully to question the old man, to find out which of his family in Bakir were still alive and which were still in the city, but the blind man, who seemed to know everything else, couldn't help him with any information here. He just said: "If there are any of them still in the city, they won't let anyone see them. They certainly won't ever appear in public."'

'They all slept on the floor, close together. Your father had nightmares and kept waking up. Once he saw that the blind man was kneeling beside him.

"You're having bad dreams," said the blind man.

"I dreamed about the hanged men under the Gate of Happiness."

"There are three of them," said the blind man.

"Are they Armenians?"

"No. Two of them are Turks and one is a Kurdish *hamal*."

"What crime had they committed?"

"They had hidden Armenians."

"Is that forbidden?"

"Naturally it's forbidden. Don't you know that the munadis have announced in the name of the government that any Muslim who hides an Armenian will be treated like an Armenian?"

"No, I hadn't heard that," said your father.'

'"I dreamed about my brother too," said your father. "It wasn't until the last morning in prison before the saptiehs took me away that I learned he'd been hanged."

"Dikran, the shoemaker?"

"Yes, Dikran."' '

'And the blind man told him the story of the boots.

"I didn't know they were your brother's boots," he said. "I only knew that when I could feel them."

"Did you sell them?"

"No," said the blind man. "I opened the heels, but there was no gold in them. And even the kid leather of the boots was worn out, and not much good any more. Yet once they'd been the best pair of boots in Bakir."

"Yes," said your father.

"I kept the boots for you," said the blind man. "You can put them on tomorrow morning."

"Keep them," said your father.'

'Your father couldn't get to sleep again. He kept seeing the faces of the three hanged men in the dark, who weren't Armenians but two Turks and a Kurd. And later, in the silence of the night of the fast, he asked himself whether they were the only ones, or whether there were other Turks and Kurds who helped the Armenians. With that question he fell asleep.

Early in the morning – it was not yet light – he was woken by the drums of the *hodjas*, calling the faithful to breakfast. One of the *hodjas* beat on the door of the hut four times with his stick. And your father, still sleepy and confused, heard the blessing of the *hodja* responsible for his flock in this poor district. The *hodja* outside the door evidently knew the beggar. He called several times: "O Mechmed, O Mechmed! It has been a happy night. Get up, Mechmed. The time of the fast is near. Allah is great and Mohammed is his Prophet. Praise be to him who created the world."' '

CHAPTER TEN

'Your father had never in his life had such a big breakfast before dawn, for in Ramadan the Muslims ate a lavish breakfast so that their stomachs would still be full all day during the fast. So they ate a lot, and they ate quickly. Then, as soon as the sun rose and the cannon on the citadel gave the signal for the fast to begin again, the meal had to be broken off and they rinsed out their mouths.

'Before your father left, he told the blind man about the question he'd asked himself in the middle of the night, when he saw the faces of the hanged men in the darkness, three dead faces that had never had Armenian eyes.

"Many Muslims help the Armenians now," said the blind man. "Only nobody sees them."

"You can see them on the gallows."

"Yes, you can see them there," said the blind man.

"Will there be more?"

"A lot of people have been arrested. And a lot will be hanged."

"Are there any well-known Muslims among them?"

"A few. Just think: the Mudir of Bakir's chief clerk."

"The chief clerk?"

"Yes."

"Had he hidden an Armenian in his house?"

"No. He had just supplied someone with false papers."

"That was a dangerous thing to do."

"You may well say that, Vartan Efendi."

"Pity he's been arrested," said your father. "I could do with some papers just now."'

'On the road your father thought about the chief clerk, and remembered that he had sometimes looked at him strangely, that

410

time in the Mudir's office. When they hang him, he thought, you won't be in the town any more.

'Your father made cautious enquiries about the Armenian who might get him forged papers. But they'd taken him away long ago. He got some other addresses in the bazaar, addresses of forgers and go-betweens who knew such and such a person, but when he knocked at the doors there was obviously nobody there. So he finally decided on the only course left to him. He went to the American consulate.'

'The American consul! A short, ordinary-looking, elderly man. Even my shadow could see from the way he moved his hands, and most of all from the way he spoke, that he wasn't one of those Americans from the Turkish picture-book. Even the last thought, who danced into the office behind your father, through the ante-room and past the secretary, between the two of us, even he noticed that this was an unusual American. But then, wasn't Vartan Khatisian an unusual American?'

'He's a Greek, the American consul,' I said softly to the last thought, and I also said it to my shadow. 'A Greek, he is, a Greek from Smyrna who's emigrated at some time. He speaks many languages, even Turkish. And above all, he knows how to get on with Turkish officials.'

'And what about the Khatisian case?'

'That's not lying in his filing-cabinet, it's out there ready on his desk.'

'He knows about it, then?'

'Of course he knows about it. He's been trying in vain for months to get something done about the case. But, as I said, in vain.'

'And the American press?'

'They heard about that remarkable case. And there it was; for weeks there were reports about the Khatisian case, but then developments in the war kept everything else out.'

'They forgot about the Khatisian case?'

'They did. Headlines have no memories.'

'And the consul?' asked the last thought. 'Did he know my father?'

'He met him twice, both times at the Hayastan, where he was a
regular visitor and always had a reserved table. He was a friend of
the proprietor's, too.'

'Of my father's brother?'

'Yes, of Haygaz.'

'And so, as it happened, the consul wasn't at all surprised to see
the man who was thought to be dead standing in front of his desk,
and actually in the uniform of a Turkish saptieh.

"Did anyone recognize you when you came in?" he asked.

"No," said your father.

"You've been forgotten," said the consul. "You don't exist any
more."

"Yes," said your father.

"Even the world press has forgotten you. You've become as
unimportant as anyone else who isn't needed any more."

"That's quite right," said your father. "They're not looking for
me any more."'

'"We can smuggle you out of the country," said the consul. "It
won't be easy."

"And my family . . . my wife, and my child?"

"Not them," said the consul.

"My son hasn't been born yet," said your father.

"I understand," said the consul.

"I can't desert my wife and my son," said your father. "I must
do something for them, though I don't really know what I can do."

"Yes," said the consul.'

'"I could issue you with a new passport," said the consul, "but
that takes weeks, because I haven't got any passports just now.
I shall have to order them first. It all takes time. Can you wait
so long?"

"No," said your father.

"And you'll need a photo."

"A proper photo?"

"Of course, a proper photo."

"That's impossible," said your father. "And I can't wait as long

412

as that. And I must find my wife. And my son. We want to call him Thovma."

"Thovma?"

"Thovma."'

'"Where are they just now?"

"They've been in prison."

"I know," said the consul.

"Now they're back home."

"In that village, then . . . what's it called now?"

"Yedi Su."

"Yedi Su . . . the village with the seven waters?"

"Or seven wells," said your father.

The consul tried to smile. "If the village hasn't been evacuated yet," he said, "maybe you have a chance of seeing them still alive . . . your wife and your son."

"We want to call him Thovma," said your father.

"Yes, I know," said the consul.'

'"The village doesn't lie directly on the caravan road," said your father. "It's already been overlooked once, during the massacres under Abdul Hamid."

"And you think it might be overlooked again?"

"I don't know what I ought to think," said your father.

"Very well," said the consul. "You want to go back to your village. Listen carefully, now. I suppose you know what happened at Van?"

"A revolt?"

"It wasn't a revolt," said the consul. "The Armenians just refused to let their men be shot and their families abducted. They armed themselves and even managed to defend their quarter of the town successfully for quite a time. They were completely surrounded, of course. But then, in May, the Russians came. And the Armenian volunteer battalions with them. They were the first ones there."

"So the town was freed?"

"Yes," said the consul. "But then the Turks advanced and re-took Van. Most of the Armenians fled with the Russians, and the few who stayed behind were slaughtered."

"Van," said your father.

"Van," said the consul.

"And what about Van now?"

"The Russians have occupied it again. But that isn't what I wanted to say. The Russians are advancing now. There's going to be a large-scale offensive. If I've got it right, they'll roll over the whole of this area in the autumn."

"Does that mean the Russians will take Bakir?"

"Yes," said the consul.'

'And the consul said: "I've got a suggestion. Fetch your wife and your son before the saptiehs kill all the men in the village and before they abduct the women and children and old men. But you'll have to hurry. Bring your wife and your unborn son to this consulate. You can stay here yourself. No one can arrest you or apprehend you here. No one would dare to take you away from here. This consulate is under diplomatic protection, it's United States territory."

"And what shall we do here?"

"Wait till the Russians come."

"Till the Russians come?"

"Yes, that's it."

"And then?"

"Then we'll take you and your wife and your son to one of the liberated Black Sea ports, to Trebizond perhaps, which will have been evacuated by the Turks by then, or we'll take you further, to the old Russian ports. And you can take an American ship from there."

"Yes," said your father.

And the consul nodded and said: "Yes. But you must hurry. I'll get you a fast horse, a few blankets and some provisions. Will you hurry?"

"Yes," said your father.'

'However, they sat together for a little while, for the consul didn't want to go and fetch the horse until it was dark, and he had to get the blankets and provisions. And he also didn't want your father to go out on the streets before dark.

"Morgenthau has done everything possible to persuade Enver

414

Pasha," said the consul. "And Morgenthau is the voice of America here."

"I've heard of Morgenthau," said your father.

"And a German priest called Lepsius has talked with Enver on behalf of the Armenians."

"Lepsius?"

"Yes," said the consul. "That man Lepsius is a German saint. The German consul in Bakir told me he was the true voice of the Germans."

"What about the Kaiser's voice?"

"That's the Germans' other voice."'

'"Only the Germans can do anything to help you Armenians now," said the consul. "They're the Turks' most powerful allies. A single really serious threat from the Kaiser's side, addressed to the Committee, would be enough to stop the massacres. But the Kaiser says nothing. And the German press also says nothing."

"So the Germans aren't doing anything?"

"That's not absolutely true," said the consul. "There are people like Lepsius. And there are hundreds of reports to the ministry in Berlin from German consulates and imperial embassies . . . reports on the massacres. There are petitions in front of the Committee for Unity and Progress, and mild warnings in the name of the Kaiser and senior officers. In the Committee they just laugh at them. They know very well in Constantinople that the Germans won't take any drastic steps, that they're determined not to get involved in Turkey's domestic affairs."

"So there will be no real help from the Kaiser?"

"No help."'

'"The Germans are an extraordinary nation," said the consul. "Often it looks as if the conscience of their poets and thinkers has got lost behind the monocles of the generals and disappeared into the jackboots of the soldiers. And there it can be trampled down easily enough."

"So no help from them," said your father.

"No help," said the consul.'

* * *

'"The American government," said the consul, "has given the Turks to understand that continuation of the massacres will not be without consequences. On the matter of our country's neutrality, I mean. The Turks know that the massacres hit the headlines in the American papers and have even displaced the war communiqués. They know too that President Wilson is indignant and that our senior officers are pressing the president to undertake concrete measures to control the Turks. But, believe me, it's all had very little effect. The extermination of the Armenians seems to have absolute precedence with the Committee. Often you could believe it was more important to them than events on the front, American neutrality, even the course of the war."

"You just can't understand it," said your father.

"Nobody can understand it," said the consul.'

'Then the consul said: "The reports on the massacres are on my desk."'

'"In the last report," the consul said, "there was something about twenty-five thousand Armenians massacred in the Kemach gorge. That's on the Euphrates. Twenty-five thousand! Those are just figures, and we can't tell whether they're correct. They say the massacres were mostly carried out by Kurds. But saptiehs and *chettes* also had a hand in them. Also, the report says, cavalry units of the Turkish regular army. It says in my report that they simply chucked little children into the Euphrates. And the women jumped after them. Many of the women actually threw their own children in because they were afraid the Kurds would rip them open first. They say the Euphrates is so choked with dead bodies that Turkish cavalry regiments on the way to the southern front can't ride across the river any more because the horses shy and vomit shoots out of the soldiers' mouths. It says in my report that the Euphrates and the neighbouring rivers are as red as the flow of blood in a slaughterhouse in a big town. Have you ever seen a slaughterhouse?"

"Not such a big one," said your father. "In our village everyone slaughtered their own beasts. Generally behind the house."'

*　　*　　*

416

'So that was how it was,' said I, the story-teller. 'The consul provided a fast horse, also the blankets, the provisions and full wine-skins, quinine pills and all the other things needed on a journey. So, when darkness fell, your father was able to leave the town well equipped. He'd actually got everything a saptieh would need. All he hadn't got was a rifle and valid papers.'

'Your father knew it could attract attention if he were seen riding into the mountains without a rifle. And the fact that he was alone would be sure to make people notice him, for saptiehs didn't often ride alone, and even the saptieh at Yedi Su never dared leave the village unless the saptiehs from the neighbouring villages were there too. But your father was cautious. The consul had given him some rags and an old flour sack, with a big knife to cut the sack up. So your father cut up the sack and bound up the horse's hooves. He rode all through the night. By day he slept, out of sight in the ravines. Your father was behaving like the old *fedayin*, the legendary freedom-fighters whom the Kurds feared even more than they feared the Dashnaks. Around the turn of the century there were many reports of the *fedayin*, who came secretly across the Persian border to avenge themselves on the Kurdish robbers and would always appear when the Kurds had raided a village and shot the men and carried off the women. The *fedayin* too only rode at night and slept in their hideouts by day, so that they often disappeared into the mountains unobserved.

'Your father didn't get on as fast as he'd planned. In those confusing heights, the mountain paths wound their way between bare rocks through the Kurdish area. Often the horse stumbled, and snorted with fear on the edge of the pitch black slopes. Your father held the reins firmly in his hands and talked to the animal softly, soothingly and gently. His journey took two days and two nights. The consul had given your father some cigarettes, but your father didn't dare to smoke for fear that the Kurds would see. By day he slept, restlessly, mostly just dozing. And he rode all through the night.'

At the end of the second night he was no longer so far from the village. Being impatient, and afraid too that something could have happened to his family, he drove his horse hard, hoping to get to the village before it was light. But the day was quicker than the stumbling steps of the horse on the winding, stony paths. It was already dawning the other side of the village, the birds were waking up all round and giving their first calls, and the sun, unleashed, stretched its fiery red head sleepily over the horizon. Your father took no notice of it. And when the sun, round and glowing, rose over the village of the seven wells, he rode on into the new day. He forgot all his caution, for it was as if his pregnant wife were calling him. Even his unborn son seemed to be calling him. He rode on, full of fear and anxiety, and, dazzled by the glaring sun, he didn't see the plumes of smoke behind the last hills before Yedi Su, nor all the saptiehs and *chettes* waiting for him at the entrance to the village.'

'The *chettes* knew that no saptieh would ever ride through the mountains without a rifle. And this one, approaching them on his tired, sweating horse, didn't have one. The saptiehs, standing with the *chettes* at the entrance to the village, also noticed it, though they didn't usually worry about such things. But the *chettes* recognized your father mainly by his eyes, for Armenian eyes tell quite different tales from the eyes of Turks. The *chettes* were specialists, and they recognized the victims they had been sent to deal with.'

'All that followed now happened in a few minutes, beneath the silent sky, cloudless on this morning. The *chettes* seized your father and tore his trousers off him. And they laughed when they saw that he was uncircumcised. They grabbed his penis and one of them took a knife to cut it off. But he never got round to it, for one of the saptiehs standing nearby had already aimed his rifle. And he shot your father through the head. And the others shot him, and the *chettes* went for him with knives.'

CHAPTER ELEVEN

When the Kurd woman Bulbul, very old now but still full of energy, rode into the village late in the afternoon on her shabby old donkey, what she saw was so appalling that she vomited all the spiced and fragrant Armenian tea and *lavash* bread spread with mulberry syrup that people in that part of the world call a good breakfast. It just shot out of her old stomach all over the neck of the shabby old donkey. And she pissed where she was sitting on the donkey's back, from sheer shock and horror. For a time she searched for friends and acquaintances among the dismembered corpses, some of which had no heads, but then she gave it up and went to the hut on the edge of the village where the only Turkish family lived, who – so she thought – would surely not have been killed. Nor had they; but the Turks were sitting behind locked doors and windows, and hard as she knocked, no one opened to her. Then she spotted the village policeman, Yuksel Efendi, who had served in Yedi Su ever since 1902, ever since the pockmarked saptieh Shekir Efendi retired. The saptieh Yuksel Efendi had evidently been hiding somewhere, but now that the coast was clear he reappeared, and suddenly he was beside her.

"Hey, Yuksel Efendi," said Bulbul. "When did all this happen?"

"Yesterday afternoon," said the saptieh.

"And why have they burnt down the Armenian church?"

"Because they had locked the women and children in it," said the saptieh.

"And you were there?"

"I was there, Bulbul. But I didn't take part in it. What was I to do? Those chaps would have killed me if I'd said anything. After a bit I went and hid."

"And who did all this?"

"Those foreign saptiehs did it. And the *chettes*." The saptieh Yuksel Efendi pointed to the burnt-out church and then to th mountain track on the way into the village. "There's another mar up there. It's Vartan Khatisian. He got here very early thi morning. They killed him."

"Vartan Khatisian?"

"Yes."

"And he's lying up there?"

"Yes. Up there."'

'Vartan Khatisian was naked. And he was bleeding from countles wounds. But he was not dead. When she saw that he wasn't dead she suddenly got very active.'

'Do you know, my little lamb,' I, the story-teller, say to the las thought, 'no one knows why the good God sometimes holds up man's death . . . as it were puts off death to a later moment.'

'Don't you know that, Meddah?'

'No.'

'Couldn't God put off death for ever?'

'He can't do that. Death is more cunning than God and alway comes back by roundabout ways.'

'So it's just delayed?'

'Yes.'

'So why didn't the good God want my father to die up there o the mountain path?'

'I don't know, my little lamb. Perhaps he still had somethin more in store for your father. That's possible.'

'Yes, you're right. It would be so.'

'Yes,' say I, the story-teller. 'That must surely be it. How els could it be? God certainly intended something more for him. But w mustn't bother our heads with that. And we ought not to as whether it was a miracle or just chance. The fact is, your fathe was alive . . . in spite of everything. And it is also a fact that Bulbı was so active, and so was the saptieh, for help was needed quickly

'The foreign saptiehs and the *chettes* had gone. When Bulbul ge down to the village with the saptieh Yuksel Efendi and the badl

420

wounded man, the shocked Turks had just opened their house again. They had got out their spades and were burying the dead. The old patriarch Suleyman, whom the Armenians used to call Tashak on account of his rupture or his big scrotum, stood outside his door and gave instructions. When the old man saw the shabby old donkey with the severely wounded man, and the wizened Bulbul leading the donkey by a rope, and the saptieh Yuksel Efendi holding the motionless body on the donkey's back, he seemed to forget the bodies in the village streets and seized his stick and hobbled towards them.

"It's Vartan Khatisian," Bulbul told him. And the saptieh also said: "It is, really. Vartan Khatisian!"'

'They took your father into the Turkish family's house.

"He'll die," said the patriarch's wife.

"He won't die," said Bulbul.

"He needs a doctor urgently."

"What he needs most of all is strength," said Bulbul. "And he also needs the help of that curious saint he believes in . . . the one who died on the Cross because he had known too much and wouldn't keep silent . . . the one the priest Kapriel Hamadian once said was the incarnate son of Allah."

"So what does he need?" asked the patriarch's wife.

"A good digestion," said Bulbul, " a couple of good belches and a loud fart, to let me know he's still alive. All the other things he needs I'll get for him."

"What do you want to do, Bulbul?"

"All that's necessary," said Bulbul. "This isn't the first time I've taken bullets out of a man's flesh and out of his bones. And knife wounds I can deal with too. Only I must go and get my herbs. They're up in my hut."'

You see how dark it is in old Tashak's hut,' I, the story-teller, say to the last thought, 'for they've never put any windows in. And it's full of noise and full of people. Yet there are only the wives and children of their youngest sons still living with them. All the others moved out long ago. Some of the men are at the war, including Gög-Gög, your father's boyhood friend, Gög-Gög as they named him

421

after the way he called the chickens to be fed.

They nursed your father back to health. By the time he firs
opened his eyes the dead in the streets had long been buried, the
pillars of smoke had died down, the glowing ashes had been put out

"He's got his eyes open," said the saptieh Yuksel Efendi, who
came to see your father several times a day. "Hey, Bulbul. He'
actually got them open. Allah is my witness." But Bulbul, bending
over your father, didn't answer him.

"The air is clean, efendi," said the saptieh now to your father
"It's really clean, for those foreign saptiehs and *chettes* were dirtie
than the dirtiest eaters of pork."

And the saptieh swallowed and belched and let out a fart, as i
he himself had eaten something unclean.

"They only burnt the church down," he said to your father then
"because they thought the women and children would burn bette
in a church than on the bonfires out in the fields. And in the field
it might rain, and then they wouldn't burn so well."

"What women and children?" said your father.

"Well, just the women and children," said the saptieh Yukse
Efendi. "They'd locked them in the church."

"What church?" asked your father.

"Your church," said the saptieh. "Don't you know the churcl
any more?" The saptieh shook his head in surprise.

"Not all the women and children were burnt," he then said
"They laid the fire during the night. So a few women and childre
escaped through the window unseen, although the church hasn't go
any windows."

"How was that, efendi?"

"Well, the church had a sort of ventilator shaft. I suppose th
smaller children and women may have been able to crawl throug
it."

"And have they run away?"

"Yes. The nights are dark, even the mountains are dark at night
although the fires were burning brightly. So they escaped into th
mountains."

Your father didn't ask about his family, not even about his wif
and his unborn son, for he couldn't remember anything. Th
saptieh talked to him for a little while, and spoke of the miracle

of Allah, who made it possible that even pregnant women and their unborn children could crawl through a narrow ventilator shaft unhindered by their big, swollen bellies, if that was the will of Allah. And Bulbul said the same. Then your father went to sleep and heard no more and said no more.

"He's lost his memory," said Bulbul. "He doesn't know anything any more. He doesn't remember anything."

"But he's a poet," said Yuksel Efendi, the saptieh. "Didn't his priest Kapriel Hamadian once tell us that poets are our memory?"

"Yes, that's what the priest said."

"So he can't have lost his memory?"

"I don't know," said Bulbul.

"Well . . . they've beaten him about the head pretty well," said the saptieh. "And those bullets you extracted, they weren't made of cowshit."

"They were not made of cowshit," said Bulbul.'

'Now and then one of the saptiehs from the seven villages came over. They hadn't taken any part in the massacres, for they had served in the seven villages in the Armenian area for years and were pretty friendly with the Armenians. Since there were now no Armenians in the seven villages, they were bored. One of them said to Bulbul: "The *mohajirs* will be coming soon to move into the Armenians' houses. Probably they'll be emigrants from the eastern border this time, who have run away with our troops. In the past the *mohajirs* came from Macedonia and other countries I don't know. The government supports them because they're Muslims like us." Then the saptieh went on: "My village is as dead as the Armenians who used to live there. The *djinn* talk to me, even by day. But you don't see the *djinn*. I'm the only person left in the village, and I'm bored."

"I can understand that," said Bulbul.

"If the *mohajirs* come here, it won't be so boring any more."

"No," said Bulbul.

"It's a bad thing to be all by yourself," said the saptieh.

"It is a bad thing," said Bulbul. And she said: "What do you do all day, the only person in a dead village?"

"I wait for the end of my boredom," said the saptieh.

"Do you think the *mohajirs* will be able to play cards and *tavla*, like the Armenians you used to play with so often in the coffee-house?"

"I don't know," said the saptieh. "And I don't know either whether they'll give me the usual *baksheesh* that the Armenians used to give me."

"I don't know that either," said Bulbul.

"We got on well with the Armenians," said the saptieh.

"They're people who know what *baksheesh* is, and they know what's right."'

'And when after a time one of those saptiehs came to the village again, one of the ones who had been friendly with the Armenians, he told Bulbul: "They say the *mohajirs* are coming this week. They're coming with all their bags and baggage. And with their wives and children and parents and grandparents and their parents and grandparents and goodness only knows who else. And there're a lot of foreign saptiehs riding with them, escorting them and showing them all the Armenians' land and houses. If those foreign saptiehs see that wounded man there and find out that he's an Armenian, they'll finish him off. And they'll kill you too, and the Turks who are looking after him and hiding him. That's forbidden, you know."

"What had we better do?" asked Bulbul.

"You'd better get rid of him," said the saptieh.

"In my hut would be best," said Bulbul, who had known the saptieh before. "What would you think about that? Those lazy dogs won't ride that far into the mountains."

"They surely won't ride that far," said the saptieh.'

'And so Bulbul, with the aid of old Tashak, tied your father to the back of the shabby old donkey. And Tashak's wife gave Bulbul another sack of provisions and some blankets for your father. It was a rocky path up to Bulbul's hut, a dangerous, narrow path, because it led over that damned gorge that you'll never get out of once you fall into it. But that didn't worry Bulbul, nor her shabby old donkey; they knew the path. This donkey looked exactly the same as the other donkey that Bulbul owned when your father came into

424

the world. And he was just as clever as the old one, which shows that it's no insult to call a man an ass.'

'As they went up, broken sunlight played over the gorge, dancing before them like will-o'-the-wisps with all their lovely, tempting colours. The clouds were broken up over the rocks of the gorge, and the *djinn* whistled furiously in the wind. The donkey didn't hurry. And Bulbul walked behind. She waddled as she always did, with her crooked legs and crooked back, a long stick in her old hand. Often, when she stumbled, she caught hold of the donkey's tail with her other hand. Bulbul cursed softly all the way, and because the Committee in Constantinople couldn't hear her, she consigned them all to hell, Enver and Talaat and Jemal, the whole of the triumvirate. And the new Sultan too, who was no more than a puppet in the hands of the Committee. She cursed the foreign saptiehs and the special units of *chettes* and even the rapacious Kurds, who hadn't in fact taken part in the slaughter at Yedi Su, though they had in the neighbouring villages. She cursed the German Kaiser and his assistants. And she cursed all the drummers and town-criers who proclaimed in Allah's name things that could not be. At the cave which had always been called the Kurds' cave, quite near her hut, the donkey stopped, as it always did. From there on the mountain path climbed more steeply towards the clouds and the sky.

"Somewhere over there is Mount Ararat," she told your father, and waved her wrinkled hands in an indefinite direction. "They say an eagle's eyes can see it from here." She grinned to herself a little while, then she gave the donkey a hefty kick and pinched its tail. When the donkey started to go on, puffing, she said: "It's not really much further to the hut, my son, you've often been there before, when you were little. Do you remember, you rode on my lap and played with my teats?"

But your father could give no answer.'

'When the shabby old donkey finally stood puffing before the entrance to the hut, Bulbul saw that your father was unconscious. His head dangled lifelessly on the donkey's sweating flanks, his eyes were closed, his mouth open. That was to be expected, said Bulbul

to the donkey. It doesn't matter. I'll wake him up again later. She
spat, and wiped her mouth, and stroked the donkey she'd just
kicked and whose tail she'd pinched. It's just a pity, she said to the
donkey, that he can't see the hut, because that might have helped
to bring his memory back all at once.

She pulled the unconscious man off the donkey, and cursed
because his body landed heavily on the ground, and she hauled him
over the threshold still cursing. Then she made a soft bed for the
sick man, and despite the summer heat she covered him with thick
lambskin and with the blankets Tashak had given her, because she
believed that he wouldn't get the shivers if he was well and truly
covered up.'

'When your father woke next morning he heard the sound of voices,
and when he opened his eyes and looked round him he got a bad
shock. Sitting round the *tonir* and chatting with Bulbul were three
Turkish soldiers. Their uniforms were as muddy as if they had just
climbed out of the grave. But Bulbul came over to his bed and spoke
to him reassuringly.

"You needn't be afraid of them," she said. "They're Armenians.
They were soldiers in the Turkish army. They were discharged in
the spring."

"How is it they're still alive?" whispered your father, shocked.

"Because the Turks are such bad shots," said Bulbul. "Especially
when they're trying to shoot down too many at a time. Those three
crawled out of the mass grave and made their way over here so that
I could put them straight."

Bulbul laughed and lit her *chibouk*. "They live up in the
mountains," she said, "but they often come over this way."'

'The men took no notice of him. They drank schnapps out of their
water-skins, grunting with every sip, talked rather quietly as if they
had something important to discuss, passed the *narghile* round, then
got up and left the hut, leaving nothing behind them but their smell
and a room full of tobacco smoke.

When the men had gone Bulbul had thrown fresh *tezek* on the
fire. Now she stood in front of the open hearth and busied herself
there cooking pumpkin seeds in a sooty, dented frying-pan. In her

426

baggy trousers, her grey sackcloth wrap and her loose, coloured cummerbund, she looked like one of the scarecrows at Yedi Su, which the superstitious peasants used to say would come to life in bad times. She was rather bent, leaning over the frying-pan, sniffing. Her face was a little flushed from the reflection of the flames; it had a sunken look under the black headcloth, as furrowed as Armenian soil in the summer when there's no rain.

Your father lay still on the floor, a few paces away from the old woman. His eyes had got accustomed to the half-darkness and the tobacco smoke, and it hadn't been long before he could distinguish individual objects from one another in the hut; dirty straw mats on the floor, a pair of big round cushions serving as a divan, a store cupboard with no door with shelves of poplar wood, with all sorts of odds and ends piled up on them, even tobacco-leaves and foodstuffs. Brass pots and clay jugs, basketwork bags, tapestries and donkey's harness were all hanging on the wall. He also noticed the little oil lamp on the floor by the *tonir*, next to the still warm *nargile*, whose long tube stretched out towards the fire in the *tonir* like a snake.

Now and then his eyes strayed to the open doorway, beyond which the outlines of the mountains stood out, hazy in the misty clouds . . . dark grey outlines. Outside, in front of the hut, the hens ran up and down in the thin grass. A big speckled cock sat silently on the wheel of an overturned handcart. He also spotted two black goats grazing peacefully by the entrance to the hut, like the shabby old donkey, which Bulbul had not tied up.

Bulbul had told the men just now: "I used to know a cock called Abdul Hamid. It belonged to the Khatisian family down in the village. But mine has a different name. It's called Enver Pasha."

The men had laughed. One of them asked: "Don't you want to chop his head off, then?"

"Yes, I do," said Bulbul. "Today, in fact."

"But why?"

"Because he's too old, he's no good any more."

"What's wrong with the cock, then?"

"He can't crow properly, and the chicks hatch too soon."

"Too soon?"

"Yes, too soon."

427

The men laughed, but they didn't say any more.'

'There was an old gnawed bone on the spit over the open hearth, though where it came from nobody knew. Bulbul pulled it off the spit and threw it out into the yard. Then she took two flat round loaves of bread out of the store cupboard, dipped them in sesame oil and spread them with salt and green pickles, and gave them to your father.

"I'll kill Enver Pasha later," she said. "If those men come back, they'll be hungry." She took the frying-pan with the roasted pumpkin seeds and put it down on the floor by your father's bed. Then she squatted down by the pan and grinned at your father.

"Why did you really come back from America?" she asked. "How can anyone be so foolish? Over there you'd have been safe." She giggled. "And that trial! And the time you were in prison in Bakir! You wouldn't have had to go through any of that." But then she saw that your father couldn't remember anything and didn't even know he'd been in America. And he didn't know anything about a trial and an interrogation and a prison in Bakir.'

'Towards evening it began to rain. The animals came into the hut for shelter, for there was no cover for them outside. First the shabby old donkey came stamping in through the doorway, sniffing like a great mouse. The two black goats followed him. One after another the hens also came tripping over the threshold of the open doorway. Last of all was the speckled cock.

Bulbul stirred the fires, looking furtively at the cock Enver Pasha, which she wanted to slaughter because he was old. The cock had flown up to the top of the store cupboard and was watching Bulbul with its head twitching, as if it knew what she intended.

Your father took a couple of pumpkin seeds out of the frying-pan and began to crack them open and throw the shells in a wide arc, as people in this area have always done. He noticed that Bulbul had taken away the fire-guard and was standing by the open fire with her arms folded. As Bulbul didn't move, the cock seemed to calm down. His attention was now transferred to a particular hen whiter and fatter than the others. The hen was strutting round the dresser looking for seeds. The cock raised its head, then stretched it out, lying in wait, and suddenly . . . with a single fluttering movement . . . it jumped on to the hen.

Your father laughed, and he thought: "That's a good cock. Why does she want to kill it?" He saw the big white hen spread its wings invitingly, crouch down close to the ground and cackle, while the cock made scratching movements as if it wanted to tear the hen to pieces. At that moment Bulbul struck. She seized the cock by the wings and lifted it up. The cock gave one sharp cry. Bulbul seized the chopper, which was lying on the floor, and threw the cock on to the dresser in such a way that its neck lay on the hard wooden surface. Then she raised the chopper and gave the cock a powerful blow behind the head.

Your father stopped chewing. The cock's head had fallen on the floor and rolled near his bed. Its beak was wide open, as if it wanted to crow. Your father pushed the head away in disgust and looked up at Bulbul again. He saw the headless cock hopping madly round the dresser, flapping its wings. It was spraying a lot of blood, and had even stained Bulbul. At the sharpest corner of the dresser it slipped and fell down right on top of the big hen, which, flattened and hurt by the impact, sat down by the dresser, its beak in the dust. The hen's white wings began to turn red. Cock and hen fluttered. They looked as if they were making love for the last time.'

'Bulbul had hung the cock Enver Pasha on the long washing-line to drain. She had put a round washing bowl under the cock, and the dripping blood made a noise like rain on the hut roof.

"That's how they cut the heads off the Armenian men in Yedi Su," said Bulbul to your father. "Just like that."

"I thought they were shot."

"Not all of them," said Bulbul. "The saptieh in the village, who didn't join in but was on the spot, he told me about it."

"And what did you see?"

"Not much," said Bulbul. "When I went into the village on the next morning I saw the headless bodies in the streets. And I saw some heads that had rolled away, too, and most of them were unrecognizable."

"Have they all been buried?"

"Yes, all of them."

"And the heads too?"

"And the heads."

"And is it true about the women and children?"

"Yes, that's true. They were burnt in the church. They shut them in. Not all of them. A few were able to get away."'

'When the rain stopped, Bulbul chased the livestock out of the hut with curses and kicks. The three Armenian soldiers came back late, long after Bulbul had plucked the cock, gutted it and hung it over the fire. The men were hungry and looked at the sizzling cock greedily.'

430

CHAPTER TWELVE

Your father was getting better. Weeks and weeks passed. Bulbul cared for him and fed him. As long as it was summer you could hardly feel the wind that blew so mildly out of the mountains, fanned the roof of the hut, sometimes slightly shook the wooden sheds, rotten and creaking with age, and could hardly find its way over the threshold into the big, soot-blackened room. But as autumn approached the wind grew stronger. Chubby-cheeked *djinn* blew cool air over the gorges. The wind didn't whisper now, but whistled round the hut, and the *djinn* that rode on the wind told stories of foliage that was fading and leaves that were changing colour. When it was winter outdoors, your father could already walk without a stick.'

Because your father had forgotten everything that had happened before . . . before the shot in his head and all the blows, because he didn't even remember his own name – because he was like a child, who asks questions and is answered or not answered, therefore old Bulbul talked more and more about the past, in her own special way. She told him all about the Khatisians, about the family, about the villagers, described each individual, told him the names of his parents and his grandparents and all the others who were related to them. Most of all she emphasized his own name to him day after day, until she was sure he had understood what he was called and would remember that that was his name. Bulbul took enormous trouble, although she was often irritated by his great lack of understanding and inability to remember. During the autumn weeks she had visits more often, Armenians she had rescued, soldiers and others, even women and children. They all seemed to have crept out of the deadly gorge. They lived in the

mountains and came surreptitiously to the hut when they were i
or when they needed something. Or else they just came to tell Bulbu
they were still alive. And they left just as surreptitiously as they ha
come.

"They're all waiting for the Russians," said Bulbul to your father
"They're advancing, they'll be here sooner or later."'

'Once she had a visit from an Armenian priest. He was the only on
from the seven villages who had survived. When he saw your fathe
and learned that he had forgotten everything, he told Bulbul th
story of Sodom and Gomorrah and Lot's wife who was turned int
a pillar of salt.

"Why did the good God turn her into a pillar of salt, of a
things?" old Bulbul wanted to know.

"Because he was sorry for her," said the priest. "For she had see
dreadful things, and the good God knew that no human being wh
had seen such things could ever go on living with the memory o
them."

But Bulbul didn't take the priest's word for that. Those Christian
talk a lot, she thought. They exaggerate and lie, like that story o
the Holy Virgin, whose slit was never opened, never penetrated, an
who still bore a child. Those Christians are story-tellers. And thi
Vartan is a Christian, but he certainly isn't a pillar of salt. It's hi
head injury. That's all.

"What do you think?" she asked the priest. "Is it possible tha
Vartan Khatisian has sealed up his memory somewhere, perhap
in the holes those damned saptiehs and *chettes* made in his skull
Could he be deliberately holding it back to annoy me?"

"If anyone at all has hidden his memory behind those holes," sai
the priest, "then it is God's will."

"Well, yes," said Bulbul, "that may be so." And she grinned
little, thoughtfully, before she said to the priest: "We have the sam
God, priest. Perhaps we should both pray together for this man wh
can't remember?"'

'And then it happened: in the winter the Russians advanced. Th
great offensive had begun some time before and had only been hel
up by the rainy weather and the muddy roads. In 1916 the Czar'

troops occupied a large area of Anatolian territory. Trebizond had fallen, and Erzurum, and Bakir. One morning Bulbul rode down to the village. And when she came back on her donkey, she told your father: "The Russians are there."'

'There were different people living in Yedi Su now. Many of them really were *mohajirs*, Muslim emigrants who had been promised the Armenian houses by Enver Pasha's government, but Kurds and Turks had also moved in, landless peasants and riff-raff from the bigger towns. The Russians couldn't talk to the people, but they drank vodka with them and, when they'd had a few drinks, sang strange, sad songs that said more than comprehensible words could. The wives of the new settlers were raped as soon as the foreign soldiers marched in; people said they were no different from the *chettes* and saptiehs and the Kurdish brigands who had taken the Armenian women without asking permission. Yet that wasn't entirely true, for the foreign soldiers didn't carry the women off and hadn't killed any of them. And they were good to the children, and never touched them. The wives of the new settlers reported that the Czar's soldiers had big, pale mushrooms between their thighs which bored through every kind of moss whether or not the mouth called on Allah. Many women said they weren't mushrooms at all, but stiff keys of bone and skin that would open every secret lock, while others said they were ugly worms that had found their way into the women's barns. Those women's husbands were furious and swore vengeance.'

'With the Russians, the Armenian volunteer battalions had marched into the land. They wore Russian uniforms. Many of the Armenian volunteers had lost their whole families during the massacres. And so many of them sought revenge and, in their turn, killed Turks wherever they found any. But most of them didn't do that, and told their people they should never repay like with like.'

CHAPTER THIRTEEN

'In the spring the Turk, Tashak, harnessed his mule to his old *araba*, which had stood in his shed for years. And he told Bulbul and Vartan: "It's a strong mule, and I've sprinkled flour on the axles of the *araba*. You can go off now and look for Vartan's wife."

"And his son," said Bulbul, "who must surely have been born by now."

"Wasn't he going to be called Thovma?"

"Thovma," said Bulbul.'

'"My wife was certainly not burnt in the church," said Vartan. "They say some women escaped from the fire. They went up into the mountains. Bulbul told me about it."

"Yes," said Tashak. "That's what they say."

"If they weren't burnt in the church with the others," said Bulbul, "then they could still be alive."

"And his son could still be alive too," said Tashak.

"But she was pregnant," said Bulbul. "She was in her eighth month, even her ninth. I saw her not so long before. She had a fat, swollen belly, too fat to let her crawl through that narrow ventilation shaft."

"If it is Allah's will," said Tashak, "a camel can pass through the eye of a needle."

"That's true," said Bulbul.

"She was big and strong," said Vartan. "Bulbul has described her to me, for I'd forgotten it all. And if she was big and strong, then she could surely have got through it. And I'll bet you she was among the first to get through the ventilator in time."

"That's possible," said Bulbul.

"We'll find her," said Vartan. "And we'll find my son. And I shall recognize them both."

"Yes," said Bulbul.'

'And so they set off, the old woman and the younger man with no memory, who had lost every important image and recollection.

"We'll find them," said Bulbul. "I believe it now too. We'll go through every town and village. And we'll go along the deportation route. And we'll ask the peasants."

"Yes," said Vartan.

"No one forgets your wife once they've seen her," said Bulbul. "She was very big. And she had no face, only eyes."

"Yes," said Vartan. "That's how you've always described her."

"The peasants are sure to remember her. I'll say to them: you must have seen her. She was very big. Her face was burnt. Actually she didn't have a face. But she had big Armenian eyes, the biggest and most beautiful you've ever seen."'

'First they went to Bakir to see if they could find any relatives, for if Anahit had survived she might well have made for Bakir and hidden with her relatives there. And if that hadn't been possible, someone there would surely have learnt something about her escape. Someone must know about it. Bulbul knew the Hayastan, and she also knew Vartan's eldest brother Haygaz.'

'In Bakir they discovered that, just before the Russians marched in, the *chettes* and saptiehs had liquidated all the Armenians still in the city, even the craftsmen who had been needed until then, and all the Vali's favourites. It was on the last day before the surrender of the city. The Russians were already at the gates of the city; not only could people hear the Russian artillery – they had heard the machine-guns for several days – but they had even heard the Russians farting and yelling when the wind was in the right quarter. Actually the Russians were nearly there when the last Armenians were shot. But they hadn't really got there. And during that time the regular Turkish army was withdrawn and only a rearguard was left in the city, the *chettes* and saptiehs who were under command of the Mudir, though of course he took his orders from the Vali and the Mutessarif and the Kaimakam. When the last Armenians had been killed on the ramparts, the officials had packed their trunks, and their well-sprung *yaylis* and *arabas*, complete with bullet-proof sandbags, were waiting outside the *hukumet*.'

'During the shooting by the eastern gate of the city, so people in the streets of Bakir said, armed Armenians had suddenly appeared. They came from the mountains and wore Turkish uniform. No one knew who they were or where they had got their weapons. There weren't many of them, seven or eight perhaps. They had tried to stop the executions, and they had shot some of the *chettes* and saptiehs. But, as I said, there were only a few of them, and in the end the more numerous *chettes* and saptiehs had killed them.'

'Yes. It's true. Those armed Armenians did not die in vain, for during the shooting by the eastern gate some of the victims were able to get away, and they ran back into the city and hid with Turkish and Kurdish friends. There weren't very many of them. But there were still a few, and they were able to tell their story later.'

'None of Vartan's relatives in Bakir were still alive. The surviving Armenians, who emerged from their hiding-places one after another, weren't related to the Khatisians. However, one of them knew Haygaz from the Hayastan, and he also knew Vartan, whom he'd seen there once.

"I knew you at once," said the Armenian to Vartan. "Do you remember me? We once sat at the same table at the Hayastan. In the summer of 1914. You were newly married, or at least that's what you said. Your wife was with you."

"My wife?" said Vartan, who wasn't able to remember anything.

"Your wife," said the Armenian.

"Have you seen her since?" asked Bulbul. "She was called Anahit, and she had a burnt face and big eyes."

"I know what her name is," said the Armenian, "and I know what she looked like."

"Have you seen his wife . . . seen her again at any time?"

"No," said the Armenian. "I haven't seen her again."'

*   *   *

'After that Bulbul and Vartan drove in their *araba*, with the mule, through the villages and towns of the liberated areas. They drove on squeaking wheels, which in spite of the flour made the usual noise made by a two-wheeled cart on wheels that don't rotate round their axles. They were neither specially noticeable, nor entirely unnoticed. There were many people on the roads in the same sort of *arabas*, and many too on foot or mounted on some riding animal. Most of them were in search of someone. The peasants gave them such information as they could. Even in the smaller towns, and in the larger, people took the trouble to answer their questions. For it was a period of asking and answering. But no one could remember Anahit. No one had seen her.'

'One day, in a little village on the banks of the Tigris, a peasant woman said that she had seen a woman who answered to Bulbul's description. She had seen a column of women and children and old men being taken through the village. A saptieh had told her that there were some women in the column who had been hiding in the mountains, but had been recaptured. One of the women in the column had struck her particularly. She was bigger than the other women and she was pregnant, probably in her ninth month. And the woman had had a burnt face, like the one Bulbul had described . . . and big black eyes. She hadn't been wearing a veil. She'd probably lost it.

The peasant woman pointed towards the Tigris. That's the way they were being taken.'

Then, on the banks of the Euphrates, they got further information. Where earlier they had only shaken their heads, suddenly some people nodded. Everyone who had been there said they knew something. Many people had seen pregnant women on the march, even women who were bigger than the others and had burnt, scarred faces, often not proper faces at all but a mass of flesh and bones, with big eyes.

"Just here the Euphrates was red," said a peasant woman, "probably with the blood of the little children thrown over the cliffs by their mothers," and she added, "so that the *chettes* and saptiehs and the Kurds shouldn't get them. For they were killing children before their mothers' eyes." Another peasant woman laughed and said: "Nonsense. The Euphrates wasn't red from the blood of all the little children but from the bellies of their mothers, which had been slit open before they were thrown over the cliffs. The children," said the peasant woman, "were chucked in the river by their mothers, so they were drowned, but they didn't have bleeding wounds." Others said that wasn't quite right, the guards had thrown children into the water too if the mothers weren't quick enough to do it before them, and they had cut their little throats first.

"And the woman with the burnt face? Did anyone see whether she was drowned in the Euphrates?" But nobody had seen that. A Turkish peasant said: "We didn't see anything at all. We merely know about it."'

'Once they met a Turkoman peasant who said that an Armenian woman had hidden in his house during the massacres. She was pregnant, and gave birth shortly after the massacres. She still lived in his house, slept in his bed, and had a burnt face. Actually she had no face, but that didn't matter to him because she was good in bed and always obedient. They visited the woman in the Turkoman's house. Vartan's heart began to pound. Even Bulbul's old face glowed with excitement.'

'It wasn't her. "No," said Bulbul. "This woman isn't Anahit. It's a different woman."'

'In the villages of the semi-nomadic Kurds, and even in the black tents of the wild tribes, they met Armenians who had lived through the massacres, and they were astonished that Kurdish tribes should have hidden Armenians. One of the Kurdish beys told them: "My tribe is a peaceful tribe and took no part in the massacres, for I told my men to keep out of it."

"But many of the Kurd tribes did take part," said Bulbul. "Often they were even more cruel than the *chettes*."

"That may well be," said the Bey. "But the Turkish authorities had sent messengers into the mountains to tell the Kurds about all the rich booty there would be. And no one would be punished, the messengers said. The government guaranteed it. And those officia messengers told the beys and their people and even the shepherds on the mountain pastures about all the fine clothes the Armenians had, and their wives' jewels, and they said the women had holes filled with honey."

On the way back to Bakir they met a Turk who had lost one leg. He was unshaven, wearing a threadbare uniform.

"I didn't know anything," said the cripple, "even when I rode over the Euphrates with the Fourth Army cavalry. They told us we were going to Syria. The English and the French might be anywhere, but they were still a long way away. And when we rode our horses into the water to swim across the river, the horses shied and we couldn't control them. The Euphrates was full of bodies. Most of them were women and children. And the water was as red as the fire in a *tandir*. I still had my two legs then; it was at the front I lost my leg. And as I'd still got both legs, I swam through the water without the horse. Some others took my horse back, and it was rearing and whinnying like old horses at the slaughteryard. And believe me, friends, I saw it all, and yet I didn't know anything. None of us wanted to know anything."'

'One night, on the way back to Bakir, Vartan got up and said to Bulbul: "I'm just going to piss. I'll be back in a moment." And he never came back.'

CHAPTER FOURTEEN

'They were astonished in the village when Bulbul came back alone. As old Tashak unharnessed his mule, Bulbul said: "Vartan simply got down and never came back."

"That's extraordinary," said Tashak.

"He said he just had to go and piss."

"I don't understand," said Tashak, "how it can take so long to piss."'

'The foreign peasants in the village hardly knew Vartan, so they'd soon forgotten him. Only Tashak's family still mentioned him now and then, and Bulbul. It was another hot summer, food was short in the village, and the drought and the locusts over the whole country really scared the peasants. Homecoming soldiers had brought cholera and typhoid fever with them. None the less traders still came from the city to sell any old thing. The traders had used to speak Armenian, but the new ones were Turks and Kurds and even a few Jews and Greeks. Only once did an Armenian trader come. Then the *mohajirs* laughed and said: "You can't get rid of those Armenian traders. Here they are again, you see."'

'And the summer drought came to an end, and with it the plague of locusts. A few of the peasants died of cholera and typhoid. The peasants hung the dead people's clothes on the village's holy tree and were convinced that the evil spirits in the clothes of the deceased would never return to the homes of the survivors. And even the fireplace of the Armenian *tonir*, which the Muslims called *tandir*, and anything boiled or roast over the flames and eaten by the dead person's relatives, would be free from infection. Soon the winter came and was as cold as ever, and the spring was just the kind of spring they were used to. The fresh grass and the young flowers and the buds on the trees seemed to care nothing for the war. Towards the end of 1917 the traders brought the news of the Russian revolution on the other side of the Caucasus, of the mutiny of the soldiers in the Russian Czar's great army, and a lot more news of the kind.

"But that just isn't possible," said the peasants. "We don't believe such a thing could happen, private soldiers killing their own officers. How can it possibly be? Who ever heard of a servant killing his master?"

"Soon there won't be any Russian army any more," said the traders, "and when that happens the Turks will come back."'

'In a way the traders were right. But it wasn't quite like that. The Turks didn't come back at once. The Czar's army was weakened, but in this part of the world it was nearly enough intact to hold the fortified front a little longer. And when another winter, and after it another summer, passed over the land, the British and French arrived from Syria.'

'When the news of the Turkish capitulation reached the village, it scared the peasants even more than the cholera and the typhoid, the drought and the locusts. They had heard that the Russians had withdrawn, that the French and British would also withdraw. And, said the traders, the country would now be occupied by the Armenians.

"But the Armenians are all dead," said the peasants.

"Not all of them," said the traders. "The Russian Armenians are still alive. And so are the Turkish Armenians who escaped across the border in time. And even here, in this district, Armenians keep cropping up. They come like *djinn* out of caves and ravines and other hiding-places. And above all there are the Armenian volunteer battalions who joined the Czar's army. After a time the Russians disarmed them, because they began to be afraid of them themselves, but they've got hold of weapons again. And now they're everywhere. They want to establish a new state here. Hayastan, they call it."

"Hayastan?" said the peasants. "We've never heard that word before."'

441

*   *   *

'Many of the Armenians who had taken refuge in the Caucasus or had been hidden by the Turks and others had come home to reclaim their property. In Yedi Su that was not the case. There was no one left who could say he used to live there – except Vartan Khatisian, but he had left nothing behind and now had completely disappeared.

"If the Armenians take power here," said the Muslim peasants, "then their officials will come to Yedi Su too, and they'll want us to give back the houses to the dead people."

"You'll even have to give the dead people back their cattle," said the traders, "and absolutely everything that belongs to them."'

'And again it worked out differently. When the Czar's empire ceased to exist, the Tartars in Azerbaijan had got together with the Georgians. And they also took the Armenians on the Russian side into their alliance and, in the vacuum on the new map, they founded a provisional state which they called the Transcaucasian Federation. But as the Muslim Tartars didn't get on with the Christian Armenians and Georgians, and as those two had also disagreed among themselves and neither cared for the other's style of living, consequently, for those and other reasons, the alliance collapsed. The Georgians declared their independence and founded their own state. And the Tartars and the Armenians followed their example.'

'When, on 28 May 1918, the Armenians proclaimed their own state for the first time in many centuries, the free and independent state of Armenia, which was actually to be called Hayastan but hadn't been called that yet, the only people in Yedi Su who rejoiced were the dead who had died a natural death before the great massacre. The report of the founding of an Armenian state on the other side of the old Russian border only reached the village in the following year, and it wasn't until 1920 that the peasants learned more details from travelling Greek traders who came from the Caucasus. The traders told them that the American President Wilson, who they said was the most powerful padisha in the world, even more powerful than the Kaiser, the Czar, Abdul Hamid and Enver

Pasha had ever been . . . well, the great padisha from America had promised the Armenians that they would be considered in the peace conference of the nations, because no people on earth had suffered as they had during the war. The traders said that Padisha Wilson had promised the Armenians, in their tiny but free state the wrong side of the frontier, the whole of the Armenian territory that had once belonged to Hayastan, including the territory on the right side of the frontier, the Turkish side. Wilson had even promised Mount Ararat to the Armenians, the traders said, as well as the cities of Erzurum and Trebizond on the Black Sea and Bakir and the greater part of all the mountains as far as the Mediterranean, even the parts where Turks and Kurds were now living, not to mention Gypsies and devil-worshippers and other peoples. But this promise, said the traders, was still only on paper, for two great armies were said to be on the march to break up the ephemeral little state of Armenia before the cartographers had time to draw the true boundaries of the Armenian state conscientiously.'

'And that indeed happened. At some time the defeated Turkish army came back to life and drove the foreign troops out of Anatolian territory. They had a new leader now, whose name was Mustafa Kemal. The traders said that this Mustafa Kemal would certainly one day be called Atatürk, for he was not only the father and liberator of all Turks, but was also a conqueror, whose troops had already crossed the old Russian border with the object of freeing the people of the Caucasus and all the little new states in that area, even the Armenian state. The traders said there were other troops on the march from the other side of the Caucasus, from the opposite direction, who were also going to free the people. This other army, said the traders, was also approaching the Armenian border, only coming the other way; it was the new army of workers and peasants, with their red flags and the hammer and sickle on the old Russian caps. These two great armies – the Turks from one side and the Reds from the other – would simply crush the weak Armenian state. And when the peasants wouldn't believe that, for they hadn't much imagination and couldn't see how a state could be crushed, one of the traders took a fresh egg from a young hen in his big, greedy hands and crushed it, slowly and gloatingly. Like that, said the trader. Just like that.

Pity about the egg, said the peasants. They understood now what the trader had meant, but it annoyed them because it was a good egg from a hen still young, and what the trader had done was a deliberate waste in the eyes of Allah.'

'And a few months later, when people were still talking about the independence of the short-lived Armenian state, an epilogue to the Great War, an incident in the chess-game of the peace talks and the establishment of new frontiers – that sort of thing takes time, it does go on and on, true enough – the traders came from the Caucasus again and told the peasants the story of the tired legs.

"The soldier's legs were tired," said the traders, "Kemal's soldiers and also the soldiers of the workers' and peasants' army, for the Great War had lasted a long time and they had been marching nearly all the time. But the tired legs of the workers' and peasants' army were faster than the Turks' tired legs. So it turned out that the little independent Armenian state was swallowed up by the Reds before Atatürk had marched in."

"That was bad luck on the Armenians," said the peasants.

"No, they were lucky," said the traders. "For Kemal had arranged a great bloodbath among them. He would have wiped out all that was left of the Armenian people."

"And where did you hear that?"

"An Armenian mother told me."

"What did she say?"

"Well, what do you think she said? She said it's better to nurse a living child under the Reds than a dead one under the Turks."

"Did she really say that?"

"That's what she said."'

CHAPTER FIFTEEN

'Bulbul heard nothing more about Vartan until 1921, when some relatives of the Armenians who died in Yedi Su made a pilgrimage to the village to pray for the souls of the dead before the mass graves in the Armenian graveyard. One of them was a very old man. He knew Bulbul from earlier days. And he had also known the Khatisians, for he was the uncle of the red-headed smith who was Vartan's godfather. The old man had visited the village more often in the old days, and he'd been present at Vartan's first wedding and also at his second. So he not only knew Anahit, but he also knew that her son, of whom Vartan had often spoken, was to be called Thovma. Now it came to pass that Bulbul too had grown very old and feeble in the last years, and lived more in the past than in the present and didn't always understand what was going on around her. She followed the old man to the graveyard and, when he had said the prayer for the dead, sat down beside him on the ground in the graveyard, which was silent, without the usual whispering of the *djinn*, and both of them chattered a lot because it was so quiet; they chattered as old people will, and neither of them knew whether what they were saying was really true or whether it was dreams and memories, and illusions woven from dreams and memories.

"I should have liked to know whether Anahit suckled little Thovma," said Bulbul, "for who would have suckled him if she'd given birth to him at that time . . . wherever it might have been!"

"But I heard that she was burnt in the church that time with the others," said the old man, who was trying to imagine how the church had been burnt down with the people locked in it – "so where would she have had the baby? Did the flames give birth to it?"

"But Vartan always believed she wasn't burnt," said Bulbul.

"She took refuge in the mountains." said Bulbul. "Only nobody saw. She jumped through the flames and forced her way through that narrow air-hole with the unborn child, in spite of her swollen belly. And she put out her burning clothes with sand. And later, after she'd been wandering about the mountains for some days, she was picked up. And she was deported, going towards Syria and Mesopotamia. She was on a death-march. And she must have had little Thovma on some country road. And I'll bet you little Thovma is alive, even if his mother died later. That little Thovma must be a tough little kid, as tough as his forefathers, who all lived a long time and grew very old."'

'"And Vartan?"
"I don't know."
"I heard something from people who knew Vartan."
"What was it you heard?"'

'"They say he joined the Armenian volunteers." said the old man. "But later, when the Russians began to distrust the Armenians because they wanted to found a state of their own, in territory that the Russians controlled and wanted to hang on to, they disbanded the volunteer battalions. A few Armenian officers who had ordered their soldiers not to hand in their arms were arrested. Vartan was an officer too, for he was a poet and could read and write and draw plans and read maps, all that sort of thing. Then they arrested Vartan and put him in chains. He was sent to Siberia with the other officers.

"And he was there, in Siberia," said the old man, "when the Revolution broke out and the Reds came and released all the prisoners. After that he fought for the Reds. And later he suddenly turned up in Yerevan, the new Armenian capital, where the Russians have raised the red flag now, and he spent quite a long time there. I suppose he must have been to Syria too, trying to find the deportation camps, because he wanted to find out something about his wife and his son Thovma, who must have been born some time before that."'

'"And then he went back to Yerevan," said the old man. "In the spring of this year the Armenians mounted a revolt against the Reds while the Russians had sent their troops into Georgia to put pressure on the Georgians. Vartan was apparently one of the leaders of the revolt. But the revolt was only temporarily effective, the Reds came right back. They say they're finally going to stay there now."

"What does finally mean?" said Bulbul. "Have you ever seen anything in your whole life that was really final?"

"No, not really," said the old man.

"We don't even know whether death is final," said Bulbul, 'because the faithful say there will be a resurrection."'

"And who told you all that?" asked Bulbul.

"People who knew Vartan."

"Did he know them?"

"No," said the old man. "They said he didn't know anybody."'

"And where can Vartan be now?" asked Bulbul.

"Anywhere," said the old man.'

CHAPTER SIXTEEN

'At some point even I, who call myself Meddah, lost track of Vartan Khatisian,' I, the story-teller, say to my shadow. 'So all I could do was to follow the track of that other man who said one day that he was his son.'

So I say to my shadow, I who call myself Meddah: 'Soon after the World War was over – very shortly after – they were preparing for a new war. For the historians wanted to give a number to the Great War, which they were just calling the World War, so that it wouldn't get lost in the files of all the other wars. But if they were going to call the Great War, which was an unnumbered world war, the First, there would have to be a Second. And there was no difficulty in that. It just had to be invented. Like most inventions, it had been invented long ago, and all it wanted was a pretext and a trigger to make it clear to the historians that the Second World War actually existed, and they could now put the word First before one of them with a clear conscience, and Second before the other. They could also be called No.1 and No.2, for everything must have its proper order, and even the spelling must be correct.'

'But I don't want to digress,' say I, the story-teller, 'and I'll just follow the track of Vartan Khatisian, which had been lost in wind and time and which suddenly reappeared in the form of his son Thovma. For this Thovma existed. There really was a Thovma. No one knows whether he was only a romancer or a lunatic who dreamed up something that he really believed he knew. But just ask the priests and parsons, the rabbis and the mullahs and all the others there are of that kind, ask the saints and the

preachers on the mount and in the valleys. They'll all tell you
that belief is knowledge. And this Thovma believed very seriously.
He believed he was the son of that Vartan Khatisian from the
village of Yedi Su, whose inhabitants have disappeared, their
names wiped out. So this man who called himself Thovma –
Thovma Khatisian – he used to sit in the cafés in Zürich and tell
his extraordinary story to the well-fed, portly burghers of that city.
Of course not all the burghers of that city were well fed and portly.
Many were not. And there were also some Armenians, survivors of
the massacre, some with memories and some who preferred to
have none – and they were glad enough to listen to this Thovma.
For nearly sixty years, this Thovma Khatisian said, he'd been
searching for clues. And he would go on searching until he'd finally
learnt the true story, for, so he said, he was an orphan, born on
a country road during the massacre of 1915. He would go on and
on searching.'

'And that's how it was,' said the story-teller. 'That man never
wearied of his search. And when he was already old, nearly seventy-
three, he was still searching.'

'He was on the verge of a heart attack. He could already feel it, for
death had often knocked at his door in his dreams. He was sitting
in a café. And, as usual, he was telling his story to the man sitting
opposite him, the story that grew from day to day, often changed
but always went the same way. But the man opposite him was an
Armenian.

"I once knew a man called Vartan Khatisian," said the
Armenian. "It was a long time ago. He was a man who could never
settle down. He'd lived in several countries after the First World
War, and often changed his nationality. In the end he got a Swiss
passport."

"A Swiss passport?"

"Yes. Though it was under some other name, for the Turks had
suspected him of espionage and he was afraid that would make the
Swiss distrust him."

"Why shouldn't they trust him?"

"Well, no one here loves a spy."

"So he had a different name?"

"Yes. The name Vartan Khatisian wasn't registered any-where. But that's what his real name was. And he did come from Yedi Su. And he told me about his wife, who had a burnt face – no face at all, really – only eyes, very big, dark eyes. This Vartan Khatisian used to say her eyes had a special gleam – as if she had seen Christ."

"That is my father," said the man who called himself Thovma. "And the woman with the burnt face and the holy light in her eyes, she's my mother."'

'He discovered an address. And he went there that same day. But there was no one there called Vartan Khatisian. An elderly lady opened the door. When he mentioned his father's name and explained to her who he was, she only said: "There was an Armenian living here. That's right. A long time ago. It must be over forty years. When did he come here, now? 1942, it was."

"During the war, then?"

"Yes. During the war . . . from which we Swiss, thank God, were spared, you know . . . at that time there was someone like that living with my parents as a lodger . . . here, in this house. I was young then, very young. That's right. I remember, his Armenian friends called him Vartan Khatisian, but he had changed his name."'

'And the lady said: "This lodger, Vartan Khatisian, who was actually called something different, he disappeared a few months later, leaving no trace. In the spring it was . . . spring 1943."'

'And the lady said: "There was a Jew with a beard who came to see him and knocked on his door. He was one of those odd ones. You know, the orthodox ones, with side-whiskers and a beard and a fur cap and a smell of garlic . . . such as I've never smelt . . . but I know those people do eat garlic. So he came. And knocked at his door. And then the two of them left."'

'"Vartan Khatisian," said the lady. "He came back once. He told me he was going to Poland. I don't know why."'

*   *   *

'So we just have to guess what happened,' say I, the story-teller, to my shadow. 'For often there's nothing else one can do but look for the final truth in one's imagination.'

'Have you found it?' asked my shadow.

And I say: 'Well, I don't really know.'

CHAPTER SEVENTEEN

And so I tell my shadow a story, because I don't know what final truth I've been looking for.

No. This isn't one of those Turkish fairy-tales. And it doesn't start the way all Turkish fairy-tales start . . . *bir varmish, bir yokmush, bir varmish*. Once upon a time there was somebody, once upon a time there was nobody, once upon a time . . . This story begins quite differently, it begins like a Jewish story or any other ordinary story. So now I'll tell it to you:

'Once upon a time there was an old Polish Jew. He knocked at Vartan Khatisian's door, for he knew him, they had often chatted in the café.

"I should like to offer you a business deal," said the Jew.

"I'm a poet," said Vartan Khatisian. "I don't make deals."

"Even poets sometimes make deals," said the Jew. "And this deal I'm offering you is an honourable deal."

"There are no honourable deals," said Vartan Khatisian.

"Yes, there are," said the Jew.'

'"Listen carefully," said the Jew. "My whole family is in Poland. Most Polish Jews are poor, but my family is an exception. They're very rich."

"Rich?" asked Vartan Khatisian.

"Yes," said the Jew. "They've got gold and jewels and great bags full of money. Some day my family will be arrested. And when they're arrested, they won't be able to take their gold and their jewels and their money with them."

"Yes," said Vartan Khatisian. "I understand."

"You've got a Swiss passport," said the Jew. "I haven't got one

452

so I can't go over there to rescue the valuables."

"Do you want me to rescue the valuables?"

"Yes," said the Jew. "That's just it."'

'And the Jew said: "I know the Swiss consul in Warsaw. They'll take you over the frontier in a diplomatic car. With your Swiss passport you won't have any trouble with the visa or anything. You'll collect the jewels and the gold and the money, and then they'll bring you back over the frontier in the diplomatic car. Nothing will be checked. Nothing will happen to you."'

'And the Jew said: "You'll do all that for nothing. From pure generosity. We shan't give you anything. No percentage, no commission, not even an advance. Nothing at all."

"Yes," said Vartan. "I understand."

"You don't understand at all," said the Jew. "Not at all."'

'And the Jew said: "You will keep the bags of money and the gold and the jewels. If my relatives survive, you'll give it all back to them after the war. And really the whole lot, for in this strictly honourable job you get no commission."

"And if they don't survive?"

"Then it belongs to you. All of it."

"What are the chances?"

"It's hard to say," said the Jew. "No one knows exactly where the Jews in Poland are being sent and whether or not they'll ever come back."'

'"My relatives don't stand to lose anything through this deal," said the Jew, "for how else could they smuggle their valuables out of Poland?"

"I'll give it all back to them," said Vartan Khatisian. "Even if only one of them survives, I'll give that one back everything that belongs to him."

"You have understood," said the Jew.

"But if they've all died," said Vartan Khatisian, "if none of them survive, then I keep the valuables and the gold. All of it."

"That's it," said the Jew. "You're a poet. You've understood it correctly."'

'"No one has anything to lose through this deal," said the Jew. "Not even you."

"I've got nothing to lose by it," said Vartan Khatisian.

"You see . . . "

"And what do you get out of it?"

"Don't worry about me," said the Jew. "Even if only one of my family survives, he won't let me starve after I've worked this all out for him."

"And suppose none of them survive?"

"Then you will care for me, Vartan Khatisian."

For the first time, the Jew smiled. "I know the Armenians," said the Jew. "And I know the Jews. They're both peoples that never forget those who have harmed them, but they also never forget those who have done good to them."

"That is the truth," said Vartan Khatisian.

And the Jew said: "That is the truth."'

'And so in 1943 Vartan Khatisian drove to Poland. In the diplomatic car. With a Swiss passport. He arrived at a small town where they hadn't yet arrested the Jews. They lived in a separate reservation, but they were still all there together. He quickly explained to the Jews what it was he was going to do. And since he had a letter of recommendation and kind eyes, the Jews trusted him. Not only did the family of the Polish Jew who lived in Zürich give him their money and all their valuables, but other people gave him what they had. And the story of Vartan Khatisian's mission got around the country, and messengers were sent to him from every part of the country where there were still Jews living, bringing him gold and valuables. The Jews embraced him and kissed him, for this was just the sort of business deal they appreciated. They knew this Armenian was an honest man. He had been sent by the Jew in Zürich whom the faithful looked on as a saint, so they had no reason to distrust him.

"If we survive," they said, "we'll get it all back. And if not, well, then we shan't. For then we shan't need it any more." They gave

Vartan schnapps and clinked glasses with him. And they wept for
joy over this good man and the honourable mission he was carrying
out.'

'The diplomatic car came punctually to take Vartan back. He
stowed the bags and bundles, each marked with its owner's name
– all the money and the valuables – in the diplomatic car and told
the driver to go to Warsaw and take it all to the consulate.

"The consul is going to Switzerland the day after tomorrow," he
told the driver. "Then we'll pack everything in again."

"Are you going back to Switzerland too?" asked the driver.

And Vartan laughed and said: "Obviously."'

'They unloaded the baggage at the consulate. Not until Vartan had
made sure that it had all been taken off and was in locked
cupboards behind barred doors did he go off to his hotel.'

'Vartan Khatisian hadn't slept so well for a long time. When he
woke in the morning, he found that his papers were missing. He felt
through everything, his coat, his suit, his little suitcase. It was no
use. He went downstairs to the receptionist, complained to the
management, but no one knew anything.

He rang the consulate.

"Do you sleep by an open window?" the consul asked.

"Yes," said Vartan Khatisian.

"And were you in your room the whole time?"

"Just once during the night I went to the toilet. It's outside in the
corridor."

"Someone must have got in," said the consul. "Someone's been
your room. The cleaning woman, perhaps, or someone like that.
Who knows? A lot of Poles are living underground just now. They've
disappeared, you see, and they want new papers urgently."

"What shall I do?"

"Nothing at all," said the consul. "Don't worry. We'll give you
provisional passport temporarily. It might be best if you came to
the office."'

So Vartan Khatisian left his hotel to go to the consulate. It so happened that there was a raid being carried out at the same time in the same part of the town as his hotel. It was nothing special, the New Order and its agents just wanted to pick up a few Jews, stateless riff-raff as they called them, who often had false papers or even none at all and who often hung about outside their reservation. Vartan was arrested too, since he was a dark-haired type and hadn't got his papers on him. The agents of the New Order took him and a handful of others to the railway station – just an ordinary station, quite near his hotel. It all seemed to happen without attracting the attention of the passers-by, who weren't worried about it, since their papers were in order. Most of them didn't even look up, but others smiled and many grinned gloatingly. Even at the station, where there were bigger groups of people under guard waiting to be evacuated, everything went ahead briskly without any great excitement, no crying and screaming, for the travellers knew there was no point in upsetting the New Order and annoying the New Orderers.'

'The overcrowded, bolted goods trucks left the station without incident. It was suffocatingly hot in Vartan's truck, although it was not yet summer; the closely packed people heated the truck with the warmth of their bodies. They behaved calmly, even the children. Even the babies didn't dare to howl, and suckled silently at their mothers' breasts. The further the train got from the town, the quieter the people became, for it had become clear to them that their fate could not be avoided. This was not the time to complain. Vartan knew that too. He said to himself: "You could complain to the Swiss consul, but the consul isn't here. And there isn't a telephone here, or a post office. And no one can talk to the guard on this train."'

'Vartan looked at the Polish landscape through the barred windows, and recognized that it was the same landscape he had seen from the car not so long before. Even the scent of the early year and the pale sky were the same. Under the few clouds, in the sharp wind, there were swarms of birds flying. They came here from a long way away, and he knew that they were the first to return to Poland in the spring, but the last he would ever see in this life.'

*   *   *

`he train went straight on for days. At least, that was how it
emed. A few old people died of hunger and thirst and of
:haustion. And they were left lying where they fell. Since there
ere no toilets and the doors were never opened, the people relieved
emselves where they stood. There was no room to sit or lie down,
› the travellers had to shit themselves and piss themselves standing
ɔ. It didn't seem to distress anyone.'

ome time, somewhere, the train stopped. Here there was a
fferent landscape. Here there was barbed wire. And behind the
arbed wire stood big furnaces that roared incessantly. Since the
ople in the truck were hungry and thirsty and had hallucinations,
ey thought the furnaces were the ovens of a bakery. And where
ere was bread, there would surely be water.
One of the Jews said: "They're taking us to a bakery."
Another said: "They promised us work. Probably we shall have
bake bread."
"Are you all bakers?" asked Vartan.
"No," said one of the Jews. "But anything can be learnt. Even
king. They'll train us."'

`he train stood in the siding a long time. Nothing stirrred. Even
e hissing of the locomotive ceased. Since the doors weren't opened,
me of the Jews peered out of the barred windows, and one of them
t the right scent. "It smells strange," he said to the others. "But
doesn't smell like bread." Now the others seemed to notice it. One
the Jews suddenly shouted: "It smells like human flesh!"
Some of the Jews began to weep, others to shout. But Vartan
mained silent. "Be quiet," he said. "There's nothing to get excited
out. Listen to me. I'll tell you a story."'

nd Vartan told them the story of Max and Moritz. When he'd
iished, the Jews were quiet. Some of them even laughed. One of
em said: "It's only a story, really. Nothing like that ever
ppened."
"They made bread out of Max and Moritz," said Vartan. "The
ker turned the two of them into dough and put them in the oven."

"A story," said the Jews. "Just a story."

"Of course it's only a story," said Vartan.

"Who wrote it?"

"A German called Wilhelm Busch."

"A German story," said the Jews.'

'"We ought to put up a memorial to that Wilhelm Busch one day,"
said one of the Jews, "for he's convinced us that with the German
things like that only happen in stories."

"True," said another, who looked like a rabbi. "That Wilhelm
Busch ought to be the Jews' favourite German poet, for he's taken
away our fear of the Germans."

Vartan had to tell them the story of Max and Moritz all over
again, all about baking the bread. And the Jews listened to him,
and when he'd finished they began to laugh heartily. They weren't
frightened any more. They were reassured.

Then the doors were flung open.'

CHAPTER EIGHTEEN

'Among the souls of the gassed and burnt Jews sitting that day on the chimney of the incinerators, there was also the soul of a Turk and that of an Armenian called Vartan Khatisian.

"How did you get here?" Vartan asked the Turk.

"And how did you get here?" asked the Turk.

"I had business in Warsaw," said Vartan.

"Are you a businessman?"

"No," said Vartan. "I'm a poet."'

'"I had business in Warsaw too," said the Turk. "And I'm a poet too."

"Did you lose your papers?"

"Yes," said the Turk. "I'd lost them, and they just picked me up during a raid."'

'"What are we actually waiting for?" asked the Turk.

"For the signal to take off," said Vartan.

"And where are we going to fly?"

"I don't know," said Vartan.'

'"Strictly speaking, a Turk ought not to be flying to heaven with an Armenian," said the Turk.

"Why not?"

"Because of that story the Meddah has been telling in one of the big bazaars."

"What story is that?"

"Just a story," said the Turk.'

'And the Turk said: "Once upon a time there was somebody. Once upon a time there was nobody. Once upon a time . . .

"Once upon a time there was a dead Turk whose soul flew up to heaven with the soul of a dead Armenian.

'What makes you so happy?' asked the Armenian.

'It's because I'm going to heaven,' said the Turk. 'All faithful Muslims go to heaven, and indeed to paradise.'

'And the unbelievers?'

'They go to hell.'"'

"'But you won't really appreciate paradise,' said the Armenian, 'for you can only value the good if you know about the bad.'

'What do you mean by that?'

'Well, put it like this,' said the Armenian. 'Anyone who has glanced just once into hell can then enjoy the pleasures of paradise two or three times more, for he knows what the other side looks like.'

'You're right there,' said the Turk. 'I do see that.'

'I'm sorry for you,' said the Armenian, 'for you won't really be able to enjoy the delights of paradise, because you've never been through hell.'

'So what should I do?' asked the Turk.

'I don't know,' said the Armenian. 'But think it over. Perhaps something will occur to you.'"'

"'And the Turk thought about it, and said: 'How would it be if you and I exchanged clothes? I'll put your black cloak on and peep into hell for a fraction of a second, just so I shall know afterwards what it's like. – And you, Armenian, you can put my white cloak on and look into paradise for a fraction of a second.'

'Not a bad idea,' said the Armenian.'"

"'And so they did that. When the two of them approached Allah's gate, the archangel Gabriel wasn't there. His deputy, a young inexperienced angel, wasn't really in the picture.

'We've exchanged clothes,' the Turk told the angel. 'I just wanted to have a peep into hell for a fraction of a second, and this Armenian wanted to have a look at paradise. It will be good for me. I shall be so much happier in paradise afterwards. And it will do this unbeliever good too, for he ought to know what he's missed.'"'

* * *

'"The angel didn't mind. He took the Turk into hell, and the Armenian into paradise. And since there's no way back from those two places, the Turk burns in hell for all eternity, and the Armenian suns himself in paradise."'

'"A fine story," said Vartan. "But why did you tell it to me?"
   "Because the Turk can't trust the Armenian," said the Turk. "Not even after death."
   "Are you really afraid to fly to heaven with me?"
   "Yes," said the Turk. "I am."'

The Jews had heard the story, and didn't know what to make of it. One of them said: "There you are. Even the souls of the dead still have prejudices. If the souls of the dead don't trust each other, what are we to expect?"
   The Jews grumbled a bit among themselves. But then they calmed down, for the good God gave them all the signal to take off.'

'And all those souls rose up and flew together into the sky. Only the last thoughts of their mortal bodies remained behind, for they are immortal and remain on the earth for ever, with every wish and every hope that has moved a human being in the course of his life.'

'Vartan's last thought was also there on the chimney of the incinerator. When all the thoughts had polished their wings, they set off. Many of the Jews flew back to the land of the Final Solution, because that was their home. Others flew to other countries. But most of them flew to Jerusalem.'

'Vartan had lost sight of the Turk. He leapt into the air and flew after the Jews who were making for Jerusalem. He flew very fast, faster and faster, and at last he caught up with the Jews.
   "Where are you flying to?"
   "To Jerusalem."
   "Jerusalem?"
   "Yes."
   "Will you fly over Turkey?"

"Of course. That's the way to Jerusalem. Don't you know the map?"

"I've forgotten so much."

"What are you looking for in Turkey?"

"The land of Hayastan."

"Hayastan?"

"Yes."'

'As they were flying over Mount Ararat Vartan heard a voice. It came from space. "I will send an eagle to you," said the voice. "And you will descend on the eagle's wings."

"And suppose there isn't an eagle," said Vartan. "Suppose there's only a gnat for me to land on, what shall I do then? The flies will eat the gnat, and I shall never reach Hayastan."

"You Armenians are a suspicious people," said the voice. "You are like the Jews. No faith in the world!"

"How could we have any faith?" asked Vartan.

"You're not entirely wrong there."'

'"Will you really send me an eagle?"

"Yes, an eagle."

And Vartan flew on the eagle's wings to Mount Ararat. And from there down into the wide Armenian country that is called Hayastan Vartan saw that he was not the only thought that wanted to live there. The thoughts of Armenians were everywhere. They were on every flower, on every blade of grass, on all the buds on the trees.

'And the day came to an end. And it grew dark. Then a whisper arose from the petals of the flowers and the buds of the trees. And whispers came from the grass, and indeed from the whole countryside.

"When the Armenians whisper at night, the Turks have night mares," said the voice – "anyway, all those in this area."

"Where are my parents?" asked Vartan. "Where are my brothers and sisters? Where are all those I loved? And where is my wife?"

"They are here," said the voice.'

'And suddenly Vartan saw his family. And he saw his wife to

sitting on a flower.

"Have you come back to me?" asked Anahit.

"I've come back," said Vartan.'

'Vartan greeted all those who had been dear to him, then he came back to Anahit.

"It's a pity our son Thovma isn't here," he said to Anahit.

"A pity," said Anahit. "I miss him so much."

"I should like to have seen him."

"I've dreamt of him for years," said Anahit, "and tried to picture what he might look like."

"I too," said Vartan.'

'"Actually our son is not called Thovma," said Anahit, "for that time, when they burnt me in the church, I had a dream."

"What did you dream?"

"I dreamed I'd risen through the flames to rescue Thovma, the little Thovma in my womb. The flames didn't touch me, because what I had in my womb was holy. There was a great crowd in front of the only ventilator – everyone wanted to be the first through it – but they all made way for me when they saw I was pregnant. And after I'd passed through the flames unharmed and crawled through the ventilator without difficulty in spite of my big belly, I escaped into the darkness of the night. For a time I wandered about in the mountains, until one day the soldiers caught me. And day after day the sun rose and set. And I dreamed of a death column on a country road by the banks of the Euphrates. I saw myself there, in the middle of the saptiehs and all those unhappy people. I dreamed that the labour pains had already started, for I was in the ninth month then and should have to give birth somewhere. When my time had come, I simply lay down in the road. And one of the saptiehs slit my stomach open with his bayonet. And lo and behold! little Thovma crept out. He was lovely to look at, so small and soiled and innocent. Then I heard a voice, and it said: 'This child shall not be called Thovma, but Hayk.'"

"Hayk?" asked Vartan. "Like the first of the Armenians?"

"Hayk," said Anahit.'

*   *   *

'"That wasn't a dream," said Vartan. "That was reality."

"What reality?" asked Anahit.

"That other reality, which the flames could not destroy."

"Then was I really on that country road?"

"Of course you were there."

"And I gave birth there."

"Yes, Anahit."

"And I bore you a son?"

"You bore me a son."'

'It was not to be many years before Thovma, now called Hayk, found his parents. But since thoughts have no sense of time, Vartan and Anahit didn't notice how many years passed. They often talked about their son. And one day the two of them raised their eyes to the sky. And, lo and behold, the last thought of Thovma came flying down. He was called Hayk now. He was actually called that. They waved to him, and Thovma, now called Hayk like the first of the Armenians, recognized them at once.

Hayk kissed and hugged his father. Then he fluttered over to his mother and settled on her great milky breasts.

"I never suckled you," said his mother. "You ought to become small again now, so that I could give you my breast at last."

"I am quite small again now," said Hayk. "Don't you see? And I'm drinking your sweet milk."'

'On a nearby flower there was a former Armenian priest. He saw how Anahit, the mother of Armenia, had found her lost son. Hayk will be fruitful and have many descendants, he thought. And the children of Hayk, and their children's children, will people this land, which was always meant for them.

And he thought those thoughts for a very long time. And all the other thoughts heard the voice of his thoughts, and thought the same.'

EPILOGUE

'You've opened your eyes again,' said the voice of the story-teller in Thovma Khatisian's head.

'Is it the last time?'

'It is the last time.'

'Where is my last thought?'

'It's still in your head.'

'And the story?'

'Perhaps it wasn't a story.'

'What do you mean?'

'I've only told you how it could be, and possibly will be, with the last thought after it's finally left you.'

'When will it leave me?'

'Soon.'

And the story-teller's voice in my head grows softer. Soon it will fade out altogether, and I shan't hear it any more. It will be very quiet.

I know that my last thought will fly back into the gaps in the Turkish history books. And because I know that, I shall die more peacefully than others before me who didn't know it.

'Minister, I'm flying back!'

'Where to, Mr Khatisian?'

'Into the gaps in your history books.'

'But, Mr Khatisian, you mustn't do anything like that!'

'Why not?'

'Because it might upset me.'

*　　*　　*

'It will upset so many people,' I say, 'if the last thoughts of all the dead Armenians in the land of Hayastan begin to whisper.'

'Do you believe that, Mr Khatisian?'

'Yes, Minister.'

'But whispering is infectious,' says the minister. 'If the dead Armenians whisper, it could cross the border and be heard everywhere.'

'That is possible.'

'Other voices could begin to whisper, even those that have never dared to whisper aloud. It would be a great whispering if everybody in the world who's been persecuted suddenly began to whisper their complaints. The whole world would be smothered by their whispering. Where should we go from there? That mustn't happen, Mr Khatisian. So many of us would get stomach-aches, for the victims' whispering voices are bad for the digestion. We might become thoughtful, and our thinking might give us headaches. And think of the nightmares that would keep us awake. Who wants that? And what's the sense of it?'

'Who says everything has to make sense?' said Thovma Khatisian. And then he breathed out his soul.

GLOSSARY

New Turkish spelling has not been used for the transliteration of
Turkish and Armenian words, since it had not been introduced in
the period covered by most of the book, i.e. up to the First World
War. Turkish was at that time written in Arabic script, and
Armenian has its own script. The words have here been rendered
in straightforward spelling that, to a reader of English, will echo
the pronunciation of them insofar as that is possible. Different
sources will doubtless offer different versions. Certain words in the
text, notably Persian and Arabic loan-words, are no longer used in
modern Turkish.

The plot of this novel, and all the characters in it, are fictitious, the
historical backgrounds are true.

Alk (*Arm*).	ghost
Araba (*Turk*.)	coach
Arabachi (*Turk*.)	coachman
Atar (*Arm*.)	dried cow dung used as fuel
Achket louis (*Arm*.)	light in your eyes (congratulations)
Avukat (*Turk*.)	lawyer
Badiv (*Arm*.)	honour
Bairam (*Turk*.)	religious festival
Baklava (*Turk*.)	sweet cake, sweet dish
Bashibazouk (*Turk*.)	guerilla, mercenary
Bash-Kiatib (*Turk*.)	chief clerk
Bedel (*Turk*.)	military service exemption tax
Bey (*Turk*.)	title given to superior person

Binbashi (*Turk.*)	major
Bismillah (*Turk.*)	in God's name
Bulgur (*Turk.*)	boiled and pounded wheat
Chalvar (*Turk.*)	Turkish-style trousers
Chibouk (*Turk.*)	pipe
Choush (*Turk.*)	corporal in Turkish army
Dede (*Turk.*)	grandfather
Defterdar (*Turk.*)	chief accountant
Dev (*Arm.*)	evil spirit
Djinn (*Turk.*)	spirits in Muslim mythology
Döshek (*Turk*).	paillasse
Dudun chorbassy (*Turk.*)	soup served at weddings
Duhne menatzaz (*Arm.*)	old maid (lit. left at home)
Efendi (*Turk.*)	sir
Efendiler (*Turk.*)	gentlemen
Ekmek (*Turk.*)	bread
Endanig (*Arm.*)	family
Fedayin (*Turk.*)	Armenian freedom fighters
Frank (*Turk.*)	nickname for European
Frankistan (*Turk.*)	nickname for Europe
Gatnachpiur (*Arm.*)	milk-well, also a milk dish
Gelin (*Turk.*)	young bride
Giaour (*Turk.*)	unbeliever
Ginka mair (*Arm.*)	godmother
Hadig (*Arm.*)	sweet porridge, pudding
Hafiz (*Turk.*)	teacher of the Koran
Hamal (*Turk.*)	porter
Hamam (*Turk.*)	steam bath
Hamamji (*Turk.*)	bath attendant
Hamidiye (*Turk.*)	Kurdish soldiers in Turkish army

Harissa (*Arm.*)	Armenian national dish of meat and pearl barley
Hars (*Arm.*)	bride
Hayastan (*Arm.*)	Armenia
Hodja (*Turk.*)	teacher
Hukumet (*Turk.*)	government building
Inshallah (*Turk.*)	God willing
Kadi (*Turk.*)	judge in Muslim community
Kahvehane (*Turk.*)	coffee-house
Kahveji (*Turk.*)	coffee-seller
Kaimakam (*Turk.*)	district governor
Karagös (*Turk.*)	Turkish shadow play
Kasah (*Turk.*)	district
Kaval (*Turk.*)	Yezidi (devil-worshipper) priest
Kelim (*Turk.*)	tapestry, carpet
Kertastan (*Arm.*)	clan
Khible (*Turk.*)	direction of prayer
Kismet (*Turk.*)	destiny
Konak (*Turk.*)	building
Kühla (*Turk.*)	pointed woollen cap
Kuthan (*Arm.*)	plough
Lavash (*Arm.*)	bread
Madsun (*Arm.*)	yoghurt
Magus (*Pers.*)	priest
Mahalle (*Turk.*)	ethnic quarter of town
Mahdi (*Turk.*)	saint
Mashalle (*Turk.*)	miracle
Meddah (*Turk.*)	story-teller
Meron (*Arm.*)	holy oil
Milet (*Turk.*)	Armenian district
Mobeds (*Pers.*)	priest
Mohajir (*Turk.*)	emigrant
Mukhtar (*Turk.*)	mayor
Mudir (*Turk.*)	chief constable

Muezzin (*Turk.*)	official of mosque who calls the faithful to prayer
Munadi (*Turk.*)	drummer, town-crier
Munj (*Arm.*)	enforced silence of young bride
Mustahfis (*Turk.*)	reservist second class
Mutessarif (*Turk.*)	district administrator
Namaz (*Turk.*)	ritual prayer
Nargile (*Turk.*)	hookah, water-pipe
Narod (*Arm.*)	charm worn by bridal couple
Oda (*Turk.*)	living-room
Oghi (*Arm.*)	schnapps
Ojid (*Arm.*)	trousseau
Okka (*Turk.*)	weight
Osmanli (*Turk.*)	subject of Ottoman Empire
Padisha (*Turk.*)	ruler
Pag (*Arm.*)	farmyard
Para (*Turk.*)	small coin
Parvana (*Arm.*)	kind of moth
Patat (*Arm.*)	cabbage stuffed with rice and meat
Pokhint (*Arm.*)	sweet dish
Raki (*Turk.*)	strong spirit distilled in Turkey
Raya (*Turk.*)	unbeliever
Rediff (*Turk.*)	reservist first class
Sanjak (*Turk.*)	administrative district
Sapkai (*Turk.*)	hatter
Saptieh (*Turk.*)	armed policeman
Sarma (*Turk.*)	cabbage stuffed with rice and meat
Saz (*Arm.*)	musical instrument
Sebil (*Turk.*)	mosque well; also, free distribution of water
Selamlik (*Turk.*)	larger living-room

Seljuk (*Turk.*)   name of early Turkish dynasties
Shekerli (*Turk.*)   sweet like sugar
Shekerli party   sweet party, also first-step party
Sinek kagidi (*Turk.*)   fly trap
Sofra (*Turk.*)   tray
Stamboul (*Turk.*)   district of Constantinople
Sunechi (*Arm.*)   man who performs circumcision operation

Tan (*Arm.*)   dish made from yoghurt
Tashak (*Turk.*)   testicles
Tavla (*Turk.*)   trictrac, dice game
Tebk (*Arm.*)   special event; also massacre
Teskeré (*Turk.*)   inland pass
Tezek (*Turk.*)   dried cow dung used as fuel
Tonir (*Arm.*)   fireplace, stove
Tramojid (*Arm.*)   dowry

Vali (*Turk.*)   provincial governor
Vartapad (*Arm.*)   priest
Vijak (*Arm.*)   children's festival on Ascension Day
Vilayet (*Turk.*)   province
Vishap (*Arm.*)   evil spirit

Yaylis (*Turk.*)   carriage with springs
Yedi Su (*Turk.*)   seven waters
Yezidi (*Turk.*)   religious sect of Kurds, devil-worshippers
Yorgan (*Turk.*)   blanket
Yusbashi (*Turk.*)   captain

THE PERIODIC TABLE

Primo Levi

'We are always looking for the book it is necessary to read next. After a few pages I immersed myself gladly and gratefully. There is nothing superfluous here, everything this book contains is essential. It is wonderfully pure, and beautifully translated'
Saul Bellow

'I was curious to know what a book of 21 chapters, each having as its title the name of a chemical element, and written by an Italian industrialist chemist, would comprise. In five minutes I was captivated but I also knew that no words of mine would do this book justice. Each chapter (and element) resonates with some feature of the human condition. It is allusive and metaphorical, yet crystal clear in meaning and always re-affirmative, often subtly and tangentially, of those values essential to a civilised society. Nominally it is prose; in actuality, it is a narrative poem of magical quality' Frederick Dainton, *New Scientist*

0 349 12198 2
FICTION

THE BEAUTIFUL MRS SEIDENMAN

Andrzej Szczypiorski

The beautiful Jewish widow Irma Seidenman has three attributes that keep her out of the Warsaw ghetto: blonde hair, blue eyes, and excellent forged papers. But one day in 1943 an informer denounces her to the Gestapo – and in the thirty-six hours following her arrest unlikely links are forged between a chain of disparate people – Poles, Jews and Germans, with motives righteous and base – in the attempt to rescue her.

Ranging back and forward in time, by turns tender, ironic, sad and funny, Szczypiorski constructs a pattern of intersecting lives in a masterly and deeply compassionate exposition, not just of Warsaw, but of all victims, persecutors and spectators alike in a world at war.

0 349 10094 2
ABACUS FICTION

THE WHITE CUTTER
David Pownall

In the thirteenth century, an age half-crazed in its quest for certainty, King Henry seeks solace in the building of cathedrals. But Christians do not make good architects. To create the illusion of permanence – those soaring wonders in stone – Henry knows to rely on the masons, the secret brotherhood whose very craft disguises a dangerous heresy and creates a blasphemous beauty.

THE WHITE CUTTER is the confession of Hedric, son of an itinerant stonemason, reared in a tool-bag, who becomes the greatest architect of his age. It tells of rumbustious adventures; of his sexual apprenticeship; of his unique education; of rogue clerics, singular nuns and The Four, a secret cabal teetering on the brink of genius and dementia.

It is a book which reveals much about light and stone, God and the Devil, father and sons, the Church and the State, love and murder, our need for secrecy and our need for uncontradicted truth in an age of chaos.

0 349 10117 5
ABACUS FICTION

GO TELL
THE LEMMING

Bernice Rubens

'Dear Angela. I can't stand it any more, so I'm going to put my head in the gas oven . . .'

For Angela Morrow the death of her marriage is the ultimate in rejection. She debates whether to address her suicide note to her parents, to her son or to David, her defecting husband – and ends up writing it to herself. In fact, Angela writes to Angela quite a lot.

But David, a successful film producer, is beginning to prefer Angela's unpredictability to the vacuous calm of his mistress. He invites her to work on location in his new film. So Angela postpones killing herself and instead goes to Rome . . .

0 349 10147 7
ABACUS

Abacus now offers an exciting range of quality titles by both established and new authors. All of the books in this series are available from:

Sphere Books,
Cash Sales Department,
P.O. Box 11,
Falmouth,
Cornwall TR10 9EN.

Alternatively you may fax your order to the above address. Fax No. 0326 376423.

Payments can be made as follows: Cheque, postal order (payable to Macdonald & Co (Publishers) Ltd) or by credit cards, Visa/Access. Do not send cash or currency. UK customers and B.F.P.O.: please send a cheque or postal order (no currency) and allow £1.00 for postage and packing for the first book, plus 50p for the second book, plus 30p for each additional book up to a maximum charge of £3.70 (7 books plus).

Overseas customers including Ireland, please allow £2.00 for postage and packing for the first book, plus £1.00 for the second book, plus 50p for each additional book.

NAME (Block Letters) ....

ADDRESS ....

....

☐ I enclose my remittance for _____

☐ I wish to pay by Access/Visa Card

Number ☐☐☐☐☐☐☐☐☐☐☐☐☐☐☐☐

Card Expiry Date ☐☐☐☐